Legacy of the Tigers

Iris Yang

Open Books

Published by Open Books

Interior design by Siva Ram Maganti

Cover image © Nova flickr.com/photos/fox3nova

ISBN-13: 978-1948598323

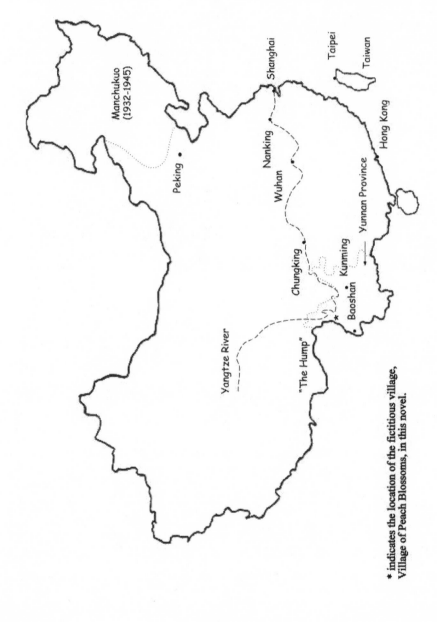

Manchukuo
(1932-1945)

Peking •

Shanghai

Nanking

Wuhan

Yangtze River

Chungking

"The Hump"

Kunming

Baoshan

Yunnan Province

Hong Kong

Taipei

Taiwan

* indicates the location of the fictitious village,
Village of Peach Blossoms, in this novel.

Part One

Life and Death in Wartime

Chapter 1

▬ ▬ ▬ ▬ ▬ ▬

Jasmine Bai was still alive. A kick from the baby in her womb jerked her out of unconsciousness.

She lay curled up on the snow at the top of a cliff, holding a garland of dried forget-me-nots to her chest. The icy wind blasted through every crevice of her clothing, making her teeth chatter. She had no idea how long she'd lain there passed out. *I'm still alive!*

The baby kicked again as if he were trying to remind her that he too was alive and fighting for his chance. But she knew she could not keep him. He was the enemy's child.

For thousands of years in Chinese culture, female purity had been upheld as a virtue greater than life itself. Even victims of rape were condemned. Any woman who could live through such humiliation without killing herself was an affront to society and a shame to her family. And giving birth to a bastard child was unforgivable. It was now the end of 1942, but the tradition was deep-seated and ongoing. Jasmine had struggled with unbearable guilt during the past few months, even in this isolated area of southwest Yunnan Province.

When she was in Chungking years earlier, she'd kept in touch with Professor Valentine, who had saved thousands of people, including her, during the Nanking Massacre. The American had told her horrible stories of what had happened afterward. Countless women

1

being raped by the Japanese soldiers had committed suicide once they found out that they were pregnant. Babies had been killed by their mothers or by family members. Some had been smothered to death while others had been drowned. They were the children of the enemy, undeserving of life.

"For all I know, not a single baby survived!" Professor Valentine had written in her letter. "I've been in China for twenty years, and I know the culture well. Women are shamed for being assaulted. A girl who chose to have a Japanese bastard child was not protected by her family. Instead, they implored her, 'Why didn't you kill yourself?' I was speechless."

Jasmine replayed what the professor had said. "How could anyone be so cruel to his or her family member? I felt sad, yet I had no power to change minds. What can one person do in the face of a thousand-year-old tradition? Nothing! I've tried my best to save lives during the massacre, but I've saved so few. And now it's even worse. Women and infants are still dying as the aftermath of the event."

What would Professor Valentine say to me, wondered Jasmine? *He is innocent!* She could imagine the professor's sad cry.

Jasmine had panicked when she found out that she was pregnant. She'd run down the mountains, hoping to get help from her family, wanting desperately to abort the unwanted child. *What was I thinking?* There were one thousand miles between her and her uncle and cousins. She didn't even have a penny to make a phone call. She'd been so focused on stopping the pregnancy that she hadn't considered any alternatives.

Perhaps I could give him away. He'd be okay if no one knows he's a product of a gang-rape. Japanese and Chinese look similar. Nobody could tell that he's half-Japanese. I could still go home one day without bringing shame to my family. The baby delivered another kick as if he'd agreed with this arrangement. At least he would be alive.

By now, Jasmine was so numb that she couldn't feel her limbs. The wind howled like a voracious wolf, and the branches of snow-laden trees rustled around her. The icy air bit her exposed face. Rubbing her gloved hands on her cheeks, she tried to soothe the numbness.

Death seemed only a breath away.

A deep voice echoed in her mind, "Don't let the Japs kill you." Her beloved cousin Birch had said that. "If you die, you just let the Japs kill one more innocent person without even using their guns or knives. I know it's hard; it's very painful. Being alive can be harder than dying. You've got to be strong, Jasmine."

For months, his words had kept her alive. Birch was right. She wanted to live to see the day that the Japanese army was defeated. She longed to reunite with her family. She dreamed of being with Danny Hardy.

Danny! Her heart swelled. She loved this courageous American pilot and had protected the Flying Tiger with her life. *How wonderful if I could see him again!* Jasmine wished he would hold her and kiss her. *On my lips next time...*

She thought as she shivered on the snowy ground. *If I don't get up soon, I'll freeze to death, along with the baby.* Her life wasn't just hers, and her survival was vital to this innocent child. He hadn't asked to be conceived.

Her eyes had adjusted to the darkness; she could make out the cliff in front of her. It was high and steep. Even in daylight, she couldn't climb down. Returning to the cabin was the only option. The hunters were among the kindest people she'd ever known, and they'd already rescued her once.

Jasmine attempted to stand, but her legs would not support her. So she started to crawl uphill. A line appeared on the flawless carpet of snow behind her. She gasped for air. Icy-white breaths plumed from her mouth, and droplets of sweat beaded her upper lip and turned to frost. Despite a homemade fur coat, the vile cold penetrated to her bones. Before long, the numbness spread throughout her body. She lay motionless. A bitter smile crept over her face. *After all, I'm going to die, and I can't save this baby whether I want to or not.*

With one arm holding the garland of forget-me-nots, she stretched her other arm and pulled forward a step, and then another. *At least I'm going to die trying.* She could feel her strength failing, but she fought with all the remaining energy within her.

Uphill, a faint light flickered. At first, Jasmine thought she was hallucinating, and then the light grew closer. She tried to scream, but no sound came out. She hadn't spoken a word for months since the torture and rape. It seemed that she'd lost her voice from shrieking too much during the ordeal. Or she hadn't dared to open her mouth for fear that if she found her voice, she wouldn't stop screaming.

She tried again. "Help…"

Eventually, she found enough volume. "Help… Please!" Her voice echoed through the vacuum of the night.

The light floated closer and closer. Outlines of two people with an oil lamp loomed out of the darkness. When she saw the hunters' weather-beaten faces, her breathing eased. Pain and exhaustion clouded her eyes. She could hear their approaching footsteps and the call of her name, but the sound ebbed away. Everything faded as a bottomless pit opened to swallow her.

Jasmine lay on her cot in the tiny wooden cabin, covered with a thick fur throw. The hunters stood by her bedside.

"You're awake!" said the wife as she sat on the edge of the cot. In her early sixties, she was thin and petite. Even inside the cabin, she wore a heavy coat. "We were so worried about you."

"Da…Ma," murmured Jasmine, using the title of reverence for an elderly woman.

"Dear Guanyin! Thank you, the Goddess of Mercy! You found your voice!"

Jasmine grasped Da Ma's hands. The back of Jasmine's hands and fingers were blistered and swollen. "I'm sorry."

"It's okay," said the husband. He was several years older than his wife. Hard living had carved deep lines onto his weathered face. "You're safe. That's all that matters. You have some frostbite, but it'll heal."

Jasmine's cheeks were red and mottled. She felt the stinging, prickling sensations in her face, fingers, and toes. Lifting her hand, she tried to scratch before Da Ma stopped her.

"Let me rub a bit more cream." The hunter returned with a jar in his hand.

The cooling salve gave her relief from the itchy feeling. "Thank you, Da Shu." Again, she used the title of reverence, this time for an elderly man.

Her heart was filled with gratitude. If it were not for this couple, Jasmine would not be alive. Several months earlier, they had found her at the bottom of a cliff where she'd jumped down to escape from the Japanese soldiers and to protect the whereabouts of the American pilot. They'd nursed her. Now, they'd rescued her again.

Applying more salve to her hands, Da Ma asked, "What's your name? We've called you *Gu Niang*—Girl for months."

"Bai Moli—White Jasmine."

"What a lovely name!" The old woman removed the lower part of the heavy coverlet and smeared the ointment on her toes. "It's freezing out there. Why did you go out? Did you get lost?"

"I was...afraid."

"Of what?"

"I'm..." Jasmine answered with a stutter, sounding ashamed. "I'm...pregnant." Embarrassment deepened the redness on her cheeks.

"I noticed that you'd gained a bit of weight. I thought you were just recovering—"

"Yeah," said Da Shu. "Nothing to worry—"

"No!" Pain twisted Jasmine's features. She closed her eyes briefly before saying, "I don't...don't want..." Her voice trailed off on a fragile, whispery moan.

An awkward silence fell between them.

After a moment, Da Ma cleared her throat. "Being a single woman with a child is hard." Concern made the creases in her tanned face more noticeable. "I'm sure the young man meant to marry you. He'd be so happy if he knew you're having his child."

Da Shu nodded his agreement. "Everyone in the village died. You should save this seed."

Indeed, everyone in the village had been killed by the Japanese when they refused to give up Danny Hardy, the American pilot. The couple, however, assumed that she'd become pregnant out of wedlock with one of the young men in the village before the massacre. Jasmine opened her mouth, wanting to say that she would never do such a thing. But then she hesitated. What could she tell them? That the baby was the product of a gang-rape? She couldn't bring herself to relate the ugly truth. "Could you please find…find an orphanage?"

"No!" Da Ma said as her husband shook his head.

Jasmine buried her head in her pillow to hide her shame.

Chapter 2

▬ ▬ ▬ ▬ ▬ ▬ ▬

In mid-April 1943, Jasmine went into labor at the hunting cabin. Although the baby had fought for his life, he was reluctant to leave the comfort of his mother's womb, seemingly afraid of the outside world. Jasmine couldn't blame him, knowing how ugly the world could be. For hours, she clenched her fists and bit down on her lip as waves of agony rolled over her. Da Ma kept encouraging her, "One more push. Come on, just one more push!" By the time the baby was born, Jasmine was soaked in perspiration.

The old woman wrapped the infant in a rag towel. "Look." She showed him to her husband. "What a fine boy!"

Da Shu beamed. His smile accentuated the wrinkles around his mouth and eyes.

Da Ma handed the infant to Jasmine.

She hesitated, knowing she shouldn't become attached to him. She'd already decided to give him away. With an aching heart, she shook her head and closed her eyes.

"Just for a while…" Da Ma placed the bundle in front of her.

Just one look, Jasmine told herself. She took the baby and held him in her arms, half expecting him to look like a little devil.

But he was no devil. He had a chubby face with pink cheeks. His eyelids flickered as he strained to open them. Once he succeeded, he fixed his innocent gaze on Jasmine as if trying to figure out who was holding him.

She touched his translucent cheeks. When her index finger grazed his lips, he opened his mouth and sucked hard.

"Feed him," urged Da Ma.

Da Shu walked away, giving her privacy.

After another moment of hesitation, Jasmine lifted her shirt and placed the newborn upon her chest. It took him a little while, but once he found her nipple, he sucked so hard that it was almost painful. She'd never expected a tiny life to have such strength.

The urgency of his need shocked her. Her motherly instinct took over, and she pressed him closer to her heart. Her cheeks turned pink, and a smile made its way across her face.

"Isn't he beautiful?" Da Ma said, an enchanted look upon her face as if the infant were her grandchild.

Jasmine caressed his soft black hair. A feeling, foreign yet primal, swept through her. It was so strong that it caught her off guard. She'd never expected to feel this way toward a baby, especially a baby with the enemy's blood.

Soon, I won't be able to hold him. Tears welled in her eyes.

"I know it hurts. But you'll get used to the sucking," said Da Ma.

Not trusting herself to say anything without breaking down, Jasmine barely managed a weak nod. She could hardly believe she'd already fallen in love with this child.

"He's too young to travel." Da Ma said, "You must keep him, at least for a while."

―――――――

For the next few days, Jasmine spent her waking hours staring at the infant. She noticed how his tiny arms and legs moved, how his mouth twitched, how his eyelids fluttered. As a talented artist, she had a sharp eye for details; she could always recall a person's face with precision.

She beamed when the boy curved his lips upward in a smile. She couldn't resist singing to him when he fussed or just cooed. Her heart ached when he cried, and she would bounce him up and down in her arms in gentle movements. Now, she understood what her mother and aunt had meant when they'd talked about maternal instinct.

Knowing they had limited time together kept Jasmine up in the middle of the night. The pain grew stronger as she spent more time with him. One day, he curled his fingers around hers and wouldn't let go. When she finally extricated herself from his grip, he wailed. His need for her broke her heart.

The war against Japan was still raging across the nation. Children were dying. Even children with families to protect them were not safe. How could she expect an orphanage to keep him safe? How could she trust strangers to raise her baby?

Naturally, Jasmine was apprehensive about his Japanese blood. *Lao shu de er zi hui da dong—A baby rat knows how to dig a hole instinctively.* Perhaps he would be as evil as his father. *Is a monster born a monster? Or does one learn to be monstrous?*

She could teach him well so that he might turn out to be a decent human being. To convince herself, she recited the famous *Three Character Classic:* "Man on earth, good at birth. The same nature, varies on nurture."

But what would Uncle, Birch, and Daisy think? Would they accept a child of the enemy? So many of their loved ones and friends had been killed by the Japanese during the war. Would they allow a boy who was half Japanese to be part of the family?

She knew they were kindhearted people. Surely, they would look past the pain and accept this innocent child. Even so, if anyone found out that the boy was half Japanese, the family would be shamed. It hurt Jasmine to think that she might bring disgrace and dishonor to them. Both her uncle and cousin were well-known military officers. Her family was highly respected in their society.

And what about Danny Hardy? If she kept this boy, she could never be with him. *Danny!* Jasmine cried out his name.

Chinese culture upheld female purity as a virtue above all else, and for thousands of years, there had been a double standard. A man could have several concubines, but a woman was supposed to marry one man for life; and she had better be a virgin when she married, otherwise she would be humiliated. A widow was often encouraged to live the rest of her life alone. Although this traditional value had started to change in recent years, the idea was still entrenched in the culture.

Jasmine felt tainted and broken. Her body and spirit had been gravely injured. She was no longer the young, virtuous woman that Danny had met, and she could not love him the way he deserved to be loved—with her clean body and pure heart.

Yet, she'd believed their love was so strong that nothing would come between them.

But a child would! Not just any child. An enemy's child. He would be a constant reminder of the pain and the humiliation she'd endured. How could she let the Flying Tiger suffer?

Danny deserves to be happy. To live a wonderful life without the relentless reminder of the war. To be with a beautiful sweet girl, a girl like Daisy. Jasmine remembered seeing the infatuated gaze in her young cousin's eyes. *Daisy loves him. Without me, she might have a chance to fulfill her dream.*

Back and forth, Jasmine debated what to do. Whether she kept the baby or gave him up, she was going to lose part of herself.

Chapter 3

Each night Jasmine went to sleep determined to let the hunter take the baby away the next day. Every morning she awoke resolved to keep him one more day. A week had passed, and she still couldn't make up her mind.

On the seventh day, she noticed something odd. The newborn was fussier than usual. He cried almost nonstop even after she fed him and changed his diaper. Later, he refused to eat, and his face contorted in pain. "What's wrong with him?" she asked.

Da Shu took the infant and touched his forehead with his lips. "He's hot." Together they checked his naked body and soon found the problem: his back was discolored. Da Ma lifted her head and exchanged a worried look with her husband.

"What is it?" Jasmine asked.

"We must cut open his skin," said Da Shu.

She was so astonished that she stammered. "What...do you... mean?" She took the boy back. Holding him tightly, she asked in an unsteady voice, "Why?"

"There's pus under the skin." Da Ma plopped down on the edge of Jasmine's cot. "We have to get it out."

"I'll go down the mountains... I'll take him—"

"We don't have money. Not enough for surgery. The clinic won't do anything—"

Jasmine struggled to get out of bed. "I'll beg them. I'll—"

"They won't care!" Sadness loomed in Da Ma's eyes. "I knelt in front of them... I—" She couldn't finish her sentence.

Jasmine's eyes widened.

"Our daughter had the same problem," the hunter took over. His Adam's apple slid up and down before he continued. "I took the best fur we had. They wouldn't take it. Told me to sell it first, but by then..."

Knowing the couple had only one son, she guessed the outcome. Her disbelief was mixed with sorrow and sympathy.

"After our daughter's death,"—Da Ma smoothed Jasmine's hair with her calloused hand—"he talked to several herbalists. He wanted to know—"

"...If I could save her. Besides, we're hunters. We live in this remote place. We have to take care of our injuries. There are ways our ancestors taught us." Moments later, Da Shu returned with a wooden box full of bottles and jars. He picked up one of them. "Magic White Powder is similar to—"

"The famous White Medicine from Yunnan!" Jasmine blurted out. "You got it from Doctor Wang!"

The couple nodded in unison.

She let a breath escape through her teeth. Doctor Wang had used the herbal remedy to save Danny's leg. Knowing how potent it was, she nodded her consent.

"Let us take him. You shouldn't..." said Da Shu while his wife went to boil water.

Jasmine shook her head. She kissed the baby's cheeks, and still sitting on the bed, laid him on his stomach over her lap.

The hunter cleaned the infected area with cooking wine. A boiled knife in hand, he signaled his wife to hold the infant down.

"Wait!" Jasmine waved her arms. "You don't have anything...to numb..."

"He's too young—"

"No!"

"There isn't any other way."

"No!" Tears sprang to her eyes. Nine months earlier, Jasmine had been tortured by a group of Japanese soldiers. One of them had slashed her chest and cheek with a sword. The pain was so excruciating that it was beyond words. How could a week-old newborn endure it?

"Don't wait," said Da Shu. "The longer we wait, the more danger..."

"Listen to him," choked the old woman. "Perhaps our daughter died so that we could save this child."

Jasmine could no longer resist. With a nod, she held the boy and squinted as if in this way she wouldn't witness the misery.

As the blade slit his skin, the baby howled. With every ounce of energy, he wriggled and thrashed. He cried so much that by the time they drained the pus, his voice cracked, and he could hardly breathe.

His bloodcurdling wails pierced through Jasmine and filled her with terror. She once again felt the tip of the blade plunged into her chest. But this was even more painful than the torture she had endured. *I'm so sorry!* In her mind, she cried: *Dear Guanyin, the Goddess of Mercy, don't hurt him anymore! He's just a baby. He's not responsible for his father's crime.*

Finally, Da Shu sprinkled the white powder on the laceration and wrapped it with clean gauze.

For the next several weeks, Jasmine held the infant in her arms most of the time so that he wouldn't have to lie on his back. The couple continued to attend the wound with the Magic White Powder and other homeopathic medicines. It was an agonizing process, but finally, his fever broke.

It took several months for the boy to completely recover. Once again, the pink color returned to his cheeks. His face was no longer contorted with pain. His lips twitched upward from time to time. Seeing the fragile life going through this ordeal, Jasmine made up her mind: she would keep the child.

This was one of the hardest choices Jasmine had ever made. She knew it would change the course of her life; by keeping the baby, her chance to reunite with her family and Danny ended. She would raise him in this remote area, isolated from the outside world so that he wouldn't be scorned, her family wouldn't be shamed, and Danny Hardy would have an opportunity for love and true happiness. With a soft smile, she rocked the infant in her arms. But deep inside, she wept.

"What name are you going to give him?" Da Ma asked, bouncing the infant up and down in her arms. They'd been calling him Bao Bao—Treasure. It was a common endearment for babies.

Jasmine hadn't considered it. She'd planned to give him away.

It would be perfect to combine her father's name with her uncle's. *Wen* meant intelligence or education, while *Wu* meant martial arts or military. *Wen wu shuang quan—Good at both books and martial arts* was often used to describe a person who was intelligent and strong. Bai Wenwu would be ideal. Yet, Jasmine hesitated. She didn't think her father or uncle would have approved of her keeping this boy.

What about a tree name?

Her aunt was fond of flora. She had been the one to suggest Jasmine's name, and she'd called her daughter Daisy, and her son Birch. After the death of her parents, her aunt had treated her like a daughter, and Jasmine would have loved to follow her tradition. Yet, she doubted her aunt would have been happy for her or the child.

How about Hui Guo—Repentant? No, that wouldn't be fair to the boy. He hadn't done anything wrong; there was nothing for him to repent.

"Bai Ge," she lifted her head and replied.

"White Dove? How lovely!" Da Ma was pleased.

Da Shu took the baby. "Fly!" he said, lifting the baby above his head. "Soar like a dove!"

By giving him this name, Jasmine hoped that the war against Japan would end soon, her son would have a peaceful life, and she could look past the pain and the humiliation she'd suffered and could make peace with the past.

Chapter 4

The joy of being a mother had taken Jasmine by surprise. Before Bai Ge was born, she hadn't smiled for months, and she'd often suffered nightmares of her torture in the summer of 1942. The pain, loss, and regret always haunted her. But now, the mere existence of the boy kept her fear and suffering at bay and brought a sense of happiness that had become alien to her. His smile warmed her heart; his soft touch reached her soul.

The couple adored the boy as much as she did. It wasn't easy to live in the small cabin in this far-flung area, but the family of four managed a simple and peaceful life, untouched by the ugliness of the war or the menace of the outside world. Besides gardening, gathering, and sewing, Jasmine had started to paint again. She signed her name as Bai Wenwu, combining her father and uncle's names. The sale of her paintings provided additional income for the family.

Throughout the years, she'd fought the urge to call her uncle and cousins. She missed them terribly and wanted to know how they were doing. Occasionally, the hunters would bring rumors about the famous and victorious Flying Tiger, and each time the news stirred the deepest part of her.

So far, she'd managed to control her impulse. She was determined to live here with the boy, without shaming her family, or making life difficult for Danny. Not a single human being would know her secret—that she'd kept the enemy's child.

One day in September 1945, Da Shu returned from a trip to Anning—Town of Peace at the bottom of the mountains—with delicacies like sweet rice wine, rice cake, and firecrackers, items that they wouldn't usually buy. A smile bloomed on his weathered face. "You won't believe this," he said, his eyes shining with an eagerness he couldn't hide. "The war is over!"

"What?" Jasmine and Da Ma exclaimed in unison.

"We won. The Japanese Devils are out!"

"Oh, God!" cried Jasmine. "Are you sure?" She was afraid that the news was too good to be true.

"Yes! The Japs are gone. We're free."

"Thank God!" Jasmine lifted the two-and-a-half-year-old boy and twirled him a few times. She let out an ecstatic hoot as a surge of exhilaration coursed through her body.

Bai Ge giggled.

"Thank you, Guanyin, the Goddess of Mercy!" Da Ma gripped her husband's hands. Exultation made her tanned face look younger than her age. "Finally, our son can come home!"

Da Shu nodded. He opened his arms and pulled everyone into a fierce embrace. With tears in their eyes, the four hugged each other, cheering nonstop.

That evening, they ate the rice cake and drank the sweet rice wine. When it was dark enough, they lit the firecrackers in the yard. Bai Ge was startled by the first boom, but then he let out a whoop of glee. Clapping his hands, he jumped up and down. A smile lit his face, and his undiluted joy mirrored what everyone felt. The ordinarily quiet mountainous area came alive.

After the boy went to bed, the three adults continued drinking and talking.

When Jasmine went to sleep in the wee hours, her face was red and ached from smiling so much. She could hardly believe the war had finally ended with the Japanese surrender.

As early as 1931, Japan had launched an undeclared war on China and conquered the Northeast Territory of the country. Fourteen years! Millions of people had died, including many of her family members and friends. She'd prayed countless times for the Japanese to be defeated.

She wished that her mother, her father, her aunt, and Professor Valentine were still alive! She wished that Doctor Wang and all the villagers could experience this. They would be thrilled. She also wished that Jack Longman, Danny's best friend, and all the Flying Tigers who had sacrificed their lives for her country could witness this moment. They hadn't died in vain. Their bravery had meant something.

Danny must be on cloud nine right now. She longed to share the moment with someone special. Tears of joy, longing, and sadness trickled down her cheeks. Wiping the salty streaks from her face, Jasmine beamed again. When was the last time she'd gone to bed deliriously happy? On Danny's twenty-eighth birthday, perhaps? It had been three years. The Flying Tiger would be thirty-one by now.

Will he go back to America soon? Did he fall in love with Daisy? Will he take her back to the States with him? While Jasmine projected happiness for her younger cousin, she couldn't help feeling sorry for herself. She would spend the rest of her life in this isolated hunting cabin without the man she loved.

———————

Life became routine as the excitement subsided. At times Jasmine could see the rest of her life unfolding before her eyes—like the couple, she would stay in this cabin, gardening, gathering, painting, and selling her art. It would be a hard but peaceful life.

The shabby hut lacked any modern conveniences. It was small. A curtain separated her cot from the couple's quarter—a handmade bed, a rough-hewn table with two chairs, and a clay stove. There was no electricity. No heating. In the winter, they wore heavy coats inside the house. A nearby creek was their water source. In the summer, they stepped into the stream to bathe. On cold days, they boiled water to sponge themselves. Washing dishes or clothes in freezing water was torturous. But life in a peaceful place was what she needed.

What about Bai Ge then? One day he would grow up, and Jasmine often wondered what she should advise him. Should she keep him here for the rest of his life? Or should she encourage him to go out and see the world? A well-known saying came to her mind: Great ambitious men travel far and aim high.

Ambition, however, should not be her son's priority, for he was different. It would be hard for a naïve young man raised in a remote area to survive, let alone to strive in the outside world. Jasmine decided that she would follow in the hunter's footsteps. His family had lived in this place for generations. Da Ma had been an abandoned orphan. She'd been rescued by the hunter's parents and had become part of the family.

But the future could wait; Bai Ge was just a youngster.

Chapter 5

— — — — — — —

In the spring of 1947, Da Shu came back from Anning with a torn-away piece of newspaper. "I was told that this is the famous Flying Tiger." With a smile, he pointed to a picture. "The paper is old, but I figure…"

One look at the photograph caused Jasmine to feel a great tenderness in her heart. In their flight jackets, two men stood side by side in front of an airplane painted with Tiger Teeth. The photo showed Danny Hardy and her cousin Birch Bai. The American had his left arm wrapped around Birch's shoulders; her cousin placed his left arm on the wing of the aircraft. Radiant smiles spread across their youthful faces.

What had happened, she wondered? *How did the two of them meet? Was Birch now the Flying Tiger's wingman?* She'd heard that the American had formed a tight bond with his Chinese wingman, but not in her wildest dreams could she imagine that her beloved cousin was that man.

Jasmine was familiar with their postures. She'd painted a similar scene in a cave where Danny, Daisy, and she had lived for several days. *My God! How incredible!* She was delighted for both.

Another look of Danny's face brought a warmth that started in the pit of her stomach. A telltale pink stained her cheeks. With amazement, she read the article.

Then her eyes widened. The news struck like a thunderbolt. Her lips started to tremble, and her hands shook. In the end, her whole body shuddered.

"What's wrong?" asked Da Shu. Concern drew his brows together. Illiterate, he had no idea what was revealed in the article.

"Tell us," said Da Ma.

Jasmine couldn't speak. She could hardly breathe. The newspaper slipped from her fingers and fell to the floor. Feeling the full force of her grief, she wailed and then ran out of the house.

Bai Ge called out and started to follow her, but Da Shu grabbed him and held him tightly. "Let Mommy be alone now."

Jasmine wandered along the trail. Cold winter had turned to a warm spring. New shoots emerged, and the area was covered with different shades of green. The season's first wildflowers dotted the edge of the lilting stream, their scent delicate and subtle. Rays of sunshine fought through the overhead branches, sending golden beams onto the path. The forest was enchanting.

But the beauty didn't belong to her. It didn't belong to Danny. Nor to Daisy. Life was anything but predictable. Snippets of the article flashed through her mind, turning her world upside down.

The death of Birch's two younger sisters had brought them together, and Danny Hardy and Birch Bai had become best friends and sworn brothers. They had flown many missions together.

During the summer of 1945, both airmen's planes had gone down in Yunnan Province, and they were captured, imprisoned, and tortured by the Japanese for information about the atomic bomb.

Days before the war against Japan ended, the Flying Tiger had made an irreversible decision to save his brother. He was buried in an unmarked grave with six other prisoners near Dashan; the exact location was unknown.

Losing a leg, Birch had barely survived. He had been in a coma for six months.

It was a long article, but those words burned in her head. *Two sisters? Daisy is dead! How could it be? What happened?* The report didn't reveal any details. *Not Daisy! So sweet and vivacious, and only seventeen!* Jasmine hoped and prayed that someone had made a mistake and that the news was wrong.

She felt sick. Bending forward, she took one deep breath after another. Not a day had passed that she hadn't thought of Danny, and the very idea of him buried in a cold unmarked grave chilled her soul. Everything about him—high spirits, infectious smile, handsome face, gold-speckled brown eyes—was etched into her memory. He should look like the one in the photograph, which was credited to another news article published several years earlier. It was inconceivable to think of him dead and gone. All the suffering she'd experienced resurfaced, and she was plagued by the dark thought that life had no meaning. Otherwise, how could someone like Danny die so needlessly?

Poor Uncle! Nothing was more painful than a parent having to bury his child. Being a mother now, Jasmine could not imagine his grief. And poor Birch! He must feel irrevocably guilty. The Chinese culture viewed an elder brother as a fatherly figure to his younger siblings.

I must go home, she screamed silently. *I must be there for Uncle and Birch.* Her family needed her. No more hiding. Over a thousand miles stretched between the cabin and Chungking, where her uncle and Birch lived, but she would return home even if she had to crawl.

She had to find Danny. She would ask Birch for more information. She could not allow the Flying Tiger to remain forever trapped in an unmarked shallow grave in a foreign land. *I'll send you back to America,* she swore. *I'll send you back to your family.*

This was an almost impossible promise, but Jasmine was determined to spend the rest of her life, if necessary, to achieve her goal. *Only death will stop me.* Wiping tears from her face, she lifted her head. For the first time in years, her eyes illuminated with an unbreakable fortitude.

When she returned to the cabin, she told the couple the sad news and informed them of her decision.

"Leave the boy with us," suggested Da Ma. "He's only four, too young to travel."

Jasmine shook her head. It was hard to believe that four years earlier, she'd planned to send the boy to an orphanage. Now she couldn't even leave him with the two people who had saved her life.

"Much too hard to bring a child along." The old woman made an earnest effort to convince her.

"And the road isn't safe," said Da Shu. "The country is in the middle of the Civil War." He emitted a long-winded sigh. "When will we have real peace? Now, the Chinese are killing each other."

"You should not leave," said Da Ma. "But I know you've already made up your mind. But don't bring the boy. We'll take good care of him."

"I want to go with Mommy." Bai Ge clutched Jasmine's pant leg.

"Da Ma, Da Shu, I appreciate your offer, but I can't go without him."

"At least wait for a few days," conceded the hunter. "Let me sell those furs and your paintings first. You'll need money."

The old woman sighed. She took off a jade bracelet from her wrist and handed it to Jasmine.

"No! I can't—"

"It belonged to his great-grandmother." She took Jasmine's hand and slid it onto her wrist. "I was going to give it to our son. But..." A cloud ran over her face.

Jasmine lowered her head. She understood Da Ma's pain. It had been a year and a half since the war against Japan had ended. Yet, their son had not returned home. Either he'd been killed, or he was in the middle of another war. The chance of them ever seeing him again was next to none.

"Thank you!" Jasmine knelt on the floor in front of the couple and signaled for the boy to follow her. A lump formed in the back of her throat as she bowed down. The hunters were like her parents, saving her twice, sheltering her for years. *We'll come back.* She swore in her mind, but she didn't say it aloud. Considering the uncertainty of her life thus far, she was afraid to make an empty promise.

Chapter 6

–– –– –– –– –– –– ––

Between the hunting cabin and Chungking lay a thousand miles of treacherous mountains. There was no direct route. When Jasmine came to the village with Daisy in 1941, Birch had taken them flying to Kunming and then on an overnight train to Anning, the town sitting at the edge of the wilderness. From there, young villagers had carried Daisy and Jasmine in bamboo-pole sedan chairs up to Tao Hua Cun—Village of Peach Blossoms.

The hunters accompanied Jasmine and Bai Ge to Anning. After that, the mother and the son would be on their own—taking a train to Kunming, then riding a series of buses to Chungking.

Saying goodbye was extremely hard for Jasmine, now that she'd just lost two more loved ones. Hot tears singed the back of her eyelids. She had no idea if or when she would see the hunters again. But for her son's sake, she didn't allow herself to cry and forced a smile until the couple was out of sight. In her mind, she gave her thanks again and again.

She called her uncle at a payphone first. Her hands quivered as she dialed the number. She hadn't spoken to him for five years and was eager to hear his voice. *Maybe Birch will pick up?* From the article, she'd learned that her cousin had been seriously wounded. Although the newspaper was months old, he would still be recovering at home.

Her excitement was replaced by a stab of disappointment when she heard that the number had been disconnected. But why should she be surprised? These were turbulent times. She hurriedly dialed the operator and was even more dismayed when no information was available.

The coach class of the overnight train was crowded. Jasmine got there early enough to find an aisle seat. Some passengers traveled with domestic animals; others carried their baggage using shoulder poles. A handful of men started to smoke as they settled, the musty smell filling the air.

This was the first time Jasmine was out in public since her torture. She noticed that most people avoided looking at her face directly. Some switched their gaze back-and-forth from her smooth right cheek to her scarred left one. Different people displayed different expressions: curiosity, contempt, sympathy, compassion, even admiration.

She held Bai Ge in her lap. After a long day of walking down the mountains and waiting at the train station, the boy was exhausted. Momentarily he fell asleep.

Jasmine was exhausted as well. But she was in that ironic state of being too tired to fall asleep. Her mind raced a hundred miles per hour, mimicking the rhythmic, *clickety-clackety* sound of the wheels on the tracks. She grieved for her loved ones. She was nervous about their long trip. She missed the hunters and their peaceful life.

The report of Danny being tortured and killed in a Japanese prison had left her heartbroken. She recoiled as she conjured fearful scenes in her imagination. When she banished those grisly thoughts, images of Daisy crept into her mind. Jasmine didn't know how her young cousin had died, yet she knew the void created by her death would never be filled. Only in the wee hours did she surrender to her exhaustion and sleep.

Sometime in the middle of the night, the brakes let out an ear-splitting screech as the train lurched to a sudden stop. Jasmine sat bolt upright and jerked her eyes open.

"Mommy..." Bai Ge raised his head from her chest. Rubbing his drowsy eyes, he asked, "Are we there?"

Jasmine shook her head. She wasn't sure. It was still dark outside. They were not supposed to arrive in Kunming before daybreak.

"What the hell?" grunted a soldier in a Nationalist uniform.

"For crying out loud!" complained another man in a business suit as he checked his watch. "It's only one o'clock."

"I'll be damned. What on earth is going on?"

Fellow passengers clucked their agreement. Some yawned and rubbed the sleep from their eyes, while others stood and stretched their arms and legs. Babies squealed, kids whined, and mothers tried to soothe them.

Then the metallic sound cut through the chatting. The doors rattled open. Half a dozen men barged inside, their faces covered by dark bandanas. Each was holding some kind of weapon—a knife, a pistol, or a rifle. For a wild moment, the car was silent.

"Are they bad guys?" asked Bai Ge. His voice wasn't loud, but in a quiet place, it was clear. Jasmine put a hand over his mouth. "Shhh…" she whispered. The feral gleam in those men's eyes put her on guard.

"We can do this the easy way, or we can do it the hard way," said one of the robbers, holding a pistol in his right hand. In black clothing, he was short in stature, stocky, dark-skinned, and looked like a bear. His deep voice boomed with unquestionable authority. "Now, move out. Single file. Start from this side. Put all your money and jewelry in the bag." He pointed to a wiry man with a knife and a sack. "When I say all, I mean everything. If I see—"

The Nationalist soldier straightened and reached up. But before he could grab his weapon on the overhead rack, a slim robber moved in and smacked the side of his head with the butt of the rifle. The soldier slumped onto his seat. Blood trickled from his temple.

The captives let out a horrified gasp.

Jasmine clutched the boy closer to her chest in an attempt to block his view, but he fought to see what was happening around them.

"Don't do anything stupid like that again," said the man in charge. "Next time—"

"Hey, the country is at war, but there's still a system of law." The businessman madly waved his arms. "You can't—"

25

Bam. Bam. The robber fired two shots toward the ceiling.

Fearful screams filled the enclosed space.

The outlaw smirked. *"This* is the law." He swung his gun toward the crowd, madness glinting in his eyes.

Everybody ducked and cried.

"If you don't obey, you'll find out that my bullets have eyes."

There wasn't any choice. The passengers moved out. They handed their valuables as they exited the door as a bright flashlight shone in their eyes. Several travelers were caught hiding money, and they were beaten mercilessly.

When it was her turn, Jasmine took out all the money from her patchwork bag. Fear and anger throbbed through her, making her shudder. *What will we do without money?*

"Hey, don't you forget something?" The ringleader pointed to her left wrist. He stepped closer and exuded an air of menace that was as strong as his body odor. "Take it off."

Jasmine covered the jade bracelet with her right hand. She looked up, but the flashlight blinded her. "No, you can't—"

"Take it off!"

"It belongs to my family—"

"We don't care."

"I've already given you all our money." Frustrated and hurt, tossing caution to the wind, Jasmine raised her chin defiantly.

The robber slapped her across the face with his open palm, knocking her to the ground. Her ears rang from the blow. Blood dripped from her nose and the corner of her mouth. A purple-red imprint formed instantly on her right cheek. Snatching her arm, the man yanked the bracelet off her wrist.

"It's my grandma's!" Bai Ge growled and waved his thin arms. When the robber paid no attention to him, he grasped the hairy hand and took a big bite.

"Little bastard!" roared the man. He lifted his fist and swung toward the boy. Jasmine flung herself over her son. His fist landed on the back of her head.

Pain stole her breath. "You scum!" Through clenched teeth, she hissed, "You're not any better than the Japs!"

The leader studied the scars on her cheek. Then, unexpectedly, he turned and walked away.

———————

After the robbery, the thieves commandeered the train. It coughed and groaned as it crawled away, leaving a cloud of smoke that reeked of coal and the stunned passengers behind. A concoction of cries, shouts, and screams of obscenities filled the night air and lasted for several minutes. Then, gradually, it quieted down. Some passengers started walking along the rail tracks while others settled to wait for daybreak.

It seemed they were in the middle of nowhere. Without a flashlight, Jasmine didn't dare to walk. She found a fallen log and sank by its side. The night was chilly. Taking all the clothes from the patchwork bag, she wrapped both of them with everything they had.

The area became eerily quiet. Crickets in the nearby field chirped, and the familiar rhythmic sound gave her comfort. Overhead, stars glittered like diamonds in the velvet-black sky. In the dark, Jasmine listened to muffled voices.

"I doubt this is a simple robbery," said a man.

"What are you talking about?" asked a woman.

"I bet the Communist guerillas had something to do with it."

"Hush!"

"Think about it. Why would robbers need a train? They only want money. But the Communists—"

"Oh, shut up! Don't you think we have enough trouble?"

Is it true? Is it possible that those thugs were Communists? Although the conversation had stopped, questions lingered in her mind. Jasmine wasn't political, but she'd read all the newspapers the hunters bought for her. She wanted only to find out anything related to the Chinese Air Force and the American pilots. As a result, she'd learned about the Civil War as well as recent history.

Since 1927, the Nationalists and the Communists had fought for control of the country. The Japanese attack had brought the two parties together in 1937 to form a united front to counter the foreign invasion. But once their common enemy was defeated, the two sides resumed fighting. Once again, the country was in chaos.

Because her uncle and cousin had worked for the Nationalist government, she didn't know any members of the opposing party. Yet she doubted the robbery had been conducted by the Communists. Most passengers were ordinary people, not the Communists' enemies. *But why take the train?*

"Mommy, look!" cried Bai Ge.

Jasmine looked up in time to see a bright light streaking across the sky. "A shooting star!" she exclaimed.

Without taking his eyes off the sky, he said, "I'll wait for it to come again."

She leaned against the log and relaxed. Her son's sense of wonder made their predicament a little easier to tolerate.

Chapter 7

▬ ▬ ▬ ▬ ▬ ▬ ▬

Except for a few hidden bills, all her money was gone. Jasmine thanked Da Ma in her mind countless times. The old woman had sewn some cash into the hem of Bai Ge's coat. Without it, they couldn't have lasted a day.

But what will we do when the money is gone? Jasmine had no way to support them. She didn't know anyone. Even though she knew the number had been disconnected, she called her uncle again in the hope she could find new contact information. She looked for a job. But with a little boy, no one was willing to hire her. She even considered panhandling. Xiao Mei, their housemaid, had walked hundreds of miles to Chungking and begged for food along the way. Growing up in a high-class family, even when she was desperate, Jasmine was too proud to ask for money.

"I'm hungry," said Bai Ge, his eyes fixed on a nearby food stand.

It was a phrase that the boy said most these days. Whenever he said it, it felt like a dagger stabbing her heart. Looking at his thinning face and body, Jasmine felt helpless. She was down to the last bit of money, enough to buy only a few steamed buns.

It was noon. The streets were teeming with shoppers and sellers. Smoke wafted from the chimneys of restaurants, and steam rose from the stands of sidewalk vendors. The savory aroma made her stomach grumble. Trying to save money for the boy, Jasmine hadn't had anything to eat for two days. She was thin. Her cheeks were colorless.

Ever since her suicidal jump from the ridge five years earlier, she had walked with a slight limp. As they trudged through the street full of all kinds of shops, an idea came to her. Quickly she looked around and found what she was looking for. She stepped into a stationery store. Using the last bit of her precious money, she bought a pencil and a sketchbook.

Sitting by the curb, Jasmine wrote Live Portrait on the sketchbook, tore the paper out, and set it on the ground in front of her.

"Come here." She told the boy to sit by her side. Inhaling deeply, she started to sketch him. At four, Bai Ge was cute, with delicate features like hers, except his eyes were narrower.

On this noisy street, and in the dire situation in which they found themselves, Jasmine felt peace for the first time since she'd left the hunting hut. Art was her passion. She was at her best when she was immersed in it, and it showed.

Soon, a girl with a lithe figure strolled by. She was pretty—creamy skin, flashing black eyes, two pigtails hanging over her shoulders. "Oh, this is so nice. Wait!" she called out to a woman dressed in a high-necked lilac cheongsam and high heels. "Mama, may I have my picture drawn?"

The woman with curly hair and heavy makeup looked at her watch before asking Jasmine, "How long will it take?"

"About twenty minutes."

"No, it's too long." Impatiently, she looked at her watch again. "If you can't finish in ten minutes, I'll pay half." She sashayed toward a restaurant across the street.

The girl rolled her eyes after her mother and turned back to Jasmine. "Take your time. Don't worry about her. She just wants to play mahjong with her friends. Nothing important. I'll make sure you get paid in full."

"How old are you?" Jasmine asked as she started to draw.

"Thirteen. I'll be fourteen in a month."

"What's your name?"

"Jin Ling."

"Lovely. You have a voice just like your name—Jingle Bell."

A grin created two dimples on the girl's round face. Jasmine's pencil stopped moving. For a split second, she thought she was looking at Daisy. Tears welled in her eyes, and she had to blink a few times to clear them. *How could someone like Daisy die at such a young age? How did she die?* She'd asked these questions a million times. *Daisy was with Danny when I left the cave.* The Flying Tiger and Birch had returned home safely. *How come she didn't?* How did Birch handle the pain of losing his sister? He adored her so much.

Ten minutes later, the girl walked away with her portrait and a dimpled smile. Jasmine looked at the money in her hand. It was enough to buy several steamed buns. She sighed, but she was thankful that at least her son wouldn't feel hungry today.

———

"Would you like to hear a story?" asked Jasmine while they were waiting for customers.

Bai Ge took a big bite of a steamed bun and nodded.

"Let me see." She tilted her head, debating which story to tell.

Jing Zhong Bao Guo would be the right choice. Many boys were taught to *Serve the Country with the Utmost Loyalty* at a young age. Almost a thousand years earlier, a mother had tattooed these four characters on her son's back with an embroidery needle and smeared the writing with ink, encouraging him to fight for his country. Yue Fei, sixteen at the time, had later become a famous military commander and a national hero.

Jasmine remembered Birch had told her that one of his early memories was his father telling him this story. "From the time I could crawl," he'd said, "I learned that the highest duty is to sever our nation."

Yet she hesitated. Japan had been a threat to China throughout history and their biggest enemy in recent years. But the boy was half Japanese. Whether she admitted it or not, he had Japanese blood. Should she teach him to hate the people who were his relatives?

And what is a country when it's in the middle of a civil war? Now, the Chinese are killing the Chinese. Brothers are slaughtering brothers. Which "country" should one serve? If she had doubts, how could she teach her son? Jasmine decided *Kong Rong Rang Li* would be a better choice.

"Once upon a time," she began, "there was a boy called Kong Rong. He had six brothers, five older and one younger. One day his father bought pears for the family. Kong Rong picked the smallest one. His father was surprised and asked, 'Why did you pick the smallest one?' Can you think of any reason?"

Bai Ge shook his head, his tiny eyes wide open.

"Kong Rong said, 'I'm younger, so I should eat the smaller one. My big brothers should eat the larger ones.'"

Bai Ge nodded. Then he scratched his head. "What about his younger brother?"

Jasmine was pleased. "Kong Rong said, 'I'm older than him. I should give the bigger one to my little brother.' Do you understand why he did that?"

A smile came over his face as he stuffed the rest of the bun into his mouth. "He didn't like pears."

"Oh, he loved pears."

The boy's little eyebrows furrowed.

"He did it because he loved his brothers. You see, he wanted his brothers to eat something nice more than he wanted it for himself. He was kind. When he grew up, he became a great scholar."

"May I be a great scholar when I grow up?"

"Yes, of course. You—"

Just then, the girl rushed back. She thrust something in Jasmine's hand. "They're sweet," she called out as she scurried away.

Jasmine looked down—several colorful candies lay in her palm. She felt as if her skin were burning by fire and quickly handed them to Bai Ge.

The sweets reminded her of the village kids and their innocent smiles. They were all dead, slaughtered by the Japanese soldiers. Using candies, a Japanese officer had bribed and tricked a simple-minded villager. As a result, Jasmine was singled out as the caregiver of the American pilot. *Poor Mutou!* The image of the teenager's ripped stomach appeared in her mind, and she grimaced. The candies he hadn't had a chance to eat were scattered around his body.

"Mommy," Bai Ge exclaimed. "This is so good. So sweet! Here…" He handed one to her. "Try it." He licked the candy again, grinning from ear to ear. "What's it called?"

Jasmine had never bought candies for her son. When they lived in the hunting hut, it had been far from any town. Purchasing the absolute essential materials was hard enough. She couldn't bother the old couple for luxuries like candy. When they were on the road, she had no extra money; keeping them from hunger was already a difficult job. And even if she had money, she couldn't stand the thought of candy.

Without hearing an answer, the boy handed her another piece.

"Don't you want to have it?" she asked.

He nodded.

"I thought you liked it."

"Yes, very much!" He licked his lips. "But I want to be a scholar."

"A scholar?"

He puffed up his scrawny chest and declared, "Yes, like Kong Rong."

Jasmine's heart turned over. She took the boy in her arms.

Chapter 8

Jasmine made enough money by drawing portraits to have warm meals and sometimes a roof over their heads. They moved slowly from town to town, occasionally by bus, other times by hitchhiking a ride, but mostly they walked. Traveling without money was hard, and having a young child made it even harder.

The mountainous scenery was breathtaking—green valleys plunged thousands of feet, and steel gray granite soared into the sky. Jasmine had marveled at the beauty on her way to Yunnan Province years earlier. Now, she had no energy to enjoy it. Reaching Chungking safely was her only goal.

One day they stayed in an inn with a dozen people in one room. The window had no screens. When they were closed, it was stuffy and hot. In the middle of the night, someone couldn't stand it anymore and opened it. The situation became worse. Although it was cooler, masses of mosquitoes swooped in. Without a mosquito net, the high-pitched hum buzzed in her ears and kept her awake the rest of the night. The boy slept through it, but he was full of bug bites. Jasmine felt terrible that she had no means to protect her son.

The path was unpaved. It was narrow, rough, and with hundreds of sharp curves that hugged the steep mountainside. As they passed a stretch with many potholes, the bus rocked from side to side. With one hand pulling Bai Ge close to her, she covered her mouth with the other but still heard her involuntary gasps. A few passengers threw up. The putrid smell made the ride even tougher.

Looking down from the top of the mountains, she thought the road looked like a serpent and wondered how they could navigate it. It was so narrow that she watched a truck tumble down a sheer cliff. Her face was frozen in shock and terror.

"It happens once in a while. No sweat," said the bus driver. Then he started telling hair-raising stories that had happened on the route. He held everyone on the bus spellbound.

The path was part of the Burma Road, which was over seven hundred miles, connecting Kunming in Yunnan Province to Lashio in Burma. It had been built during the war against Japan so that military supplies could be transported from the outside world to China.

Jasmine knew that the Flying Tigers had protected this supply artery until Burma was occupied by the Japanese. She remembered the Salween Gorge Battle that Danny had talked about. The only thing standing between Kunming and the Japanese Army on this road was the American Volunteer Group. The Flying Tigers alone had stopped the enemy's rapid advance at the gorge. Without Danny and his friends, most likely, the Japanese would have crossed the river, and Chinese history might be vastly different.

"A few foreign companies said they could build the road, oh say, eight or nine years if we provided modern machinery." The driver smirked. "Guess how long it took us to build it?" He paused and then said with a proud voice, "Less than a year! Without machines. Only farm tools and bare hands. But we did the job. When I say 'we,' I mean villagers, mostly old men, women, and poor kids! Hard to believe?"

The white-knuckle ride continued from Kunming to Chungking, passing more mountainous regions. Some parts were so hazardous that they were impassable during winter, but it wasn't much better in spring or summer. Monsoons started in May and continued well into July. Torrential rain often created mudslides. Once, they were stranded for several weeks before they were able to leave. Luckily, the nearby villagers opened their doors. Without their help, Jasmine and the other passengers would not have survived in the wilderness. She drew as many portraits as they wanted.

Another time, they were in the back of a truck when they drove through an overhanging waterfall. Both of them were drenched. Even though it was summer, the spring water was freezing cold. She shivered and grunted. Wiping the water from his face, Bai Ge grinned. "Now, my hair is clean." Sitting in the back of the truck, their hair had been white with dust. Nothing seemed to sour this boy's spirit, and his sense of adventure made their journey tolerable.

It was the fall of 1947 when they finally reached Chungking.

Jasmine had been eager to return to her family, but as she stood outside her uncle's house, she hesitated. The air smelled of the familiar bittersweet magnolia. Two stone lions perched at the side of the gate had guarded the house for decades. Stepping closer to the one on the right, she rubbed its nose as Daisy had done whenever she passed.

Tears filled her eyes. Daisy was gone; she would never grow older than seventeen; she would never touch the lion in this life…

The lions, which were supposed to keep them safe, had failed her. Jasmine, as an elder cousin, had failed her. *Zhang xiong ru fu, zhang jie ru mu—An elder brother is like a father and an elder sister a mother.* When her uncle sent them to the village in Yunnan, he'd asked her to take care of Daisy.

"Mommy, I'm hungry." Bai Ge gripped her pant leg.

Jasmine shook herself out of her daze. It was almost dinner time. Smoke wafted from the chimneys of the nearby houses. The smell of delicious food permeated the air, and the aroma made her stomach growl.

She felt awful. At four, the boy seemed to be in constant hunger. Wiping tears from her eyes, she squatted down and picked him up. "We'll have something delicious to eat very soon. Grand-uncle has lots of goodies for you."

"Who is he?"

"Grand-uncle is a wonderful man. He's my uncle. Your grandpa's brother. Don't you remember? I've told you before. He loves a good boy like you." *I hope he'll love you,* Jasmine thought wearily. *I hope at least he'll accept you.*

The boy grinned, innocent, and trusting.

"What would you like first? A steamed bun or a baked sweet yam?" Jasmine asked. The smile was still on her face, but concern knotted her brow.

A gaunt-faced old man opened the door. He was in servant's clothes that seemed too large for his stick-thin body. "Go. Go away. Beg somewhere else—"

"I'm not a beggar!" Jasmine cut him off. She stood taller. Even in dirty clothes, she exuded a sense of dignity. "I'm here to see General Bai. He's my uncle."

The old man looked her up and down, skeptical. "General Bai moved away. This house belongs to—"

"Moved away?" She staggered half a step back. Stabilizing herself, she asked in a hurry, "Where did he go? Is it far? How can I find him?"

He shook his head. "I don't know. I'm just a doorman."

"Please! Ask someone else! Ask the new owner. He should know."

The doorman shook his head again. "I've already asked him before. Someone else wanted to know, too."

"Please! It's important. Let me talk to him." Jasmine stepped inside the gate.

"Hold on. Hold on." The doorman raised his hands, blocking her. "I'll ask him again. Just wait here." He pushed her out and closed the door in front of her.

She was so close, standing right outside her home, yet she was so far away. Where had they moved? Would she find them? She had no money left. How would she feed her son?

A few minutes drew out like days. Finally, the door squeaked opened. "As I told you, Mr. Qian doesn't know. They left a year ago, but Mr. Qian doesn't know where they moved to."

"Oh, no! What about their…mail?"

"General Bai sends someone to pick up his mail from time to time. If you leave your address, we'll tell the person to get in touch with you when he comes again."

Tears rolled in her eyes, but she refused to cry. She'd been through worse. "May I ask a favor? I'm not a beggar, but I've lost everything. Could you please give us a couple of buns?"

The man looked at her again, shaking his head, even more skeptical.

"My son—"

He didn't allow her to finish. The door slammed in her face—the door of her former home.

Chapter 9

— — — — — — —

Jasmine sat down by the side of the stone lion. She had to rest. She hadn't eaten anything for two days. With the little money she had, she'd bought food for her son.

Late afternoon shadows slanted across the land. Above them, two house finches fluttered past, playing tag in the clusters of white flowers and the golden leaves of the magnolia. She propped herself against the stone lion and shut her eyes. "I'm going to take a short nap," she said as she circled her arm around the boy. Bai Ge sat quietly. Before long, she heard his soft snore. A lump formed in her throat as she pulled him closer.

Jasmine couldn't fall asleep, even though she was dead tired. Too much was on her mind, and hunger made her feel hollow and jittery.

Where have Uncle and Birch gone?

Her aunt had decorated the house, and everything had remained the same, even after her death. If her uncle and cousin were still in Chungking, they would not have moved to a different location.

Had they gone back to Nanking? Before the Japanese invasion, the capital of the Republic of China was their home. But why would they go there? *Mom and Dad are gone. There isn't any incentive for them to go there.* She couldn't imagine what had happened to her parents' house. Ten years earlier, she'd fled from her home in haste and left her parents' bodies behind. The Japanese soldiers could have looted and destroyed the house as they'd done in many places. And if it was still standing, someone must have already occupied the space. Uncle and Birch wouldn't go there just to chase other people out of their home when they had a perfectly good house here in Chungking.

Could they have moved to the Village of Peach Blossoms?

The idea crossed Jasmine's mind only briefly before she dismissed it. Why would they choose to live in a poor, remote community when they had comfort here in the city? Besides, no one would be there. All the villagers had been slaughtered by the Japanese soldiers. By now, most likely, it had been turned into a ruin with only ill-fated ghosts around. Remembered images of mangled bodies in Doctor Wang's front yard made her wince.

Her mind spun in another direction. The article stated that "Both General Bai Wu and Major Bai Hua had retired from the Chinese Air Force." Could they have immigrated to America? Her uncle and aunt had encouraged her to marry Peter Peterson, her art teacher from the U.S. Her aunt had mentioned many times that one day she wanted the family to immigrate to a more developed country. Sadly, she'd never had the chance. *Could Uncle and Birch have actually moved to America?* If so, she would likely never see them again.

But the most pressing short-term issue was where she and Bai Ge could spend the night. The days were getting colder, and Jasmine did not want him to spend another night outside if she could prevent it. Sitting in the last glow of the sunset, she emitted a long-suffering sigh. A stab of loneliness struck her. *What am I going to do?* No answer came to her.

She missed the tiny cabin in that remote area in Yunnan. She missed the hunters, the green hills, the fresh air, the simple life.

People passed by, looking at her with curiosity or dismay.

"I'm hungry," said Bai Ge, shaking her sleeve. He looked up with his sleepy eyes.

Jasmine's stomach was grumbling. Her hand squeezed the last few coins left in her pocket. It was only enough to buy a bun.

"Grand-uncle is bad," grunted Bai Ge. "I don't like him."

"Oh, no. That man isn't Grand-uncle. Your Grand-uncle is very kind. He'll love you and feed you lots of delicious food." *If we can find him!*

By then, the sky glowed amber, rose, and pink. But the beauty didn't belong to her. She had no luxury to enjoy such splendor. *I should go. But where?* She sat there too exhausted to move. Gradually, her eyelids began to droop.

Then, she heard someone knocking at the door. "It's me again. Any news?" a man asked. For an instant, she thought she was dreaming. The voice seemed so familiar.

"Someone else was looking for General Bai as well. Look, she's still over there…"

Jasmine looked up. She sucked in her breath as she caught a glimpse of the back of a tall man in the Nationalist Army uniform. She couldn't see his face, but the familiarity was enough to make her heart skip a beat.

She surged to her feet, as if the man would disappear into thin air if she did not hurry. But hunger caught up with her; she felt dizzy. Stars swam in front of her eyes, and she fell backward. Her head hit the side of the stone lion, and darkness swallowed her. The last thing she heard was her son's cry: "Mommy! Mommy!"

Jasmine lifted her eyelids with a groan. She had no clue how long she'd lain passed out. She moved her head, and pain washed over her. A wave of dizziness engulfed her. She whimpered and closed her eyes.

"Don't move too fast," said a woman. "Let me give you some pain reliever."

A nurse with a soft smile came into her view. An acrid smell of antiseptics pervaded the air. Jasmine knew then that she was in a hospital. "Where is my son?" She struggled to sit up, but the headache pushed her back down.

"Don't worry. Your cousin took him to breakfast. You're lucky. He's nice."

"My cousin?"

"A good looking fellow."

Jasmine's jaw dropped before she said, "Are you sure?"

"That's what he said. He's coming back soon—" The nurse stopped, and her smile broadened. "Speak of the devil…"

Jasmine turned in time to see a tall, broad-shouldered man step into the room. He was holding Bai Ge in his arms. His face was in the shadow of his army cap. For a moment, she thought he was Birch. *Can it be? Am I dreaming?* Her beloved cousin had come to rescue her, just like he'd done after the Nanking Massacre. "Birch?"

"You're awake!" said the man in a cheerful tone. "I *was* Cousin Birch, but there is no need to pretend anymore. The doctor said you have a concussion, but you can go home now. You just need rest." A smug grin turned his mouth up in amusement as he put the boy down. "Only family members can stay here overnight. So, I used our old trick."

"*Li Ming Ge—Big Brother Li Ming?*" Jasmine could hear the doubt in her own voice.

"Yes!" Li Ming stepped closer and seized her hand with both of his. "I can't believe this. It's been nine years! Why are you here without your family? Where is your uncle? Where is Birch? Father John told me he'd sent you home not long after I left Professor Valentine's house. Who hurt you like this? What happened?"

"*Li Ming Ge!*" Jasmine pulled herself to a sitting position. So much had happened in the past nine years that she didn't know where to start. Tears rushed down and dripped from the end of her chin. The pain she'd suffered. The terror she'd experienced. The desperation she'd felt. And now the relief of seeing a friend when she had no one. A great weight had been lifted off her chest, and holding on to this Big Brother, she allowed herself the luxury to cry her heart out.

"Don't cry, Jasmine. No matter what happened, you're safe now. I'll protect you as you protected me."

"Mommy, look," said Bai Ge, lifting a handful of candies. "Uncle Li bought them for me. Don't cry. Here…you can have them."

"Your son is a good boy." He ruffled the child's hair. Then he turned to Jasmine. "Can you stand?" Seeing her nod, he pulled her to a standing position, and bending down, he picked up Bai Ge. "Would you like to go home with Uncle Li? I've got lots of goodies for you and your mommy."

The boy gave a series of little nods. His face spread into a radiated grin.

"Home?" Jasmine turned her tear-stained face to look up at him. "You found your wife and son? They're here in Chungking?"

Li Ming's face darkened. A muscle ticked in his jaw.

"Where are they? How—"

"I'll tell you when you feel better. We have much to tell one another."

Chapter 10

▰ ▰ ▰ ▰ ▰ ▰ ▰

Li Ming, a lieutenant colonel in the Nationalist Army, lived in a military dormitory. The one-level building had eight units, each with two rooms, and all shared a common kitchen at one end of the building and a bathroom at the other end. The front yard overlooked a tracking field, and a wooded hill sat at the back. He moved his belongings to the living room where there was a sofa, a desk, and a table with a few chairs so Jasmine and Bai Ge could use his bedroom.

After dinner, they put the boy to bed and sat down together on the sofa.

"I'm sorry." Jasmine patted the leather cushion. "This can't be comfortable. It's probably not long enough for you, either. You're so tall."

"Better than the trenches." He flashed her an enchanting smile. "Remember where I slept in Professor Valentine's house?"

She nodded. During the Nanking Massacre, the American woman had sheltered them. Seven people camped in her bedroom. Li Ming slept on the floor.

"She's such a kind person. The things she's done for us, for all those people in Nanking—"

"She took her own life," Jasmine blurted out, a thick ache swelling in her throat.

"What? Why? She saved so many people. Thousands and thousands. How come—"

"The pain was too much. She had nightmares. She couldn't handle it. Even after she moved back to the States, we kept in communication, but the last letter was from her nephew. He told me she'd..."

Li Ming's jaw tightened, and anguish darkened his eyes. "What she had done was above and beyond. I admired her. I've always wanted to thank her again. I guess I'll never..." He lapsed into silence.

"She knew we were grateful."

He sought a more comfortable position. "How is Xiao Mei? How's her family? Have you heard from her?"

"She survived, but her entire family died." Swallowing the lump in her throat, Jasmine told him of the housemaid's harrowing journey from Nanking to Chungking. "She's such a tough girl. I hope she's still with Uncle and Birch, wherever they are..."

Li Ming nodded. He hesitated a beat before asking the same questions again, "So, what happened to you? If...if you're not ready to talk, I understand." He plowed his fingers through his crew-cut hair. "I'm so sorry. I just can't imagine how—"

"I'm ready." She sat straighter, her chin tilted upward, and her teeth clenched.

In the next hour, Jasmine told him about what had happened after they parted: her narrow escape from Nanking; her unexpected encounter with Birch in Wuhan; the death of her aunt during a Japanese bombing in Chungking; her uncle's decision to send Daisy and her to a remote village in Yunnan; her rescue of a severely wounded American pilot who had crashed in the area. She told him of the torture she'd suffered when the Japanese demanded the whereabouts of this Flying Tiger, and about the slaughter of all the villagers by the Japanese soldiers. She also mentioned the kind hunters who had nursed her back to health, the newspaper article, and her treacherous trip from Yunnan to Chungking.

Purposely, she skipped her rape and the fact that Bai Ge was the product of the sexual assault. Rape was a taboo subject. Any woman who lived through such horror without killing herself was an insult to society, let alone allowing a bastard child to be born. Jasmine wasn't ashamed of Bai Ge, especially now that the boy had given her so much joy, but she wasn't proud of his background. If Li Ming asked her, she wouldn't lie to him. She simply wasn't willing to volunteer the information. Luckily, he never pressed for anything she didn't readily share.

Grief, pain, and anger passed over his face in rapid successions as he listened. His features reflected the turmoil with which he was wrestling. He looked up and stared at her scarred cheek. His eyes turned soft. "You're the most gorgeous girl I've ever met. How could anyone…" Lifting his right hand, he meant to touch her face, but in midair, he stopped. Instead, he lowered his head and wrung his large hands until the joints cracked. Silence fell between them.

"Sometimes I envy Professor Valentine. It takes guts to…" muttered Jasmine. She leaned against the back of the sofa. "I did it once. I was so determined that I didn't think twice before jumping. Since then, it's come across my mind now and then." Her closed eyes were quivering behind her eyelids. "Life is too hard!"

"Don't think that way." Li Ming sat straighter. "There is life, there is hope. You—"

"Hope for what?" Her eyes were empty.

"To have a better life. To reunite with Birch and your uncle. They're remarkable men. And to watch your son grow up. He's a sweet boy. And you have me. I'm your Big Brother."

His overwhelming emotions took her aback. Like Birch, Li Ming had a mild and calm demeanor. She gave an almost imperceptible nod. Her throat ached with the effort to hold back tears.

He leaned forward and squeezed her arms. "You're brave. I respect you so much. You look like such a delicate girl, but you're tough. Promise me…"

Jasmine nodded, forcefully this time. She narrowed her eyes and stared at him. In a crisp, clean army uniform, Li Ming was even more handsome than when she'd met him in Nanking ten years earlier. Every time she looked at him, his angular face, straight nose, and captivating dark eyes reminded her of Birch. "You're like my cousin in so many ways." A trace of a smile broke through her grief.

"I hope I'll meet him one day."

"How old are you, anyway? Professor Valentine thought you were a couple of years older than my cousin."

"I'm thirty-three, a Tiger. I was born in January 1914."

"Only five months older than Birch!" Worn out and in ill-fitting clothes, he'd looked much older. No wonder the professor had been mistaken.

He raised his arms and crossed his fingers behind his head. A mischievous sparkle came into his eyes. "I'm curious about my 'twin brother.' Even Professor Valentine thought I looked like him."

Feeling relaxed for the first time that evening, Jasmine stood up, went to the table, and poured two cups of hot water. She handed one to Li Ming and sat back down. Blowing air to the cup a few times, she took a sip and asked, "So, what happened to you? How did you get away? I saw a group of young men collecting bodies along the Yangtze River. Did you find the Communist guerillas? How come you're back to the Nationalist Army? I thought you were so fed up with them."

He didn't speak. His eyebrows knitted.

"I was so worried. All those years, I wondered about what happened to you."

Li Ming stood up. With the cup in his hands, he paced back and forth in the small space of the living room before sitting again. He looked into her eyes and said, "I don't want to lie to you, but there are things I can't tell you, things larger than my life."

"I understand." Even though she didn't know his story, from his hesitation she could make an educated guess. He didn't want anyone to know he'd had connections with the Communists. That was understandable. The Nationalists and the Communists were adversaries now.

"Don't worry." She touched his arm. "You're alive! That's all that matters."

"When the time is right, I'll let you know. I give you my word."

"I'll hold you accountable. I have a fairly good memory, you know."

A faint smile graced her lips. "But you have a better memory. I can't believe you remembered my uncle's address. It's been over nine years."

"Look." From his inner breast pocket, he took out a piece of paper with her handwriting. "I was transferred to a unit in Chungking several weeks ago. I went to the house right away, but it was too late. I don't know where they moved to. The doorman said he would pass on any news, but somehow I don't trust him."

Jasmine nodded.

"I've been stopping by there almost every day, but who knew I'd run into you?"

"You can't imagine how happy I was." She took a sip of the hot water. "Without you, we'd be homeless. Oh, is that why your wife and son are not here? You just got here, and they're on their way?"

Li Ming shook his head. "My wife..." All the light vanished from his face. Profound sadness lurked in the depth of his black eyes.

"You don't have to tell—"

He swallowed a few times. Taking a shuddering breath, he started, "Her name is Lu Fang..."

Chapter 11

▬ ▬ ▬ ▬ ▬ ▬ ▬

After the Japanese invasion of Peking in the summer of 1937, Lu Fang left her comfortable house in the occupied city and fled to her parents' home in a nearby village, hoping it would be safer for her and Bao Bao, her two-year-old boy.

The village had a couple of hundred people, mostly women, children, and old men. Young men had either joined the Nationalist Army, the Communist guerillas, or simply fled.

With acres and acres of flat wheat fields, there was no natural hideout. Her parents dug a shallow hole in the ground and covered it with twigs and hay for an emergency. For weeks it remained quiet, and life went on as usual. Farmers worked in the fields; children played in the yards; women sat around, gossiping, sewing, knitting.

Then, one day the Japanese came, driving through the village in trucks full of soldiers with bayonet blades shining upon the barrels of their rifles. "*Hua gu niang—pretty girl. Hua gu niang,*" they yelled, searching for the young women in the village.

Lu Fang's father shoved her and the boy inside the shallow hole and covered it with the twigs and hay. He pulled their wooden waste bucket closer to the stack of hay seconds before their door was being kicked down. A group of four soldiers searched their mud-brick house inside and out but didn't find her. One soldier stepped near the hideout. Luckily, the foul smell drove him away.

They left, eager for their next target.

An older couple and their eighteen-year-old granddaughter Lian Hua lived across the street. The young woman was as pretty as her name—Lotus Flower—with translucent cheeks, cherry-red mouth, and eyes that could tell stories. Her grandparents hid her under the bed, but the soldiers found her and dragged her out of the hideout. Her eyes went large and round. Her delicate features dissolved into a mask of terror. Even so, her youth and beauty couldn't be disguised.

"*Hua gu niang!*" the Japanese cheered and tossed her onto the bed. Four of them took turns raping her. Her screams mixed with the men's groans and laughter.

An involuntary shudder rippled through Lu Fang's body as she listened. She quivered, and the haystack above her head shook with her. Paralyzed by terror, she crouched down even further and folded herself along with her son into a ball. She held on to him so tightly that he cried out. Immediately, she covered his mouth to stifle his cry.

The boy kicked and wiggled. But the more he struggled, the tighter she held on. "Shhh… Hush…" she whispered to his ears, begging. "Don't make any noise. Please don't make any noise!"

Time lapsed into eternity as she listened to the never-ending horror that was unfolding nearby. Fear consumed her. She couldn't move. She could hardly breathe. Warm liquid from the boy wet the front of her shirt. The musty smell of urine filled the cramped space.

Finally, the men stopped. But the girl's cry revved up another notch as they carried her naked body outside. She kicked and squirmed. They slapped her face and tossed her onto the truck that was already filled with weeping young women.

Her grandparents didn't fight until then. It was meaningless. Without batting an eye, the Japanese soldiers stabbed the old couple.

Later, the villagers learned that the Japanese had done this throughout the area. At their camp, they allocated each girl to ten or twenty soldiers for sexual assault. Some girls suffered for days while others lasted only a few hours, for they were stabbed to death when they cried too much. Then the Japanese went out to hunt again to quench their animal hunger.

When everything was quiet, Lu Fang let out a huge pent-up breath of relief. She was sad for the other women, but she was safe. Her son was safe, and she had been spared the unimaginable pain and humiliation. They were alive!

Her father removed the haystack. He pulled her out of the hideout as she held the boy in her arms.

"What's wrong with Bao Bao?" her mother cried out.

Lu Fang looked down. Her son's face was gray and purple. His eyes were open, but there was no movement.

"Bao Bao!" Lu Fang shrieked.

He didn't answer. Nor did he stir. The two-year-old boy, *Bao Bao—Treasure* of the family, had died without uttering a sound.

Lu Fang wailed and wailed until she collapsed. She was carried inside her room and placed on her bed. That was the last time anyone would ever see her. She disappeared in the middle of the night.

———

"I have no idea what happened to her." Li Ming finished by saying, "Did she kill herself because of grief and guilt? Did she lose her mind and wander off? Her parents said her eyes seemed so empty before she passed out. Was she killed somewhere by the Japs? Died of hunger or disease? She could be under a pile of rubble or in a mass grave. It's been ten years, and I have no way of ever finding out what happened to her." His face contorted in agony. "I wouldn't have blamed her. It wasn't her fault. She didn't mean to hurt our child. It was a tragic accident."

Jasmine listened with great sympathy, blinking hard to beat back the tears. At times she had to fold her arms around her chest to prevent herself from an uncontrollable tremor. The story reminded her of her own terror-filled experience. The pain, the humiliation, the scream! How many women had been assaulted by the Japanese soldiers? How many were still suffering the aftermath of the attacks? "I'm sorry," she murmured, lowering her head, unwilling to see his pain-filled eyes or allow him to see the misery in her own eyes.

"I miss her," Li Ming said in a tormented voice. "We met when I was stationed in Peking. I was sad about losing my mother. It was Lu Fang who comforted me." He paused. His hands clenched and unclenched. "I wish I could see her again, even if it's just her body. I want to bury her, to let her rest in peace."

Suddenly it hit Jasmine. Her loved ones—Danny, Birch, and her uncle—must have suffered the pain of not knowing where she was. Her cowardice and shame had robbed them of the chance for closure.

Chapter 12

－ － － － － － －

Staying with Li Ming brought a sound sleep that Jasmine hadn't enjoyed for years. She didn't have to worry about her safety; she was under the protection of Big Brother. Feeling well-rested, after Li Ming left for work, she went to the Air Force's base with Bai Ge, but they were not allowed to approach. Although she'd expected the outcome, she was still disappointed. After shopping for food and art supplies, she returned home and wrote a letter addressed to her parents' house in Nanking in case Birch and her uncle had moved back to the city.

For now, all she could do was wait—for a letter from Nanking or any news that Li Ming might find out.

"Is Uncle Li a dove?" asked Bai Ge. He was standing beside an easel Jasmine had set up in the shared yard in front of their unit. She looked up, confused. At four, the boy seemed to come up with all kinds of bizarre questions or statements. She found herself fascinated by what was inside her son's little mind. "No, Uncle Li is not a dove. Why do you say that?"

"I'm a dove." Bai Ge tilted his head, his eyes luminous. "You call him *Li Ming Ge*. How come he is not?"

Jasmine laughed and realized how much joy this child had brought her. She'd rarely smiled before he came along. At moments like this, she often wondered about her inclination to abort him or to give him away. What kind of life would he have had in an orphanage? And what kind of life would she have had? By keeping him, she kept her sanity and saved her life.

"Those are two different words, even though we pronounce them the same way," she said. "Your *Ge* means *dove*. But when I call him *Li Ming Ge*, that word *Ge* means *Big Brother*."

The boy's tiny eyebrows puckered. Seeing his bewildered look, Jasmine leaned down, picked up a stick, and wrote two characters on the ground. "See, this is your name. And this is Big Brother."

Bai Ge picked up another stick. Squatting down, he traced the lines.

It occurred to her that she'd been so focused on survival that she'd overlooked the fact that he was old enough to begin his education. "Would you like to learn to read and write?"

"Yes."

"Why?"

"I want to be a good boy." He turned up his nose. "I want to help Mommy when I grow up."

His innocent words touched Jasmine's heart, as he'd done countless times. She pulled his tiny body into her arms. "You *are* a good boy." Her lips pressed onto his head full of soft black hair. "You're Mommy's good boy. You've been more help than you will ever know."

———————

That evening, Jasmine handed the painting she'd finished earlier to Li Ming. "This is gorgeous!" he exclaimed.

"I hope others will think so, too."

"Who cares about other people?" He moved closer to a lamp, studying it. It was a picture of a turquoise lake surrounded by colorful wildflowers at the bottom of a mountain with its snow-capped peak jutting straight into a crystalline sky. "Where have you seen a place like this? It's out of this world!"

"In Yunnan, near the village that I told you about."

"It makes me want to go there. I love it. That's all that matters, don't you think?"

"Not that you want someone to buy it."

"What?" Li Ming exclaimed, moving the picture away from Jasmine. "You're not thinking—"

"Yes, I am."

"No! This is too beautiful to sell. We don't need money."

"*Li Ming Ge*," Jasmine stepped closer to him. "I can't stay here without…"

"Of course, you can! Dead positive. You can use the money for whatever you need." He pointed to the desk. "I'm your Big Brother. Mine is yours. You saved me—"

"Don't keep bringing that up. You saved me, too. Saved us! You put a roof over our heads. Because of you, I don't have to worry about Bai Ge being hungry all the time. If anything, we're even now."

"Okay, then, why do you want to sell it?"

"Think about it from my perspective. My parents taught me, even as a woman, to be independent, and not to be a burden to someone else. I can't stay here without doing something. Without contributing…"

Li Ming responded with a head bob. "You're so different," he said without taking his eyes off her. "Okay, you'll contribute. But not this one! We must keep the first one." He held the picture to the wall above his sofa. "Now, is this a perfect spot or what?"

He was right. The colorful painting brought life to his dull bachelor's dorm.

———

From then on, Jasmine and Li Ming lived in separate rooms under the same roof. They were more than friends, but not lovers. They were brother and sister; they were family. This was exactly what Jasmine needed.

Before she left the cabin, Jasmine had cut her long hair to a short ponytail. Now, she let it grow. Her shiny black hair fell to her back. She even applied light makeup to cover the scars on her cheek. A phrase came to her mind as she did it: *Shi wei zhi ji zhe si, nu wei yue ji zhe rong—A warrior would die for the one who recognizes his worth; a woman would dress up for the one who touches her heart.* Li

Ming commented on how gorgeous she looked. For the first time since the torture, she felt pretty and desirable.

What about him? As an intuitive woman, Jasmine could tell that Li Ming was fond of her. Whenever he stared at her, his eyes were so warm and intense, overflowing with emotions. She could see light dance on his dark pupils. His smile was infectious and enchanting. One had to be a fool not to notice how much he adored her.

But he'd never openly expressed his feelings. *Does he still love his wife like I love Danny? So much that he can't accept someone else? Was he hurt so badly by his family's tragedy that he's afraid to have another one? Perhaps he knows I'm not ready.*

No matter what his reason for reticence, Jasmine was content. She cared about Li Ming and wanted to make him happy. Since the day she'd arrived, she'd cooked, cleaned, and decorated his place. He was busy, leaving early in the morning and coming back late at night. Whenever he was home, though, he praised her dishes and thanked her for making his place feel like a real home.

Li Ming never talked about his work, and Jasmine didn't ask. She was used to military men keeping their lips sealed. They shared their past experiences and their visions for the future. A peaceful and prosperous life was their shared dream.

For the first time in a long time, she had a semblance of a family. When Mrs. Liu, a neighbor, called her "Mrs. Li," she just grinned. The days were getting colder, but the winter months passed in a haze of contentment. Jasmine had been bone-tired and soul-weary for years, and now she allowed herself the leisure to enjoy these rare moments of serenity while she waited for the news of Birch and her uncle.

Chapter 13

It was now February 1948, and the Chinese New Year was fast approaching.

Jasmine stepped out of the bedroom one morning and found Li Ming home. Instead of his uniform, he wore a thick brown twill jacket. There was no heating, so the temperature inside was just as cold as outside. "Hey, how come you're still here?" She was pleasantly surprised.

"I'm taking a day off," he replied. Crouching down, he faced Bai Ge. "Would you like to go to the Fair? We can buy lots of goodies there for the New Year."

The boy gave a series of rapid nods.

"What would you like to have for the holiday?"

"Rice Cake." Bai Ge paused, looking up at Jasmine with his innocent eyes. "May I ask for one more thing?"

"You bet. Ask for as many as you want," said Li Ming. "Uncle Li will buy—"

"No," she interrupted. "You can't spoil him." Kneeling, she put herself at eye level with the boy. "Yes, you can ask for one from Uncle Li, and one from Mommy."

A smile split his face. "I want some firecrackers."

"Well, I'm going to get both. Mommy has to think of something else." Li Ming winked.

Bai Ge chortled.

Li Ming picked up the boy and carried him on his shoulders. "Let's go!" Oozing with confidence, he offered his right arm to Jasmine. A faint blush stained her cheeks when she noticed the glittering heat in the dark irises of his eyes. She lowered her head as she took his arm. Through the twill jacket, she could feel the lean muscle of his bulging bicep. The three of them walked out together. The winter sun was cold, but her heart was filled with warmth.

"Colonel Li. Mrs. Li," called out a neighbor. "Going out shopping for the New Year?"

"Yes, Mrs. Liu!" chipped the boy. "We're going to buy lots of goodies at the Fair."

The blush on Jasmine's face deepened as she nodded to the neighbor. She'd learned to cook from the middle-aged woman.

Once they reached the main street, Li Ming flagged down a taxi. "No need—" she said.

"For Bai Ge," he interrupted her.

Like most kids, her son had never sat in a car. She tipped her head in gratitude.

Li Ming took the middle seat and directed the driver to circle the city before going to the Fair. Bai Ge pressed his forehead against the window and fastened his gaze to the scene outside. He was brimming with jubilation. Li Ming held him upright, preventing him from falling over. He was as animated as the boy.

Jasmine looked at them with a mix of joy and sorrow. She was happy for her son and thankful to Li Ming. At the same time, knowing his son's tragic death, she felt a pang of sympathy for him. *He must be heartbroken, holding someone else's child.*

Her grip tightened on his forearm.

———

Before and during the Chinese New Year, there were Fairs in every city and town throughout the country. With a dazzling variety of food, calligraphies, paintings, performances, and acrobatic shows, the Fairs usually lasted for days. Even amid the Civil War, New Year was a time when people celebrated, and hope and happiness flourished.

The festive décor adorned the area—red lanterns dangled high above their heads while red posters bearing golden LUCKY characters and door gods decorated storefronts. Inappropriately, banners like "Patriotism requires anti-communism," "No compromise in the anti-communist stance," and "No mercy to Communist Bandits and their followers," were amongst the festive decorations—they served as the poignant reminders of the ongoing Civil War.

People swarmed the narrow cobblestone streets. Vendors offered their goods in high-pitched cries. Kids laughed and yelled, running through the crowd. The mouth-watering aroma of food permeated the air. Li Ming bought lots of food—Rice Cakes, *La Rou*—*Salt preserved meat, Xiang Chang*—*Sausage*, baked sweet yams, roasted peanuts, and chestnuts.

He stopped at a Tanghulu stand. Bai Ge's smile broadened when he sucked the red sweet-and-sour hawthorns. "This is so good!" he exclaimed and handed it to Jasmine. "Try it, Mommy. Better than candy!"

They joined a crowd circling several street performers. Two young men fought in the center. A wooden rifle in hand, the taller one wore the Nationalist Army uniform. The short man had an ugly mask, holding a wooden spear. He was dressed in black, white cloth with dripping crimson red "Communist Bandits" circling his head. They twisted and turned and jumped high in the air. Their weapons swooshed and thumped together. A middle-aged man banged a drum, making loud noises, creating excitement.

Bai Ge, who was sitting on Li Ming's shoulders, clapped his hands and cheered with the crowd when the taller man won.

From the corner of her eye, Jasmine noticed the change in Li Ming's reaction. His smile diminished to a grimace. She was baffled. *Perhaps the young men reminded him what his son could do if he'd had the chance to grow up?* She moved closer to him.

Firecrackers sizzled and popped everywhere. The booms rumbled like thunder, and the smell of smoke permeated the air as if the area were on fire.

"Do you know why we light firecrackers during the New Year?" Li Ming asked Bai Ge.

The boy shook his head.

"Well, according to legend, there is a mythical beast called *Nian*— *Year*. He lives under the sea or in the mountains. Once a year, at the beginning of a new year, he comes out of hiding to eat. Since food is hard to come by in the winter, he goes to villages to eat people, mostly kids."

Bai Ge circled his arms around Li Ming's head. "What does he look like?" he asked, his voice a bit shaky.

By then, the clouds had moved in and obscured the sun. The sky was cat-gray. With a sharp bite to the wind, the day grew chilly. Jasmine tilted her head and then nudged Li Ming. "Maybe we should go home?"

He tipped his head but continued talking. "He looks like a flat-faced lion, but he has a dog-like body. And many ugly sharp teeth." He wriggled his fingers like animal claws.

The boy inhaled sharply.

"However,"—Li Ming lifted his hand—"like all bad guys, he has a weakness. He's afraid of loud noises, fire, and red color. That's why we wear red clothes and put up decorations in red during the New Year. We also use firecrackers to chase him away."

"Oh!" Bai Ge heaved an exaggerated sigh of relief. Then he pointed ahead and asked, "Are those the bad guys? The beasts?"

"What?"

"There!" The boy pointed again over the heads of the crowd. On Li Ming's shoulders, he had a clear, unobstructed view and saw something neither adult could see.

They moved along with everyone, almost like being carried away by running water in a flood. Then abruptly, Li Ming stopped. It was too late. The grim scene unfolding before them was apparent—they had walked right into a public execution.

Surrounded on three sides by hundreds of onlookers, a dozen bodies lay on the ground in pools of crimson red. Behind them stood another dozen prisoners in shackles. Shoulder to shoulder, against the wall, they faced the crowd. Their names and crimes were being announced. A stocky man with a snake tattoo on his neck was a gangster who had committed a triple murder. A slim man with a mole on his chin was charged with rape. The third man was a thief who had stolen jewelry; he had a reddish-purple birthmark on his right cheek. The rest of them, seven men and two women, were *Gong Fei—Communist Bandits.*

With a sick sneer, the heavyset gangster hollered, "You'll see me again. Mark my words! In twenty years, another fighter will return." Spittle flew from his mouth, and his face turned purple as he snarled in contempt. The rapist shook so much that he could hardly stand up straight. Before being shot, he slumped to kneel on the ground. The thief leaned against the wall and faced the crowd with dazed incomprehension in his eyes. In tattered and blood-stained clothes, the Communists stood tall and proud. They shouted slogans like "Down with the Nationalist Counter-revolutionaries!" and "Long live the Communist Party!"

The rifle shots rang out like firecrackers. One by one, the prisoners crumpled like rag dolls and sprawled slack on the ground. Blood dripped from the wall behind them and pooled around the bodies, draining into the brown dirt.

The mob broke into wild cheers as if it were part of the festival celebration. A faint voice next to Jasmine grumbled, "Damn cruel. One day they'll taste their own medicine." His voice was drowned out by bloodlust and cheering.

Jasmine twisted her head away from the gruesome spectacle, a frown creasing her brow. The smell of blood and death was thick in the air. She didn't understand communism, nor did she care. The official newspapers had painted an appalling picture of the Communists—they were brigands, crooks, and ruffians; they would take people's property and share it with everyone; they were vicious and would destroy the country.

She didn't know any Communists. She just hated the concept of killing. *These Communists looked like factory workers, teachers, or students. That middle-aged woman was very poised and lady-like.*

As she turned again, Jasmine noticed Li Ming's reaction. His face darkened. A succession of emotions passed his face so swiftly, she could not identify them. *Anger? Grief? Worry? Determination?*

Chapter 14

Qing Ming Festival fell on the fifth of April in 1948. During this Tomb-Sweeping Day, families cleaned their loved ones' gravesites, prayed for them, and made ceremonial offerings. Since neither Li Ming nor Jasmine had deceased family members nearby, they decided to pray for their families at a Buddhist Temple on top of the rounded hill behind their house.

During the past few months, Jasmine had learned more about his family. Li Ming had grown up in northern China. His father was a successful businessman who drank a lot, partly because it was required to make business connections. When he was four, his father passed away; heavy drinking played a role in his death. Life wasn't easy for a young widow with a child, but since his father had made enough money, they got by without too much trouble.

In 1931, Japan invaded northeast China. A year later, his hometown, where he was studying at a local college, was occupied. Along with hundreds of thousands of refugees, Li Ming and his mother fled the region and migrated south, carrying everything they could on their backs. The road was treacherous; the journey was dangerous.

One morning, as Li Ming was still sleeping, the Japanese airplanes flew over and dropped incendiary bombs on the village. Debris flew everywhere, and rubble showered down. To protect him, his mother flung herself over his body. A beam fell and crushed her skull, killing her instantly. At eighteen, Li Ming joined the Nationalist Army. Revenge consumed him.

But Chiang Kai-shek, the leader of the Nationalist government, focused on fighting the Communists instead of the Japanese. In December 1936, he was forced by his subordinates to agree to an alliance between the Nationalists and the Communists. This history-turning event was called the Xi'an Incident, and afterward, the two parties formed a united front to counter the foreign invasion.

Li Ming hadn't had a chance to face the enemy until December 1937 when his regiment was ordered to protect Nanking. Several days later, however, they were instructed to retreat. If it weren't for Jasmine, he would have been killed, as were thousands of trapped Nationalist soldiers in the city.

"I can't believe you run up this hill every day with sandbags strapped to your thighs. There are three hundred steps, right?" Jasmine said as they hiked up the hill. The early morning was fragrant with the rich scent of earth and pine trees. A breeze stirred the nearby forest, making the branches sway and sigh.

"It's an old fashion way to exercise," replied Li Ming, his runner's build powerful beneath his navy-blue blazer and black slacks, a book bag full of offerings on his back.

"I read of it, but had no idea that people actually do it."

"You like to read martial arts or military books? How about *Romance of the Three Kingdoms?* It's my favorite."

"It's my cousin's favorite, too." Jasmine panted, her cheeks flushing. She'd never been a sporty person. With a slight limp, she held on to his upper arm and plodded uphill, one step at a time.

"How many things Birch and I have in common!" He unleashed his famous smile. "Hey, slow down, Bai Ge," he called out to the boy who was twenty yards ahead of them. "Don't run too far away from us."

"It's not my favorite, though," said Jasmine.

One of Li Ming's eyebrows arched.

"I love stories about heroes, but somehow the characters seem… unreal in this book. Guan Yu allowed a doctor to cut open his arm to scrape off the poison from his bone. Without any anesthesia! He played a board game with his men and never even flinched. Now, if he had no fear, he was a fighting machine."

He nodded.

"I admire heroes like Danny, my cousin, and…you." The redness on her face deepened. "You guys have fears. I know Birch is afraid of pain."

"I'm definitely not a fan of pain either."

"But you still do what needs to be done for the country. How many times have you been injured? Three? I admire heroes like you."

"Jasmine, you're a true hero!"

"No." She shook her head. "I was just trying to protect Danny."

"I want to be a hero like Uncle Li," cheered Bai Ge, bouncing up and down on the irregular rocky steps by their side.

"Why?"

"I'm afraid of pain."

The adults laughed.

Then her smile faded, leaving only the sadness in her eyes. "He died anyway."

Li Ming faced Jasmine. "But he lived three more years. Do you know how many Japanese aircraft he shot down during that time?" He laid his free hand on her arm. "And think about Birch. He gained a terrific brother. It's not the length of our lives that matters; it's the experiences we have." He took a deep breath before continuing, "Life is worth living, even just for a few more years, months, or days, if we can have such incredible bonds. If only I could meet Birch. In my mind, he's already my brother."

"I told him about the massacre…and you. Of course, he has no idea that you're back in my life. I hope you'll meet him soon."

They reached an opening in the woods. A Buddhist Temple stood on top of the hill, and the path kept going down on the other side. The sun rose, its upper edge peeking between clouds and distant horizon, bathing the forest below in vibrant golden-yellow color. The smell of incense hung in the air.

Half a dozen people milled around the front yard while a handful of pigeons fluttered overhead. A poster was tacked outside the temple, flapping in the breeze, and it read: No Prayer for the Communist Bandits and Their Followers Is Allowed. Any Violation Will Be Punished Severely.

Jasmine emitted a sigh as she stepped inside. She didn't like the constant reminder of the conflict between the two parties, especially in a peaceful temple.

In the courtyard, they placed offerings, lit incense sticks, and bowed.

Silently she prayed for her parents, for Danny and his friend Jack, for her aunt and Daisy, for Doctor Wang and all the villagers, and for Professor Valentine and the Nationalist soldiers she'd met in Nanking. She also prayed that she would reunite with her family soon. She wished that Birch would have Li Ming as a Big Brother. *The pain of losing his siblings won't be replaced, but at least he'll feel better having another close friend.*

Before they stepped down the hill, Li Ming hesitated then said, "If you ever need help, contact the cook here. He's a…good friend. He'll help you."

Why would I need help from someone else when I have you? Jasmine wondered but didn't bother to ask.

———————

Ten days later, Bai Ge turned five. Li Ming took the family to a restaurant to celebrate. A cry of delight burst from the boy as he watched a white linen-covered table full of dishes—Longevity Noodles, Lion's Head Pork Meatballs, Nanking Salted Duck, Pan-Fried Shrimp, Yangzhou Fried Rice, Steamed Pork Bun, Eight Precious Pudding… The smell of delicious food hung in the air.

Red lanterns dangled from the ceiling and glowed. Below, several timeless oil paintings were hung on the cream-colored wall. Being the wartime capital, Chungking was westernized. Soft lighting complemented by soothing music—Chinese and Western, and a plate glass window provided a stunning panoramic view overlooking the night lights of the city.

Dressed in a toffee-brown corduroy jacket, Li Ming handed the boy a leaf-green toy truck. "Want to be an engineer when you grow up?"

"No. I want to be an army officer like you."

Li Ming shook his head. "The war will be over soon. No need to be a soldier anymore. Afterward, our country will need people to rebuild."

Bai Ge bobbed his head. He held the truck with one hand and touched it with the other, eyes twinkling.

Jasmine was dressed in a purplish-blue, ankle-length cheongsam that hugged every inch of her slender body. Light makeup covered the scars on her cheek. She gave her son a set of Chinese folktales.

"Is *Kong Rong Rang Li* in here?" asked the boy.

"Yes." She was pleased that he remembered the story she'd told him almost a year earlier.

Li Ming showed Bai Ge how to slurp a mouthful of the Longevity Noodle. It reminded Jasmine of Danny's birthday party. She'd been concerned that he would bite the noodle, which symbolized long life. She sighed silently and hoped that her son would have better luck.

Deliriously happy, Bai Ge gobbled up the food.

Then the music changed. Jasmine was captivated by a soulful voice. When she heard the lyrics, "Oh, Danny Boy, I love you so," she couldn't help but burst into tears.

In this song, it was "Danny Boy" who came to visit the girl's grave. If Jasmine had died as everyone assumed, then the song would have fitted perfectly. She would have waited for Danny to visit her grave and to tell her how much he'd loved her. But now it was she who hoped to find his grave and to tell him how much she loved him.

"What's wrong, Mommy?" asked Bai Ge. One brow hoisted high.

Jasmine wiped her tears, her cheeks burning with embarrassment. "I'm sorry. I…" She didn't know what to say. Honesty was one of her guiding principles. She looked up at Li Ming and saw a flicker of sympathy on his face. She knew that he could speak only a little English, but he didn't need much to understand some of the lyrics.

"Mommy is thinking of a dear friend," He told the boy. "We're sad when our friends are no longer with us. We miss them." He put his hand on her arm. "Don't worry. I promise to make Mommy cry less."

Bai Ge tipped his head.

Jasmine nodded in gratitude.

"Are you going to be sad when I'm gone?" asked the boy.

"You're going to live a long time, much longer than my life," Li Ming said with a hearty laugh. "Hey, I hope you'll remember me and think of me when you grow up."

"How can I forget about you?" Bai Ge stretched his eyes wide, lashes fanning in innocent perplexity. "You're my uncle!"

Chapter 15

▬ ▬ ▬ ▬ ▬ ▬ ▬

Jasmine had grown up in Nanking, where people liked to eat rice. Li Ming, on the other hand, had grown up in northern China, where people ate anything made of flour. Soon after she came to live with him, she'd learned from his neighbor to make flour dishes. Noodle, *Cong You Bing—Chinese Flatbread with Scallion*, Wonton, Dumpling, *Bao Zi—Steamed Bread with Fillings*…she made them all, even though they were not her favorite. Luckily Bai Ge wasn't a picky eater. He loved everything she made. Seeing how much Li Ming enjoyed her cooking gave her great satisfaction.

One day in mid-May, Jasmine woke up with a headache. She hadn't been in good shape ever since her torture, and the long journey filled with stress and insufficient food had made it worse. Even so, she chose to make dumplings—it was everyone's favorite. She used ground pork, leek, mushroom, and a handful of shrimps.

Bai Ge's face opened into a wide grin when he tasted it. "It's so good!" he mumbled with his mouth full. "May I eat more?"

"How about five? Wait for Uncle Li. He should be home soon. We'll eat together."

He gave a series of little nods. Afterward, he licked his lips and asked, "May I play with Liu Gui?" The boy next door was a year older than Bai Ge.

"Sure. Don't go outside. It's too wet and muddy." It had been

69

raining for days. Known as the "Fog City," Chungking could be covered by a thick layer of clouds, sometimes for months at a time.

"I know."

"Come back when they start their dinner, okay?"

While the boy was gone, Jasmine "stole" one dumpling, and the tasty fillings brought a smile to her lips. Her headache became worse, so she took an aspirin. After taking a short break, she started cleaning the rooms.

As she was mopping the floor, the door flew open. Li Ming rushed in. "Let's go!" He looked around and added in a hurry, "Where is Bai Ge?"

Jasmine was startled. She'd never seen him so stern. "Mrs. Liu's place." She pointed to the next door. "What's going on?" Before she could finish, he was already out the door. She followed. To her astonishment, she watched him walk inside the neighbor's room without knocking. Two seconds later, he dashed out with Bai Ge in his arms. "Go! Go!" He pushed her inside their room and locked the door.

"What's wrong?" asked Jasmine, a claw of anxiety digging into her.

"No time to explain. Just come with me!" Li Ming pulled her along and hurried toward the back window. He handed Bai Ge to her. Shoving the window open, he crawled through the opening. Once he was on the ground, he reached up and grabbed the boy. "Come on, Jasmine!" With his left arm holding the child, he waved his right hand: "Hurry!"

Normally a man of unwavering calm, his urgency frightened her. She didn't know exactly what the problem was, but she knew it was serious. Holding onto the frame, she bent her upper body and swung her legs through the window. As she lowered herself to the ground, she felt Li Ming's arms circle her waist.

Before she could stand still, he grasped her hand and pulled her along. They sprinted up the wooded hill behind the house. Moments later, she heard the wail of sirens coming toward their direction. *What's going on?* It seemed that Li Ming was in trouble with the authorities. *Why?* What had he done? He hadn't told her what had happened after Nanking, probably because he'd made connections with the Communists. Had someone found out?

They raced up the hill. Adrenaline coursed through Jasmine's body as she heard shouting and whistleblowing from their home. The recent rain had turned every piece of exposed ground into mud. A thick white mist swirled among the hardwood trees.

Limping and slipping, she huffed and puffed in just a few steps. She was in a pair of black cloth shoes and a maroon cheongsam with a side slit that clung to every curve of her body. Her footwear was too slippery for the muddy path, and the dress prevented her from moving freely.

"Come on!" Li Ming urged.

"Go ahead," she wheezed. Her chest seemed about to burst. "Don't wait..."

He wouldn't leave her behind.

Her heartbeat revved another notch as the noise came closer.

"Stop!" barked a man behind them. More voices joined him, "We'll shoot if you don't."

The only thing separating Jasmine and Li Ming from the men was the fog.

Gunshots rang out.

"Bend down!" With one arm holding the boy over his shoulder, Li Ming let go of her hand. He took out his pistol and returned fire.

Bullets whizzed over their heads. Jasmine guessed their intention—to slow them down and capture them alive. Overwhelmed with fear, all she could do was run as fast as her legs allowed.

She was a step behind Li Ming as they reached the top. Her chest rose and fell with labored breathing. Her lungs burned. Her legs, especially the injured one, were sore. *Where are we going from here? If we hide inside the temple, we might be trapped and have nowhere to go from there. If we run down the mountain, the fog may help us get away. If only I could run fast enough!*

Distracted by the thoughts, Jasmine paid less attention to her steps. As a result, she kicked hard on a rock sticking out of the ground and tripped. Falling face down on all fours, she scraped her palms. Her toe hurt badly since her cloth shoe offered little protection. Her right knee crashed against the rocky step. She cried out.

As she struggled in vain to stand upright, out of the corner of her eye, she watched Li Ming turn back. With the boy flung over his shoulder, he grabbed her forearm and pulled her to a standing position. "Run!" he yelled and shoved her forward.

Jasmine limped on, hot breaths thundering in and out of her lungs.

More shots fired. Then, she heard Li Ming's gasp. She whipped around. For a moment, everything stopped. The area became eerily quiet.

Twilight had fallen. In the fading light, Bai Ge lay lifeless in Li Ming's arms, staring at her with unseeing eyes. Blood and tissue sprayed from a hole on his forehead.

Oh, God! No! Jasmine opened her mouth, trying to call her son's name. But no sound would come. It stuck in her throat, frozen there by a bone-deep terror. Through the mist, she looked up at Li Ming as if he could wake her up from this nightmare.

His eyes mirrored her own: sheer unabated fright. Fright and sorrow.

Seconds later, she found her voice and shrieked. "No! Bai Ge! No!" Hysterical, she took the boy, his body sagging in her arms. In every fiber of her being, she felt chilled and shaken. Sparks appeared before her eyes, and her vision blurred. Then, a sea of darkness enveloped her. She fell to the ground, taking her son's limp form with her. The last thing she heard was Li Ming's cry of apology.

When Jasmine awakened, she was lying on a hard bed inside a dim room. Handcuffs restricted her wrists. For a moment, she was disoriented. *Where am I? Is this a prison cell? What happened? Where is Li Ming? And Bai Ge?* The thought of her son brought back a flood of memories. *Bai Ge is gone!* The last image she remembered was his blood-covered forehead.

Anguish squeezed her heart like pincers with vicious teeth. Jasmine wept. Bai Ge, this unplanned life, had come to the world because of one war; now he was gone because of another war.

It was his kick that had brought her back to life. Now she was still there, yet he was forever gone. He'd brought happiness once alien to her, but during his short life, he hadn't experienced true peace. He'd been hungry most of the time and had to make the long hard journey. He'd been a good boy, but he would never be a great scholar or an engineer or an officer.

Jasmine curled into a ball and hugged herself, trying to stop herself from trembling. On top of her grief, she felt guilty. She'd loved and cared for Bai Ge as much as any mother could. In the back of her mind, though, she'd always had a reservation. If he were Danny's son, she would have raised him with pure joy and pride. But Bai Ge wasn't her pride; she'd had to raise him out of duty, and out of decency.

Even though she'd never allowed her feelings to show, she'd blamed the arrival of this child for preventing her from being with the man she loved. Deep down, she knew that it had been her cowardice and insecurity that had stopped her from being with Danny. Now that Bai Ge was gone, all she wished was to hold him and to tell him how much joy he'd brought to her life, and how proud she was of him.

I didn't even allow him to eat as many dumplings as he wanted on his last day. At that thought, she felt a dagger plunged into her chest.

Jasmine tried to get up; the action brought on a surge of dizziness and headache. She fell back onto the bed. After lying still for a moment, she tried again. Stumbling, she reached the door. "Let me see my son!" She yelled as she gripped the metal bars.

"Shhh..." a female voice from the next cell warned her. "Be quiet. You'll get yourself in big trouble."

"I want to see my son," she replied and continued shouting.

"Stop yelling!" bawled a hoarse voice. Soon, a man in the Nationalist Army uniform showed up, holding an iron baton. He looked like a bear—husky, heavyset, with dark skin and thick back hair.

"Please! My son is injured. He needs—"

"Be quiet." *Thump.* He hit the door with the baton. The iron bars clanked and rattled. The metallic sound echoed in the empty hallway.

"He's just a child. He's—"

"One more time, be quiet!" He struck the door again, creating a spine-tingling noise.

Jasmine wouldn't stop. After she pleaded a few times, the man lost his patience. He brought down the baton again, and instead of hitting the door, smacked her left hand on the bar.

Instantly, her knuckles bled. Pain shot through her arm. She drew in a sharp breath. Holding her hands together, she demanded again, "I want to see my son!"

"Bring her to me." A deep voice came from the end of the dark hallway. Jasmine couldn't see the man. If she weren't in jail, she would have thought that he was an opera singer.

Chapter 16

▬ ▬ ▬ ▬ ▬ ▬ ▬

The stocky jailer brought Jasmine to a windowless but well-lit interrogation room. He shoved her onto a chair. Standing on her left
side, he clamped his hand upon her shoulder, pressing her down.

A Nationalist Military Secret Police officer sat behind a desk with
a notebook. He was in his thirties, medium build, rectangular face,
sharp eyes, and with crew-cut hair. Immediately, she sensed that this
was a man of principle and unwavering determination. Behind him,
a slogan hung on the wall: "Patriotism requires anti-Communism.
No compromise in the anti-communist stance. No mercy to Communists and their followers." The room was disconcertingly empty.

He jammed a cigarette into his mouth, lit it, and took a long draw.
"My name is Tan Yin," he said with his deep singer's voice. "I'm in
charge of the investigation. Tell me, Miss Bai, what—"

"Where is my son?"

"He...he didn't make it. You know that, don't you?"

"Where is he? Let me see him."

He gave a slight shake of his head. "He's been...cremated."

"No!" A mournful wail came from deep inside. "Oh, dear God! No!"

"I'm sorry. It was an accident. We didn't mean to... We were
supposed to scare..."

"Let me have his ashes, please!" She looked up with pleading eyes.
"Help me! I beg you. Let me—"

"Do you know how many Communist Bandits we kill every day?"

"He's not a Communist Bandit. He's just a boy!"

"I'm sorry. Truly. I have a son. He's six," Tan Yin said. He looked genuinely saddened. "I wish I could help. It's too late."

Sobs wracked Jasmine's body. Her son had died. She'd lost the boy forever. The room spun as a wave of dizziness swept over her.

"Now," the officer cleared his throat, "Li Ming is a Communist spy. I need to hear your side of the story. What did you do to help him? When did you become a Communist?"

Her suspicion was confirmed. Li Ming not only had connections with the Communists but also worked for them. "I'm not a Communist! I didn't know he was a spy."

"You better come clean."

"What would you like me to say? My uncle was a general in the Air Force. My cousin was a fighter pilot, a well-known hero. Both have worked for the Nationalist government. I don't know any Communists."

"Li Ming is a Communist. That's a fact. Now tell me his contact."

"I don't know. I didn't even know he worked for the Communists until now."

"Miss Bai," he gawked at her with eagle eyes, "tell the truth. No need to stick your neck out for him. He's already confessed."

"Why ask me if he's already confessed?"

Tan Yin shook his head. His lips formed a subtle smirk. He stood and marched toward her. Once next to her, he grasped her hair with his left hand and tilted her head upward. He took another drag off his cigarette. Then he held the burning cigarette close to her right cheek—so close that she could feel the heat.

Bile rose in her throat. Jasmine couldn't believe that she would have to endure torture again—this time, at the hands of the Nationalists. She was more heartbroken than afraid. *Is this the government that my cousin and uncle have supported all their lives?* Every time she'd encountered a Nationalist combatant, she thought of Birch. She'd helped several of them during the Nanking Massacre, including Li Ming, a lieutenant in the Nationalist Army.

"You have a pretty face. You must have been a rare beauty before... It'll be a shame to have the smooth cheek scarred as well." He paused and then demanded, "Who cut you up?"

Tamping down her anger, Jasmine told him how she'd saved an American pilot. She had nothing to hide. Americans and the Nationalists were allies.

Tan Yin let go of her hair. "Do you have any proof?" His voice softened. "Can anyone besides Li Ming verify your story?"

"There are newspaper articles about Major Hardy and my cousin. You'll find a copy in the dorm. In the middle desk drawer..."

"Good, I'll double-check. I appreciate your cooperation, Miss Bai. So far, I believe you're telling the truth. Now, did anyone visit Li Ming while you were there? If so, what are their names?"

"He had no visitors."

"Your boyfriend is in deep trouble." He bore down on her. "You can help him, do you understand?" he said with an aggressive edge in his voice. "You don't want to see him suffer, do you?"

The officer sucked hard on his cigarette, waited a moment, and then nodded to the jailer. The heavyset man grasped her handcuffs and, with a violent motion, jerked her up from the chair. The shackles pressed deep into her flesh. He shoved her to the far side of the room so hard that she stumbled and lurched forward. Before she fell, Tan Yin seized her arm. He pulled her upright in front of a blind and rolled it up. Through a small glass window, Jasmine gaped at the next room with unruly horror. Her hands flew to cover her mouth as a cry ripped from deep inside her.

Li Ming was tied to a chair. His eyes were closed, head cocked to one side. Naked from the waist up, his broad chest was crisscrossed with bloody whip marks. Blood was trickling from his nose and the side of his mouth.

A man with a full beard stood close to him with a bucket. Another man positioned himself near a burning clay-stove tucked in the far corner; he wore a black patch over one eye. Spots of congealed blood stained the floor. Rusted shackles, heavy tongs and blades, whips of different sizes made of various materials, and other devices were bolted to the walls.

"The contact person," demanded Tan Yin, his mouth next to her ear. "Spill it out."

"I don't know." Jasmine started to shiver. "How can I tell you something I don't know?"

The bearded man flung the bucket of water in Li Ming's face. He gripped Li Ming's hair and slapped his cheeks, coaxing him back into consciousness. Leaning closer, he said something, and without getting the answer, he signaled to the other man. The one-eyed man snatched the handle of a hot iron from the stove.

"Stop! Stop!" Jasmine yelled, her voice climbing to full pitch.

The man strode toward Li Ming with measured steps, the glowing hot iron in hand.

She whipped around. With a haunted expression, she grasped Tan Yin's arm. "Please!" she pleaded. "Stop this madness. I beg you!" Tears poured down her face. "For God's sake, he worked for the same government!"

"He's a traitor," barked the jailer behind her. "Everyone hates traitors."

"He fought the Japs. He was wounded by the Japs." Jasmine didn't take her eyes off the officer. "This is insane. He fought for the country. Please don't hurt him!"

"You can help him." Tan Yin paused for dramatic effect, peering into her eyes as if trying to see the secret she concealed. "Just say the name—"

"I don't know. I don't know!"

The one-eyed man was right next to Li Ming now.

"No! No! No!" Jasmine cried hysterically. She felt as if her heart had splintered into a thousand pieces. "Stop him. Please!" She shook his sleeves. Her features dissolved into a mask of pure terror.

The one-eyed man asked a question, waited for a beat, then thrust the hot iron onto Li Ming's bare chest. Smoke sizzled from his flesh. He screamed; his face distorted in suffering before he passed out.

"*Li Ming Ge!*" wailed Jasmine. Her heart was too weak for such horror. Her fingers on the sleeves loosened, and she slumped onto the floor.

Chapter 17

—— —— —— —— —— —— ——

"Run, Jasmine, run!"

Unwilling to leave the safety of Li Ming's embrace, she hesitated. A group of men in the Nationalist Secret Police uniforms surrounded them and wrestled Li Ming to the ground. "Run! Find Danny. Only he can help."

"Jasmine!" The voice sounded familiar. *Is that Danny?*

She ran toward the voice. Jagged rocks were in her way. Tree branches scratched her arms and blocked her path. Ripped by undergrowth and pricked by thorns, her skin burned. As she ran through the woods, animal eyes, gleaming with jade-green light, glared at her. But she had to reach Danny.

"I'm here." She heard him. His voice was faint and filled with terror. Ignoring the pain, she shoveled the dense shrubs apart. There he was—Bai Ge lying on the ground, blood still oozing from his forehead. Jasmine held his tiny body in her arms, her lips forming silent words of sorrow.

A woman's voice was whispering to her. *Is that mother? Or perhaps Aunt?* Jasmine wanted to find out, but her eyes were so heavy. When she finally pried them open, to her utter surprise, Daisy stood in front of her.

"Danny is gone," she said, wrapping her arms tightly around Jasmine. "I'll find him. He must be freezing in that grave. I'm going to warm him up." Her voice was shaky and pitiful.

The news yanked Jasmine's heart out. *Danny is in a grave?*

As she grappled with the sad news, Daisy spun around. Fear and sorrow marred her beauty.

"Don't go." Jasmine stretched her arms, trying to grab her cousin, but the girl disappeared, and only her soulful voice echoed in the dark. "I'll never leave Danny. I'll find him. I'll bring him home to America."

Shackled inside the nightmare, Jasmine couldn't escape the words, which acted as a sword, thrusting deep into her chest. All the air rushed out of her body. She woke with a start, drenched with sweat, breathless. Sodden sheets twisted around her frail body.

Jasmine didn't know how long she'd been unconscious. Nor did she care. She rolled into a fetal position, wishing the darkness would swallow her, and she would never see this awful world again. But even with her eyes closed, images of Li Ming's torture haunted her. Her heart palpitated wildly as she conjured still more petrifying scenes in her imagination. *Life is not worth living.* The familiar thought returned, poisoning her mind. *This world is too ugly.*

Then she heard Birch's deep voice. "Don't let the Japs kill you." He'd said that after the Nanking Massacre. "Don't let them win so easily. Live! Do the things you love to do… Live a productive life…"

She'd tried to live according to the highest standards—be kind, be helpful, be caring… She'd loved, and she'd been loved. She had cherished friends. But most of her loved ones were now gone. What did she have left? A scarred body. Recurring Nightmares. A broken heart…

Glimpses of her past appeared—her parents' blood-soaked bodies, her aunt's stiff figure, the news of Danny's and Daisy's deaths, the massacre in Nanking, the slaughter in the village, her torture… Sliding back into unconsciousness, she hoped that death would claim her.

"Thank God, your fever is gone," exclaimed a woman. "How are you feeling?"

In the early morning light, a lady in her mid-forties sat by the side of her bed. She was slim, with a fine-boned face and pale skin.

Her body was encased in a turquoise cheongsam. She was holding a damp towel in her hand, eyes brimming with kindness and concern.

———————

"You were in and out of consciousness for three days. I was worried you wouldn't make it," said the woman with the towel. "My name is Leng Xue—Snow. Can you sit up?"

Jasmine tried but failed. She had no strength.

"Don't worry." Leng Xue picked up a bowl from the floor. Other than two beds, there was nothing else in the small cell. Using a spoon, she fed Jasmine watery rice porridge.

She swallowed one gulp and started to cough. The women waited patiently before lifting the spoon. Jasmine shook her head and closed her eyes, hoping she would never open them again.

"You need to get your strength back."

She wanted to argue but had no energy to speak. She was bone-tired and soul-weary.

"Life in prison is…hard. But you'll get used to it."

Jasmine noticed a couple of sentences carved upon the wall near her bed: "The will of the Communists is made of steel," and "Heads can be chopped. Limbs can be cut. The spirit of revolution is indestructible."

She wondered if all Communists had such a calm and steely mentality regarding imprisonment and death. "How long have you…?" Her voice came out as little more than a breath.

"I'll tell you later. My son will be here soon."

"Your son?"

"Yes. He lives with his father in the male quarter. He's allowed to visit once a week."

Just then, the door rattled.

"Here he comes," said Leng Xue, her voice full of joy.

A young boy stepped into the cell. He was as thin as a twig with a head too big for his frail neck.

"Shen Shen!" Len Xue opened her arms and embraced him. She checked him up and down before she said, "Come over here. I'd like you to meet Auntie Jasmine."

The boy gazed at her with his shiny eyes. An innocent smile split his face. "Pleased to meet you, Auntie Jasmine."

Jasmine watched the boy interact with his mother. For hours, they talked, read books, and played cards. She was impressed with his behavior and wished that Bai Ge could be here to meet Shen Shen.

After a lunch of more porridge with pickled vegetables, the door opened. The mother and the son hugged before he left. Jasmine was astounded that there was no whining, no fuss, no emotion as if separating from their loved ones for a week at a time was of no concern. It was only when Leng Xue turned around that Jasmine noticed the tears in her eyes. "I'm sorry."

The woman shrugged. "It's been two years. They took him away when he turned five."

"He's been here for two years?"

"No." Leng Xue paused a beat and said, "He was born here. He's seven now."

Jasmine couldn't believe her ears.

"My husband and I were arrested when I was six months pregnant. Shen Shen has never seen the world beyond these walls." Leng Xue looked calm. Only her tightly clenched fists revealed her true emotions.

Chapter 18

With the help of Leng Xue, Jasmine slowly recovered, at least physically. Emotional damages would take a lot longer to heal if they could ever be healed.

Bit by bit, she got to know the woman and her family.

Since 1927, the Nationalists and the Communists had fought for control of the country. Even after Japan conquered the Northeast Territory, Chiang Kai-shek, the leader of the Nationalist government, still focused on fighting the other party rather than the Japanese. His campaigns against the Communists became increasingly unpopular.

In December 1936, Chiang Kai-shek was detained by his subordinates in Xi'an. Two generals, Zhang Xueliang and Yang Hucheng, held him captive until he agreed to an alliance between the Nationalists and the Communists. After the Xi'an Incident, the two parties formed a united front to counter the foreign invasion. Later, General Zhang Xueliang was detained and kept under house arrest. General Yang Hucheng was imprisoned, along with his wife, children, and some of his staff members. Leng Xue's husband was one of them.

Jasmine remembered reading the news about the incident. At seventeen, she'd never imagined that one day she would meet one of the participants of this history-turning event. She felt sorry for Leng Xue, a woman with a cold name but a warm heart. Her calm and graceful demeanor reminded Jasmine of her mother and aunt—both had died in their forties. Even her cheongsam looked like the one her aunt was wearing the day she'd been killed.

Jasmine felt even worse for the boy. A boy who had never seen the outside world or an animal other than birds. He'd never run free in the fields, or climbed a tree, or picked berries, or played with other kids, or tasted food besides the terrible prison rations. The child reminded her of her son. Bai Ge had died at a young age, but when he was alive, at least he'd done some of the things a normal boy would do.

Why is an innocent child punished for his parents' crimes? Personally, Jasmine didn't think the Xi'an Incident should be labeled as a crime. The two generals' actions might have been radical, but their motivations were pure—to promote the unity of the nation to fight the foreign attack. *And even if it was a crime, what did that have to do with a boy?*

"May I have a couple of sheets of paper?" she asked Shen Shen when he came to visit. Paper was invaluable in prison, but he tore several pages from his notebook without hesitation. Jasmine nodded her appreciation. She stayed busy while the mother and the son spent their precious time together.

Before he left, Jasmine handed the few sheets back to him. His face burst into a big smile. Leng Xue leaned over to look. Instantly, tears filled her eyes. Jasmine had drawn portraits of them.

Shen Shen gave his portrait to his mother and kept her portrait and the one with the two of them together. With a gap-toothed grin, he gave Jasmine a big hug before he walked away, holding the pieces of paper tightly in front of his scrawny chest.

Birch was right, she thought. She had a gift. Her talent could bring beauty to this not-so-beautiful world, but more importantly, it might brighten someone else's day and make their miseries a bit more tolerable.

Jasmine crept through each day and was haunted by nightmares at night. She grew weak and gaunt. She missed her son terribly. His death had sucked the life out of her, and she didn't know how to go on without him. She was worried about Li Ming but had no way of knowing how he was doing. Had he survived? Were they torturing him again? How did he handle the unbearable pain?

Not a day went by that she wasn't plagued with loss and misery. She woke up in the middle of the night, whimpering at the agony that possessed her. Once again, she was confronted by the dark thought that life had no meaning. She got up, she ate, she went to sleep—a cycle repeated again and again, blind to hope for the future. The only bright moments came from Leng Xue and Shen Shen. Often, she wondered if she could live through this confinement without these two companions. When summer gave way to cool autumn, Jasmine was once again brought to the interrogation room.

Not being questioned for four months, she was anxious. Every muscle in her beleaguered body clamped tight as she entered the room.

Tan Yin, the same stiff-backed officer, sat behind the interrogation desk. He lit a cigarette and offered it to her.

She shook her head, holding her breath.

"Your story checked out, Miss Bai." He leaned on the table with his elbows. "I'm quite familiar with the Flying Tigers. What you've done is...incredible. I'm impressed. We'll let you go."

Jasmine couldn't believe her ears. It was the last thing she'd expected. Doubtfully, she stared at him. "What about Li Ming?"

"He's a Communist spy and a traitor. He'll never be freed."

"How...how is he?" She could hear the tremor in her voice.

"He's a tough man. I have to say," Tan Yin stated, a hint of admiration lurking behind his stern face.

"Let me see him—"

"I'm afraid I can't."

"Please!"

"It's out of my hands."

Disappointment shot through her. She knew she would probably never see him again. She closed her eyes, and then slowly stood up. "May I go now?"

"Wait." He waved his arm. "I'd...I'd like to"—hesitantly, he took

85

a drag of his cigarette and lowered the volume—"ask you a favor."

Jasmine backed off a step, bumping into the chair, which made an unpleasant squeaking noise. Terror rushed through her. She would never allow herself to go through such pain and humiliation again. That was a promise she'd made to herself. Her eyes darted around the room, trying to find a weapon.

"Not that kind of favor. Sorry to frighten you." Embarrassed, he hurried to say, "Could you please draw a picture for me?"

She stood speechless. Panic was replaced by astonishment.

"Truth is, I look awful in photos," he explained. His mouth curved into an awkward smile. "Whenever I have a photo taken, for some reason, I tense. A portrait would be better. Could you please draw one?"

Jasmine would never have imagined a Secret Police officer making such a bizarre request, especially here in prison.

"I've seen your paintings. And the sketches you've done for Shen Shen are flattering. He showed them to everyone, you know. Miss Bai, you're very talented. I'll pay you, of course. Whatever your standard fee, I'll double it."

"No," Jasmine answered quickly. She didn't have a single coin and surely could use the money once she got out, but the idea made her sick to her stomach. Tan Yin was the one who had forced her to watch her loved one's torture. The image of Li Ming's bare chest sizzling under the hot iron appeared in her mind, and she cowered.

"I'm sorry about your…boyfriend. I was just doing my job. Communist Bandits will destroy our country. I must do my best to prevent that. If I were lenient to a few crazy Communists, more people would be hurt in the end."

Jasmine wanted to argue with him but decided not to provoke him. She was still in jail and at his mercy. And her knowledge of communism was limited. With her head held high, she stood her ground.

Tan Yin shifted his weight from one foot to the other. "I wish we could have met under different circumstances. I'd love to talk with you about the Flying Tigers. My brother was a fighter pilot in the Air Force. That's why I'm familiar with the American pilots. I also wanted to be a pilot, but my eyesight wasn't good enough for it."

Her face softened.

"Your cousin probably knows my brother. He was killed by the Japs. His death was heroic and...tragic."

Jasmine gave a small nod.

They sat back down. The officer took out the fine drawing paper and pencils he'd prepared. "Could you please make me look happy? Who knows how long I'll still be kicking?" He crossed his legs and then uncrossed them. "The Nationalist Army is doing a rotten job. I'm prepared. *Bu cheng gong bian cheng ren—Die for the righteous cause if we don't succeed.* But I want to leave a smiling image for my family."

Jasmine was once again startled. *No one is safe.* No one knew when he would die and never see his family. Sullenly, she picked up the pencil and paper and started drawing.

Chapter 19

——————

Jasmine was blindfolded and put inside a car. The ride was bumpy and seemed to take forever. She didn't know for sure that the Secret Police would let her go. Maybe they had tricked her. Perhaps, they were transferring her to a different location. Or maybe she would be secretly executed. It was rumored that many people had disappeared without a trace in recent years.

Being blindfolded heightened her anxiety. She wrung her hands and chewed her lower lip. Thirty nail-biting minutes later, the car stopped. When she stepped outside, she found herself in the middle of the city center. The vehicle sped away, leaving her behind engulfed by black diesel smoke. She was free. But utterly alone.

Her parents, aunt, and younger cousin were long gone. Danny Hardy had been killed. Doctor Wang and all the villagers had been slaughtered. Her uncle and Birch were out of her reach, and she had no means to find them.

Now, her son was dead. Li Ming, the Big Brother who had sheltered her for months, was in jail, and most likely, he would be executed soon. A Communist spy working in the Nationalist Army would be considered a capital crime.

Jasmine regretted not asking the Secret Police officer about her uncle and cousin. Tan Yin might have known where they'd moved, but under stress, she'd forgotten to ask him. It was too late now.

There was no way for her to find him.

Aimlessly, she wandered around the streets. The murky sky cast the city of Chungking in an ominous gray and mirrored her mood. A year and a half after she'd learned the tragic news, she was nowhere close to finding Danny or her family. If anything, she'd slipped even further away from him. The article stated that he'd been killed in Yunnan. If she'd stayed with the hunters, at least she would have been in the same province where Danny had died.

And Bai Ge wouldn't have been killed…

When it started to rain, she took shelter in front of a fancy hotel. "Go away," barked a doorman in a yellow and blue uniform. He seized her arm and shoved her sideways. "Go! Do your business elsewhere."

Jasmine stumbled and fell on the slippery pavement. Her face turned red with humiliation. She stood up. Mud stained her already dirty maroon cheongsam. With leaden steps, she moved to stand under a low window awning. The wind picked up and blew sideways. Even with the shade, she was soaked. The gust was biting and sneaked through the thin layer of her clothes. Cold and hungry, she shivered. Tears of despair mixed with raindrops dripped down her cheeks.

"Come inside," called a man's hoarse voice.

An old man with a bald head stood in a nearby doorway. He waved his aged-spotted hand and repeated, "Come inside." She stepped into a tiny shop with four empty tables. The smell of delicious food filled the air.

"Come here," said an old woman with silver hair. She put a steaming bowl on a table. "Have some hot noodles. It's so cold out there."

Tears stung Jasmine's eyes.

The old man pointed to the bench near the table. His wife snatched a washcloth and handed it to her. "You must be freezing. Why do you stay outside? Why didn't you go home?"

Jasmine didn't know where to start. And she didn't dare release the emotional floodgates for fear they might never close again.

"Don't talk to her. Let her eat first," grunted the man.

She ate in silence. The lump in her throat burned each time she swallowed.

The old couple brought back fond memories of the remote cabin. Jasmine missed the hunters. She missed the green hills, the fresh air, and the peaceful way of living. No gunshot. No jail. No torture. No death.

There and then, she decided to return to Yunnan, to the hunters' home. Even if she couldn't find Danny, at least she would be closer to him. At least she would be with the kind-hearted people. Perhaps, just perhaps, she could find the location of his grave once she was there.

Jasmine paid the old couple extra for being kind to her. What they had done for her was *xue zhong song tan—give a gift of firewood on a cold day.*

But where would she spend the night?

Jasmine didn't bother to go back to Li Ming's dormitory. It belonged to the Nationalist Army. Now that he was no longer part of the organization, his place must have been taken over by another officer. Their personal belongings? She didn't want to knock on the door of an Army officer to find out. She wished she could get Bai Ge's stuff and the first painting she'd done at the dorm—Li Ming loved it so much. What she missed the most was the newspaper article, but she was sure the Secret Police had already confiscated it.

She wondered if she should get in touch with the cook at the Buddhist Temple. Li Ming had told her to contact him if she ever needed help. He might be one of Li Ming's contacts. He might be the traitor, or the one Li Ming tried to protect. Either way, Jasmine didn't think it would be safe to get in touch with him.

Tan Yin had been so satisfied with the portrait that he'd paid triple the amount she would typically make. She could stay in a cheap inn. Instead, she bought a few essentials, such as an extra set of clothes, a light jacket, a bag, and art supplies for her trip.

Known as the "Mountain City," Chungking was built on hills and surrounded by rivers. After the fall of Nanking, it had become the wartime capital and, at the same time, the target of the Japanese terror campaign. Numerous air-raid shelters had been dug deep into the hillsides. Jasmine checked a few, but to her dismay, every single one was locked.

That night, she found a dry spot on the riverbank under a bridge and lay on the ground against a stone pillar. Dampened by the afternoon shower, the air was chilly and dense with humidity. It was dark—thick clouds stole the moon from the sky, only dim light from the houses on the hillside across the river twinkled here and there. Sleep eluded her for hours.

In the dark, she listened to the rhythmic sound of rushing water. She wondered how long it would take for the water to claim her if she jumped into the river. She'd had a similar thought while escaping from Nanking. It was her fond childhood memory of Birch that had saved her. *Don't worry, Birch. I won't do anything stupid. I gave Li Ming my word as well.*

Thinking of her Big Brothers, she turned away from the river with a tired sigh. At least she was free. No walls to lock her in. No guards to hit her or yell at her. No handcuffs to hurt her wrists. No fear of being tortured or humiliated. No pain of being forced to watch a loved one's torment.

In the darkness, Jasmine thought of Li Ming, Leng Xue, and Shen Shen, those without freedom, those with a constant threat of death hanging over their heads. Between the insufferable cold, nightmares of the prison, and the images of her family and friends, she barely slept that night.

When a pale sheen of daylight appeared on the eastern horizon, Jasmine began her journey back to Yunnan. She drew sketches along the way as she'd done before. Practically, it was much easier to travel without a child, but his smile, his innocent remarks, his curiosity about the world had brought joy to the difficult journey.

Now, she had no choice but to soldier on, alone.

Part Two

Struggles in Time of "Peace"

Chapter 20

It was late November 1948 when Jasmine returned to Anning, the sleepy town at the foot of the mountains. Dog-tired, she longed to settle down so that she didn't have to worry about where to stay the next day.

As if everything were against her, winter had arrived earlier in the area this year. A thick blanket of snow covered the path going up the mountains. Even if she were in good shape, she couldn't make it to the hunting hut so high up and hidden in the forest. She had no choice but to wait for the snow to melt, most likely until next spring. She was so close—only a day away—yet she was still a world apart from her loved ones.

As she'd done along the way, she drew sketches and sold her paintings for a living. But the cold weather made it almost impossible. No one wanted his portrait drawn, and few people would shop for art in such lousy conditions.

One late afternoon, Jasmine shivered by her stand on the street. She hadn't sold anything. A light flurry was falling from the darkened sky, adding to the carpet of snow already on the ground. She touched her pocket and heaved a deep sigh. *Where will I live if I don't sell anything tomorrow?*

As she was getting ready to call it a day, a middle-aged man in a long, one-piece garment strode toward her. Jasmine grinned. She knew him. Mr. Zhao was Bai Fu's butler. Bai Fu, the richest man in town, had brought several of her pictures.

"Come with me, Miss Bai," said the man with droopy eyes.

"Oh, Mr. Bai wants to see more paintings? You can take these and return the ones he doesn't want, like what we've done before."

"No. Mr. Bai wants to speak to you."

"Really? Why?"

"He just told me to fetch you. You'll find out soon."

Jasmine was curious, and Bai Fu had a good reputation. She gathered her paintings. Through crooked cobblestone streets and blind alleys, she followed the butler and trudged through the snow.

———————

Bai Fu sat behind an ornately carved redwood desk full of notebooks. Bookshelves lined two sides of the study. "Miss Bai," he said, motioning her to a chair. In his early forties, he was attractive in a scholarly way. "I really like your paintings." He pointed to the wall behind him, where one of her landscapes hung. "My son is only five, but he has a special interest in art."

She listened.

"I'd like to hire you to teach him."

"To paint?"

Bai Fu shook his head. "That's only one part of your job." He paused for a beat, his fingers drumming the cluttered desk. "Besides teaching, I'd like you to work for me. You can paint whatever you like, but I'll own them. I can sell them to whoever wants to buy, at whatever price I think fit. In exchange, I'll provide room and board and spending money." He named the amount of salary.

Jasmine lowered her head as she considered his offer. It wasn't a generous one; her paintings could sell for a lot more than he was offering. Still, this way she wouldn't have to constantly worry about where her next meal would come.

"You'll get a day off every week. Any paintings you generate on your off days are yours. I could sell them for you if you like. Oh, our term is for one year, just so you know."

"I can stay for the winter."

Bai Fu seemed a bit taken aback. He pushed his glasses up the bridge of his nose and gave Jasmine a slow once-over. "How about half a year?"

It was longer than she wanted to stay, but she nodded her affirmation.

"Good. We have a deal. I'll write up a contract. Meanwhile…" He looked at his watch and then turned to Mr. Zhao, who stood patiently near the door. "Show Miss Bai her room, will you? Dinner will be ready in fifteen minutes. I'll introduce her to the family."

———

The dining area was well lit by porcelain lamps with white lampshades. Oil paintings of stunning landscapes, one of which was done by Jasmine, decorated the walls. A three-panel floor screen with birds and flowers painted on glossy black lacquer stood at one corner of the room. Long bamboo blinds had been lowered to keep out the winter cold.

Mr. Bai's family sat around a large round table full of delicious dishes—for an ordinary household, this was better than its holiday meal. His mother was seated on his right-hand side, and his wife and son sat on his left. "So, where are you from?" asked Bai Fu after his introduction. "You don't speak our local dialect."

Jasmine didn't like this simple question. "Nanking." Standing, she shifted her weight from one foot to the other.

"Everyone wants to live in a charming city like Nanking, Well, at least before the massacre. Tragic. Just tragic. How come you're here in this remote part of the country?"

"I'm here…for the beauty of nature." She hated lies and decided to tell a half-truth.

"Oh, I see." Bai Fu seemed to get it. His features revealed intelligence and discernment. "You're one of those artsy types. Well, we've got plenty of beautiful nature around here."

"Who cares about art nowadays? The Communists will probably take over the country soon," grumbled An Kong, his wife. With heavy makeup, she was slender in a high-necked black cheongsam embroidered with primrose-yellow flowers and birds. She wore many rings and sapphire bracelets.

"Nonsense. Art is timeless, no matter who oversees the country."

"This is too hard to chew," the boy complained and prodded at the tenderloin. Bai Long—White Dragon was a pretty child with chubby cheeks. He scrunched his nose and wiggled it from side to side before spitting out a mouthful of meat.

Jasmine sighed silently. Her son would have been thrilled to have any of the dishes on the table. Bai Long also reminded her of Shen Shen, who had tasted nothing except prison rations.

"Tao Zhao," said An Kong, turning to the butler, "tell the cook he must improve. Many would be happy to take his job."

"Yes, ma'am," Mr. Zhao replied submissively.

"Nothing is wrong with the tenderloin. Don't spoil the child too much," said Bai Fu, chewing the meat. "Now," he faced his son and ordered, "Miss Bai is going to be your teacher. *Yi ri wei shi, zhong shen wei fu*—teacher for one day, father for life."

"She's…poor. And ugly…" The boy gaped at her left cheek.

"Yeah. Look at her clothes…" An Kong shook her head with contempt.

Jasmine was wearing a dark blue cotton jacket and trousers of a peasant.

Bai Fu turned to his butler. "Tao Zhao, take Miss Bai to our tailor tomorrow. Tell him to make three sets of clothes for different seasons."

"Three sets?" grunted his wife. "That's a lot of money. You should take it out of her salary."

"No." Bai Fu dismissed it with a wave of the hand. "We've made a deal. This is extra. It's on me. Now"—he turned to his son—"kneel and bow to *Bai Lao Shi—Teacher Bai.*"

"She's a woman. She can't be a father."

"Bow!" He lightly smacked the back of his son's head. "She can't be a father. But she can be a mother."

"You wish!" barked his wife, slapping her husband's arm.

Realizing his slip of the tongue, Bai Fu flashed a sheepish smile.

"Just bow to *Bai Lao Shi*. She is your teacher."

The boy didn't move. He just sat there and rolled his eyes.

Jasmine wished it were Shen Shen she would teach. She'd considered teaching him when she was in jail, but she didn't have the heart to take away his precious time with his mother.

Chapter 21

— — — — — — —

The next few months were uneventful, except for Bai Long's temper tantrums from time to time. Even though he had great potential as an artist, he was a spoiled brat. Teaching him was a chore, not a pleasure, and he was a constant reminder of the loss of her son and Shen Shen.

When the summer of 1949 came, Jasmine thanked Bai Fu and left her job. He tried to persuade her to stay by offering a higher salary but bid her good-bye once he sensed her determination.

Bai Fu was polite. He'd offered her lodging and warm meals during the cold months. His wife, on the other hand, was less friendly. She hadn't been openly rude, but she seemed adept at finding the smallest fault. Not long after her arrival, Jasmine had overheard a rumor that Mr. Bai had considered taking her as a concubine. She'd scoffed at the gossip. Nevertheless, Mrs. Bai had been jealous of her.

Leng Xue, who had a cold name, reminded Jasmine so much of her mother and aunt. Bai Fu's wife, who had the same title as her mother and aunt, turned out to be far from a graceful woman.

Jasmine was ready to leave. She missed the hunters.

———————

After a long hike up the mountains, Jasmine was elated to see the hut in the opening of the dense forest. The sun had already slipped behind the hills, and the sky had turned orange and lavender. In golden rays, the wooden cabin gave the impression of peace and serenity. "Da Ma! Da Shu!" she yelled, her eyes glowing and her cheeks flushed.

No one answered.

Disappointed, she pushed open the door. The room was dark. It took her a few seconds to adjust. Squinting, she scanned the small space and, to her surprise, saw a figure lying on the hunters' bed. She rushed over.

"Da Ma?" She could hear the trembling in her own voice.

Under a heavy blanket lay the old woman. Her eyes were closed, and her cheeks were hollow. Her coarse skin had a gray pallor.

Jasmine placed her right index finger under her nose and feared the worst. Her eyes widened when she detected weak breathing. "Da Ma!" she called out softly, touching the coverlet.

Slowly, the old woman managed to open her eyes. She gazed at Jasmine with a blank look on her face.

"It's me, Jasmine." She put her arm underneath the blanket and gripped Da Ma's thin hand.

"Jasmine?"

"Yes! I'm back."

Tears welled in Da Ma's eyes.

"Don't be sad. You're going to be okay. I'm home now." Jasmine took off the bag she was carrying and rummaged through the contents, trying to find the food she'd bought. "Would you like a banana? How about a mooncake? What about—"

"Jasmine!" Tears rushed down the old woman's hollow cheeks.

"What's wrong? Oh, dear! Where is Da Shu?"

Da Ma seized Jasmine's arm. "We've lived here all our lives. Sixty years. We've always hunted together. A year ago, I became ill, and I couldn't go out with him anymore." She wheezed. Dragging in a labored breath, she continued, "It's dangerous out there, and he's getting old. I didn't want him to hunt alone, but he insisted. It's been three weeks. He's gone. I know it."

"Three weeks?"

"He's out there. I'm here. Can't do anything for him," Da Ma choked, her withered face devoid of any hope.

"I'll look for him. Now, you must eat."

"No! Promise me you won't go into the woods. You're not familiar with the forest. It's too easy to get lost. Don't do anything stupid. You're a mother. You need to think of your son." Da Ma looked behind Jasmine and asked, "Where is Bai Ge? Let me see him. It's been two years. I miss him so much."

Jasmine hesitated. She didn't want to lie, but she didn't have the heart to tell the truth either. "He...didn't come." Tears swam in her eyes as she said it.

"He's a good boy. Don't leave him with others. Bring him home." Da Ma stroked Jasmine's head.

Anguish darkened her eyes, but she didn't allow herself to wallow in grief. She had a dying woman to care for. Wiping tears with her knuckles, she picked up the mooncake. "Da Ma, please eat."

"I'm so tired." Her eyes had sunk into the dark circles surrounding them.

A torrent of emotions hit Jasmine. Without thinking, she said, "Would you please be my...*Gan Ma—Godmother*?"

Da Ma opened her eyes. Her pale lips parted in wordless surprise. Then she shook her head. "No, you're a heroine. You're from a rich and educated family. We're too poor—"

Jasmine knelt on the floor and bowed down. She knocked her forehead on the floor three times, showing her sincerity and reverence.

The old woman smiled; the wrinkles around her eyes and mouth became more pronounced. "Now, I can rest." She closed her eyes.

Two days later, Da Ma passed away. Jasmine was sure that grief and loneliness had played the biggest part of her illness.

———

Jasmine remained at the cabin, waiting for Da Shu to return. She believed her godmother's intuition—that her husband was dead. But to be on the safe side, she decided to wait for a while. It would be terrible if he returned, and only a new grave waited for him.

She found some rice, flour, and pickled vegetables. But there wasn't much growing in the garden. Luckily it was summer, so she could pick wild berries and mushrooms. Living with the hunters for several years, she'd learned how to live off the land. But she didn't dare to venture far from the path. The forest was dangerous. She could be swallowed by the dense woods, and no one would find her body.

Three chickens roamed freely in the fenced yard. Jasmine wondered if, in the future, she would have to kill them to survive. That idea made her wince.

One day she became violently ill after eating mushrooms. She'd been careful, but wild mushrooms were tricky. Some of the poisonous ones looked very much like the edible ones. All night long, she vomited.

When she went outside, she saw eyes in the dark. *Animal eyes!* The hairs pricked on the back of her neck. No one was around. No one could help her if the animal charged her. She was utterly alone and defenseless. Her legs turned weak with fear. From then on, she remained inside the cabin and had to use the wooden washbasin. Fortunately, she felt much better in the morning. At thirty, she was still young and resilient.

Within three months, the supplies were exhausted to the point that she had to consider the chickens. She had seen chickens being killed. It seemed easy enough.

She chased them around the yard and caught one. She twisted its head back. Adrenaline pumped through her, and her hands started to shake. Fending off a rising panic, she slit its neck with a kitchen knife. It squirmed and thrashed so much that she couldn't hold it and let it go. Blood dripped from its throat as it scurried around the yard.

Jasmine felt terrible. But she didn't have any choice. With a frown, she snatched the chicken again. To ward off the unpleasant scene, she squinted and tilted her body sideways before cutting off its head. It wasn't the right way. She was supposed to drain the blood, which was nutritious and tasty. But all she wanted to do was end its misery as fast as she could.

Chapter 22

Jasmine hadn't had meat since she'd left Anning. The chicken tasted delicious, especially with the mushrooms she'd collected. But she didn't have the heart to kill the other two. And even if she killed them, the food would last only a few more days. The hunter was long gone and wouldn't return.

But winter was approaching. Although she'd lost track of the exact date, Jasmine knew that it was late autumn already. The weather had grown colder and the days shorter. Most of the wildflowers were gone. She could find fewer and fewer wild berries or mushrooms. The lush green hillside had turned to a mixture of yellow and brown. If surviving the summer in this remote hut had been hard, surviving the bitter cold winter alone was inconceivable. She knew she had to leave. But where could she go?

There weren't many options. In the end, she decided to return to Anning to work for Bai Fu. The boy had shown great promise as an artist, and there were many books in the house, and reading took her away from her miseries.

She left a note for the hunter, just in case he returned one day. Although she'd never met his son and doubted that he was still alive, she included him in the note. Calling them Godfather and Brother, respectively, she thanked Da Shu again for saving her and accepting her as part of his family. She also jotted down Bai Fu's address.

Even as she was writing, she doubted that either of them would ever read it. Most likely, the old man had met with an accident, and he was already dead. As for the son, he hadn't returned after the war against Japan. A dull and all-too-familiar ache settled in her chest.

Jasmine closed the door behind her. Intentionally she left the front yard gate open. The chickens ran for their freedom and instantly disappeared in the nearby woods. She wished that they would be luckier to survive in the wilderness than she'd been in the human world.

A lump formed in the back of her throat. The cabin was tiny, with only bare necessities, but it had been her home and sanctuary. Now, once again, she was thrust back into the world—homeless and penniless.

She limped through a tunnel of trees along the narrow path. The autumn-wind tossed fallen leaves and twigs around her, and the land shivered beneath a gloomy sky.

Jasmine decided to stop by a cave before going to Anning. This place had sheltered her, Danny, and Daisy for several days. The last time she'd seen them was at the cave. She'd never taken this route, but when they went down the mountains, Da Shu had pointed out a trail going up to the Village of Peach Blossoms. She knew how to go from there to the cave. Yet she grimaced at the thought of going through the hamlet. *Did anyone ever bury those bodies? Who cared enough to take the time?*

According to her estimation, she could reach the cave before dark. She would spend the night there as they'd done before. She'd prepared enough food for three days, and there was plenty of water along the way.

But the path was longer than she'd expected. And she'd picked the wrong day. By midmorning, it started to rain. How could she have known? The weather was hard to predict in the mountains. It had been sunny and dry for a couple of weeks. Now, thunder echoed off the distant peaks, and thick raindrops came down. The track became muddy. Jasmine slipped and fell. Luckily, she wasn't seriously hurt, only her elbows were bruised, and her clothes tainted with mud.

By late afternoon, she was exhausted. Her toes, calves, and thighs were cramped. She dragged her feet, fatigue slumping her shoulders. The rain had stopped. The sun fought through the clouds and slanted toward the western horizon, but she hadn't even reached the village.

She would never get to the cave before dark. A tired sigh escaped her lips. It had taken her half a day to go to the cave from the village when she was in good shape years earlier, and now the thought of walking in the darkness frightened her. She would have to spend the night in the village. Images of the carnage in Doctor Wang's front yard rushed to her mind. She shivered, and she knew it wasn't just from the cold. *I'll go around Doctor Wang's front yard. It'll be okay if I don't see it.*

As determined as she was, she grew anxious once she got close to the village. Every step was a test of will. When she reached Tao Hua Cun, to her utter astonishment, it was peaceful. And alive!

Tiny beads of water covered the leaves and sparkled in the late afternoon sunlight. The terraced fields looked like golden ribbons laid out over the hills, and waves of rice stalk flowed with the wind. Men and women worked in the rice paddies. Children ran around the adults, chasing each other, yipping, and laughing.

Jasmine didn't know any of them. Was this a dream? She spun around, making sure this was indeed the Village of Peach Blossoms. Everything seemed so familiar, yet somehow different.

"Auntie, what are you doing here?" asked a little girl, her voice filled with curiosity. With two pigtails, she wore a raspberry-colored jacket covered with small yellow flowers. "I don't know you. Are you looking for someone? Are you sick? My dad is an herbalist. He'll help you. Would you like me to find him for you?"

Jasmine was too astonished to think. She just stood there. Her mouth hung open, but she couldn't find anything to say.

"Dad! Dad!" The girl called out while she sprang toward a man in the nearby terraced field. "This auntie needs help. I think she's sick."

In a peasant's smock and straw shoes, the girl's father was in his mid-twenties, short but sturdy with a round face. "May I help you?"

he asked as he took off his conical straw hat to fan himself.

Jasmine backed away two steps. A look of disbelief passed over her face.

The young man stilled. He pulled his daughter closer to him as if to protect her from harm.

"Linzi!" She stepped forward with outstretched arms. "I'm Jasmine!"

Chapter 23

The young villager's eyes went wide, first with disbelief, and then with elation. He let go of the little girl and grasped Jasmine's arms. "Miss Jasmine! It is you. You're alive! How in the world…?"

She broke down. Years of pain and suffering erupted in her chest and ripped through her throat, robbing her of words. Only mournful sounds escaped from deep inside her.

"It's all right." Wang Linzi patted her bony shoulders. "It's all right now."

Gradually, her sobs subsided. "I thought everyone had died." She wiped her tears with her sleeves. "I forgot your grandpa had sent you to call my uncle and cousin. You were away from the village when…"

"Yes, it took me a while. The Japs were everywhere in Anning. So, I walked to another town to make the call. When I came back…"

"I'm so sorry about your grandpa and brothers." Jasmine reached out and wiped the tears on the villager's suntanned face. "I can't believe it! I'm so glad you survived. A sole survivor!"

"No, there was another girl. Ding Xiang. She—"

"Ding Xiang?" She tilted her head slightly, thinking. "I remember. She was dragged away by the Japs. There were three girls. What about the other two?"

"They didn't make it."

"How did she get away? The Japs were taking us to their camp."

"After the soldiers had their...fun with her, they offered her to a translator. He set her free."

The image of a Japanese man dressed in a black V-neck tunic over loose-fitting trousers came to her mind. Jasmine recoiled. She'd begged the man to help her, to prevent the torture and rape.

"Ding Xiang told *Bai Hua Ge—Big Brother Birch* about you... and the massacre."

"Birch knew about this?" Her grip on the young man's arms tightened. Hope ignited within her as she asked, "Where is he? Is he still here?"

"They were here but left—"

"They? Who are they? Birch and Daisy?" Even though she'd learned from the article that her younger cousin had passed away, she couldn't help but hope. Maybe the article had been mistaken.

But her hope was shattered in seconds. No, Daisy hadn't survived. Linzi didn't know how she'd died. It had happened when she left the area with Danny and Birch. General Bai and Birch had never brought up the subject.

"I think it has something to do with...Birch," mumbled the villager. He lowered his head to avoid looking Jasmine in the eyes. "Whenever anyone mentioned her, Birch had that look. You know, pain. Guilt. After a while, we didn't dare to say her name. No one was willing to hurt Birch. We all love him. And look up to him."

She nodded in appreciation. "When did they come here? When did they leave?"

"They came here in the fall of 1946. Your uncle said he didn't want to live through another war—a war that the Chinese were killing each other. He and Birch also wanted to rebuild the village. They couldn't let the Japanese destroy a piece of heaven on earth. They left only a few months ago."

Jasmine had been in Yunnan until the spring of 1947 and returned in the fall of 1948. The hunting hut and the village was only a one-day hike away. If she'd come here earlier, she would have met up with her uncle and cousin. She would have had a family. If only she'd known! If only she could turn back time. The thought released another downpour. "Why did they have to leave?"

"You don't know?"

"About what?"

"The Civil War. The conflict between—"

"Yes. It seemed the Communists were winning. At least that was the case a while back. I haven't—"

"The Communists won."

"Really?"

"They've taken over the Mainland. A new country—the People's Republic of China—was established several weeks ago. On October 1, Mao Zedong, the Chairman of the Communist Party, announced it in Peking. He said, 'The Chinese people have stood up.' I'll show you the newspaper."

Jasmine listened in bewilderment. So much had happened in the last few months, and she had a lot to process. She shouldn't be surprised by the result. Being the main force and after fighting the Japanese for eight years, the Nationalist Army had been significantly weakened, while the Communist guerillas had gained power since they'd had time to recuperate from Chiang Kai-shek's campaigns against them.

How did she feel about the news? Although her uncle and cousin had worked for the Nationalist government, a part of her felt excited. She'd never been political, but she'd seen things that she didn't particularly like about the old government, especially what had happened in prison.

A new world. A new beginning. A place where everyone is equal and sharing all the commonwealth—Leng Xue had shared some of the ideas. Although she wasn't a member of the Communist Party, being in jail for many years, Leng Xue was knowledgeable.

It could be a turning point in history. At least the war is over. No more senseless death. But more crucial to Jasmine was how the new government would affect her family. She asked in a hurry, "What about the Nationalists?"

"They retreated to Taiwan."

"That's where Uncle and Birch went?"

"Yes. They had to go. It's not safe for them here. But don't worry, Miss Jasmine. They'll be back. General Bai said Taiwan was only a temporary stop. They'll come back"—Linzi looked around, making sure there wasn't anyone within earshot—"when the Nationalist Army reconquers the Mainland. Or the Communist government forgives their former enemies."

She nodded, hoping to God that the new government would be lenient to its former enemies. *If the Nationalist Army reconquers the Mainland, that means there will be a war between the two sides.* Millions would die. She prayed earnestly that she would never witness another war in her lifetime.

"How is Ding Xiang?" Jasmine asked.

"Your uncle and Birch helped her find a factory job in Chungking. She..." He hesitated before continuing, "gave birth to a boy after... you know. She really shouldn't do that."

"The kid is innocent."

"Not in our society. He's a bastard. He has Jap's blood! If anyone finds out, he'd be looked down upon for the rest of his life. Why bring a child to the world where he'd be shunned? She really should have aborted him."

Jasmine sighed silently and decided not to bring up her son. Bai Ge was no longer there anyway.

"Enough about other people. What about you? How did you survive?" Linzi asked his previous question again. "Birch and Major Hardy searched for you...many times. Ding Xiang took them to the ridge where you...jumped. I thought you were a ghost when I saw you a moment ago. Oh, too bad! Major Hardy would be so thrilled!"

Chapter 24

––– ––– ––– ––– ––– ––– ––– –––

General Bai's house had a courtyard surrounded by rooms on all four sides that connected by a pathway with an overhang. The small room next to the gate was the kitchen. The side rooms were used as bedrooms—they had been taken by Jasmine and Daisy. The largest one facing the entrance was designed as a dining area.

When Danny was there, the big room had been given to him. Jasmine just learned that Birch had also stayed in the same place. It was an obvious choice for her. After seven years, the room was unchanged, except for a row of cardboard boxes on the floor along the wall. She suspected that they were books. Both her uncle and cousin enjoyed reading.

That night she lay on the bed that Danny had once used. He'd been there for a couple of months, but the memories he'd left behind could fill a lifetime.

Lying on the same bed, even though it had been seven years, she could imagine his scent and the heat from his body. How could a man like Danny—courageous, energetic, and passionate—be dead? Overwhelmed with emotions, Jasmine tossed and turned, and sleep evaded her for hours. Only in the wee hours did she cry herself to sleep.

In her dream, Danny appeared. He was as dashing as he'd been, a white scarf wrapped around his neck. "Would you like to fly with me?" he asked as if they had never been apart.

"Of course!" She beamed, unable to suppress her delight.

He pulled her up, and hand in hand, they walked out. The night was quiet, and a dazzling full moon hung in the sky. Wondering where his plane was, she remembered that his fighter plane had been shot down and destroyed by the Japanese.

"Ready?" He turned to her, tightening his grip.

She nodded.

Danny grinned. With one hand holding hers, he circled his arm behind her back and held tightly to her waist. "Here we go!" With that, he lifted her off the ground, and they soared into the sky. The light from the full moon cast a glow upon the landscape. The scenery was out-of-this-world, and Jasmine was walking on air. The wind rushed by, but she didn't feel cold. In fact, her face was burning. Landing in a meadow full of forget-me-nots, she recognized this place as the location where she'd first found Danny, severely injured and unconscious.

He sat by her side. His hand never let go of hers. "You kissed me that night, didn't you? You brought me back with your kisses."

"I…fed you herbs. Sweet wormwood. I had to chew it first. I—"

Danny gave a hearty laugh. "I'm such a fool." He brushed a loose strand of hair from her face. "That doesn't count." His hand moved down and cupped her chin. "May I?"

The intensity of his gaze sent a ripple of exultation through her body. She nodded and closed her eyes.

He eased her down onto the soft grass. He kissed her cheeks, lingering longer on her left side with the three ugly scars. When he unbuttoned her blouse, she grabbed his hand. She was worried that he could see her scar-covered chest in the silver light.

"Let me see them, Jasmine. They're *my* scars! If you didn't take them for me, they would have been all over my body."

Tears welled in her eyes.

Slowly, Danny brushed open her blouse. Leaning down, he placed his mouth on the left side of her upper body, where a Japanese soldier had used his sword. Over and over again, he kissed her with feather-light touches.

Jasmine shivered with desire.

Minutes later, he lifted his head. "Done."

She opened her eyes, still deeply immersed in the ecstasy she'd never experienced. Her mouth opened as she looked at her body—all the wounds were gone. Moonlight turned her naked skin silver. And smooth. "What did you…?"

"They are mine," he said matter-of-factly. "I took them back."

In haste, she lifted his shirt. Scars covered the broad plane of his masculine chest. "No!" She tilted his face so that it wasn't in shadow. Three long jagged scars etched his left cheek.

"No!" she cried again, feeling pain in her heart.

Danny's eyes were brimming with tenderness. "Crazy as it seems, I'm one of the Gods now. I have the power to ease your pain."

Jasmine was speechless. The depth of his love overwhelmed her, and she placed her lips to his.

Ever since her torture and rape, she'd been fearful of intimacy. The idea of a man entering her body terrified her. That was one of the reasons why she hadn't returned to Danny. And she'd had other opportunities for intimacy. Li Ming adored her and wouldn't have hesitated to marry her. She knew it. She'd felt it.

But now, without hesitation, she gripped his hip and pulled him inside her. The pleasure was so intense that she cried out.

Immediately, he stopped. "Are you okay?" Concern drew his brows together.

"I'm okay. I'm more than okay." Jasmine dug her fingertips into the lean muscles of his back, pulling him closer to her. Her body arched up, eager to receive him. "Don't stop, Danny. Don't stop!"

Each smooth thrust sent him deep inside, carrying her to new heights of sensation, and the intensity of the pleasure increased until every nerve in her body tingled.

It was almost dawn when he finally rolled over to her side. Folding her in his arms, he kissed her hair.

She snuggled closer. Hearing the thudding of his heart, she smiled. A wholehearted smile she hadn't shown since the day they'd parted. Her face was gorgeous and delicate as she'd been before the torture.

The moon slipped beneath a cloudless horizon. Faint light rimmed the mountains around them, and the sky turned gray with the encroaching dawn. Reluctantly, he let go of her and sat up. "I… have to go."

"No!" Jasmine bolted up. Circling her arms around his neck, she wouldn't let him go. "Don't leave me, Danny. Don't ever leave me!"

He patted her back. "I don't want to leave." He took her right hand and lightly planted a kiss on the back of it, just as he'd done seven years earlier. "But I'll be back. Trust me."

With that, he soared into the sky, the white scarf flapping behind his back. "I love you, Jasmine!" he shouted. His voice echoed off the nearby mountains.

Jasmine reached up, trying in vain to bring him back. She woke with her hand still high in the air. Lying in tangled sheets, she was breathless. Tears trickled down her cheeks, then she smiled, and cried some more.

She knew it was just a dream, some of the scenes she'd already daydreamed a thousand times. But the bittersweet dream was different from reverie. It was tangible and sensual. She felt the emotions more intensely than in real life. The heat of his touch made her body tremble, her pulse race, and her heart sing a joyous song. His declarations of love echoed in her ears. Now she knew that the Flying Tiger was with her. She'd made love to him and could make love to him again in her dreams. A blushful smile broke through her grief, and her cheeks—one smooth and the other scarred—grew hotter at the thought.

Chapter 25

▬ ▬ ▬ ▬ ▬ ▬ ▬ ▬

Jasmine had lived in the village once for a year, so everything was familiar to her. But the situation was very different. She'd come from a wealthy family and had no need to do anything. Her uncle had paid Doctor Wang's daughter-in-law to cook and clean for her and Daisy. She was free to explore the area, to draw or paint. Now, penniless, she needed to learn to take care of herself and make a living.

"Good morning." She stepped through Linzi's gate. She had to turn her head and narrow her eyes halfway when she passed the front yard, where the massacre had happened.

He greeted her with a lopsided smile. "I was about to send Lili to get you. Breakfast is ready." He pointed to a table.

It was the same table Jasmine had sat at before she was captured by the Japanese soldiers. The thought made her cringe, but she forced her attention away from the painful reminder. Since she was going to live here, she would have to get over the hurtful feelings. Knowing it would be impolite to refuse his kind offer, she sat down. "Thank you." She took a bowl of rice porridge from him but didn't hurry to eat. "I can't believe you have a daughter now," she said, looking at the girl at the table.

"Two girls. The other one is only a year old. Her name is Yaya." He gave his daughter's pigtail an affectionate tug. "Lili is five."

"Six in a month," the girl lilted, eyes glittering with curiosity.

Jasmine touched Lili's glossy black hair. Turning back to Linzi, she asked, "Have you heard anything about your father?"

"No. So many never returned. I'm sure he's dead."

She heaved a soundless sigh. Li Ming's wife had never returned home—missing for years, most likely dead.

"So much to tell you." He lowered himself onto a chair. "Xiao Mei was here, too."

"Xiao Mei?"

"Yes. She left for Taiwan with General and Birch."

"Great! She loves my cousin. I could tell."

"Even I could tell." He grinned.

She's lucky, Jasmine thought. Although a maid like Xiao Mei could never marry her Young Master, at least she was living under the same roof with the man she loved.

"I'd like to ask you a favor, Linzi," she said.

"Anything!"

"I'd like to plant a vegetable garden and raise some chickens. I don't have anything, so I need to borrow—"

"Miss Jasmine, you don't need to do those things. You're not supposed—"

"No. I'm not a *Xiaojie*—Miss anymore. I must learn to support myself. I can't let you—"

"You'll always be Miss Jasmine," said the villager. "General Bai was like a father to me after Grandpa's death. Birch is my Big Brother. You are family. I'll take care of you."

An unanticipated tenderness welled inside her. In this world, she didn't have many family members left, and the last two were far out of her reach. "Thank you, Linzi! It means so much to me. I…" She swallowed the dryness in her throat. "But I want to learn to take care of myself."

"Birch taught us the concept of *Yi*—morality, duty, loyalty, decency, brotherhood. Taking care of you is my duty to General, to Birch, to society. You almost died for our country."

This farmer's simple words touched her deeply. She grasped his hand with both of hers. "Birch would be so proud of you. Not many people care about the concept of *Yi*, let alone follow it."

"Birch left all those books to us," he said with pride in his voice. "I kept reading."

"Linzi, think of it this way—it'll make me happy to be independent. I want to be useful. My parents taught me to always try my best to contribute to family and society. Could you please help me?" She'd already learned to cook, garden, and raise chickens when she lived at the hunting hut. Now, she just needed tools and a little assistance to start.

He nodded his understanding.

"I also want to work around here…as your helper. I may not be able to go out collecting herbs with you, but I can learn to sort, clean, and make the medicines. Will you teach me? I may slow you down at first, but I'm a fast learner."

Linzi responded with another head bob.

"Wonderful!" Jasmine picked up the bowl of porridge and ate several spoonfuls. "Delicious. Once I settle into a routine, I'll teach kids in the village to read and draw. Maybe even teach them English."

And I'll paint more pictures so that I'll have the funds to look for Danny, she vowed.

―――――――

For the first time in seven years since she'd been taken away by the Japanese soldiers, Jasmine had a place to call home. She decided to wait there for her uncle and cousin to return. Meanwhile, she would work hard so that she would accumulate enough money to make a proper search for Danny.

She still suffered nightmares. The pain and fear were like animals lurking in her subconscious, always wanting to break out. But ever since the day she'd dreamed of Danny, at least she wasn't so afraid to fall asleep. She knew that in her dreams, and only in her dreams could she meet him again, and she lived for that opportunity, even if it meant she had to endure the nightmares.

Other than helping Linzi with his herbs and attending her vegetable garden, Jasmine spent most of her time painting. But the cold months were not suitable for selling art. It wasn't until the summer of 1950 that she had enough money to ask Linzi to take a long trip with her to Dashan. If she'd asked earlier, he would have agreed and spent all he had to help her. Life in this remote village was tough; no one had extra money. She couldn't bring herself to burden the kind-hearted villager.

During the past few months, Jasmine had learned of Birch's relationship with an old couple in Dashan. She decided that her first stop would be to visit Ding Fang's family. Mr. Ding had been a Communist and was imprisoned with Birch and Danny. His parents might have learned from the Communist government the whereabouts of his grave, where seven prisoners, including Danny Hardy, were buried. It took them an exhausting long day to hike up to Angel's Pass and walk down the other side of the mountains to Dashan.

Blending naturally with the environment, Dashan was a mountainous town with ancient huts perched on the lush hillside. Linzi guided Jasmine through a maze of narrow streets paved with large inlaid cobblestones. Everywhere they went, they could see slogans and banners: "Down with the Capitalists," "Exterminate the Counter-revolutionary Nationalists, the Enemies of the People," "Down with the American Devils," "Build a New Communist China."

Colorful, cartoonish posters hung on every street corner. On one of them, a pockmarked man in the Nationalist Army uniform was hanging by the neck. A smoking pistol, a bloody knife, and pieces of documents were scattered around him. "He Who Tries to Harm the People Will Be Punished Severely" read the title. On another, a skinny man wore dark sunglasses. "The Enemy of the People" was written on his shirt. He was running away from an oversized hand that clasped the back of his clothes. One of his shoes was gone. A "Made in the USA" camera was strapped to his right leg. Under the spotlight, he was visibly shaken. "Where Can a Nationalist Spy Run?" was printed on top of the image.

Jasmine was stunned and hurt by the images. She'd learned from the newspapers that the Communists had recently launched a campaign to suppress the Counter-revolutionaries, which was designed to eliminate their former enemies—the Nationalists. But seeing all the slogans and posters made her worry. Birch and her uncle had worked for the Nationalist government. Danny Hardy was an American. Would they be labeled as the Enemy of the People from now on?

Chapter 26

Jasmine was still in deep thought when Old Ding, Mr. Ding's father, opened the door. "Come in." The gentleman beamed when he spotted Wang Linzi.

His one-bedroom apartment looked homey and tidy. Knowing that Birch had helped this poor couple to move from the degraded place where they'd lived, Jasmine's heart filled with warmth and admiration for her cousin.

The old man's smile broadened when he learned that she was Birch's cousin. With both hands, he clutched hers. "He's a fine young man. My wife couldn't say enough good things about him. I wish she could be here. She'd be so happy to meet you. Too bad, she passed away nine months ago."

"I'm so sorry."

"She had a hard life, especially after our son was captured by the Japs. Not knowing what happened to him and where he was had killed her long before she died." Hard living had carved deep lines of sadness into his complexion.

Jasmine knew their family story. Both Ding Fang and his wife had been slain by the Japanese, but his parents hadn't heard anything about him for three years before Birch found them. By then, the country was in the middle of the Civil War. The old couple was kicked out of their home by the Nationalist government simply because their son was a Communist. Birch helped them, even though he and Ding Fang had worked for opponent parties. She felt sorry for the old woman. Thinking of Danny, she wondered how his death had affected his family.

Old Ding motioned Jasmine and Linzi to chairs around a wooden table. "So, how is Birch? I haven't seen him for a while."

"We don't know. He and my uncle left for Taiwan before..." She hesitated. She didn't like the term "liberation."

"Before the liberation," Linzi finished. "We haven't heard from them for months. They said, in their last letter, that they'd bought a house in Taipei. That was last fall."

The old man poured hot water from a thermos into cups to make tea. "They made the right decision. The Mainland isn't safe for them."

"What do you mean?" asked Linzi, unable to resist.

"Well, we all know that the Nationalists are the enemies of the Communists, but the things they did..." He shook his head.

"Who are they? What did they do?"

"Let me tell you a story." Old Ding picked up the cup and blew the tea leaves away before taking a sip. "Two months ago, I was invited to a meeting with hundreds of people. I didn't know what the meeting was about, except that they were going to honor my son. In the middle of the meeting, the man in charge wanted me to talk. I don't know how to give a speech."

The old man chuckled, his smile accentuated the wrinkles around his eyes and mouth. "But he encouraged me by saying, 'Tell us how you found out about your son's death.' So, I started talking."

Jasmine wondered if Old Ding had said the right thing. Why would the organizers of a Communist Party meeting allow him to share a good deed done by a Nationalist military officer?

He rambled on, "I told them about Birch and everything. When they found out your cousin had been a fighter pilot, they hurried me off the stage."

She gritted her teeth. Unfortunately, her instinct was correct.

"It turned out that the meeting was part of the Campaign to Suppress Counter-revolutionaries."

"Oh, my goodness," said Jasmine. "The campaign is designed to get rid of the former Nationalist members."

"Yes, I said the wrong thing. The exact opposite of what they wanted to hear. I praised a man who had worked for the former government." Old Ding heaved an exasperated sigh. "I was just telling the truth. When I was young, we were taught to be grateful to the people who help us. A drop of water shall be returned with a burst of spring—that's our ancient philosophy."

Linzi agreed.

"What Birch has done for us is above and beyond. I'm forever grateful. But I can't thank him. Can't even talk about him to anyone anymore—that's what they told me. Birch fought the Japs more than most of the Communists, surely more than my son."

"*Lao Ye Zi*," said the villager in earnest, using the title of respect for an elderly man. He touched Old Ding's age-spotted hand. "Don't talk about Birch anymore. It'll get you in trouble. Just remember him…" He pointed to his heart.

This conversation made Jasmine miss Birch even more. They'd been very close, and he was like a brother to her. In fact, she called him *Ge—Big Brother*. She wished her cousin and uncle were here with her. But now she was thankful that they'd left the Mainland. At least they were safe in Taiwan.

"Did the officials say they'd look for your son's…grave?" said Linzi.

"No. I asked, but no one gave me a straight answer. I haven't heard anything from them since that day."

———

Jasmine and Linzi had a lengthy conversation after the visit. They decided that it was risky to search for the remains of the American pilot right now. The United States had sided with the Nationalists during the Civil War. So by default, they were enemies of the Communists. They were double enemies because they supported South Korea in the current Korean War while Mainland China assisted the northern Communists. It wasn't just their safety that Jasmine and Linzi had to think about, it was their families' well-being as well. They left Dashan without doing anything else.

This visit had stirred Jasmine so much that she kept thinking about how to contact her uncle and cousin. She missed them and just wanted to make sure that they were truly safe. Try as she might, though, she couldn't figure out a way. By then, the country had been separated into two unbridgeable parts—the Communist-controlled Mainland and the Nationalist-governed Taiwan. There was no communication between the two sides. No phone calls. No mail. They were living on two different planets.

Chapter 27

——— ——— ——— ——— ——— ——— ———

One night in the fall of 1950, Jasmine flipped through newspapers before going to sleep. Although she had no interest in politics, she habitually read all the papers that Linzi could bring back whenever he went to Anning. She wanted to find any news related to Taiwan, hoping to learn something about her uncle or her cousin.

She skimmed the headlines, expecting to find nothing exciting as it had been the case for months. So far, all she'd learned was the Communists' desire to "Liberate Taiwan from the Nationalists' White Terror" or to "Save the Taiwanese from their suffering under the cruel Nationalist government."

Suddenly, Jasmine stopped scanning. Her eyes sprang wide, and she sat bolt upright. In the dim light from the oil lamp, she stared at the headline "Major Hu Chen Defects to the People's Republic of China from Taiwan." She moved closer to the light and read the article carefully.

Once she was done, she stood up. After pacing back and forth in the small room a few times, she put on her jacket, took the lamp, walked toward Linzi's house, and knocked on the door.

"Something's wrong? Are you sick?" asked Linzi as soon as he opened the door.

"No! No! I'm fine. Sorry to bother you at such a late hour. But"— Jasmine waved the newspaper—"have you read this article?" Her eyes glowed with an eagerness she could hardly hide. "A pilot from Taiwan just defected to the Mainland. Major Hu Chen. I don't know him, but I think I should get in touch with him. He may know a way to contact people in Taiwan. He may know something about Birch or Uncle. My cousin is a well-known hero—"

"No, you can't—"

"I know it takes money to travel. He may not even live in"—Jasmine held the newspaper closer to the lamp and checked—"Peking by now. But I'll work harder. We can sell more paintings," she said.

"It's not the money I'm worried about. Yes, we need money. But you can't go looking for Birch or your uncle." Linzi turned and looked around. Even in the middle of the night, when no one was there, he lowered his voice. "You know the political situation—"

"But I'm just looking for my relatives, my family. It has nothing to do with politics."

"Everything has to do with politics nowadays. You've seen things. You should know."

"But..."

"No, Miss Jasmine. Forget it. Get the idea out of your mind. You shouldn't attract attention to yourself. People get into trouble for nothing. You are a relative of two Nationalist military officers. Don't go looking for trouble. Please, don't give anyone an excuse to hurt you!"

"I know. I was just hoping..." She threw her head back and let out an exasperated sigh. Above them, millions of stars burned against the ink-black sky. "We live on the same planet, under the same sky. Birch might be looking at the stars right now. But I have no way of letting him know I'm still alive."

His expression softened, matching his voice. "I'm sorry to disappoint you."

"But look at you." Turning back, Jasmine fixed an unblinking stare on Linzi. A feeble smile spread across her face. "You were a teenager when I first met you. You could hardly read or write. Now, you're as wise as your grandpa."

"I'm just telling you what your uncle told me."

126

Surprise widened her eyes.

"He told me to lie low. Even though we're not blood-related, my closeness to him and Birch could get me in trouble. Originally, he wanted to transfer the title of the house to my name, but he changed his mind. He told me to use the place, but a deed in my name might not be a wise idea. The Communists despise rich people. Being rich is equivalent to being evil, and being poor is equivalent to being good. He said I'd better stay poor. Of course, as smart as he is, he had no idea that you'd come back, and now you're looking for them!"

January 1951 was unseasonably cold. A penetrating northern wind swept through western Yunnan with icy blasts, lowering the temperature to below freezing. Snow blanketed the village and buried the surrounding area.

"Miss Jasmine, may I come in?" Linzi knocked.

She opened the door and pulled the young villager inside. "Come in." She shut the door. The room was cold, barely warmer than the air outside. She was in the oyster-colored coat she'd brought with her to Yunnan ten years earlier.

The wind groaned. The snow painted a cobweb of ice on the pane of the window, which rattled with each strong gust.

"How are your hands and toes?" he asked. "I see your cheeks are better."

Jasmine stuck out her hands, palms facing down. Her fingers were discolored and swelling with a few blisters. "They still hurt, but they're much better. I hate the stinging, itchy feeling. I know I shouldn't scratch, but..."

"Keep using the cream. I'm sorry. I should have—"

"Don't be silly. It's not your fault. I had frostbite every year when I lived with the hunters. It's painful, but no big deal. I should've asked you earlier, though. I forgot your grandpa had this wonderful cream."

"You need to be careful. We're far in the south, but the mountains are so high in this area. Deep frostbite can cause serious damage."

"Look at you," she said with a prideful note in her voice. "Your grandpa would be so proud of you. Hey, sit down." She picked up a mint green aluminum bottle with two rose-pink peonies on it, the same thermos Birch had used, and poured hot water into a china teacup.

Linzi didn't sit down. He shifted his weight from one foot to the other.

"What is it?" asked Jasmine, rubbing her hands together to generate heat. "Someone is sick? This weather—"

"No." He shook his head. "Don't worry. No one is sick."

"Then what's wrong?" Her tone grew apprehensive. "Tell me, please."

He bowed his head, averting eye contact. Shadows fell across his face. "I'm going to join the People's Volunteer Army."

"To fight in Korea? No!"

"I must."

"No, you don't have to volunteer."

His mouth twisted into a bitter smirk. "We're expected to join. It shows our political alliance and support to the new government. I don't have any choice. A certain percentage of people are expected to join within every town, every village—"

"But *you* don't have to go!"

"I do." Lifting his chin, Linzi stood straighter. "When General Bai and Birch rebuilt the village, they asked me to be the village head. I'm younger than a lot of people, but I'm one of the two survivors. I gave them my word to protect the village as much as I could. This is my duty. It's *Yi—morality, duty, loyalty, decency, brotherhood.*"

"But you're going to fight against Americans." Jasmine had to pause to clear the sudden hoarseness from her throat. "Americans helped us. They fought the Japs for us. Some of them died here. They're Danny's brothers. You can't—"

"I know you loved Major Hardy. I loved him, too. I don't want to fight his countrymen. Believe me. I'm grateful for their help. Without Danny and his friend Jack, the course of our history might have been changed. General Bai told us that. But I have to go." He emitted a long-winded sigh. "The Chinese are killing Americans. Brothers are killing brothers. But I won't kill anyone. I give you my word."

"How can you go to war without—"

"I'm an herbalist. I'll join a medical team. I'll save people."

Jasmine nodded and then shook her head again. "I don't want you to go, Linzi!" Distraught to the point of tears, she said, "You're family. You're the only family I've got left here. You can't leave—"

"I'll be back. I promise."

Just then, another gust of wind swept through cracks in the house.

Chapter 28

Selling art had always been difficult. In a poor country where most people struggled to stay alive, only a few fortunate individuals were able to afford paintings, and even fewer appreciated them enough to spend money on them. For months, Jasmine had trouble selling her paintings. She blamed the weather. It had been cold.

When the warmer seasons arrived, and she still had no luck, she became worried that it was because of Big Chen. The broad-faced young villager had been recommended by Linzi to help her. But perhaps he wasn't as good a salesman as Linzi, who had assisted his family selling herbs since he was a teenager. Big Chen didn't seem to have trouble selling herbs or vegetables, though.

"Honestly," the young man told her, "the folks in town don't buy art." He pointed to one of her elegant landscapes. "These are for capitalists, they say."

"For capitalists?" Jasmine frowned with perplexity. In recent years, the term "capitalists" was equivalent to evil persons. It made sense that no one would purchase things appreciated only by bad people. But it boggled her mind how beautiful nature could be associated with capitalists. *Perhaps only capitalists could buy art?* "What do they want, then?"

The young man scratched his badly-cut hair. "Men, women, people doing things, you know. Just look at the posters; they're all over town."

Jasmine couldn't afford to lose her side business, so she decided to go to Anning.

The next day, she left the village before sunrise. The July morning was crisp and fragrant with the rich scent of the earth. Clusters of colorful wildflowers dotted the grass along the trail. Birds flitted among the pine trees and sang in the woods. She hadn't been to the Town of Peace for several years.

Around noon, she reached Anning. Big Chen was right; posters were everywhere. Since the autumn of 1949, the Communist Party had launched several movements—Land Reform, Campaign to Suppress Counter-revolutionaries, Combat Illiteracy Campaign, and Three-Anti/Five-Anti Campaigns. They were all intended to strengthen support for the Party, to eliminate various enemies, to cultivate the new ideology, and to promote economic production. Those posters reflected the political themes of the movements.

Many were similar to the images she'd seen in Dashan, which portrayed the Nationalists as devils and demons. Although Jasmine hated the Secret Police who had tortured Li Ming and imprisoned her, she couldn't bring herself to draw anything that demonized the Nationalists. Both Birch and her uncle had worked for the old government, and they were among the most decent people she'd ever known.

Other propaganda images were easier for her to accept. The posters depicted factory workers and farmers working diligently to build a new country, or ordinary people enjoying life and family. She made a few quick sketches of the posters which she could later adapt to her own ideas.

The dogmatic propaganda didn't interest Jasmine, but she would force herself to adapt. She had a goal. *I'll do whatever it takes.* In the back of her mind, though, she feared that it was just a dream and would remain a dream. It had been four years since she'd started her journey, and she was no closer to Danny or her family. But she would never allow herself to give up.

In the town center, several tables were set up with banners hanging overhead—"Join the People's Volunteer Army; Guard Our Homes and Defend Our Country; Resist U.S. Aggression and Aid North

Korea." Young men stood in line, waiting to sign up. They reminded her of Linzi. They had communicated by mail, but the last letter she'd received was two months earlier. He'd said that the war was growing more intense, and he might not have time to write as often in the future. She prayed for the umpteenth time that he would return home safely.

Feeling hungry, Jasmine stopped by a food stand and bought a bowl of porridge and a steamed bun. Sitting on a nearby bench, she drank the porridge in a hurry. She was still hungry, yet looking at the steamed bread, she couldn't bring herself to eat it.

Images of Bai Ge swirled through her mind. This was the same food stand where she'd shopped with him many years earlier. *He was so happy eating that bun.* His innocent smile flashed in her mind, and her heart contracted with pain. She didn't even know where his ashes were buried.

Her thoughts jumped to Danny, the one without a proper burial like her son. She couldn't imagine how his family had coped with their grief. He'd been left in an unmarked grave in a foreign land thousands of miles away from home. No one was looking for him. No one was allowed to look for him. Old Ding's words, "Not knowing what happened to him and where he was had killed her," echoed in her mind.

With a heavy heart, she wrapped the bun in a handkerchief, put it in her patchwork bag, and left. She visited a stationery store to replenish her supplies. Before going back, she decided to stop by Bai Fu's house. She hadn't seen Bai Long for several years and wondered how the boy was doing. He wasn't the most pleasant child, but he was her former student.

———————

Being one of the richest men in Anning, Bai Fu had a mansion. Every time Jasmine entered the residence, she'd felt a slight twinge—above the gate, two golden characters on a scarlet wooden banner stated the owner of the place: Bai Residence. They shared the same last name, but she didn't belong to this place. This had never been her home.

She drew up short before the house. Two guards in the People's Liberation Army's leaf-green uniform stood by the side of the gate. A different banner hung above the doorway—Anning People's Government. Goosebumps cascaded down her arms. This house was now occupied by the Communists!

There was a handwritten announcement on the wall. Jasmine stepped closer. As she read the message, her hand covered her mouth to stifle a gasp. Bai Fu had been executed. Being a rich man, a capitalist, a Counter-revolutionary, he'd taken advantage of the poor and exploited his workers. He'd been found guilty of his 'confessed' crimes. All of his assets had been seized and returned to their rightful owners—the people.

Jasmine couldn't believe what she'd just read. Bai Fu wasn't the kindest man she'd ever met, but he wasn't an evil person. He was simply a polite businessman. The arrangement that he'd offered her was in his favor, but she'd willingly accepted it. At least he offered a roof over her head and warm meals during the coldest months. When she resigned, he tried to make her stay, but he never forced her and offered her better pay if she ever decided to return. Whenever he passed by, he always nodded and smiled. He'd told his son to call her *Bai Lao Shi*—*Teacher Bai* when she was just a starving artist.

Since the establishment of the People's Republic of China, Chairman Mao had initiated a series of political movements designed to target the wealthy classes—landlords and capitalists. Living in a remote village, Jasmine hadn't seen the results of the actions until now.

Why did a man like Bai Fu deserve to die? Simply for being rich? He might not always have acted fairly, but he'd worked hard to earn his wealth. Even if he'd committed crimes, he shouldn't have been punished so severely.

"Do you know him?" asked one of the guards, moving closer to her, his face stern.

Jasmine jerked herself out of her stupor. She shook her head and fled as quickly as a hunted animal. She was in such a hurry that she bumped into a beggar. "I'm sorry," she mumbled without looking up and resumed running.

The beggar in tattered clothes opened her arms and thrust a dirty clay bowl in front of Jasmine.

Having been in similar circumstances, she felt sorry for the beggar and took out the bun she'd saved.

"Anything else? Help us!"

The familiar voice made Jasmine jerk her head up. "Oh, my God! You..." She was so stunned that she couldn't finish her sentence. The woman was An Kong, Bai Fu's wife, the one with heavy makeup, fancy clothes, extravagant jewelry, and who had complained about the pork tenderloin.

"*Bai Lao Shi? Teacher Bai?*"

"Yes, it's me. What has happened...?" She swallowed the rest of the question. She knew what had happened. The announcement stated clearly—all assets of the Bai Residence now belonged to the government.

"Bai Fu is dead. They killed him." Tears cut paths through the dirt on her face.

"I know." Jasmine patted An Kong's bony shoulders. "Shhh..."

"They killed him. They took—"

She steered her away from the guards, fearing for more trouble. "I'm sorry." She looked around. "Where is Bai Long? Where is his grandma?"

"There..."

Jasmine followed An Kong to a row of low, shabby shacks in the back of the Bai Residence. Along the base of the wall, water over-flowed from the drainage and formed murky puddles, producing an odiferous smell.

Drifters and beggars had built the wooden sheds. "One can live off Mr. Bai's garbage" was a running joke. Bai Fu had destroyed the primitive structures, but they returned like mushrooms after a shower. After a couple of attempts, he decided it was not worth his effort. A tall wall was constructed to separate the mansion from the dwellings. No one in the family was permitted to go to this area.

Before his death, had Bai Fu known his family would live there— the place he'd tried to demolish? Jasmine scowled as she stepped into the low-ceiling wooden shack with teetering walls.

In the dim light, a wizened old woman lay on a pile of hay near the back wall. Her eyes were closed; a dark blue bandana encircled her head. Even though it was a warm day, she was covered with a blanket. A boy sat on the ground next to the old woman. He was stick-thin and filthy. Jasmine could hardly recognize them as Bai Fu's mother and son.

"Nobody helps us. Nobody dares to help us." An Kong gave a harsh, bitter laugh. "Everyone wanted to be close to Bai Fu as if one could grow rich just by standing next to him. Now, no one wants to be near us. I can't blame them. Who would want to be associated with the family of a Counter-revolutionary?"

A lump grew in Jasmine's throat. She hadn't been particularly close to the family, yet their suffering saddened her. "Here." She took out the little money she had left, and the art supplies she'd just bought, and handed them to the boy. "Draw pictures. You can sell them. You have talent. Use your talent to help your mother and grandma. You understand?"

The eight-year-old boy gave a weak nod.

"Don't draw landscapes, or flowers, or animals that I taught you." She fished out the sketches she'd done and thrust them into his dirty hands. "Draw something like these. Have you seen the posters on the streets?" She swallowed past the painful lump in her throat. "Follow them. Follow their themes. Okay?"

Bai Long's eyebrows furrowed in incomprehension.

Jasmine sighed. She knew the boy didn't fully understand. How could he? How could he draw pictures of people enjoying life while he now lived in this shabby place?

Chapter 29

On this balmy autumn day in 1952, Jasmine worked as usual in her vegetable garden. As a city girl, she'd never enjoyed farming. But she'd learned a lot along the way. She was pulling weeds when she heard her name called. She straightened and stood transfixed as if she'd seen a ghost.

"It's me, Li Ming!" The man walked toward her. He stretched out his right arm, his left arm curled upward at an odd angle. Warm sunlight highlighted his handsome features.

Jerking herself out of her daze, she clasped his hand with both of hers. "You're alive! I thought…I thought…" Tears of joy blurred her vision.

"Yes, I'm still kicking." He checked Jasmine up and down, his dark eyes luminous with a tenderness he couldn't hide. "I had no idea where you went. Since you talked so much about this village, I thought I'd try my luck. I'm so glad I found you. How are you?"

"I'm okay, all things considered."

They exchanged more basic information before Li Ming said, "When we ran into each other in Chungking, you asked me about my life after the Nanking Massacre. I—"

"You told me you didn't want to lie to me, but you couldn't tell me the truth."

"Now, I can." He spent the next few minutes telling his story.

At the end of the massacre in February 1938, along with two former Nationalist Army soldiers, Li Ming had joined a burial group. There were a lot of bodies along the Yangtze River that needed to be collected and buried. Doing this gruesome task, at least they could go outside the city without much trouble from the Japanese. It took them three weeks to find an opportunity to escape. One man decided to go home first and left his companions. Li Ming and his other friend searched for the Communist guerillas and joined them.

Because of his experiences in Nanking, he fought the Japanese with determination and courage, and due to his knowledge as a former lieutenant in the Nationalist Army, he conducted many skirmishes, ambushes, and moonlight raids with great success. For the first time, he felt he was genuinely contributing to the fight for his motherland. His achievements convinced him that the Communist Party was the future of China.

Soon his bravery was acknowledged—he became a member of the Communist Party as he'd hoped. Then one day, a Political Commissar approached him. The middle-aged man talked to him at length and, in the end, asked, "Would you go back to the Nationalist Army?"

Li Ming shook his head decisively.

"I don't mean for you to work for them. I mean to work for us while you're back in the Nationalist Army."

Li Ming was surprised and baffled. "I'm just a soldier," he replied. "I'm not a spy."

"No one is born a spy." The Political Commissar chuckled. "The job is important. You can do a lot for us over there. We'll train you, of course."

So, Li Ming went back to the Nationalist Army. He told them he'd been injured and had gone home to recover, which was a half-truth since he'd been wounded while fighting as a Communist guerilla. Since tens of thousands of soldiers had been killed in Nanking, and the Nationalist Army desperately needed people, they took his word for it and accepted his return without question.

Li Ming finished the story by saying, "So, I became a Communist spy working in the Nationalist Army. I'm sorry. I couldn't tell you the truth."

Jasmine nodded. She pointed to a large tree by the side of the garden. They sat on the ground. She drank a few gulps of water from a bamboo water carrier and handed it to him. "How did you escape?"

Involuntarily, he touched his left arm. "This is what happened…"

———————————

Li Ming had worked as a Communist spy in the Nationalist Army until a traitor gave him up. When he received a message urging him to leave, instead of fleeing right away, he went back to his dorm, hoping to take Jasmine with him. If he'd escaped right away, he wouldn't have been captured by the Nationalist Military Secret Police, but then she would have been detained as an accomplice of a Communist. Li Ming was interrogated after his arrest. He didn't hide his identity as a spy since they'd already found out the truth from the traitor.

"Jasmine Bai is innocent." That was the first thing he stated. "She doesn't know anything about my work. Her uncle and cousin have worked for the Air Force for many years." He gave the Secret Police their names and ranks so that they could verify his story. He told them how she'd saved an American pilot, a Flying Tiger. Americans and the Nationalists were allies. "The Japs tortured her when she refused to give up the information about the Flying Tiger. She's a heroine. You can see the scars on her face."

But Li Ming wouldn't hand over his Communist contacts. "I can't tell you. That's our party's secret."

They tortured him relentlessly for days—whipping, spicy water, electric shock… They deprived him of food and sleep. They injected him with "Truth-Telling Potion." Semiconscious, he kept repeating the same statement: "Jasmine is innocent. She saved an American."

They threw him into a dark cell. His wounds became infected, and he was gravely ill for weeks. Many times, he thought he wouldn't make it, but miraculously he recovered.

Before the People's Liberation Army approached Chungking,

the Nationalist Military Secret Police started killing the political prisoners one after another, dissolving their bodies in nitric acid. On October 1, 1949, Mao Zedong declared the founding of the People's Republic of China in Peking. Yet, two months later, Chungking was still occupied by the Nationalists.

On November 28, the Secret Police carried out a massacre, shooting detainees with machine guns. A couple of hundred people were slaughtered; a boy with a big head was among them. A sympathetic officer opened a few cells, which enabled a small group of prisoners to escape. Several ran into the nearby forests, but most were gunned down. Li Ming was one of the lucky ones. Later, he was awarded a medal by the Communist Party for his bravery.

"The pain was so intense that I passed out many times," added Li Ming. "Every time I came to, I cursed my consciousness. I knew they wouldn't stop. I was terrified that I might crack." He closed his eyes, seemingly trying to block the images.

Jasmine's chest contracted. She understood what he was talking about. The pain was so excruciating that it was worse than death. But the fear of giving up something or someone precious was even worse.

"Believe it or not, I kept thinking of you. I told myself that if you could live through it, I could, too."

Jasmine wrapped her arms around him and wept. "They made me watch…"

"What?"

She could hardly breathe. "I saw them…I saw them use the hot iron…"

"Son of a bitch! I'm sorry. I'm so sorry!" Li Ming held her tighter. "I heard that they'd let you go. I didn't know…" His eyes went wide before a look of horror distorted his features. "Did they hurt you?"

"No, they didn't," Jasmine reassured him. "I passed out. Bai Ge had just died, and I was sick and too weak to handle more misery. Seeing you suffer like that broke my heart."

Chapter 30

"This is something else," said Li Ming as they stood at Angel's Pass. "You talked about this place so many times, but without being here, it's hard to fully appreciate its beauty."

Jasmine stepped closer to a statue of an angel on one side of the canyon. "Birch had this built because of Daisy...and me."

Tilting his head backward, Li Ming gazed at the figurine. Placed on pedestals, the angel looked larger than life. She faced the gorge. Her arms stretched out and wings spread upward, ready to fly across the chasm. "He did a great job. The resemblance is hard to miss."

Jasmine lightly caressed the ivory-white marble. "Now I'm here, but he doesn't even know I'm still alive." Her voice trembled. A welter of emotions filled her. It happened every time she was there.

"You'll meet him one day."

"How? We're in two separate worlds."

Li Ming gave Jasmine a sympathetic look. "No matter where he is, he wants you to be happy, to be safe." He moved a step closer to her. "I'm worried about you."

"Don't worry. The village is small, but I've got everything—"

"No, I'm not talking about everyday life." He swallowed a few times, debating how to say it. "Because of my work for the Communist underground and my bravery"—he used two fingers of his right hand as quotation marks—"I'm now a party official working at the provincial government in Chungking—"

"An important position!"

"Yes! It's an honor. But…but…" He jammed a cigarette into his mouth, his hand shaking as he lit it. Sucking in the smoke, he tried to maintain his composure.

"What's wrong?" she asked.

"There are things…things that concern me a great deal. I can't tell you the details, but I'm worried about you."

"Why? I've done nothing wrong."

"You've done everything right. And more… But…" Li Ming looked around. "You saved an American. Don't you realize that Americans are now our enemies?"

"Who doesn't know the Korean War? I told you about Linzi. He joined the People's Volunteer Army. But…Americans helped us during the war against Japan. They came halfway around the world to fight the Japs for us. Some of them died here!" She pointed to the statue across the gorge. "It's the truth. It's history. We can't rewrite history just because we're at war with them now."

"I know. That's why I'm concerned. Have you read the newspapers lately?"

Jasmine shook her head. She hadn't read any newspapers since Linzi had left. She didn't have any means to obtain them, and politics were never her interest anyway. But she wasn't completely ignorant. She'd seen the posters and slogans. She knew at least one family that had been severely affected by politics.

"People were put in jail, people with any connection whatsoever to the Nationalists or Americans. Many were executed. Thousands! Hundreds of thousands! Others killed themselves. More will die in the future. It's getting out of hand."

Since the establishment of the People's Republic of China three years earlier, there had been a series of political campaigns, targeting people who were wealthy, such as landlords and business owners, or those who had connections to the former Nationalist government.

But the sheer number of people affected, and the severity of the situation shocked Jasmine.

Despite everything, she'd clung to a thread of hope that her family would return to the Mainland one day. Now, the dream was shattered. The Communist government hadn't treated their former enemies leniently as they'd promised, and she now understood that Birch and Uncle would never return. Suddenly she shuddered from an array of emotions too complicated to name.

Li Ming took off his jacket and draped it over her shoulders. In deep thought, he paced back and forth in front of her. Smoke drifted through his fingers. "Don't tell anyone what I just said. Not to a single soul. You understand? If it weren't for you, I'd never—"

"I won't."

A breeze stirred, ruffling the nearby treetops. Except for some wispy clouds, the autumn sky was cobalt blue. The area was fragrant with the rich aroma of wildflowers. A chorus of birds sang in the woods.

After a while, Jasmine murmured, "This is a remote area. It'll be safe. Who—"

"I bet your uncle had the same thought when he sent you and Daisy here. Look at what happened. It's remote, true. It may take time, but eventually… Don't wait for that to happen." In a tone of exasperation, Li Ming added, "By then you'll be a target. You are from a rich family that sympathized with both the Nationalists and Americans."

She gazed across the gorge. A suspension bridge built by Birch and the villagers connected the two sides. A statue of a young Westerner stood facing her, holding a model airplane in his right hand high above his head. Tall and muscular, he wore a flight jacket, a long scarf wrapped around his neck. A pair of flight goggles rested on his forehead. She could tell that Birch had designed it based on a picture of Danny she'd drawn in the cave. The thought of the Flying Tiger being labeled as an enemy brought tears to her eyes.

"Don't be afraid, Jasmine. I'm not here to scare you. I can protect you." He tossed the cigarette, grinding it into the dirt with his rubber-soled sneaker. Lifting his right arm, he tucked a strand of her wind-swept hair behind her ear. His hand lingered over her head a moment longer than necessary. "Come with me to Chungking. Be my wife. I've always been so…fond of you. I love you, Jasmine. I didn't ask you when we were in Chungking. I couldn't offer you true safety. Now, my position in the Party can protect you. I won't let anyone harm you. I swear."

Jasmine was caught off guard. As an intuitive person, she'd sensed his love for her. But his open admission of affection still took her by surprise. An unexpected tenderness welled up inside her, and she felt the heat creeping onto her face. "Thank you, *Li Ming Ge*. It's very kind…and thoughtful of you." She lowered her head to avoid his intense gaze. "But…I can't…"

"Because I'm a Communist?"

"Oh, no! It's nothing to do with politics. I know you've been working hard for our country."

"It's because of Bai Ge, isn't it?" Bitterness darkened his voice. "You blame me. You blame me for his death. Honest to God, I loved the boy. I didn't mean—"

"No! That's not it. I've never blamed you. How could I? You were trying to save me. You shielded me with your body. It was a tragedy. I'll never blame you. Please, believe me."

He picked up her hand. "Then, why? I know you care about me. I can tell."

Not knowing how to answer, she bit her lip.

"Jasmine, why?"

"I can't offer something…I don't have." She felt her palm in his hand become clammy. She'd liked Li Ming from the first time she met him in Nanking. He was a tall attractive man like her cousin. He was kind and considerate. She admired his strength, his courage, and his determination to do his best for the country, for his beliefs, even though his beliefs might not be the same as hers. He was a Tiger, just like Birch and Danny. Rejecting someone she respected and valued was hard. She had no intention to hurt his feelings; life had already hurt him too much.

"You still love Danny?"

She gave an almost imperceptible nod.

"He was a remarkable man. I understand your love for him. I respect that. But he's gone. He's not coming back. No matter how long you wait. Life goes on, Jasmine. You can't live only with his memory—"

"Please!" She stared at him, eyes imploring. "I do care about you. Very much! You're my Big Brother. You're my dearest one. I want you to be happy. But please don't…" She couldn't say more.

Jasmine didn't want her life to go on without Danny. She couldn't tell Li Ming that she was taken, body and soul. She'd been making love to the Flying Tiger in her dreams. He didn't appear as often as she hoped, nevertheless he showed up from time to time, offering her much needed love and affection. She knew that she could never be anyone else's wife, even if that meant she would miss the protection she might desperately need. She wouldn't trade those precious moments with Danny for anything or anyone. This was her secret, and she wouldn't share it with anyone.

Chapter 31

Since Li Ming's visit, Jasmine had been consumed with loneliness, sadness, and despair. She'd already lost many loved ones, and now she had to face the prospect that she would never reunite with the only two surviving members of her family. She crawled through the days and longed for dark nights; only in occasional dreams did she taste the pleasure of love, of being a real woman, of being truly alive.

On a chilly evening in April 1953, Linzi's daughter walked into her house. "Auntie Jasmine, Mama asked me to get you."

"What is it? Is something wrong?"

"I don't know. A sick lady just came to the village."

Could it be An Kong? Jasmine immediately thought of Bai Long, and she was worried about her former student.

The sun had already set behind the mountains as she entered Linzi's front yard. Beneath the milky twilight, a woman sat in a bamboo-pole sedan chair, holding a toddler in her lap.

Even though the woman was no more than forty, she was weak and ill—her hair was short and thin, and her skin had an unhealthy pallor. Her eyebrows furrowed. Evidently, she was in pain.

"I'm not an herbalist. Our village doctor is in Korea now—"

The woman waved her arm. She looked at Jasmine with an intense stare. "Are you really Bai Moli? They"—she motioned to Linzi's wife and the young villagers who had carried her sedan chair—"they said you're Birch Bai's cousin."

"Yes, I'm Bai Moli. Birch—"

"Oh, dear God!" The woman stretched her arms. "Jasmine! Do you remember Meng Hu? I'm his wife. My name is Wang Hong."

"Of course. He's my cousin's friend. We met a few times. Where is he? I'd love to—"

"Meng Hu is dead!" Wang Hong squeezed Jasmine's hands. Tears spilled onto her cheeks.

"Dead?" For a moment, she felt nothing except blank astonishment. "How?"

"Killed." Her closed fingers on Jasmine's hands loosened and fell open. She slumped backward and passed out as the toddler at her side cried, "Mama! Mama!"

"How did you survive?" Wang Hong asked. Her shrunken figure lay beneath a heavy cotton coverlet. "Birch told us—Meng Hu and me—about your death. Birch will be so happy! Major Hardy...would be thrilled! They've searched for you up and down the mountains. How did you—"

"It's a long story. I'll tell you when you feel better." Jasmine pulled the coverlet up to her chin. "Now, just rest." She stood up from the edge of the bed, ready to leave. "I'll cook—"

"Stay," Wang Hong grabbed her arm. "Please. I have things to tell you."

"You should rest. We'll talk when you feel better—"

"I'll never feel better." She swallowed as if something in her throat was choking her. "I'm dying of...colon cancer. I don't have much time. Let me talk before it's too late."

Jasmine sat down, dumbfounded. "No! There must be a way to—"

"I'm a nurse. I know."

Tears welled in her eyes.

A flicker of a smile passed across Wang Hong's sallow face. "I'm going to see Meng Hu soon. He died such a tragic death. I want to be with him." She began to sob.

Jasmine patted the cotton coverlet, trying in vain to comfort the distraught woman.

"They killed him."

"Who?" Jasmine asked, even though she already knew the answer.

"He was killed during the Campaign to Suppress Counter-revolutionaries. Xiao Hu wasn't even born."

"Your son's name is Little Tiger? Did Meng Hu know...?"

Wang Hong shook her head again, touching the boy sleeping next to her. "Meng Hu knew I was pregnant. He told me to name him Xiao Hu if we have a son."

"How come you're here? It's more than a thousand miles from Chungking. You can't get good medical—"

"When I found out that I have cancer, I sold everything."

"Why?"

"I don't have anyone left. I don't want Xiao Hu to end up in an orphanage. That would be a miserable life for him."

Jasmine thought about her decision not to send Bai Ge to an orphanage. The toddler reminded her so much of her son. Little Tiger had a plump face with jet-black hair standing on end like a brush. His healthy, translucent pink cheeks lay in stark contrast to Wang Hong's declining health. He nestled close to her, his short arm on her chest. In his sleep, he looked achingly innocent.

"I had a small family." Wang Hong continued, "My father passed away before the war. Mom died when I was in high school. She also had cancer. We were so poor that my relatives refused to take me in. That's why I joined the Army. I was sixteen, but I told them I was eighteen."

"What about Meng Hu's family?"

Tears returned to Wang Hong's eyes. "His father was executed because he was a rich capitalist, and because of Meng Hu. His brother was arrested and is still in jail. His mother...took pills."

"Dear God!"

"I thought about asking one of our neighbors to take care of him. We've lived there for many years and got along with everyone. But I didn't want to get them into trouble. Little Tiger is the son of a

Counter-revolutionary, an Enemy of the People!"

Jasmine held the woman's hand, not trusting herself to speak without great emotion.

"Besides, I didn't know whom to trust. I've seen people turn against their family members and their best friends. People do terrible things under extreme pressure." She paused. "Birch told us we could use this place if we ever needed to hide from the Communist government. We made fun of his worry and precaution when we read his letter. The stories we heard were all positive—the Communists had treated their former enemies fairly."

Jasmine listened patiently.

"I've been here. I've met Linzi and other pure-hearted villagers. I knew they'd keep my son. They took care of Danny, a foreigner. They'd look after Xiao Hu—the son of Danny's friend, the son of Birch's friend."

"I'm sure they will."

"I didn't expect to see you. God! Major Hardy would be so thrilled."

If only she had come here earlier! Jasmine cut that thought off before the familiar surge of guilt hit her.

"I'm so sorry to bother you," said Wang Hong. "We've just met. But I feel like I've known you for a long time. Little Tiger is only two-and-a-half. He needs someone to look after him."

"Don't worry. I'll take care of him."

"I don't mean to burden you. God knows you have had more than your share of hardships." Wang Hong paused to gulp air. "It's hard to raise a child, especially for a single woman. One day you'll get married. Single women with kids are looked down upon in our society. Not many men are willing to marry a woman with a child."

"Don't worry about that." She'd just turned down a proposal from a fine man.

"Are you sure? He's the son of a Counter-revolutionary. I'll understand if—"

"Meng Hu was a hero, just like my cousin and Danny. I don't care what others say. I know them. I'll take care of your son. I promise.

Meng Hu was Birch's good friend. My cousin would—"

"Oh, we asked Birch to be our son's godfather..."

"Then I am Auntie Jasmine." Tears pooled in her eyes as she looked at the boy. A boy with no father. And soon to be without a mother. Little Tiger reminded her so much of Bai Ge, and she hoped that someone was looking after him in heaven.

Chapter 32

Jasmine spent the next few weeks with the sick woman. She killed her chickens, hoping that the much-needed nutrients would prevent, or at least delay, the inevitable. However, Wang Hong was too ill to eat much. After she learned that the former nurse had trained Xiao Mei to take care of Birch when he was in a coma, Jasmine felt grateful and even closer to this dying woman.

She also learned more about Meng Hu's death.

The Campaign to Suppress Counter-revolutionaries was the first political movement launched by the new Communist government. It had begun in the spring of 1950, and Meng Hu was under arrest in the summer.

"Do you know their policy?" asked Wang Hong.

"Yes: 'Lenient treatment to those who confess frankly; severe punishment to those who remain stubborn.'"

"When they say severe punishment, they mean death."

Jasmine nodded. Li Ming had told her a lot about the movement. Mao Zedong had implemented a quota for the executions according to local populations. The Chairman of the Communist Party had estimated that roughly 0.1 percent of the population were hard-line Counter-revolutionaries and should be killed in order to get rid of the worst anti-communist elements. As a result, hundreds of thousands of people were arrested based on assumptions and wrongful accusations, and countless cases were decided without thorough investigation.

"Many people confessed their alleged crimes under pressure. Some even pointed the finger at their friends or family members to save their own skins," said Wang Hong. "But not Meng Hu." Pride raised the chin of her haggard face. "He didn't. He insisted that he hadn't done anything wrong."

Jasmine understood. Meng Hu would rather die with honor than survive in disgrace. *Ning wei yu sui, bu wei wa quan—Better to be a shard of jade than an intact tile* was an unwritten code for noblemen.

"A small group of pilots from the Nationalist Air Force defected to the Mainland from Taiwan. The young men just wanted to help to rebuild the new China." Wang Hong had to take a break before continuing, "On the surface, the Communists welcomed them and even called them heroes. But in truth, they distrusted the young men and suspected that there might be some kind of conspiracy. Meng Hu just happened to know several pilots. The authorities pressured him to point the finger at the group. He wouldn't do it."

Wang Hong's closed eyes were quivering behind her eyelids. "They tortured him. For weeks!" Tears fell in a steady stream down her pale face. "When they told me to get him, his body was covered with all kinds of bruises and wounds. A fatal blow cracked his skull." The last few words ended on a mournful sob.

Jasmine squeezed Wang Hong's hand. An unbearable ache welled inside her.

"You met him. You know how strong and handsome he was. But I could hardly recognize him. I can't…I can't imagine…"

Neither could Jasmine. She trembled as grief engulfed her.

Li Ming had already given her an overview of the campaign. The number of people being imprisoned and killed was staggering. Now, in addition to her shock and dismay, she was saddened. She knew the victim—a fighter pilot, a brave Tiger, a good friend of Danny and Birch, a man who had come to her rescue fifteen years earlier.

The two women looked at each other, and an unspoken sorrow flowed between them. An oppressive silence filled the room.

Finally, Jasmine asked, "How did you know so much? I mean…I can understand they wanted him to confess his work in the Air Force. But…but… How did you know they pressured him to indicate the defected pilots? They shouldn't—"

"They didn't say anything."

Jasmine arched an eyebrow.

"Meng Hu was tall and heavy. There was no way for me to lift his body from the floor, even in a normal situation. I was eight months pregnant."

"Dear God!"

"A group of policemen stood around and watched me struggle. None of them gave me a hand except one. He helped me to put Meng Hu on a *ban che—wooden pushcart.*"

Jasmine wondered how Wang Hong, a petite pregnant woman, could pull her husband's body with the pushcart in Chungking, a city built on mountains.

"I fastened the strap across my shoulder. With everything I had, I struggled to turn the wheels. It was hard but doable when the road was level. Soon, there was a hill."

"Gosh! How…?"

"I couldn't. As I got stuck, someone came to my aid. It was the policeman. He pushed it from the rear and helped me all the way to the crematorium." Wang Hong took a shaky breath. "That night, Xiao Hu was born. I delivered him by myself at home."

"The same day Meng Hu died?"

"Yes. It was the Mid-Autumn Festival when families are supposed to be together."

Sorrow robbed Jasmine's ability to respond.

"I was kicked out of the hospital after Meng Hu's arrest, and I was ordered to sweep streets. Three days after Little Tiger's birth, I returned to—"

"Three days?" In Chinese tradition, postpartum recuperation was a month, and during that time, the woman wasn't allowed to do anything.

"I didn't have the luxury. I'm the wife of a Counter-revolutionary.

I worked with Xiao Hu strapped to my back." She closed her eyes briefly. "A few days later, as I was cleaning, a man jumped in front of a bus not far from me..."

"No way! He was…"

"Yes. He was the policeman. His body was badly damaged, but I could tell. He had a long scar on his forehead. I felt terrible. He was the only one who was sympathetic enough to help me. Although we never exchanged a single word, I was thankful to him. I didn't even know his name. Several days later, I received a letter. I didn't know the person until I started reading."

"It's him!"

Wang Hong bobbed her head. "His name is Mu Jing. He told me what had happened to Meng Hu in jail. He said he was touched by his bravery and integrity. If my husband wanted to save himself, he could easily point his finger at those young men who would have been in huge trouble. Mu Jing apologized for his involvement in Meng Hu's torture and death. 'It's a clear case of wrongful accusation,' he said."

Jasmine nodded.

"Mu Jing had nightmares for days afterward. He dreamed…Meng Hu took him flying, but each time he fell out of the plane and woke up in a cold sweat. He couldn't handle the guilt."

"He grew to admire his enemy. That must be hard. And dangerous."

"His job demanded that he interrogate the former Nationalists, but his conscience told him that most of those people were innocent, like Meng Hu. He was torn. He'd fought the Japanese side by side with the Nationalist soldiers. The scar on his forehead was left by the Japs. If the Nationalist Army had not shown up in time to help, he probably would have been killed."

Jasmine responded with a nod.

"Mu Jing told me to keep this letter. When the time is right, he instructed, hand it in to clear my husband's name. He said he'd use his life to attest Meng Hu's innocence. He left his fingerprint in blood." Wang Hong grabbed her jacket and tore the hem. Out came a piece of folded paper. "I don't have time…to wait for that day." She handed it to Jasmine.

"When the time is right, I'll…I'll…"

Meng Hu—Fierce Tiger had fought the Japanese for eight years. He had been injured several times. He'd received two medals. Then, in peacetime, he was beaten to death just because he'd worked for the old government. Just because he wouldn't confess his "crimes" or expose the innocent to save his own skin.

Once again, Jasmine was thankful that her uncle and cousin had left the Mainland. Meng Hu's fate could have been their fates: They might be put in jail and beaten to death. Birch had already suffered in a Japanese prison. She couldn't envision her cousin losing his freedom again. Even if he were not executed, the injustice would surely have killed him.

Chapter 33

━ ━ ━ ━ ━ ━ ━ ━

Wang Hong was getting worse by the day. She was stick-thin, but she couldn't eat much and threw up the little food she'd forced down. One night after dinner, she murmured, "One last thing," and pointed to her small suitcase.

Jasmine brought it to her bed and opened it.

"This is Meng Hu…" Wang Hong picked up a small cardboard box. "I couldn't afford a formal urn."

"I'll bury him—"

"No!" She held the box close to her chest. "Wait…wait until I…"

"No, don't say that. You…you'll get—"

"You're the sweetest person I've ever known." The former nurse lifted her arm and traced the scars on Jasmine's cheek. "You're so gorgeous. How could anyone have the heart to hurt you like this?"

"They were monsters."

"I wish we'd met years ago. We could have been great friends. Too bad. I'm…leaving soon." She held up her hand to forestall Jasmine's protest. "Meng Hu would hate to be buried. He loved freedom. He was a flyboy." Taking a ragged breath, she continued, "Scatter us at the gorge. It's his favorite place, and I love it, too. Danny and Daisy are there. Where can be better?"

With tears in her eyes, Jasmine nodded.

"When we visited, of course, we just marveled at the beauty. Who knew that one day it would be our resting place?" She picked up a journal from the suitcase and caressed the leather-bound cover. "Meng Hu kept a diary. Many pilots did. Birch had—"

Jasmine confirmed it with a nod.

"All his diaries were gone...except this one."

"Gone?"

"I tried to hide them, believe me. But where? Our apartment was small. I put one under the bed, one at the bottom of a bookshelf, one in a bag of rice... They found them all."

"But this one?"

"With diapers." A bitter smile flickered across Wang Hong's pale face. "Here." She handed it to Jasmine. "Please give it to Little Tiger when he grows up."

"Of course."

"You can read it, too."

"Me?"

"Yes. It's powerful. You'll see."

Jasmine held the journal close to her chest and felt the weight of it.

"I didn't get a chance to tell you." Wang Hong squeezed Jasmine's arm. "I'm so sorry about Daisy. She was so young... Poor Birch. I can't imagine—"

"You know what happened?"

"Birch told Meng Hu. They went up to the gorge several times. Once was enough for me. Meng Hu never told me, but he wrote—"

"In this one?"

"No. It's—"

"Tell me. Please!" Jasmine grasped the other woman's hand.

"I thought you knew—"

"No. Please, tell me!"

In the dim light, the pallor of Wang Hong's face seemed even paler. "No need to know...the details. She's gone. She won't come—"

"Would you like your son to know how his father died? You see, it hurts not to know the truth."

But the truth hurt even more.

For years Jasmine had tried to find out how Daisy had died. From the conversation with Linzi, she'd already suspected that her death had something to do with Birch. But hearing it utterly broke her heart. It felt as if a dagger had been plunged deep into her chest.

She was sorry that Daisy had died so young, that Birch had had to kill his beloved sister, and that Danny had had to witness the horror.

Her heart flew toward Taiwan. At that moment, she felt worse for Birch than for her younger cousin. Daisy was gone. She couldn't feel anything anymore. But the people she'd left behind would suffer for the rest of their lives.

As soon as she was in her room, Jasmine lit the oil lamp and opened the journal. Although she was dying to find out if there was anything about Danny or her cousin, she forced herself to start from the beginning, savoring the precious gift.

Meng Hu's writing was direct. The first several pages read like a logbook: Date, time, where and what happened, how many Japanese planes or supplies were destroyed, so-and-so was injured, or so-and-so didn't come back…

In one place, he mentioned Danny buying Lucky Strikes for everyone. Jasmine grinned and shook her head at the same time. She didn't understand why all those guys, including her cousin, liked smoking so much.

In another place, Meng Hu wrote that one of his teammates hadn't come back. "Did he survive the jump? Was he captured by the Japs? Perhaps he was lucky to be saved by villagers like many of us were. I pray to God that I'll see him again." That was as emotional as it got.

It wasn't until the fifth page that Jasmine found a long entry.

November 25, 1942

It's been a month. I haven't written anything. Sometimes I wonder why I keep a journal. Many pilots do. But why? Isn't it enough to live through hell once?

Four weeks ago, we flew a mission to Hong Kong.

We came back with only minor injuries, and most of the planes would be patched up in a short time. We walked toward our barracks, talking and laughing.

Earlier, someone from a nearby village had dropped off a case full of bottles of rice wine. Danny walked in between Birch and me. He patted our shoulders and said, "Let's go. Those bottles are calling our names."

Then Birch stopped us. "Wait, where is Tan Hu?"

I turned around and looked. Everyone was there. Everyone except Tan Hu. His plane was right behind me just a moment ago. "Has anyone seen Tan Hu?" I shouted, turning back to the runway as if I could find him there.

Just then, loud noises announced the arrival of an airplane. It was his. His plane wobbled like a drunkard, and the nose of the aircraft was on fire. I watched in horror and awe as he crash-landed.

We all ran. As I got closer, I could see fire and smoke pouring out of his cockpit. "Get out!" I yelled. But Tan Hu didn't move.

Everyone was shouting. But he just sat there. Fire shot up from his lap, flame licking his chest. Through the smoke, I watched him raise his right hand toward the side of his head, thumb up, index finger pointing to his temple. His eyes fixed on me.

I understood what he meant—he was asking me to shoot him!

We'd made a pact five years ago—we vowed that we would kill the other person to prevent him from being captured by the Japs or to end his suffering if there was no chance to survive. But how could I be sure that there wasn't any chance for him to survive? We'd laughed and joked when we made the pact. But when it became real, all I could feel was pain, indescribable pain.

Tan Hu was my best buddy. Because of our given name, people called him Xiao Hu—Little Tiger and me Da Hu—Big Tiger for being several weeks older. We were brothers.

All those thoughts ran through my mind, but in reality, it took only a millisecond. I had to react. And react fast.

I drew my pistol and aimed. In the past five years, I've killed countless enemies. But I couldn't do it. My hand was shaking, and my arm felt numb. All I could do was stare at his contorted face. I'm sorry, I screamed in my mind. So sorry!

Then, someone grabbed me from behind. With one hand, he steadied my arm, and with the other, gripped my hand. Together, we squeezed the trigger. The bullet hit right in between Tan Hu's eyes.

I spun around and saw Danny's face twisted with grief.

I threw away the pistol and rushed toward the airplane. But Danny and Birch grabbed me and pulled me back. "Wait. Stay back."

I kicked and fought, but they held me tight.

When the firemen finally put out the fire, I took Tan Hu from his seat and held him in my arms. His lower body was burned to the color of charcoal. That's why he couldn't get out. But how did he fly the plane back to the base? Why hadn't he jumped before it was too late?

"You idiot!" His life was surely worth more than that airplane.

Now I regret squeezing the trigger three seconds too late. Tan Hu had suffered three seconds longer because of my cowardice. I didn't want him to leave this world. I didn't want our friendship to end so soon. Oh, God. Forgive me.

I know I'll never talk about this again. But someone should know the truth. My son or daughter, if I live long enough to have a child, should know this part of history. The generations that come after us should know how their fathers and grandfathers fought.

This is how we live. And die.

Tears blurred Jasmine's vision. She felt sad that Meng Hu had had to make such a heartbreaking decision. She was angry that someone like Meng Hu had been beaten to death in a peaceful time. *He risked his life and sacrificed his friend's life to fight the Japs. He should have been treated with dignity and respect.*

Now Jasmine understood why Meng Hu had named his son Meng Xiao Hu. *I'll make sure Little Tiger remembers you and your friends.*

Suddenly, it dawned on her that perhaps this was why she was still alive—as a survivor of the war, to tell the truth, even if just to one child, so that he would learn that horrific yet heroic history.

Chapter 34

▬ ▬ ▬ ▬ ▬ ▬ ▬

Wang Hong was gone. She'd left very few things behind, but two of them became precious and vital to Jasmine—Meng Hu's son and his journal.

"Where is Mama?" whined the boy after dinner. "I want Mama."

A crushing sense of sorrow engulfed Jasmine. How did one tell a two-and-a-half-year-old boy that his mother was dead? She pointed to the sky. "Mama is there," she said, adding a light tone to her voice to hide the turmoil riddling her, "on one of those stars."

"May I go there?"

"One day."

"I want to see it, the star."

She held his tiny hand, and they walked outside the gate. It was a comfortable early summer night. The scent of honeysuckle and other wildflowers hung in the air. Two crickets chirped somewhere in the yard, and fireflies winked at them from the leafy shadows. Overhead was a velvet-black sky studded with glittering stars. They sat on the doorstep. Jasmine pointed to a bright star on the right side of the Milky Way. "This is where your mother lives now. It's called Weaver Maid."

The boy lifted his short arm in an attempt to touch the star.

Combating the sudden dryness in her throat, she asked, "Xiao Hu, would you like to hear a story?"

He gave a series of little nods.

"Once upon a time, there was a boy. His parents died when he was young. He made a living by herding cattle, so people called him Cowhand. A fairy from heaven fell in love with this kind-hearted young man. Her name was Weaver Maid." She pointed to the star again. "She came down to earth and married him without telling her parents. They had a son and a daughter and lived a happy life."

"What are their names?"

Jasmine paused. She'd heard this classic folktale numerous times and told her son as many times, yet this question had never occurred to her. "I don't know," she answered honestly. "What name would you like to give them?"

The boy scratched his head, looked around, and chirped, "Little Grass and Little Flower."

"Those are lovely names! Now, Weaver Maid's parents found out the truth and didn't like it. Her father, God of Heaven, ordered her back."

His breath came in short gasps.

"With the help of his celestial cattle, Cowhand chased his wife into the sky with Little Grass and Little Flower."

Xiao Hu sat up straighter.

"Before he reached his wife, her mother, Queen Mother, took off her gold hairpin and made a stroke." Jasmine waved her hand in the air and then pointed to the Milky Way. "A raging river appeared in front of Cowhand. See that? The river was called *Yinhe—Silver River.*"

His hands flew to his mouth. "Where is Little Grass? And Little Flower?"

She leaned down to his eye level and pointed to a brilliant star on the other side of the Milky Way across from Weaver Maid. "That's Cowhand. See the two smaller stars by his sides? One is his son, and the other is his daughter."

Little Tiger bobbed his head, satisfied.

"From then on, Cowhand and Weaver Maid were separated by the river. They cried and cried. Their love touched magpies. Every year

161

on the seventh day of the seventh lunar month, tens of thousands of magpies came to build a bridge for them to meet in the middle."

"What about their kids?"

"They would meet their mother, too, of course."

Xiao Hu smiled. But then he scratched his head again. "Auntie Jasmine, is *Baba* living with Cowhand?"

"Yes." As soon as the word left her mouth, she regretted it: being with a loved one only once a year would be torture. Wang Hong and Meng Hu deserved to live on the same star. Luckily, a child of his age had little concept of time.

"How do I find him? I don't know what *Baba* looks like."

Jasmine's heart turned over for the child who had never met his father and would never have the opportunity. "It's getting late." She picked him up and walked back into the house.

———

Jasmine was jerked into full awareness by Little Tiger's scream. The boy waved his arms as if fighting off something or someone. "Get away! Get away from Mama."

"It's okay, Xiao Hu." She patted him. "It's just a nightmare."

The boy squirmed for a few moments, and without opening his eyes, he stretched his arms and circled them around her neck. "Don't leave me, Mama. I'm afraid."

She held him tightly in her arms, heartbroken. "Don't be afraid. I'm right here."

"Queen Mother wants me."

"No one is going to hurt you."

"Don't leave!"

"I won't." Threading her right arm under his neck, Jasmine wrapped her left arm around his small body. She patted him and murmured in a soothing sound. The boy nestled against her and fell back to sleep. But she remained awake the rest of the night.

Early the next morning, she got up and worked until Little Tiger woke. "Look." She handed him a picture. "This is your *Baba*. Now, you'll be able to find him."

On the paper, a tall man in his twenties stood next to an airplane with shoulders back and head held high. In a flight jacket, he was attractive—a straight nose, a firm mouth, dark eyes, glossy black hair. His left arm rested on the wing of his aircraft. A confident smile spread across his face.

The boy beamed.

Fifteen years earlier, Jasmine had met Meng Hu for the first time while escaping from Nanking. He was in his early twenties. It was he who had given up his seat in their trainer plane so that Birch could fly her home in Chungking. She had always been grateful to him. Daisy had joked that Jasmine should date Meng Hu. If it hadn't been for her uncle who had adamantly objected to her courtship with any pilot, he might have become her significant other. Now, this devilishly charming fighter pilot was gone, leaving behind a son he'd never met.

"Draw a picture of Mama, please?"

"Certainly," she replied as an idea popped into her head. From then on, Jasmine started to create a picture album of her family and her friends.

Chapter 35

━ ━ ━ ━ ━ ━ ━ ━

"Auntie Jasmine," said Little Tiger one afternoon, "my tummy hurts."

"Did you go poo-poo today?"

He shook his head. His tiny eyebrows knitted.

"Where does it hurt?"

He pointed to his belly button.

Jasmine touched his forehead. It felt normal. She remembered her son had had stomachaches like this a few times. It usually went away in a couple of hours after going to the toilet. She gave him an herbal medicine for pain and kept a close eye on him. She wished Linzi were there. It was the autumn of 1953, and the villager was still in Korea.

When daylight faded to dusk, Little Tiger refused to eat, which was unusual for the three-year-old boy, and alarming to Jasmine. He folded his upper body, his hands pressing his stomach.

She touched his forehead. This time it was warm. Tensely, she asked, "Where does it hurt now?"

He pointed to the lower right abdomen.

Jasmine didn't know what was wrong, but in the back of her mind, she remembered vaguely that Daisy had had a stomachache like this. It turned out that she'd had appendicitis and needed surgery. Could the boy have the same illness? If he did, it would require medical attention that they didn't have in a remote village.

She'd promised Wang Hong that she would take care of her child. And Little Tiger was more than Wang Hong and Meng Hu's son. He was Birch's godson, and the offspring of that group of fighter pilots, including Danny and Tan Hu.

Even though it was dark, Jasmine decided to take him to the clinic in Anning. She dressed them in warm clothes and gathered every penny she had. Holding the oil lamp, she carried the boy on her back. With a slight limp, she started the long walk down the mountainside.

It was the day before the Mid-Autumn Festival, Little Tiger's birthday. The nearly full moon was high overhead, casting a silver light on the village. An owl made rhythmic *whoo-whoo-whooing* noises somewhere in the woods.

Once they were on the path, tree branches extended over the trail, forming a canopy that blocked out the moonlight. Jasmine could rely only on the light from the oil lamp. The darkness scared her, but her worry was even greater. Every time the boy moaned, her stomach cramped with fear.

Even though the night was chilly, Jasmine was soon sweating. She took off her jacket and tied it around her waist. Wiping the perspiration from her forehead, she picked up the boy. Readjusting and securing his position on her back, she moved forward.

Even in the daytime, it wasn't easy to hike down the narrow path, but it was much harder in the middle of the night with a boy on her back. Loose rocks slid beneath her feet. Several times she slipped or tripped. Her legs ached, and her arms were sore. She was dog-tired. In the end, every step became a test of will, and only sheer determination propelled her onward. Finally, she spotted the streetlights in the distance.

She approached the clinic and banged on the door. A middle-aged woman opened it. Jasmine handed her the boy before she slumped in the doorway. She was exhausted and thirsty. She'd left in such a hurry she'd forgotten to bring water with her. The woman called out, and a man with graying hair approached. He gave Jasmine a cup of water before turning his attention to Little Tiger. She drank the water in one long gulp.

It didn't take the doctor long to diagnose the problem. "He needs an appendectomy right now."

Her worry became reality.

"If the appendix ruptures, it can cause an infection," the doctor continued, "and the infection can spread, making it potentially life-threatening."

"Whatever needs to be done, please, save him!"

"We will." He picked up the boy. As he strode toward an inner room, he turned and said, "You'll need to make the payment now."

Jasmine took out all the money she had.

The woman counted the handful of small bills and looked up. "That's all? It covers only half—"

"That's all I have."

"We can't do the surgery without full payment." She yelled toward the inner room. "She doesn't have enough money."

The doctor walked out with the child in his arms. "I'm sorry," he said and handed the boy back to Jasmine.

Little Tiger whimpered. His feebleness broke her heart. "Please, help him!"

"I'm sorry. The government has taken over the clinic. We have to keep track of everything."

His reply filled her with desperation and despair. "I beg you! He's just a child. You can't...can't..."

"Last year, he saved a little girl without getting the full payment. They still remind us of the 'mistake' we made. We can't afford to get into trouble with the government again." The woman started to shove Jasmine toward the door.

With the boy in her arms, she dropped to her knees and bowed down. Grief strained her features. "Is there anything I can do? I'll work. I'll do anything for this child. Just..."

The couple exchanged a look.

"There is one thing..." The woman paused.

"Tell me."

"We're...in need of blood. If you give—"

Blood had always been in short supply. A donation was unheard of. Only people with no means to make a living would sell their blood, so it had a bad connotation associated with it.

"Yes! I will."

———————

Four days later, Little Tiger was released from the clinic. Carrying him on her back, Jasmine started their long journey home. It was a balmy autumn day with a few clouds floating in the blue sky. The soft breeze stirred the nearby treetops. Even so, she was soon soaked with perspiration.

"Mommy, I need to pee," mumbled the boy, his soft hand touching her head.

Jasmine was startled but didn't think much of it. The boy had been through a lot in the past few days, so it was understandable that he was confused about her identity.

They took a break and then moved onward. After selling blood twice in four days, Jasmine felt dizzy. The ascent in the daytime became as hard as the descent in the dark. All along the way, Little Tiger called her "Mommy."

Before going to bed that night, the boy circled his short arms around her neck. "Don't go." He tilted his head, his big innocent eyes staring at Jasmine. "Mama is on that star. Queen Mother won't allow her to come back. Will you be my mommy?"

Now Jasmine realized that he hadn't been hallucinating. He meant to call her mother. A dull ache settled in her chest, and her heart leaped to the poor boy. She folded him in her arms. "Yes!" she said, squeezing the word past the lump in her throat. "I'll be your mommy."

Her son was gone, and the boy's mother was no longer there. They became a new family.

Chapter 36

"Uncle Linzi is back! Uncle Linzi is back!" Children screeched while running around the village. Jasmine dropped her paintbrush, picked up Little Tiger, and rushed out of the door.

Villagers had already gathered at the herbalist's front yard when she arrived. Through a crowd of people, she looked at the young man. It had been two and a half years, and Linzi looked unchanged, except his skin was tanned to a coppery red. He wore the yellow-green army uniform with two shining medals. A carmine red paper flower was strapped to his chest.

With a big smile and tears in her eyes, she waited while Little Tiger played with other children. When the crowd thinned, she stepped forward, reached out, and clasped his outstretched arms. "Linzi!" Her voice caught on a small lump lodged in her throat, and she had to take a deep breath. "Let me look at you." She checked him up and down. "How are you? Did you get hurt?"

"I'm fine, only minor injuries."

His daughters ran over. "Daddy. Daddy!" cried Lili, tugging the hem of his uniform. Yaya hid behind her big sister and stuck out her head, obviously curious.

Linzi reached down and picked up the younger one. "Oh, you're getting so heavy. What did Mama feed you?"

The five-year-old giggled.

"Daddy," chirped Lili. "Mama killed a chicken for dinner."

"Good." Linzi put his daughter down. He rubbed the older girl's hair and said, "Daddy wants to talk to Auntie Jasmine. Will you keep an eye on your sister and this little brother?"

The smell of delicious food hung in the air as they entered the house. Apparently, his wife had already started cooking.

"Still the same Linzi." She grinned.

"No one is the same after being through war."

They sat around the table, catching up on each other's life. Jasmine told him about Wang Hong and Meng Hu, and Linzi cursed and sighed. He'd met them and was fond of both. He shared some of the horrible things he'd experienced while she listened, shaking her head.

"I didn't kill anyone, Miss Jasmine. I kept my word. I only saved people." He hesitated, squirming in his seat. "I...even...even..."

"What?"

He looked around, pitched forward, and spoke in a low voice as if vouchsafing a secret, "I saved an American soldier."

Her jaw dropped, and it stayed there for a few seconds before she uttered, "Goodness gracious! That's impossible. Why? How? What did you do?"

Linzi sought a more comfortable position in his chair. "Three months ago, I went to the battlefield after fighting. As usual, I tried to bring back as many wounded as I could find. After a few runs, I passed a trench and tripped over a body. He moaned and snatched my ankle. He was an American! It scared the hell out of me."

Jasmine listened in fascination.

"I didn't know what to do. I've never killed anyone and wasn't willing to break my promise." He kicked his right foot a few times. "I fought to free myself, but he held on even tighter. 'Help me. Please help me!' he begged."

Linzi picked up a cup on the table and drank a few gulps before continuing, "People called me Doctor Wang over there. Saving lives is a doctor's job. So, even though I was scared out of my wits, I asked where he was hurt." Linzi chuckled. "Birch taught us English. He could never have imagined that I'd use it in Korea."

169

"Not in his wildest dreams." Jasmine leaned back, and her face relaxed into a smile.

"The soldier was surprised. Then he pointed to his stomach. His wound was pretty bad, and I couldn't bring him back. He'd bleed to death. Besides, he'd be a prisoner, and POWs wouldn't get proper medical care. I decided to patch him up in the trench. We talked while I attended his wound."

"What did you talk about?"

"All kinds of things. He said his name was Bob. He was from San Francisco. I told him about Major Hardy. I knew that he too was from San Francisco. I asked him why he didn't shoot me when he had the chance."

She listened with a rapt silence.

"He said he was dying and terrified and didn't want someone to go through the hell he'd been through."

Jasmine shook her head in disbelief.

"I was so focused on his wound that I didn't notice a group of American soldiers moving toward us."

"Oh, no!" She sat up straighter; her hands clapped together.

"Yes, I was captured. When they dragged me away, Bob yelled, 'Let him go. He saved me.' No one listened to him. I was a soldier of the People's Volunteer Army."

"You became a prisoner?"

"We were taught that *hao xin you hao bao*—*kindness often meets with recompense*. I didn't expect rewards, but…" He twisted his lips.

Jasmine felt sorry for Linzi. A POW's life couldn't have been easy.

"Then something happened." With a wicked grin, he paused for effect.

"What?"

"Bob took out his pistol and pointed it at his head."

"You've got to be kidding me!"

"He yelled, 'If he hadn't patched me up, I'd be a dead man by now. If you take him, I'll blow my brains out, my blood will be on your hands, and I'll see you all in hell.'"

"Unbelievable!"

"I didn't want him to die because of me. So I shouted, 'Bob, don't do it!'"

"What happened?"

"The soldiers were stunned at first. Then..." One corner of his lips moved upward. "They let me go!"

Tension drained out of Jasmine's shoulders. She beamed, unable to conceal her delight. But before long, her smile faltered. Nervously, she scanned the door leading to the front yard. Several girls were playing hopscotch. Little Tiger and Yaya sat on the front step, watching them. Turning back and leaning closer to him, she said, "Linzi, you were incredibly brave and kind." She lowered her voice to a whisper. "But don't tell this to anyone! Like it or not, Americans are enemies of the country now."

He bobbed his head. "Another thing..." he stammered and fidgeted in his chair. "I became a member of the Communist Party."

"You...you wanted to...?"

He shook his head. "I had to. Everyone is eager to be a party member nowadays. It's a label to say you're a good guy."

Jasmine nodded.

"Crazy as it seems, many soldiers cut their fingers to write Blood Letters. They swore their loyalty to the Communist Party." His mouth lifted in an ironic smirk. "I was chosen. I've saved many lives." He pointed to his medals. "How could I say no? I couldn't refuse. But...but I felt betrayal to your uncle and Birch. Where is my *Yi—morality, duty, loyalty, decency, brotherhood?*"

"Don't think that way." Jasmine patted his arm. "Birch worked for the old government, but he was just military personnel. He's not a Nationalist. My uncle...he's a member of the Nationalist Party because he believed that was how he could help his country. We have a new government now. You're a decent man—that's all that matters."

Linzi nodded his appreciation.

"But listen to me. Take this to your grave. Don't tell a soul! You'd get into big trouble."

"I know. I'd be hanged."

Chapter 37

----- -- -- -- -- -- -- --

Over the next few years, many movements emerged: New Three-Anti Campaign, Sufan Movement, Hundred Flowers Campaign, and Anti-Rightist Movement. Most of them had targeted intellectuals, which had limited impacts to a remote village.

Jasmine read that any criticism, or even a mere expression of disapproval of the Party, was enough to merit arrest and imprisonment. The afflicted individuals were subjected to public humiliation, social exclusion, and struggle sessions—criticism and repentance meetings. She didn't know any of those people, but instinctively, she felt sorry for them. Her parents, uncle, aunt, and cousins were all educated individuals. If they had still been alive and lived in the Mainland, they too would likely have been affected.

She stopped reading newspapers. What was the point? What she truly cared about was her family and friends. It seemed, though, that her dream of reuniting with her family, or of searching for Danny, was slipping further and further away. The Communists tolerated neither the Nationalists nor Americans. Jasmine had to accept that reality and bury her dream deep inside. She'd built a life on her own—learned to live in this far-flung community, poured out her love to her adopted son, befriended Linzi and other villagers, communicated with Li Ming by mail, and dreamed of Danny at night. It wasn't ideal but tolerable.

The next campaign seemed lighthearted compared to the previous ones. Eliminate Sparrows Campaign was introduced in 1958 by Chairman Mao. The Communist government declared that "Birds are public animals of capitalism." According to official estimation, each sparrow pecked away four pounds of grain per year. By slaughtering the birds, "We could save tons of grain for our people." The whole country followed Chairman Mao's order.

Jasmine was told to draw a poster. In the picture, a boy raised a slingshot toward a sparrow in the sky. Next to him, a girl held a basket full of dead birds. "Let's Kill All Sparrows" was the title.

Like other kids, Little Tiger was excited. At eight, he was skilled in using a slingshot. He got up every day at dawn. Quietly, he tiptoed through the village, his footfalls muffled by the rubber-soled sneakers that Li Ming had mailed to them. And each day in the evening, the number of dead sparrows was counted in Linzi's front yard, and the one with the largest number would be praised. Little Tiger seized this non-material reward a few times. He gave a lopsided grin, unable to suppress his delight and pride.

Bird nests were also destroyed. Their eggs were broken, and chicks were slain. Little Tiger was good at this task, too. Like his father, he was athletic, even at his young age. He could climb a tree faster and higher than boys several years older. A few times, he returned home with torn shirts or pants. Once a tree branch snapped, and he fell. His right elbow and knee were scraped and bruised. Jasmine felt sorry for him, but he raised his narrow shoulders in a quick shrug. Even this gesture reminded her of Meng Hu.

Linzi told her that there was another tactic used in cities and towns. People banged pots and pans so that the sparrows had no chance to rest anywhere and would fall dead from the sky. Soon, these nationwide attacks depleted the population of the sparrows and other wild birds, pushing them to near extinction.

Jasmine enjoyed the sight and the song of birds, but if the reduction of the sparrows could save food for the hungry people like Bai Long's family, she didn't have any objections. Besides, she was thrilled to see Little Tiger happy. The boy deserved to live a carefree life without the shadow of family tragedies.

———————

It turned out that the Eliminate Sparrows Campaign was one of the first actions taken in another movement—the Great Leap Forward. Once again, Chairman Mao initiated this movement, aiming to transform the country from the agricultural civilization to a modern society through rapid industrial development and collectivization. This campaign had a direct impact on the countryside, including the remote village. Private farming was banned, and anyone engaged in it would be labeled as a Counter-revolutionary and persecuted.

Along with other villagers, Jasmine had to give up her private field to form *Sheng Chan Da Dui—Production Brigade* in People's Commune, which was controlled by the Communist Party. All jobs were centrally assigned every morning. Linzi was the *Cun Zhi Shu—Party Secretary in the Village.* He was fair and square. Problems arose, however, due to the nature of the shared duty. No one was working for himself or herself. Inevitably, some people became lazy and started cutting corners when they did their jobs.

In a typical People's Commune, everything was shared, even cooking. Private cookery was replaced by communal dining. All things in the private kitchen—tables, chairs, utensils, pots, and pans—were all contributed to the commune's kitchen. Linzi resisted this idea. It would be hard for a small village to build a separate communal dining area.

He had another concern. "I've seen things when I visited the model People's Commune. Things I don't like," he told Jasmine. "I'm afraid food will be wasted if everyone can eat for free."

"But you may get into trouble if you don't obey."

He shrugged. "*Shan gao huang di yuan—The mountain is high, the emperor far away.*"

"Let's pray you're right. Oh, I truly hope our tiny village is out of the reach of the emperor's long arms."

———————

One late afternoon, Jasmine returned home from a long day working in the fields. She was exhausted and felt dizzy. It wasn't anything new. She'd been feeling lightheaded every now and then throughout the years. She suspected that the concussion she'd sustained a decade earlier might be responsible.

She put down a hoe and wiped the cold sweat off her face. All she wanted to do was to crawl into bed and sleep. But being a mother, she didn't have that luxury. The eight-year-old boy was big for his age and needed lots of food. With a sigh, she walked into the kitchen.

In the fading light, she gawked at the small space, puzzled. There weren't many items: a clay-stove, a basket holding firewood, a bucket for water, and a wooden table. Normally, she had a kettle, a wok, and two pots on the counter. They were gone. Jasmine looked all around the kitchen but couldn't find them. There wasn't enough room to hide anything, and she didn't think anyone would steal. The village was safe, and nobody locked their doors. A headache started to build at her temples.

"Mom, I'm home," called out Little Tiger. "What's for dinner?" he asked, sticking his head into the kitchen.

"Have you seen my pots and pans? I can't—"

"Oh, I took them."

"What? Oh, go get them back."

"I can't. We're going to make steel out of them," Little Tiger said, a proud smile firmly in place.

Jasmine squeezed her fingers against her temples. "We need them for cooking." She raised her voice as her temper flared. She'd never yelled at the boy before. "You're old enough to know better—"

His mouth drooped at the corners. "Lili said our country needs steel. She said we could help. We could melt…"

She frowned as the darkened room swirled around her.

Just then, Linzi called from outside the gate, "Miss Jasmine."

"We're here."

He stepped into the kitchen, holding the charcoaled cooking supplies in his hands. "Here." He handed them to her. "Sorry. I didn't have time to clean them. I was worried you might be upset."

"Upset? You bet I am! But I'm more confused. What's going on?"

"The whole country is making steel by melting scrap metals, including pots and pans. It's part of the Great Leap Forward Movement. I'll show you the newspapers." He swallowed before continuing. "I'm afraid we may have to…" His voice trailed off.

"You must be joking! This is insane."

That night, Jasmine read the newspapers. Consistent with the blueprint borrowed from another communist country—Soviet Union, steel production became one of the major yardsticks of industrial development. Chairman Mao had encouraged the establishment of backyard furnaces in every People's Commune and in each urban neighborhood.

Tremendous efforts were made in producing steel out of scrap metals. Pots, pans, tools, and other metal artifacts were demanded so that the unrealistic targets could be met. There were pictures of people working at night using these homemade facilities. Farmers, factory workers of all kinds, teachers, office clerks, and even hospital staff were sidetracked from their jobs to help with the production.

To fuel the incinerators, countless hardwood trees were cut down. One article praised a bank clerk for donating his wooden table and chairs. Soon after, there were stories about people taking down doors and giving away their furniture to fuel the furnaces.

Jasmine was flabbergasted. *Is everyone in this government going mad? How can anyone think the country can produce usable iron or steel in this fashion?*

After the Anti-Rightist Movement, the intellectuals were silenced. They'd had enough trouble during the movement. Many had been labeled as Rightists, which was equivalent to being convicted as a criminal. A few daring scientists raised their concerns and protested the folly of such a plan. They were labeled as Counter-revolutionaries who were against Chairman Mao's ideology. They were publicly humiliated for sabotaging the modernization of the motherland and sent to jail for undermining communism.

Jasmine sighed as she put down the newspapers. Her headache was getting worse. She rubbed a bit of Tiger Balm on her forehead, feeling a mild cooling sensation on her skin.

Should I write a letter to Li Ming? Immediately, she dismissed the idea. She doubted he would agree with such a foolish policy. But if he wrote anything down, it might be used as evidence against him. The censors were everywhere. They'd made an earnest effort not to discuss politics in mail or phone calls.

Jasmine felt terrible that she'd lost her temper. Taking the oil lamp, she walked into the boy's room and perched on the edge of his bed. "I'm sorry I yelled at you earlier." Her fingers tousled in his short hair. "I was tired and had a headache. But that's no excuse to lose my temper. I shouldn't blame you without knowing the whole story. Even though it's…unrealistic, you were trying to help. I should've trusted you, Little Tiger. I'm sorry."

"It's okay, Mom." He raised his arm, his palm touching her left temple and cheek. "It's my fault. I'll ask your permission next time."

She leaned down and placed a soft kiss on his forehead. Warmth filled her heart. In this senseless world, she had a sensible child.

Chapter 38

It was now the summer of 1959. Jasmine was on her way to Anning. She was worried about Bai Long and his family. Throughout the years, she'd offered as much help as she could—giving them food or clothing from time to time.

Recently, things seemed to be worse. Extreme droughts, according to official newspapers, had spread across the nation and lasted for months, substantially impacting the ecosystem and agriculture of the country. As a result, the production of grains had dropped significantly. The government asked people to "struggle together through this difficult time."

So far, the village hadn't been affected by the droughts. However, since the Eliminate Sparrows Campaign, there were fewer birds, but more and more grasshoppers. Swarms of them had come like gray clouds and destroyed almost all their crops. The villagers were struggling to feed their families.

If Bai Long's family had trouble before, what would happen to them now? Jasmine was worried, and she had to check on them.

The cool mountain morning gave way rapidly to a rising temperature at the lower elevation. When she was close to town, she watched hordes of people spread over the fields. It seemed that they were collecting something under the beating sun. She wasn't alarmed. She'd seen strange movements in recent years—killing birds, cutting down trees to melt pots and pans or any metals to "produce steel." *Could this be another campaign?*

When she got closer, she felt a flutter of panic. The men and women looked shrunken, emaciated—as thin as scarecrows. Their faces had an unhealthy gray pallor. Many of them had tired, vacant eyes.

Jasmine uttered a sharp cry of fright when she spotted bodies lying by the side of the road, their skin pallid and mottled in death. Some corpses were torn by hungry dogs or crows. *Dear God! What on earth is going on?* The rotting stench made her gag, and the color in her face drained away.

As a well-read person, she knew that there was a long list of famines in Chinese history. Millions of people had died. Numerous books described the tragedies—people eating leaves, roots, or clay, ravenous folks lying helplessly and dying in the streets, men selling their wives and daughters into slavery, and worst of all, children being boiled and eaten.

Could this be another famine?

Jasmine planned to buy steamed buns for Bai Long's family. There was a long line at the food stand where she'd shopped before. She looked up at the sky. The sun was directly overhead, and it was staggeringly hot, so it must be close to noon. She kept going, hoping to find another stand or store. There were very few places selling food, all with long lines. In the end, she waited for almost an hour. By then, her stomach was aching, and the aroma of food made her feel even hungrier. She thought about the pancake in her bag but resisted the temptation. It was inappropriate to eat while everyone else was waiting for food.

When it was her turn, she emitted a relieved sigh and said, "A dozen steamed buns, please. The ones with pork filling." She took out a few bills from her patchwork bag and handed them to the seller.

"*Liang Piao—Food Stamp,*" said the man behind the stand. He was in navy blue working clothes. His face had a healthy color that was rarely seen around town, but his eyes glazed with tiredness.

"Food Stamp? What is that?"

"*Liang Piao* is *Liang Piao*. You don't know that?"

Jasmine shook her head. "Isn't that enough?" She thrust the few bills in front of the man.

"No. I can't sell you steamed buns without Food Stamp."

Her face held nothing but blank bewilderment. "How about..." She looked behind him. A middle-aged woman was making baked pancakes. "How about a dozen *Shao Bing*, then?"

"No, you can't!" The man lost his patience. "Without Food Stamp, you can't get anything here. Go away." He waved his arm as if he were shooing a bothersome fly.

Jasmine stepped aside, feeling like she'd just landed on an alien world.

"How on earth you don't know anything about *Liang Piao*?" asked a skinny woman next in line. "We all have it. You can't buy anything made of flour or rice without it."

"I live in the mountains." She pointed in the general direction. "I've never..."

"Oh, that explains it. You're from the countryside." The woman took out her wallet and held out Food Stamp with her frail bird-claw hands. "Depending on age and gender, each person has a certain quota of *Liang Piao*. We get it every month. Not just rice or flour. Everything needs a voucher. Here...this is for cooking oil. This is for sugar. For meat..."

Jasmine had waited an hour and left the store empty-handed. *Well, if I can't get anything made of flour, perhaps I can get some fruits or vegetables.* Pushing aside her frustration, she walked toward a market she'd been to before.

The place was empty. No fruits. No vegetables. All the shelves were bare, but people were standing in line, their downcast faces pinched with hunger, their eyes vacant.

"What are you waiting for?" she asked a slim old man.

"Vegetables. What else?" the man drawled as if speaking fast would take too much energy.

"But there's nothing. When do you expect—"

"You never know," butted in a splay-toothed woman next in line. She cooled herself with lazy swishes of a bamboo hand fan. "In the late afternoon, they may bring something. We've done this almost every day, standing in line, waiting, hoping. Yesterday, there was nothing."

Jasmine opened her mouth. She wanted to ask how people survived without anything, but she already knew the answer. *That's why there were people in the fields. That's why the nearby fields are so barren.* She'd seen the result—gaunt faces, bony figures, dead bodies!

"I'm going to see a friend. I can't go there, empty-handed."

"If you have enough money,"—the woman twirled around—"you may get cabbages from a man over there." She pointed to indicate the direction.

"He has a nice garden," added the old man. He didn't even try to hide his envy. "He guards it as if it's a palace."

"I'd guard it with my life if I had a garden like his." The woman licked her chapped lips. "I have to warn you, though, his price is…" Thumb-up, she lifted her hand a few times.

Jasmine had no choice. She paid a hefty price to get a cabbage.

———

Jasmine was quaking by the time she reached Bai Long's place. She'd seen numerous corpses near the wooden shacks in the back of the Bai Residence. The foul stench of death pervaded the air. "An Kong? Are you here?" she called out, purposely avoiding the word "home."

No one answered.

The door stood ajar. Jasmine pushed it open. The putrid odor made her gag, and she took a step back. It was dark inside and stiflingly hot. Squinting, she scanned the low-ceiling room with teetering walls. In the dim light, three people lay on the floor—Bai Fu's mother, wife, and son.

Her instinct was to flee, but she forced herself to stay. She had to check. *What if they're still alive? Perhaps they're sleeping or just passed out.* "An Kong?" she called out, raising her voice.

No one stirred.

She squatted down near the old woman. Everything about her was sunken and shriveled—her hair was thin and white, her face was as wrinkled as a walnut, and her skin had a gray pallor. Fending off the rising fear, Jasmine placed her right index finger under her nose. No breathing. She touched her cheek. It was cold.

She turned to Bai Fu's wife. An Kong was stick-thin, but strangely, her face and hands were swollen. Her hair was thin and dry as straw, most likely due to lack of nutrition in her diet. Detecting her weak pulse, Jasmine shook her. "An Kong? Wake up!"

The middle-aged woman uttered a faint groan.

"Oh, thank God!" Jasmine touched her hand. "Are you okay? What can I do? Do you want water?" She unplugged the bamboo water container she was carrying. Threading her left hand behind the sick woman's neck, she tried to give her water.

An Kong looked up, eyes pleading.

"What do you want me to do?" Jasmine had no idea how to help the dying woman.

Slowly and listlessly, An Kong took Bai Long's hand and placed it on Jasmine's arm. She felt the warmth of his skin. He was still alive! "You want me to help him first?"

The sick woman's mouth moved, but nothing came out. Only her eyes implored.

"Okay, I'll…I'll take care of him first." Moving toward the boy, she lightly shook him. "Bai Long, wake up."

The teenager stirred. He was just a bag of bones.

"Have some water." He gulped it down in such a hurry that he choked. "Slow down. Slow down!" she said and took the pancake out of her bag. It was her lunch, but she hadn't had a chance to eat it.

Bai Long snatched it and stuffed it into his mouth. "More?" he begged. "You've got more?"

She shook her head. His voracious appetite shocked her.

"Oh, no!" he cried and turned to his mother. "I'm sorry. I'm sorry!"

His mother didn't reply. Her body began to convulse. Gagging noise came from her throat.

"An Kong!" Jasmine shrieked, her tone laced with panic. "Mama!"

The middle-aged woman didn't speak. Her eyes rolled back until only the whites showed, and her last breath escaped in a prolonged hiss. Her head lolled to one side and then stilled. An Kong—her name meant Safe and Wealth—left the world, left her son.

"Mama!" Bai Long broke down over his mother's dead body.

Jasmine sobbed with him. She patted the teenager on his back. "I'm so sorry."

When his cry subsided, she said softly, "Come with me, Bai Long. The village is small and poor, but whatever I have, I'll share it with you. I'm your teacher. *Yi ri wei shi, zhong shen wei fu—Teacher for one day, father for life*. I promise you won't go hungry before I do."

The fifteen-year-old boy wiped the tears with his dirty sleeve. "Mama said that you were the kindest person in the world. She wanted me to find you. She said you'd take me in." He bowed down, knocking his head on the floor three times. Ten years earlier, that was precisely what his father had asked him to do.

"Get up, Bai Long. Get up!" Jasmine seized his bony arms.

He lifted his head, tears staining his cheeks. Taking a ragged breath, he said, "*Bai Lao Shi—Teacher Bai*, I was wrong. Would you please take me as your student?"

"Of course!" She folded him in her arms as they sat together on the filthy floor and wept.

Chapter 39

———————

Jasmine took Bai Long to the village. She didn't tell anyone about his family background and told the teenager not to say a single word. She simply stated that she'd found the starving boy by the side of the road and was happy for Little Tiger to have a big brother.

To her surprise and dismay, the younger boy wouldn't accept the newcomer. "He's not my brother," Xiao Hu grunted and refused to call him Big Brother. Whenever she praised Bai Long's paintings, Little Tiger would roll his eyes and say, "It's ugly. You'll never paint as well as my mom."

Jasmine was confused and frustrated. "It's important to get along with your family members," she reasoned with the boy. "As brothers, you should support each other. You should be polite and respectful."

Little Tiger twisted his lips and wouldn't listen.

Luckily, when she apologized to Bai Long, the fifteen-year-old was very mature and forgiving. "No worries, *Bai Lao Shi*." Adversity and the life-and-death experiences had changed him.

Still, it troubled Jasmine.

She'd kept a garden ever since she'd come to the village. It wasn't large, but it had provided enough vegetables for her family. However, since the Great Leap Forward Movement in 1958, like everyone else in the village, she'd had to give away her private field to form People's Commune, which was controlled by the Communist Party.

Private farming was prohibited, which ruined peasant life at its most basic level. Amid the Great Famine, food was getting more and more scarce.

Besides the assigned jobs, Jasmine had to find different ways to feed the family. She could no longer sell her paintings; no one cared about art when hunger was a constant threat. Her additional sources of food came from nature. She collected wild berries, mushrooms, black wood ears, and edible wild plants like shepherd's purse. In their separate ways, both boys helped as much as they could.

One day, Bai Long brought back a snake. It scared Jasmine. "Relax. It's not poisonous," said the teenager. He was no longer a skeleton. "I checked with several old villagers. We can eat it." He killed the snake and cooked it with spices. It turned out to be quite tasty, she admitted once she'd gotten past the initial fear and disgust.

Another time, Little Tiger brought home a bee brood. His face and arms were covered with nasty welts. The boys ate the white grub-like larvae, but Jasmine would rather starve than eat the creepy-crawlies. She applied Witch Hazel Extract to Little Tiger's bee stings.

Since the Eliminate Sparrows Campaign, there were fewer and fewer birds, but more and more locusts. One year, swarms of locusts came like dark clouds and destroyed almost all of their crops. But the insects were the boys' favorite catch. She had no idea that grass-hoppers could be used as food. "Anything with four legs other than a table can be eaten, and anything with wings except an airplane can be consumed" was no longer a joke.

Two months after Bai Long joined them, Jasmine came home pleasantly surprised. For the first time, the two boys were talking and playing together.

"What happened today?" She was happy for them and couldn't suppress her curiosity.

Both chuckled, but neither said anything.

———

There was no school in the village. Unofficially, Jasmine had taught the kids for several years, but since she had to work at the assigned jobs, she found it difficult to keep up. Still, no matter how tired she was, she would spend a couple of hours each evening teaching the two boys. Bai Long had shown great promise as an artist when he was little; now his paintings were more and more impressive. Little Tiger displayed a special interest in literature, thanks to all the stories she'd told him.

One night, after the boys went to sleep, Jasmine sat down as usual to check their homework. She yawned before opening Little Tiger's notebook. The titled "Brother" instantly jolted her awake.

I didn't like my brother. He's older and talented, and he gets more attention from Mom. He's not my real brother anyway. Mother made me call him Ge—Big Brother *and told me to play with him. But why? I liked to spend time with my own friends.*

One day, my buddies and I spotted a yellow bird. Nowadays, you don't see too many birds. We chased it, and it flew into an outhouse. I took out my slingshot as we fought to enter the tiny space. I'm a better hunter than most of my friends.

Before I got the chance, however, Fang Fang pushed me aside. I tripped on a wooden plank, and it slid sideways. I fell. My body slipped through the crack and into the pit full of poops and pees! Feces came to my face. I tried to press my lips as tight as I could. When I came up, I gulped for air and reached up to grab the rim. The stinky smell made me want to throw up.

"Help!" I called out. "Pull me out!"

My friends covered their mouths and fled. I could hear their screams and laughter getting further and further away. No one, not a single one of them, stayed to help me.

Hanging on the wet rim, I tried to pull myself out. But it was too slippery, and I wasn't strong enough. Little by little, I slipped back down. "Help! Help!" I yelled. I was scared out of my wits. I didn't want to drown in a filthy pit. Tears rushed down my face.

Then I heard someone calling my name. It was my brother.

"I'm here. I'm here." I'd never been happier to see him.

He ran inside and squatted down. Without the slightest

hesitation, he grabbed my arms, the arms with all the poops and pees, and pulled me out. He's thin, but thank God he's strong. He took me to the creek outside the village and washed my body, hair, and clothes. The water was cold, but my heart was filled with warmth.

Mother was right. It's great to have a brother, and Big Brother is even better.

Now I understand the concept of Yi. Perhaps I'll ask him to be my sworn brother like in Romance of the Three Kingdoms.

No, wait. I take it back. He's already my Big Brother. I'll tell him the story of two fighter pilots—one Chinese, one American—they're sworn brothers like us.

Relief flooded through Jasmine, and a smile spread across her worn-out face. She wondered how much of the story was true and which part was fiction, but she decided not to ask. She was just grateful.

Chapter 40

＝ ＝ ＝ ＝ ＝ ＝ ＝ ＝

On April 15, 1960, Bai Ge would have turned seventeen if he were still alive. Jasmine had never told anyone in the village about her biological son. On that day, she got up before sunrise, cooked a simple breakfast of porridge, and left the house when the sun was barely above the horizon.

Standing on the hillside, she faced the direction where Chungking should be. She clasped her hands in front of her chest and said a silent prayer, "Happy birthday, Bai Ge. May you fly as free as a dove in heaven. No hunger. No violence. No death. And have as many dumplings as you wish." Tears rolled in her eyes, but after twelve years, she no longer cried.

Jasmine collected a basketful of shepherd's purse before she had to work in the fields with other villagers. She stayed there the entire day, transplanting rice seedlings, only taking a short lunch break. In the late afternoon, as she was getting ready to go back to the village, she watched Little Tiger run toward her. He waved and shouted, "Mom, this uncle is looking for you." He pointed to a man behind him and added, "He brought us all kinds of goodies. Bai Long is cooking. I'm going to help." He turned without hearing from her and disappeared in a breath.

The man continued to walk toward her. Without seeing him clearly, Jasmine knew who he was, and her face lit up with joy. Wiping her hands on a rag around her neck, she stepped out of the paddy field and darted toward him with outstretched arms. *"Li Ming Ge!* What a surprise! Why are you here?"

The smile on his face was his answer.

———————

After exchanging pleasantries, Li Ming said, "May I help?" He rolled his sleeves to his elbows. "You shouldn't—" Jasmine was worried about his injured arm. But he kicked off his rubber-soled sneakers, rolled up his pant legs to his knees, and walked down the water-filled rice paddy. Water came up to his ankles.

"Be careful." She reached out to grab his elbow. As she watched him struggle to move, she remembered the first time she'd stepped into a rice paddy and how much she'd detested the thick, slippery mud on her bare feet and legs. She'd screamed whenever she was bitten by a leech on her legs or hands before the bloodsucking worm became part of her life. Now, she was more like a farmer than an artist, she begrudgingly thought.

Li Ming stood beside her. "Show me how to do it."

Using her right hand, Jasmine took the rice seedling from the bundle in her left one, and bending down, wedged it into the mud. She repeated several times, keeping the seedlings a foot apart.

"Easy as rice cakes," he joked. Since his left arm was almost useless, he took the seedlings from her. Slowly, they moved backward, planting and talking. Before long, he straightened and rotated his waist a few times to work out the stiffness. "I've had rice for forty-six years. I had no idea how much work it took to grow it."

"Shui zhi pan zhong can—Who knows food on a tray...?"

"Li li jie xin ku—Each grain comes from toiling days." Li Ming finished a famous poem and grinned. Then his smile vanished, leaving only sadness in his eyes. A deep line formed between his eyebrows. "I'm worried, Jasmine."

She looked up. She noticed for the first time that there were flecks of gray in his black hair.

"This village is lucky to have water." He glanced around. They were standing in the middle of the terraced fields. Under the late afternoon sun, the water shimmered and glowed in the gaps between the crops. Surrounded by the lush mountains, the area was serene and picturesque.

By then, all the villagers had left for the day. Yet, he lowered his voice. "The entire nation is suffering a terrible famine. Many people have starved to death. I'm afraid—"

Jasmine nodded. Images of dead bodies she'd seen in Anning appeared in her mind. Since then, she'd heard more horrid stories from the villagers, who went down the mountains regularly. She didn't need a vivid imagination to picture the dire situation. Great Famine, as the official newspaper explained, was a result of a series of natural disasters—extreme droughts one year, and then life-threatening floods the next.

Even this village was affected. The villagers hadn't had much trouble with droughts, but heavy rains had created mudslides, wiping out parts of their terraced fiends. They had produced little grain since the beginning of the natural disasters in 1958, and the small amount they'd been able to grow had to be handed over to the government. Hunger became a real threat.

Li Ming emitted a sigh. "I've seen things, unpleasant things. Dreadful things." His expression turned grave. "People are so hungry that they eat tree bark and *guan yi tu—clay!*"

"I know." A heavy feeling of sorrow settled like a blanket over Jasmine. "But I don't understand why people eat *guan yi tu*. It has no nutrients."

"It makes them feel less hungry. At least they have something in their stomachs. But if one eats too much, he suffers constipation, swelling, and eventually death. We've seen many cases of such fatality."

She quailed, remembering An Kong's body with swollen hands and legs. Bai Long had told her that his mother had eaten clay to save food for him. Jasmine prayed that her family wouldn't have to endure such suffering.

"How did we get to this point?" asked Li Ming, his eyes imploring. "People are dying." He leaned closer and said in a gruff whisper,

"Hundreds of thousands. Maybe even millions… This is so far from the communist society that I imagined."

"Our nation has experienced some terrible weather," she said.

"Weather is only part of the reason."

"What else can it be?"

Li Ming opened his mouth, but the words died on his lips. The sun slanted toward the western horizon. His face bathed in its crimson glow. Reaching up, he unfastened the top button of his official Mao suit. "So many reasons," he murmured. "I can't tell you all. But remember the campaign to exterminate sparrows?"

"I was told to paint posters." Jasmine tilted her head. "Each sparrow can eat up to four pounds of grain per year. If all the sparrows and other wild birds were killed, we'd save tons of food."

"Not true. I talked to a group of scientists." Sadness lurked in the depths of his eyes. "Sparrows eat more than grains. They also eat insects. Without birds, the population of crop-eating insects exploded, and as a result, rice production dropped. And so many trees were cut down to fuel the homemade furnaces during the Great Leap Forward Movement. These campaigns disturbed our country's balance of nature." He took a long shuddering breath before he concluded, "In truth, the Great Famine is a *man-made* disaster."

Jasmine was dumbstruck. Utterly at a loss for words, "Dear God," was all she managed.

Chapter 41

‒ ‒ ‒ ‒ ‒ ‒ ‒

On their way to her home, Jasmine asked, "How's your family?"

"My family? We're fine. Li Dong is five now. He's a rascal."

She nodded. Although she hadn't seen Li Ming for eight years, they'd kept in touch. There was no postal service to the village, but they'd arranged with the stationery store in Anning so that they could receive mail. And whenever she and the boys went down the mountains, they would call him on the payphone at the store.

When she learned of his marriage, she'd painted a picture of a pair of colorful birds soaring in a crystal blue sky as a wedding gift. Four characters "*Bi Yi Shuang Fei—Flying Wing to Wing*" were artfully integrated into the picture, expressing her sincere wish.

His wife, Huang Yun, had been a reporter before the liberation, and her articles had been pro-Communist and raised red flags. If it weren't for Li Ming to warn her, she would have been arrested by the Nationalists. After the Communists took over, she wrote an article about him and pursued him for a couple of years. Li Dong was their son.

"As a party official, I don't have any trouble. It's a privilege." He gave a self-deprecating chuckle. "I'm grateful that my family isn't starving. Believe me. But…" He paused for a beat. "Don't you think it's ironic? When we fought capitalism, when we took over the old class-ridden sociality, we envisioned a world with equality. No more rich or poor. No more capitalist exploitation. Everyone is happy. We tried hard and paid dearly, including this—" He motioned to his left arm. "But...but..."

"Whatever doubts you have, keep them to yourself!"

He shook his head. "I'm going to write a report. I have to point out the flaws of some of the policies. I—"

"Oh, don't! Please! You'll get into trouble."

"I must."

"Have you forgotten the Hundred Flowers Campaign and the Anti-Rightist Movement afterward? Thousands of people were labeled as Rightists, simply because they'd criticized the Party's policies or a party official."

"I know. The most unfair part is that they were asked to criticize our party's policies." His lips twisted into a bitter smirk as he motioned to his left arm. "Well, how much more trouble can I have? It can't be worse than this."

"*Li Ming Ge—*"

"Don't worry about me. I'm a member of the Communist Party. It's my job." He glanced around the surrounding area and asked, "What about you? I'm here because I'm worried about you."

"I'm fine. *Kao shan chi shan, kao shui chi shui—The mountain dweller lives from the mountain, and the shore dweller lives from the sea.*" Jasmine pointed to the forest around them. She was wearing a peasant's long-sleeved shirt and trousers, her thin body hiding under the loose fabric. Her face was drawn, and lately, she often felt tired to the bone.

But she didn't want Li Ming to worry about her. A ghost of a smile flickered across her face before she said, "We're lucky, considering everything." *Hopefully, they won't keep cutting down more trees,* she added in her mind. Many blocks of forest near the towns down the valley had been destroyed, leaving patches of bare earth, turning the area ugly. Huge bonfires were built to melt pots and pans in an attempt to produce steel.

A muscle in his jaw bunched. "Today is...Bai Ge's birthday. I just wanted to come, to make sure..."

"He would appreciate that."

An awkward silence descended upon them. Although Jasmine had never blamed Li Ming, her son had died in his arms.

As they got close to her house, he cleared his throat and said, "I met Little Tiger. He's a bright boy." He swallowed before continuing, "There is no school here. I could, if you like, bring him home with me. I could send him to—"

"You can't—"

"Don't you want him to get a good education? He'll forever be a peasant if he stays here."

"He'll be safe here!"

He arched his eyebrows in inquiry.

Jasmine hesitated a moment before she decided to tell him the truth. "You know I adopted the boy, but I didn't tell you the whole story. His real name is Meng Xiao Hu. His father was a Nationalist fighter pilot, a good friend of Birch and Danny..."

Li Ming didn't say anything for a while after hearing the story. By then, they'd already reached her home. Leaning against the outside wall, he took out a cigarette and jammed it into his mouth. Soon, smoke drifted through his fingers. "Jasmine, do you know you can get into a lot of trouble for this?"

Evening settled in as they stood in the twilight.

His voice dropped a notch. "He's the son of a former Nationalist. His father was killed in jail! No matter Meng Hu was wrongfully accused or not, he'd always be a Counter-revolutionary, an Enemy of the People. His son will always carry this shameful family history."

"What could I do? I couldn't abandon him. He was just a baby. Anyway, he's my son now."

"It's a shame. In our society, we treat people based on their family background, not how they act."

Jasmine paused a beat before she shared the secret she'd kept for years. "Bai Ge was...half Japanese."

"I know."

She raised an eyebrow.

At her look of consternation, Li Ming said, "His age...Your love for Danny… I put it together. There's no other explanation. You were…raped by the Japanese soldiers, weren't you?"

She tipped her head as tears gathered in her eyes. "Yet you accepted him and loved him. Why?"

"Bai Ge had no choice. He did not ask to be born."

"Most men would not think that way," said Jasmine.

"Sadly, true." Li Ming took another drag off his cigarette and let the smoke trail out slowly. "I'll send you some books. At least he—"

A faint smile blossomed upon her lips. "I guess you forget about all those boxes in the house."

"Damn, I'm getting old." He banged his forehead with the heel of his right palm. "It's been eight years…"

In the dim light, Jasmine noticed a twinkle of mirth in his eye.

"Mom, Uncle Li," called out Little Tiger from inside the house. "Come inside. Dinner is ready."

The savory aroma that she'd already detected became stronger as they walked into the house. Jasmine was hungry. The little food she'd had was long gone, and the delicious smell made her stomach grumble even louder.

They stepped into her room, and she stopped dead in her tracks. Her hand flew to cover her opened mouth as she gawked at a table full of dishes. She couldn't remember when they'd had so much food. Jasmine stood perfectly still for a few seconds before she murmured in a shaky voice, "Let's save some for Uncle Linzi."

"There is much more." Bai Long pointed to the kitchen, his eyes sparkling, a smile splitting his face. "After dinner, we need to marinate—"

"I'll help," Little Tiger chirped. The room filled with warm light from the oil lamp burning on the table, and his face lit up like summer sunshine.

She turned to Li Ming. Moisture burned her eyelids, and her chest expanded with warmth and gratitude. For her, food was more valuable than gold. "You…you shouldn't…"

"This is the least I can do. I can't help everyone, but… I'm so out of shape, otherwise, I could bring more." He eased into a chair. "Sit down, everyone. Let's eat. I'm starving."

All of a sudden, Jasmine understood what Li Ming had just talked about—the new social inequality. While ordinary people had so little to eat and some had starved to death, the prominent party officials like him had ample supplies. She fidgeted in her seat and swallowed a lump in her throat, along with the tasty food.

Chapter 42

The Great Famine, which had lasted for three years, was finally over in 1961. Official newspapers had never blamed anything except for the weather. There was no report about how many people had actually perished during that period.

In the next several years, life gradually became normal. Although nobody was rich, few deaths were known. Jasmine and the boys lived a quiet farmer's life. Both Bai Long and she painted whenever they had a break from their assigned jobs. Their landscape paintings were once again acceptable and brought them extra income. They were recognized as "Peasant Artists" in Anning and the surrounding area.

In the summer of 1964, Bai Long and Lili, Linzi's daughter, turned twenty-one and decided to get married. Their affection for each other had been an open secret, and they were constantly teased by the youngsters in the village. Both Jasmine and Linzi were ecstatic. Now the two families would be tied together as one.

The wedding wasn't elaborate, but the entire community came to celebrate, each family bringing a dish or two. Half a dozen tables filled with food stood in the herbalist's front yard, and the aroma permeated the air. A small pile of gifts lay on a side table; most were household items such as a thermos bottle, a washbowl, a few towels, and a blanket—except for a transistor radio, a luxurious thing for an ordinary family to have at the time, especially for those in a remote rural area.

Standing under a large sophora tree with strings of white flowers, the young couple wore new but regular peasant clothes. A cherry red flower was strapped to each of their chests by the same colored fabric ribbon. Hand in hand, they bowed to the crowd, to Jasmine, to Linzi and his wife, and then to a portrait of Chairman Mao hanging on the front door. Rays of warm sunlight shone on their youthful, exuberant faces.

Yaya sang a revolutionary song. Used in every gathering, public or private, "*Dong Fang Hong—the East Is Red*" was the *de facto* national anthem of the communist China. In pigtails, the sixteen-year-old girl was lit up with energy.

The east is red, the sun is rising.
From China comes Chairman Mao.
He strives for people's happiness.
Hurrah, he is people's great savior!
Chairman Mao loves the people.
He is our helmsman to a new China.
Hurrah, he leads us forward!

The villagers clapped and cheered.

Then Little Tiger stood up and read his poem, his eyes bright with childish excitement.

Be my love, forever and ever
Without separation or goodbye
Even when mountains are flattened
And oceans are dried
I promise to love you
Till thunder roars in winter
Snow falls in summer
Till the sun goes around the moon
And sky and earth blend as one

Sitting by the table, Jasmine applauded with everyone else and then fidgeted in her seat. Waves of emotions crashed over her.

She was elated for Bai Long. This once spoiled boy had turned out to be a remarkable young man. He was of medium height and slender but seemed tall as he stood to his full height. He had smooth skin and delicate features like his mother. Jasmine couldn't be happier for him to find an equally fine young woman as his wife. The newlywed couple looked like *jin tong yu nu—a golden boy and a jade maiden*. She wished that his parents were watching him from heaven.

At the same time, Jasmine missed her son. Bai Ge, too, would be twenty-one if he were still alive. She imagined him standing in front of the crowd at his wedding with his goofy grin. Blinking hard to beat back the tears burning in her eyes, she forged a flicker of a smile to match others. *This is a joyous time.* Although Bai Long had never called her anything other than Teacher Bai, he was like a son to her. *I can't ask for a better child.* She was a proud parent.

The particular location compounded her emotions.

Twenty-two years earlier, it was right in this yard that the villagers had thrown an elaborate birthday party for Danny Hardy. She could still see the happy faces in her mind, taste the delicious food in her mouth, hear the heartfelt songs, smell the fragrance of the white flowers, remember the Flying Tiger's fascinating stories...

A few days after the heartwarming celebration, it was in the same yard that the Japanese soldiers had captured the villagers, tortured Jasmine, and slaughtered everyone in the community except for three girls whom the Japanese kept for their pleasures. She could still feel the pain of every single cut on her body, hear the screams and the gunshots, see the villagers' mangled bodies, smell the blood and death...

In the past two decades, she'd tried her best to avoid being here, or at least to pass by as fast as she could manage. Now, a flood of memories rushed back. Pulled by opposite feelings, she was hanging on her composure by a thread. Jasmine lowered her head to hide the emotional roller-coaster. *Don't think about the past. Today is a happy day!* By sheer determination, she held back the tears that flooded her eyes.

Static noise brought her head up. Bai Long stood by the gift table. Turning a knob on the transistor radio, he tried to find a good reception. Once the music of a Peking Opera became loud and clear, the crowd cheered. A sweet smile spread across Jasmine's face, even though tears were still swimming in her eyes. The thoughtful gift was from Li Ming.

Throughout the years, this dear friend had kept in touch with the family and had been sending non-perishable food. Although hunger was no longer a threat, he still insisted. The difference between the remote village and a large metropolis was enormous, and after saying "no" several times, she gratefully accepted his help. She wanted to make her children happy.

Judging from the wild cheers and excitement from the people, she had no doubt that his gift was the best one received.

Jasmine didn't give the newlywed any gift until the crowd thinned. She handed them a drawing book full of members of both families. Tears gathered in Bai Long's eyes when he stared at the pictures of his parents. His lips moved a few times, but no sound came out. He'd been eight when his father was killed and fifteen when his mother and grandma starved to death.

Lili gave Jasmine a big hug after seeing her family pictures. "I had no idea what they looked like." She pointed to her great-grandfather Doctor Wang, Uncle Shitou, and Little Fatty. All had been slaughtered by the Japanese soldiers.

After the wedding, with Jasmine's approval, Bai Long moved in with Lili at Linzi's house instead of the traditional way of taking her with him. Yaya had been studying at a reputable school in Anning for years and couldn't get away from the village fast enough even though it was summer break.

Jasmine noticed the subtle changes. Whenever Yaya came back, she complained about everything in the remote hamlet. "It's so backward! No electricity. No indoor plumbing. The manure stinks. The farm work is too dirty and sweaty…"

Jasmine was dismayed. While she'd become a real villager and had fallen in love with the simple life, the girl, who was born and raised here, had grown distant. She didn't mention it to Linzi. He was so proud of his daughter—at sixteen, Yaya was the only high school educated villager. Sending her to school was one of his privileges as the Party Secretary in the Village.

Chapter 43

Life became calm. And the family had extra funds. Jasmine couldn't help but think about her dream of finding Danny again. He'd been showing up more and more in her dreams. She didn't know if it was triggered by Bai Long's marriage or because life was no longer a constant struggle. She was just thrilled.

When she brought up the subject, Linzi shook his head. "No, you can't!" He was adamant. "America is still our country's enemy. Americans are still called American Devils. It's not safe to search for Major Hardy."

She sighed, disappointment mushrooming inside. She was in her forties now. How long did she have to wait? *Until I have trouble walking and can't search for him anymore?*

"Be patient, Miss Jasmine." He called her Miss Jasmine in private, but in public, she was Comrade Bai, as Comrade was the commonly used term for everyone. "We have to wait for a better time." Reluctantly, he took a folded envelope out of his pocket and handed it to her. "Look, another movement."

It was an official letter from the Party, informing Linzi that three professors were coming to the village in the winter of 1964. It was part of a new campaign—Four Cleanups Movement, which had started in 1963.

She'd read it in the newspapers. The goal was to cleanse politics, economy, organization, and ideology, thus the name Four Clean-ups. Intellectuals had been sent to the countryside to be reeducated by peasants. Why the intellectuals needed re-education was beyond Jasmine. And what kind of education would they get from farmers?

Since the Communists took over the Mainland in 1949, there had been nearly a dozen campaigns; some had enormous negative impacts, resulting in extreme terror and millions of deaths. Her senses jumped to alert.

"Will you host one of them?" asked Linzi. "Professor Lin is a woman."

Still on guard, Jasmine nodded. She had an extra room.

———————

Lin Ling was the head of the Department of Literature at Yunnan University in Kunming, the capital of Yunnan Province. Trim and austere, she was in her mid-forties with short hair and glasses. "Oh, I love this." She entered the room Jasmine had prepared for her and stepped closer to a landscape painting on the wall. "Bai Wenwu?" She read the signature. "I've never heard his name. I love his style. Elegant. Gorgeous!"

Jasmine grinned, the lines around her eyes crinkling. Before she opened her mouth, Little Tiger said, "It's my mom. She did it."

"Your mom?" The professor was visibly surprised. She turned to Jasmine. "You painted this picture?"

She gave a small nod.

"To tell the truth, I didn't expect this. Well, that's why we, the educators, need to be reeducated by peasants."

Jasmine grinned again. She didn't say that she'd been educated at a college in Chungking, and that her favorite teacher was an American. Every time she thought about Mr. Peterson, she wondered what kind of life she would have had if she'd said yes to his proposal. No doubt, life would have been much more comfortable. Most likely, she'd have become a renowned artist. But then, she would never have met Danny, a man worth her love even twenty years after his death.

"Bai Wenwu is her pen name," explained Little Tiger. "My grandpa's name is Bai Wen, and my grand uncle's name is Bai Wu."

"Oh, good. *Wen wu shuang quan—good at both books and martial arts.* A perfect name."

"My pen name will be Bai Long Hu—White Dragon and Tiger."

"Your pen name?"

"He's great at writing," explained Jasmine, a prideful note seeping into her voice. "One day, he'll be an author."

The boy whipped around and dashed out of the room. Seconds later, he came back with a pile of notebooks and handed them to the professor.

Sitting at the table, Lin Ling leaned closer to the oil lamp, hunched over a notebook, and started to read. Twenty minutes later, she lifted her head. Pushing the glasses up the bridge of her nose, she said, "Very impressive. Which school did you attend?"

"Here."

"Here?"

A goofy grin played on his lips. "Mom taught me. I've never attended any school."

"And he read most of those books." Jasmine pointed to the row of boxes along the wall.

Lin Ling's lips parted, but she was speechless.

Later at dinner, the professor brought up the topic again. "I've been teaching literature for over twenty years and had thousands of students. Frankly speaking, I was very impressed by Little Tiger's work. He's only fourteen. And knowing he has no formal education, I still can't fathom… He has a gift."

Jasmine grinned from ear to ear, unable to contain her delight and pride.

Through her thick glasses, Lin Ling looked at the boy and then turned to Jasmine. "If it's okay with you, I'd like to take your son as my student. Unofficially, of course… But I want to offer him whatever I know."

"That's wonderful. Thank you!" replied Jasmine, folding her left palm over her right fist and raising them before her chest.

Little Tiger needed no prodding. He stood up, clicked his heels together, and snapped a crisp salute.

Both women laughed.

"I don't know what to tell him," said Jasmine. "Kowtow would be the proper way, but it's too old fashion. Young people don't do it anymore. But what is the correct way now?"

"It doesn't matter." Professor Lin was in a buoyant mood. "I'm just happy to accept an extraordinary student."

For the next three months, Professor Lin taught Little Tiger in the evenings. Even after she left, she kept communicating with the boy by mail.

Another movement, the Campaign to Destroy the Four Olds and Cultivate the Four News, began in August 1966. The Four Olds were: customs, culture, habits, and ideas. An article in *People's Daily*, the most important state-run newspaper, described the old things as anti-proletarian that had poisoned the minds of the public for thousands of years and should be swept away. The traditional culture was responsible for China's economic backwardness and needed to be reformed. Four News—new socialist customs, culture, habits, and ideas—must be established.

Almost all names of businesses, stores, and streets were changed from their original names to something like "Defending Chairman Mao Street," "Red Guard Road," "Following the Revolution Store," and so forth, aligning with the Communist Party's ideology. People also changed their given names to contain words like Red, East, Revolution... Even this village, Tao Hua Cun—Village of Peach Blossoms, was now called Tao Hong Cun—Village of Peach Red, for red represented revolution and goodness.

Jasmine read the newspapers in shock and horror. Red Guards—a revolutionary youth organization—broke into people's homes and historical sites to destroy paintings, books, furniture, and statues, all of which were viewed as part of the Four Olds.

"Linzi, help us to hide the books and the paintings in the cave.

Please!" she implored. Although the village was isolated from the outside chaos, she had to prepare for the worst. The cave was still a secret hideout.

"Of course," was the villager's answer.

Chapter 44

In the early fall, a small group of Red Guards from Anning made their way to the village. They didn't stop. Instead, they kept going up the mountains.

When Jasmine heard it, she knew instinctively that their targets were the statues. "Quickly," she told Little Tiger and Bai Long, "we have to stop them."

At forty-seven and with a slight limp, she was much slower. By the time she reached Angel's Pass, her boys had already started an argument with the Red Guards. There were four young men and three girls, either college students or high schoolers, all in olive-green military uniforms with red armbands. They looked like kids to Jasmine, but they were mean kids. A fierce exchange had broken out. Their faces were infused with hot colors. A portly boy picked up a large rock and threw it at the Angel. The loud thump broke Jasmine's heart.

She limped forward. Out of breath, she stood in front of the sculpture with open arms.

A lanky boy and a petite girl aimed again with the rocks in their hands. "Move away," barked the young woman, her short hair bouncing around her reddened face. "This is part of the Four Olds. If you protect it, you're against our great leader Chairman Mao."

"You're a Counter-revolutionary," roared the stocky student. "We'll fight all hardline Counter-revolutionaries to the death."

"We'll protect Chairman Mao and Maoism," bellowed the boy with the rock, sending a wad of saliva arching through the air.

Anger slammed into Jasmine, immobilizing her for a second. She quaked from a vast array of emotions too complicated to name. *How do I reason with a group of rabid youths?* There was madness in their eyes.

"*Gun kai—Piss off!*" The portly student muttered a foul curse and collected another rock. "If you don't, we'll destroy you with the old stuff. *Gun kai!*" His eyes were fiercely aglow.

"How dare you! My mom is a heroine," bellowed Little Tiger, stepping closer to her. "She—"

All Red Guards shouted the popular slogans, cutting him off. Their voices echoed throughout the canyon. They punched their hands with Chairman Mao's Little Red Books high in the air, and spittle flew from some of their mouths. Their enthusiasm and conviction were evident and genuine.

Insanity escalated with each violent outburst, finally sliding out of control, and the infuriated young man tossed the rock at Jasmine.

Little Tiger flung himself over her. So did the elder brother. The rock hit the back of Bai Long's head.

"Are you okay?" asked Jasmine, concern in her voice.

"I'm…all right."

She turned him around and checked. There was a lump; blood matted his hair around it. Her heart tightened. Pain, rage, and frustration bombarded her.

Little Tiger rolled up his sleeves. Spitting out a swear word, he took a giant step. His hands clenched into fists, ready to strike.

Jasmine hurried to pull him back. "Stop!" She gripped the arms of both brothers. After years of hard labor, her boys were strong. Little Tiger was almost a head taller than most of the students. But she knew that if they hurt any of the Red Guards, they would be sent to jail, and jail was no place for her children. She would use all her power to prevent such a violent outcome.

Under the blistering glare of the brothers, the Red Guards backed up a few steps. Fists in front of their bodies, however, they were ready to die for the ideology. Both brothers fought to extricate themselves from Jasmine's hold. Their eyes seethed with fury. She held on tightly, refusing to let them go.

The gangling boy paled. A muscle in his chin twitched. A dribble of sweat ran down between his eyes onto the bridge of his nose, and fretfully he wiped his face.

Jasmine's anger was replaced by sympathy. Throughout the country, millions of youths had pledged their loyalty to Chairman Mao and worshipped him above everything. Many were enveloped in a trance of excitement over revolution. She decided to use their language: *Yi qi ren zhi dao, huan zhi qi ren zhi shen—Beat someone at their own game* was ancient wisdom.

Head high, shoulders squared, she stood with grace and confidence. She said with a calm voice, "Don't you remember what Chairman Mao told us? I'm sure everyone here can recite *the Three Main Rules of Discipline and the Eight Points for Attention*. Number one, speak politely. Number five? Do not hit or swear at people."

She paused for the message to sink in before continuing, "Our leader instructed us to rely on reason rather than violence. You're his guards. You should listen to his words. He told us to 'seek truth from facts.'" Jasmine quoted a few more of Mao's mottos. Like everyone, she'd read the Little Red Book, which was required study. The entire country was expected to follow Maoism like a new religion.

The gangly boy looked at her with awe.

"Okay, let me tell you the fact about the statues."

"No," shrieked the petite girl. "She's trying to poison our minds. We mustn't listen to her nonsense."

The other Red Guards agreed. "We can't allow—"

"Poison your mind with what?" said Linzi, reaching the gorge with several villagers, including Big Chen. "With Chairman Mao's sayings?" He panted. He was dressed in his old People's Volunteer Army uniform, two medals pinned to his chest. Perspiration flowed in tiny rivers down his face.

"Young woman, what you just said is Counter-revolutionary."

Big Chen wiped the sweat from his forehead with his right wrist, a hoe in his left hand. A sneer pulled his lips back over his teeth like a watchdog. "I'm just a layman. But I know that much. Ask your friends."

"I didn't…I didn't mean…" The girl shrank, the skin tightening across her narrow face, a hand flying to her mouth. She took a quick step backward.

"I'm sure it's just a slip of the tongue." Jasmine lifted her arm. Nowadays, errors like that could have dire consequences. It could end a person's career, or even send him or her to prison.

"Okay," said Linzi, turning to the cowered student. "You should be grateful. Your life has been spared by her."

The girl nodded, shrinking even further. All her fellow Red Guards were quiet.

"I'm the Party Secretary in the Village. Now, let Comrade Bai tell you the story of the statues." Linzi stood with his feet planted slightly apart, hands on his hips. He was short, but his upright posture bespoke authority. His gaze swept the group. "Good. It is decided."

Chapter 45

▬ ▬ ▬ ▬ ▬ ▬ ▬

"I'm going to write a book," announced Little Tiger at dinner the day after the incident, "about the Flying Tiger."

"About Danny Hardy?" asked Jasmine, unsure what she'd heard.

"Yes! I've always enjoyed the stories you told me. I want to write them down. To tell the truth about the Flying Tigers. Their courage. The sacrifices they made. Did you see those Red Guards? Some of them were really moved."

"Too dangerous." Bai Long shook his head. At age twenty-three, he was a lot more mature. Although he was married, once a week, he joined Jasmine and Little Tiger for dinner. "If anyone finds out, you'll be labeled as a Counter-revolutionary."

"I don't give a damn. I just want to write. It's been on my mind for a while. I was going to tell Professor Lin. Too bad, she stopped writing..." Disappointment laced his voice.

"She might be too busy. She's the head of the department. But I support you. It's an excellent idea. I wish I'd thought of it earlier. We should record that history."

Using chopsticks, Bai Long picked up a string of noodles, his eyebrows pulled together. "What good will it be if you can never publish it?"

"No one knows the future. Who knows what the world will be like in ten years? Twenty years? Things have changed so much in my lifetime."

211

"It'll take time to write it, anyway. It's not like I'll finish a book in a few days. Worse comes to worst…" Little Tiger made a face and lowered his voice. "Have you heard *shou chao ben—underground handwritten manuscript*? I'll—"

"That's too dangerous. We'll wait." In the dim light from the oil lamp, Jasmine's eyes glowed, translucent with her hopes and dreams. "Xiao Hu, your father would be so proud of you!"

"In that case, I've got an even better idea." Bai Long paused for drama. He slurped a mouthful of noodles and made sucking noises. When he lifted his head, one corner of his mouth twisted upward.

"What?" Little Tiger took the bait.

"If you beg us nicely,"—he pointed to Jasmine and then to himself—"*Bai Lao Shi* and I could draw pictures for your book. The front cover and—"

"Please!"

"It'll be a family project." Jasmine reached out and squeezed their arms. "Don't tell anyone. Not Even Uncle Linzi."

Both young men looked at her in disbelief. "Uncle Linzi?" Bai Long stammered. Even after marriage, he still used the old way of addressing him.

"Oh, I trust him with my life. But why involve him? He can't help us with this project. The less he knows, the safer he'll be. We must protect the people we love."

The young men nodded. Their faces turned serious.

In this troubled time, Jasmine felt a sudden lifting of her spirit. "We'll wait for the right time." In the back of her mind, though, she was worried that the day would not come anytime soon. Perhaps, not even in her lifetime. Things might get worse.

———

Things indeed got worse. Destroying the Four Olds quickly descended into attacks on people. In the fall of 1966, Chairman Mao appeared atop Tiananmen eight times to greet thousands of young people from all over the country. Wearing an olive-green military uniform, the type favored by Red Guards, he endorsed the actions of the Red Guards and praised their rebellion. Facing the Red Guards' violence, the national police chief said it was "of little consequence" if they were beating "bad people" to death.

The Cultural Revolution was launched. Its stated goal was to preserve communism by purging remnants of capitalist and traditional elements such as the Four Olds and to fully impose Maoism as the ideology in the country.

"Chairman Mao is our Commander-in-Chief, and we're his Red Guards. Who can stop us?" stated a Red Guard leader. "First, we'll make China Maoist. Then we'll help the poor working class of other countries... And eventually, we'll take over the whole universe."

Chairman Mao identified groups of people as Enemies of the State, and the Red Guards followed him like mad dogs. All over the nation, they accused countless individuals. Who were the "bad guys"? Anyone could be! Anyone they suspected. Anyone who criticized or expressed the slightest complaint about the Party.

Jasmine couldn't even keep up with the news. One day a person was Revolutionary, the next day, he could be labeled as Counter-revolutionary. Intellectuals such as writers, professors, teachers, and school officials suffered the brunt of these attacks.

Party officials weren't immune. In fact, many top party officials such as Liu Shaoqi, Deng Xiaoping, and Peng Dehuai were attacked by the Red Guards. They were denounced as Traitors and Capitalist Roaders.

Jasmine was confused. How could so many people, especially top Communist leaders, turn out to be the Enemies of the State? Liu Shaoqi was the Chairman of the People's Republic of China, Deng Xiaoping was the Secretariat of the Communist Party, and Peng Dehuai was Defense Minister.

Later, she saw Lin Ling's name in the newspaper, and her heart squeezed in her chest. The head of the Department of Literature at Yunnan University was denounced—and that explained why she'd stopped communicating with Little Tiger. Like other intellectuals, she was named as *Chou Lao Jiu—Stinking Old Ninth*. Educated people were looked down upon, and they were at the end of "Nine

Black Categories"—Landlords, Rich farmers, Counter-revolutionaries, Bad influences, Rightists, Traitors, Spies, Capitalist Roaders,
and Intellectuals.

What about Li Ming? As a party official at the provincial level,
would he be in trouble? Jasmine hadn't heard from him since September, even after sending him several letters. In his last letter, he
mentioned that he'd been busy dealing with the chaotic situation
created by the Red Guards. Schools and colleges were closed; fac-
tories and plants stopped producing; everyone was participating in
study sessions.

"No one answered," said Little Tiger. He'd just returned from
Anning. It was now the end of 1966. He'd been going down the
mountain every two weeks to call Li Ming. "I tried many times." He
took off his hat and shook off the snow. His cheeks were flushed by
the freezing wind. "*Da Zi Bao—Big-character Posters* are everywhere
in town. In two days, I've seen several Public Struggle Sessions."

"Where did you see it?" asked Jasmine.

"In the town center. Hundreds of people were there. Maybe a
couple of thousand. I don't know for sure. It's crazy."

"What happened?" asked Bai Long.

"Poor men and women were forced to wear tall cone-shaped
hats. Others had big cardboards hung in front of their chests." Little
Tiger made a gesture to show the size of the sign, fear in his eyes.

"What was written on it?"

"Down with so-and-so. His or her name was crossed by bloody
red lines. They were forced to confess their crimes in front of the
crowd. If they didn't, they were scolded. And if they still didn't plead
guilty, they were beaten."

Jasmine sucked in a breath.

"Would this happen to Uncle Li?" Bai Long asked, his forehead
creased with worry lines.

The disturbing thought was uppermost in her mind. "It shouldn't,"
she stated firmly, trying to convince herself more than the others.
"He's done so much for his party. He almost died." Yet, a tight knot
formed in the pit of her stomach and then cinched down.

Chapter 46

Jasmine was on her way to Chungking, almost a thousand miles away from the village. The news had gotten worse, and the country seemed in total chaos. She hadn't been able to get in touch with Li Ming for months. By January 1967, she couldn't stand it anymore. She had to find out what had happened to him.

Both Little Tiger and Bai Long loved Uncle Li and wanted to come along. But the family couldn't afford to pay double, and Linzi had already made an exception for one person to leave the village. Although it was winter, and there wasn't much to do in the fields, the villagers, like everyone in the country, had to attend political study sessions. Reluctantly the young men let her go alone, but Little Tiger insisted on escorting her to Anning, where she could take a train to Kunming. From there, she took a series of buses to Chungking. It was the same route she'd made with Bai Ge two decades earlier. A week later, Jasmine arrived at her destination. Many public transportations had either stopped running or ran at a reduced frequency.

The layout of the city seemed unchanged from 1948 when she'd last seen it. But slogans like "Down with the hardline Counter-revolutionaries!" "Long live our greatest leader Chairman Mao!" and "Long live our unbeatable Communist Party!" were everywhere. Almost all walls of all buildings were covered with Big-character

Posters. By now, this was a familiar scene. Every city or town she'd passed unveiled the same political turbulence.

It was sunny, but the low winter sun held no heat. Despite the cold weather, lines of people stood by the sides of the streets. Everyone was carrying the Little Red Book—a pocket-sized collection of quotations from Chairman Mao. A cacophony of songs praising "our beloved Chairman Mao" echoed throughout the area. The crowd sang along, then cheered and clapped.

Several trucks drove through the city as slow as snails, displaying the Counter-revolutionaries standing in the back of the vehicles. Each had a tall cone-shaped hat strapped on his head and a piece of cardboard hanging in front of his chest. On a loudspeaker, a woman's high-pitched voice shouted the revolutionary slogans and denounced the people by name.

"What's going to happen to them?" Jasmine asked a nearby woman in a gray cotton coat and hat.

"To be denounced at the Public Struggle Session, of course." The woman stared at her beneath arched eyebrows. "Where are you from?"

"The countryside."

"That explains it. These meetings have taken place almost every day for months now."

Jasmine looked at the people on the truck. Most of them were middle-aged or older and looked like educated people who might work for the government or teach at universities. She was surprised to see a young man amongst the older generations. He was probably in his mid-twenties, thin, sallow skin with a purple bruise on the left side of his forehead. Dressed in a blue cotton jacket and black trousers that were too thin for the chilly day, he was shivering. Fear glazed his small slanted eyes. One lens of his eyeglasses was missing.

"He's just a kid," she mumbled to herself. What could he have done? If Bai Ge were still alive, he would have been a similar age. Jasmine had always felt a special feeling toward men of her son's age.

"He's not just any kid," said the woman in the gray cotton coat. She leaned closer. "He's a bastard child." She lowered her voice as if

216

it were a secret, which apparently wasn't the case. "A Jap's bastard!"

Jasmine was stunned. "A Jap's—?"

"Yes! His mother… That poor woman. She was gang-raped by the Japs during the war."

"Then how come—?"

"He has the enemy's blood. That poor woman," she repeated. "Truly stupid! How dumb could she be? She should've aborted him."

Grief and sympathy sawed through Jasmine. If her son were still alive, he would have been labeled as the enemy's child. He would have suffered the same ill-fate as this young man. At that moment, she almost felt relieved that Bai Ge wasn't alive. Humiliation and injustice would kill both of them.

It occurred to her that even if she'd had Danny's son, the boy would be in the same shoes—an American's child would be labeled as an enemy's child. American soldiers were called American Devils, just like Japanese Devils.

Such realization chilled her to the bone. *Americans helped us! They gave their lives for our freedom!* She lowered her head as if the thought weighed her down.

A woman's ear-piercing scream perforated the air and jerked Jasmine's head up.

A middle-aged woman ran along with the truck. Her hair was filthy and in a mass, and her face was covered with dirt and dust. Calling the young man's name, she waved her arms wildly as if she wanted to stop the vehicle. It was clear that she wasn't in her right frame of mind. No sane person would dare to do what she was doing.

The young man on the truck looked up briefly before lowering his head. At that moment, Jasmine detected tears in his eyes. *Poor mother. Poor son!*

The loudspeaker kept shouting slogans: "Long live our greatest leader!" "Long live our great savior Chairman Mao!"

Jasmine sucked in a breath when the deranged woman passed. Although she was in her mid-forties, the resemblance was undeniable. *Is it possible?*

The image of a teenage girl being dragged away from Doctor

Wang's front yard by a group of Japanese soldiers appeared in Jasmine's mind. She cringed. Linzi had told her that Ding Xiang had survived the massacre. The girl was the other survivor in the village. She'd been gang-raped by the soldiers but set free by a sympathetic Japanese translator. Later, General Bai and Birch had helped her to start a new life in Chungking. Was it possible that this woman was Ding Xiang?

Jasmine felt shaken as if she were looking at herself in a mirror. This woman's fate could have been hers. She staggered away. What could she do? She had no means to help this unfortunate soul. In a matter of minutes, she felt she'd aged ten years.

Chapter 47

▬ ▬ ▬ ▬ ▬ ▬ ▬

Jasmine had never seen Li Ming's house, except in photos. It was a one-story gray brick building tucked into a grove of magnolia trees in a quiet neighborhood. An ornately carved archway reminded her of the place owned by her uncle and aunt. Most likely, this house had been possessed by a wealthy man in the old society, confiscated by the Communist Party after the liberation, and assigned to him.

She knocked on the door, softly at first and then harder. No one answered. Where had the family gone?

Big-character Posters were mounted all over the outside wall. Across the nation, this type of handwritten poster was a popular propaganda tool to rabidly denounce a person. In recent years, being attacked in Big-character Posters was enough to end one's career even without a shred of evidence of a crime.

Jasmine stepped closer to the wall. Her heart skipped a beat when she saw Li Ming's name—it was crossed by bloody red lines as if he were a criminal that was sentenced to death. Quickly, she scanned the content.

All had the same tone and a similar message. They condemned Li Ming and called him names—Traitor, Capitalist Roader, Counter-revolutionary, Enemy of the People, Enemy of the State…

Li Ming was a lieutenant in the Nationalist Army—an enemy of the Communists. He sneaked into the Communist guerillas and became a member of the Party. But deep down, he's a Nationalist. He's a spy and informer. That's why he survived the Nationalist Secret Police's jail.

Comrades, do you know how many people survived during the prison break? Three! How come all those valiant Revolutionary Martyrs were killed, but those three survived? Don't you think it's suspicious?

Well, your suspicion is right on the mark. The answer is simple—They survived because the Secret Police wanted them to. They're spies and traitors. The Nationalists designed the scheme so that the three could live among us and infiltrate our party. They're waiting for the Nationalist Army to invade the Mainland and reclaim our motherland as the capitalist society.

For years, Li Ming has criticized our party. He's stained our party's reputation. Along with his co-conspirators, he's attempted to destroy our country. Look at the letter he sent to the Central Committee of the Communist Party, and you'll see how much he hates our supreme communist ideology.

Fortunately, our leader Chairman Mao is great, our party is unbeatable, and our people's eyes are sharp—we found the Counter-revolutionary, discovered his scheme, and snipped his plot in the bud.

Down with Traitor Li Ming!

Down with the hardline Counter-revolutionary!

Long live our great party!

Long live our great savior Chairman Mao!

Jasmine stared at the poster with a mix of incredulity and rage. They had wrongfully accused Li Ming—everything was upside down. Trembling with anger, she read his letter to the Central Committee of the Communist Party regarding the Eliminate Sparrows Campaign and the subsequent Great Famine.

Li Ming had been courteous in his letter and addressed the recipients as "Dearest Central Committee of the Communist Party." Citing scientific data about the effect of the Eliminate Sparrows Campaign, he pointed out that the Great Famine might be the result of this ill-planned movement, which had severely affected ecological balance across the land. His conclusion was sound and logical. His criticisms were constructive: "Before we make any important policy in the future, we should do thorough research. For the sake of our people, our party, our country, let's learn from our mistakes. Let's not take on seemingly good ideas without science to support them." His overall tone was positive. In the end, he implored the Party to lead the people to become a strong and prosperous country.

Jasmine couldn't understand why such a letter was used as proof to label him as Counter-revolutionary. And who had leaked the letter? It was addressed to the highest level of the Communist Party, not to the public. But if they could call him a traitor, then nothing would surprise her.

How can a man who has fought all his life for his country become the Enemy of the State? How can his own comrades turn on him?

Jasmine's ability to comprehend the world seemed to decline as the madness escalated. A sick feeling clutched her stomach as she silently asked the question: *Where is Li Ming now?*

———

Jasmine stopped everyone who passed and asked the same question, "Do you know where to find Li Ming?"

Nobody answered; many simply walked around her without making eye contact. Finally, a trim man with a full head of graying hair walked over. "Who are you?"

"I'm his...cousin," she replied. "Where is he? Where is his wife? And his son? Tell me if you know. Please!"

"Don't you know? She divorced him several months ago. She made him sign the paper while he was locked up." Anguish darkened his tone and eyes.

"Locked up?" Jasmine's breath stopped. "He's in jail?"

"The Red Guards have him."

"Where?"

He pointed to a four-story building not that far away. "He's in that school—"

221

"School?"

"All classes have been canceled."

"How do I find him?"

"Are you sure you—"

"Please tell me!"

"He's on the fourth floor." He leaned closer and lowered his voice to a confidential pitch. "Li Ming is a good man. He helped many during the Great Famine. But don't mention this to anyone." Panic appeared on his bony face as he glanced around. No one was there. "You...you don't know me, okay?"

With that, he disappeared faster than Jasmine could thank him.

Chapter 48

It was easy to find the classroom. Even in the hallway, Jasmine could hear shouting and beating. Following the noise, she tiptoed closer and peeked through a small glass window on the door.

The classroom was well lit by overhead fluorescent lights and the sunlight pouring in from a window. There was no furniture except for a desk. Behind it sat a moon-faced man in a muddy-green Mao suit. He was in his fifties and had a double chin, a broad nose, and flat dark eyes. It was clear that he was in charge. Two men squatted in the middle of the room. Six young men and women with Red Guards armbands surrounded them.

Although she could only see his back, she knew one of the two was Li Ming. A young man twisted his right arm behind his back while a woman pressed her palm on his left shoulder. His left arm had been damaged years earlier during the torture. Jasmine strained her ears to hear the conversation in the room.

"Confess!" A Red Guard kicked the man next to Li Ming. "You set Li Ming and the other two free because they're traitors. Spies! They've tried to destroy our party, our motherland. Admit it!" Another young man hit him in the face. "You know our policy: lenient treatment to those who confess; severe punishment to those who remain stubborn. Tell the truth!"

Jasmine flinched. She couldn't stand watching another man's torment.

The man lifted his hands above his head in surrender and stood up. His face was a mess—split lips, bloody nose, swollen eyes.

Jasmine almost fell backward, reeling from shock. She knew him—medium build and height, rectangular face, sharp eyes. It was Tan Yin, the Nationalist Secret Police officer who had forced her to watch Li Ming's torture. He was now in his fifties instead of thirties, but she could clearly see the resemblance.

What's going on? Why is he here? Was he the sympathetic officer who set the prisoners free? She regretted not having asked Li Ming the name of the Secret Police. She'd never imagined that she might have known the person.

"May I smoke?" Tan Yin asked.

The leader gave a clipped nod. A Red Guard handed him a cigarette and a box of matches. With a shaky hand, Tan Yin lit the cigarette, took a long drag, and exhaled slowly. "This is karma." He grimaced as pain showed on his face. "I used to interrogate people. I tried my best to break them, no matter what it took."

Jasmine was on pins and needles. *Li Ming's fate is sealed. The Secret Police won't say anything in his favor.* Li Ming would be labeled as a traitor forever. No one would think that Tan Yin had given a false confession. It was clear that everyone wanted him to point the finger at Li Ming.

She'd saved him once during the Nanking Massacre. But what could she do now? Her mind raced at full speed for an answer.

"I assumed they were guilty—the Communists. After all, they were sent to me as political prisoners. I grew up hearing the Communists were bandits. They were evil, and they were going to destroy our nation. Well, this was how I thought—by hurting a small number of bad individuals, I might save hundreds or thousands or even the country." Tan Yin talked without removing the cigarette while he paced back and forth in the room.

Nobody stopped him. They were all waiting for his statement.

"Truth is, it was people like him"—he pointed to Li Ming—"who moved me and educated me. I started having doubts. I began to see from a different perspective. When I saw the body of an eight-year-old boy, I knew I had to do something. Freeing the prisoners wasn't politically motivated. It was because of my awakened humanity. I didn't want to work for a government that showed no mercy, even to a child."

"You're lying," roared one of the Red Guards. "Be honest," bellowed another young man, punching his right fist in the air.

Tan Yin sucked in the smoke. "I understand why you hate me, why you don't trust me. Yes, I worked for the old government. I had the blood of many Communists on my hands. The few people I saved cannot wash away all the blood. I'm paying my due now."

He stood with his back to the window and looked down at his hands, the butt of the cigarette glowing between his fingers. Rays of sunlight streamed through the window behind him, and shadows fell across his bony face. "But I don't understand how you can treat someone like Li Ming this way. He's been through hell. For your party! He's your party's hero. He's alive because of pure luck, not because he's a traitor. Why the hell do you want me to hurt your own hero?" In a desperate voice, he added, "I didn't free traitors; I freed Communists. If Li Ming and the other two had died that day, they would have been labeled as Revolutionary Martyrs!"

"You're a diehard Counter-revolutionary. This is not—" bawled the moon-faced leader. His palm slammed onto the surface of the desk.

"Down with the hardline Counter-revolutionary," shouted the Red Guards, punching their fists high in the air. "We swear to defend Maoism to the death! Long live the rebellious spirit of the revolution! Long live the great Chinese Communist Party!"

Several young men advanced toward Tan Yin.

"I'm not done." Lifting his right hand, Tan Yin remained a black silhouette outlined against the sunlight pouring through the window. "If you want a true confession, then let me finish." Taking one last puff, he dropped the butt and crushed it on the floor. He wiped the blood from his mouth and stood taller. His head held high as if he were a proud officer once again. Staring at Li Ming, he said, "I'm truly sorry." Then, without forewarning, he leaned backward. The moment he disappeared out the window, Jasmine heard Li Ming shout, "I forgive you!"

She put her hands over her mouth to prevent herself from crying out loud.

Chapter 49

Chaos ensued. People ran toward the door. Jasmine stepped aside in time to avoid being trampled. She waited until everyone was gone and quietly stepped inside. Li Ming stood at the window. He slouched against the sill as if the weight of the world were upon his shoulders.

Her heart tightened in her chest. Just as she stepped closer, Li Ming put his right hand on the windowsill, and his upper body leaned forward.

"*Li Ming Ge*," she said in her gentlest voice, her hand on his arm. "It's me, Jasmine. Don't…"

He spun around, eyes wide with surprise. Instantly, his haggard face lit up. "You must have radar or something… You always show up when I'm in a life-or-death situation?" he joked, but the pain he was trying to hide was evident.

She was looking at him for the first time since 1960. He was rail-thin. Hollow and unshaven, his face had an unhealthy pallor, and his left cheek was swollen. His forehead was etched with deep lines, and gaudy purple bruises covered his forehead and neck. Blood was still dripping from his nose.

The sight of Li Ming, the pale reflection of the man he'd once been, wrenched a cry from her. Her heart ached for him. How could his comrades treat him this way? "You're my Big Brother. Of course, I know." She concealed her grief and dredged up a feeble smile.

He turned to look at the street. A crowd gathered around Tan Yin's body. "Did you...?"

Jasmine gave an almost imperceptible nod.

"He was one of the Nationalist Secret Police." Li Ming swallowed; his features reflected the turmoil within—shock, outrage, sadness, regret. "Can you believe it? He came to my rescue. The man who participated in my torture saved me. Twice! He set the prisoners free, but his good deed was questioned and accused in the worst possible way. If he'd tried to save his own skin as so many have done, I'd be dead."

"I was worried. I thought..."

Weighted down by guilt, his expression turned contrite. "Me, too."

Overwhelmed with emotions too complicated to define, Jasmine remained silent. After a moment, she murmured, "He was the one who made me—"

"I know. He told me. He asked me for forgiveness."

"Did you?"

"No. I told him I could forgive him for everything except for making you watch. I couldn't forgive him for that. But the moment he leaned back, I regretted—"

"I heard it."

"I hope he heard it, too." He started to cough.

Jasmine patted his back.

"You know, he told me his brother was a fighter pilot. You won't believe it. His brother was shot by his friends to save him from being burned alive."

Eyes wide, she asked, "Tan Hu? His brother's name?"

"I didn't ask."

Most likely, Jasmine thought, Tan Yin's brother was Tan Hu, the pilot whom Meng Hu and Danny had shot together.

"You would never guess who was in charge of the investigation." Anger, betrayal, and hurt burned in his bloodshot eyes. "My contact. The one I protected!"

"He must've known—"

"He knows."

"Then why…?"

"I'm not sure. I can't figure it out. He was thrown in jail five months after my arrest. I heard he went through a hard time. Perhaps he thought it was me? How could he think I gave him up five months later? Who knows what he thinks? Sometimes, people push others down just to keep afloat. By finding a Counter-revolutionary, he showed his loyalty to the Party. It's a crazy world now."

Jasmine cursed silently. She wasn't surprised, though. In recent years, disgruntled individuals obtained newfound power over the people they bore grudges against simply because the act of denouncing someone could easily land the person in jail or worse. The whole thing was too ironic, too poignant. The one who had hurt Li Ming eventually saved him, but the one who owed Li Ming his life doubted him and accused him of a crime he hadn't committed.

"Everything is upside down. I am a traitor." He looked crestfallen. "But I'm a traitor of the Nationalists, not the Communists. I left the Nationalist Army to join the Communist Party. If I'd never—"

She put a hand over his mouth. "What about the other two? They were not here—"

"One passed away three years ago. Heart attack. Lucky him. He didn't have to go through so much shame and unfair accusation. The other one…" His Adam's apple rose and fell as he worked to swallow. "He hanged himself two months ago. Couldn't handle being called a traitor after all he'd been through. I'm the only survivor."

Jasmine tightened her grip on his upper arm and moved closer to him. "Can you leave?"

"Yes." A self-deprecating snigger turned his lips down. "They let me go. You see, Tan Yin saved me again. I've been locked up for months." Li Ming swayed and coughed again.

"Don't talk." She looped his right arm around her shoulders, and with her left hand around his waist, she supported him. "Let's go home."

"Jasmine, I'm so glad you came to see me. But get the hell out of here. Leave this place. You're too…pure-hearted for this ugly, dirty place. Go back to the village. It's a safe haven. I pray it'll stay a sanctuary forever."

Jasmine shook her head. She didn't tell him about the statue incident. She didn't want to say that the village might not be a haven for long. "Let's go home," she repeated.

Chapter 50

—————

"What a mess! How could she do this to you?" said Jasmine, fighting the hot surge of anger.

Li Ming's house was in disarray. A wooden chair lay sideways. Her wedding gift to them, the painting of a pair of colorful birds soaring to a blue sky, lay on the floor with muddy footprints on top of it. Trash, old newspapers, and pieces of broken china were scattered everywhere.

There was no food in the house, except for half a bag of rice. But Jasmine couldn't cook it since there were no coals. She had to hurry outside to buy steamed buns. "How could she leave you? How could Li Dong go with her? He's old enough—"

"I was upset at first," Li Ming admitted. They were sitting at his dining table. He took a small bite of the bun. Although he was thin, he didn't seem to have an appetite. "But I understand now. She didn't have much choice—"

"Of course, she had a choice. She chose to leave you when you were in trouble, when you needed her the most. For better or worse, stay together. Isn't that what a marriage is about? You saved her when she was in trouble."

Jasmine could feel the blood in her veins warm. Before the Communists took over, Huang Yun had been a reporter for a pro-Communist newspaper. Even though she wasn't a member of the party, her articles raised red flags. If it weren't for Li Ming to warn her, she would have been arrested by the Nationalists. After the liberation, she wrote an article about him and pursued him for a couple of years.

His silence invited her to continue: "When you had power and status, she pursued you; now that you're in trouble, she betrayed you. I guess she believes *Fu qi ben shi tong lin niao; Da nan lin tou ge zi fei—Couples are birds in a forest; they fly in separate directions when disaster strikes.* How can you be so calm, and so forgiving?"

"She was trying to save our son."

His statement rendered Jasmine speechless. Sitting across the table, she just stared at him.

"You know our culture." Li Ming's mouth twisted sideways; anguish darkened his eyes. "What kind of future would Li Dong have if he stayed here? He'd be the object of scorn. He'd have a hard time finding a job. How would he make a living? He'd be the son of a Counter-revolutionary for the rest of his life. I believe Huang Yun left me to protect him. Between our son and me, she chose our son. How can I blame her?"

Jasmine's anger and contempt gave way to sympathy and sadness. For thousands of years, the family of a criminal would be labeled as bad as the guilty person. They would be looked down upon and sometimes punished for the crime for which they had no knowledge. *Zhu lian jiu zu—When a man committed a crime, the whole clan was implicated*—had applied to the worst capital crimes. The "clan" included family members, relatives, friends, and colleagues. This mentality had become worse in recent years. Chairman Mao identified groups of people as Enemies of the Revolution. Their children were singled out, treated as second-class citizens, and forced to draw a line between themselves and their parents. No matter how hard they worked, they were not rewarded for their efforts.

Jasmine's compassion for Li Ming had prompted her to berate his ex-wife. She hadn't considered alternative reasons. "Still, she shouldn't have ruined the place," she murmured.

"By destroying the place,"—he took another bite of the bun but had trouble swallowing—"she showed the world that she would have nothing to do with me. The more she disassociates from me, the safer for her and our son."

Jasmine still disagreed with what Huang Yun had done. A family should stick together no matter what happened. Slowly she chewed the bun yet tasted nothing.

"You know, Tan Yin was worse off."

"I still can't believe it."

"Right after the liberation, he was praised for saving the Communist prisoners, and he was given a low-level office job. But he'd been investigated again and again with each campaign, even though he'd been cleared previously. You know how many campaigns we had."

"More than a dozen."

"His wife couldn't handle the stress anymore. She divorced him eight or nine years ago and took their kids with her."

Jasmine winced. "How come you know so much about him?"

Li Ming's eyes became empty. "We went out from time to time over the years, just to eat, drink, and talk. It's probably hard for others to understand, but there was a weird bond between us." He coughed and had to pause for a beat. His hand pressed his chest. "I hated him. He put me through hell. At the same time, I was grateful to him for saving my life."

Jasmine nodded.

"His people detested him. And he was never truly trusted by our party. I trusted him. We were not friends, but not enemies either. Just two men who had shared some crazy experiences. Our meetings became our crime."

"Why?"

"They said we were conspiring to destroy the Party and the country."

"Groundless accusations!" fumed Jasmine.

"The saddest part is"—Li Ming inhaled deeply and expelled his frustration on a single breath—"recently his children attended the Public Struggle Sessions and condemned him. Openly. Several times. He hadn't seen his sons since the divorce. Then he saw them at those horrible meetings. Can you imagine how he felt? Perhaps that's the reason he jumped."

"A man with no family, no future, no hope," concluded Jasmine. A lump formed in her throat as she recalled that Tan Yin had asked her to draw his happy portrait. She wondered if his family had kept the picture.

Lowering her head, she felt nothing except sorrow—soul-deep sorrow for Li Ming, for Tan Yin, for Meng Hu, for all the men who had fought for their homeland but had been betrayed by their own countrymen. She grieved for her country—a country where humanity and morality had been turned upside down.

Chapter 51

Li Ming was sick. He coughed all night, and it seemed he had a vile cold. "I'm okay," he rasped, dismissing Jasmin's concern. His hand pressed against his chest, seemingly to suppress pain or discomfort. "I've been coughing for several months."

By the third day, he had a high fever and started to sweat and shake with chills. When he coughed bloody mucus, Jasmine insisted on taking him to a hospital. She suspected that he had pneumonia and needed treatment. But by then, he was too frail to walk.

She went outside. A cold wind was blowing, causing the bony trees along the street to sway and rustle. In the chilly morning, she waited for a taxi. After half an hour, she realized that she hadn't seen a single taxi since coming to Chungking. They were in the midst of the Cultural Revolution. Everything was in chaos; nothing functioned properly. Even some of the buses had stopped running.

She wished that Little Tiger were here. At sixteen, he was tall and strong. He could carry Li Ming on his back. Jasmine's forehead creased with worry lines. Tension claimed the space between her shoulder blades as she paced back and forth in front of his house. The dark sky cast the street in an ominous gray that mirrored her mood. Then she walked toward a street vendor. She'd bought steamed buns from him during the past several days. The old gentleman carried his supplies on a wooden pushcart.

"How many buns would you like today?" asked the man. His smile accentuated the wrinkles around his eyes and mouth.

Jasmine shook her head. "*Da Shu,*" she said, using the title of respect for an elderly man. "Could you please lend me your pushcart? My cousin is sick. I need to take him to the hospital."

He gave her an appraising look and then shook his head.

"Please help us! He's very sick. I don't have any way to..." The last few words ended on a sorrowful sob. An overwhelming sense of helplessness engulfed her, and tears gushed down her cheeks. In the chilly gray morning, she felt heartbroken.

The old man looked at her in a silent query. Then his head wobbled in agreement. With his age-spotted hands, he started to remove his supplies from the pushcart.

"Thank you so much!" Jasmine wiped away the tears and gave him a smile of gratitude. Warmth swelled around her heart. In this gloomy, crazy world, she felt renewed hope in humanity.

Huge feathery snowflakes started to fall, twisting and turning in the sky. Jasmine bent her head against the wind, and with Li Ming lying on the pushcart, she began the journey. Straps fastened over her shoulders, she pushed on the balls of her feet. The wooden cart creaked as it wobbled and churned through the slush. She pulled and heaved, and soon she was out of breath. A sheen of perspiration clung to her forehead by the time they arrived at the hospital.

As she'd expected, Li Ming had pneumonia. A sour-faced doctor had done several tests and ordered a shot of penicillin. He told them to come back every day for a week. Then he pulled Jasmine into the hallway. Shifting his weight from one foot to the other, he said without eye contact, "There's something else."

His uneasiness alarmed her. "What?" she asked in a small voice.

"He..." His Adam's apple bobbed.

Jasmine pressed the nails of her hands into her palms, reminding herself to stay calm.

"I'm sorry. He has lung cancer."

Her entire body stiffened. Her heart skipped a beat and then thundered against her ribs. After a moment of panic, she managed to ask, "How serious?"

"Late-stage."

"Are…are you sure?"

He nodded in affirmation.

"How long does he have?"

"Hard to say; maybe a few months…"

———

Jasmine stayed in the hallway after the doctor had left. She slumped to the floor. Bending forward, she folded herself into a ball. Rivers of tears poured down her face. She'd known Li Ming was sick. She'd seen the signs—cough, shortness of breath, bloody mucus, fever, yellowed skin, fatigue, and swollen hands and face. She'd assumed that some signs were due to flu, and others were the results of the beatings and imprisonment. But nothing had prepared her for the severity of his illness. At fifty-three, he would soon die. The gravity of his future weighed heavily on her soul.

She was sad not only for the illness but also for Li Ming's situation. He would die an accused man—Traitor, Capitalist Roader, Counter-revolutionary, Enemy of the People… Since ancient times, *qing shi liu ming—leaving a legacy in history* was of paramount importance to any decent men. Li Ming would never live to see his name being cleared.

Should she tell him the truth?

In Chinese culture, family members or even friends were informed of a patient's condition, but not the patient himself. The premise was that the cruel reality might crash the person's spirit. By keeping it a secret, he might live longer. Jasmine had never approved of such a practice. She believed that it was the individual's right to know how long he might have left in this world. If it were her, she would prefer to know the truth. But now, she faltered. She loved Li Ming and hoped he would live longer.

An acrid odor of antiseptics hung in the air, aggravating her sense of loss. In the end, after crying and debating, she decided she had to let him know. It was his life. She had no right to keep him in the dark. She should trust him to handle the final chapter of his life. With a broken heart, she walked back into Li Ming's hospital room and delivered the tragic news.

He listened. Afterward, he simply said, "It's good to know the truth."

His unshakable calm and stored reserve filled her with admiration.

Chapter 52

"Call me if you need anything," said Jasmine before she went to bed. She left their bedroom doors open so that she could hear him. That night, she jolted awake by a loud thump from Li Ming's room. Without knowing what had happened, she jumped up and dashed barefoot toward his room.

There he lay on the floor near his bed, a flashlight at his side.

She rushed over. "Are you hurt?" she asked as she squatted.

"I'm…all right."

In the weak light, she couldn't detect an apparent injury, but the frown on his face told a different story. "Where are you hurt?"

Li Ming shook his head, embarrassed.

"Let me help you." Jasmine threaded her right arm behind his neck and tried to lift him. Even though he was thin, he was still too heavy for her.

"Give…give me…a minute," he panted.

She pulled the blanket from the bed to cover him. Sitting on the floor, she lifted his head and laid it on her lap. Lightly, she patted him. "It's okay. You'll be fine." Tears welled in her eyes, but she blinked them away.

The few minutes they waited seemed like days. When he finally regained enough strength, Jasmine helped him back into bed. As she was leaving, she noticed a small puddle on the floor and understood his embarrassment.

Minutes later, she came back with a washbowl. She set it on a chair near the bed and dipped a washcloth in the warm water. After wringing out excess water, she said in her softest voice, "*Li Ming Ge*, let me…" She started to remove his blanket.

He grasped her hand and gave a slight shake of his head. Sadness tinged his eyes.

Jasmine lowered herself onto the edge of his bed. "I've called you *Ge—Big Brother* for thirty years. Let me do this…as a sister."

He tightened his grip. "You should hate me, instead of—"

"No! How—?"

"Bai Ge is dead because of me."

"No. We've been through this—"

"Hear me out, Jasmine. I don't have much time. I have to tell you." Li Ming coughed into his fist. "I was selfish. I loved you. I still do."

The veins on the back of his hands bulged, and Jasmine sensed the heat from his hand. She felt guilty that she couldn't love him the way he loved her.

A small smile broke through his lips, yet it was hollow and bitter. "I fell in love with you the moment you saved me." He coughed again and had to pause. "I was married. I had no right to express such feelings. Then you returned…"

Not knowing what to say, Jasmine lowered her head.

"I shouldn't have kept you in Chungking. It was dangerous. I knew it. But I kept you there anyway."

"You sheltered us when I had nothing, and no one would help us."

"No." Li Ming shook his head, looking miserable. His eyes narrowed as if to hide his guilt. "I gave you my word to look for your uncle and Birch, and I did. But I did it half-heartedly. In the back of my mind, I knew I didn't want to find them. Even so, I learned they'd gone back to Yunnan. It was several days before… If I'd told you earlier… I was going to, honest to God. I just wanted to…keep you a little longer."

Taking a deep breath, he continued, "Being with you under the same roof made me happy. It was the happiest time of my life. If I'd known that my selfishness would cost Bai Ge's life, I'd—"

"It's been twenty years," Jasmine sighed, feeling sad for her son and missed opportunities. She could have reunited with her family, but she wouldn't allow herself to wallow in her grief. She had a dying man to care for. "Even if you'd told me, there wouldn't have been enough time for us to leave."

"Will you forgive me?" Li Ming looked up, tears glinting in his eyes.

"There is nothing to forgive. I've never blamed you." In her mind, she added, *Love makes people do foolish things. I'm no better.* She knew that no rational person would love someone the way she'd loved Danny.

With her right hand in his grip, she placed her left one on the back of his large bony hand. "You'll always be my Big Brother."

His lips quivered.

"I love you, *Li Ming Ge.*"

Tears brimmed, and one escaped, sliding down his hollow cheek.

Jasmine felt a stab of sympathy and guilt. There had always been an undeniable attraction between them, even though they'd never been romantically involved. Li Ming was a young and handsome man when she'd first met him. He looked so much like her beloved cousin. Perhaps, unconsciously, that was why she'd rescued him out of so many soldiers in the same dire situation.

What if Li Ming hadn't been married at the time? What if she hadn't fallen so deeply in love with Danny that she resisted giving up those rare moments of being with him in her dreams? *Could I have been his wife? Would his life have been better with me at his side? Would he have been happier?*

When the answers came positive, the tears she'd fought so hard began to fall.

———

Several weeks later, Jasmine awakened to the sound of loud banging on the front gate. She hurried to get up.

Another dull dawn turned the sky from coal black to ash gray. A light flurry was adding itself to the carpet of white snow on the ground. Two young men—one tall and gangly and the other short and chubby—stood outside the house. Both wore forest green heavy coats and Red Guards armbands.

"This house is confiscated," said the lanky man.

"What?" Knocked off balance, Jasmine stood transfixed for a moment. "You can't do this! This is—"

"Yes, we can. Li Ming is a Traitor, a Counter-revolutionary. He doesn't have the privilege to use this place. It belongs to the Red Guards now. He doesn't deserve a nice house like this."

Mind reeling, she hurried to ask, "Where is he going to live then?"

"That's not our problem. We were told to let him know."

"How could you—"

"We'll be back in five days." The lanky man cut her off. "That's enough time for him to move."

She was too dumbfounded and furious to know what to say.

As they were leaving, the chubby young man turned and whispered to Jasmine, "Go to *Pai Chu Suo*. Someone there might give you some suggestions."

She had no choice but to relate the bad news to Li Ming.

"I'm not surprised. In fact, I can't believe it took them this long." He looked extremely calm. "This house was assigned to me. Now that I'm no longer one of them, they'll take it away."

But where will we live? Jasmine shouted in her mind.

Chapter 53

— — — — — — — —

After breakfast, Jasmine left for *Pai Chu Suo*, as the young man had suggested. The one-story neighborhood police station was only ten minutes away. Two police officers sat behind a desk. They were an odd couple—the woman was stout as a pig and the man as thin as a monkey. A dozen people waited in line. Some seemed to have easy cases requiring only the thumping of stamps; others were being admonished and chased away. Jasmine waited anxiously for her turn.

The heavy-set policewoman said without lifting her eyes, "*Hukou.*" She was referring to the essential household registration permit, similar to an internal passport. When she opened Li Ming's *Hukou*, she made a sound like "Oh" and showed it to her colleague. "You should've come here much earlier."

"Oh, thank you!" Jasmine said with a rush of relief. "I'm so glad you know the situation. Where is Li Ming going to—"

"No!" The policewoman cut her off. "I mean, *you* should've come here earlier. You need to register. You can't just show up and live here without proper registration."

"Registration?"

"Yes! Without it, you can't stay. We hear that you've already lived here for several weeks. That's against the law. You must leave."

"Against the law? Okay, I'll register now."

"No. He's going to lose his place. You have no address to register."

"Well, that is why I've come here." Fending off rising fear and irritation, Jasmine asked, "Where are you going to relocate him? I'll register wherever he goes."

"Wherever he goes, huh?" snorted the policewoman.

"We don't know where he's going, and we don't care," said the thin policeman. "That's not our business."

Jasmine wanted to scream at the indifference, but she knew that would be counterproductive. Banking her anger, she said, "I'll take him to Yunnan, then." It was a long trip with bumpy buses and a packed train ride, which would be harmful to his health, but they had no choice. "What kind of paperwork—"

"You can't take him to Yunnan." The policewoman shook her head and folded her arms across her chest. "His *Hukou* is here."

"He's sick. He has…cancer. He needs someone to take care of—"

"He's a Traitor, an Enemy of the People."

Jasmine was fuming. In a tone of exasperation, she hissed through her teeth, "You don't know anything about Li Ming. He's a great man, a hero—"

"Well, if you know him so well, then you should marry him," the policewoman said with scorching contempt. "If you marry him, then you can take him with you, and we'll have one less Counter-revolutionary to deal with. Happy ending for everyone…"

Jasmine had already guessed that there were rumors about her. She'd seen inquisitive and disapproving looks. She'd overheard unflattering comments. Chinese culture upheld female purity as a virtue more important than life. Living with someone without marriage rendered the foulest reputation for a woman. Although she was a guest, the gossip fed the worst of people's imaginations. She wondered how many of those people had benefited from Li Ming's generosity throughout the years.

If it had happened before, those obnoxious statements would have killed her. But Jasmine didn't care about what others thought anymore. All she wanted was to help a friend, whatever it took. She walked out of the police station, frustrated and furious.

———

Running out of options, Jasmine decided to talk to Huang Yun. She knew where Li Ming's ex-wife lived. On their way back from the hospital, she'd accompanied him to the street where Huang Yun and their son were living. They stayed in the distance. "I just want to take a look at him," he said. His longing and helplessness broke her heart.

Huang Yun opened the door. She was in her early fifties, the same age as Li Ming. With her smooth face and slender body, she looked much younger. "Yes?" she asked. Her eyes bored into Jasmine, especially her left cheek.

"I'm Bai Moli. I'm a friend—"

"I know who you are. I heard that you're living with Li Ming now. Why are you here?" Her voice was soft, but there was no mistaking the contempt.

"He's very sick. He's…dying, actually. He has…lung cancer." The last two words were barely audible.

Surprise widened Huang Yun's eyes. A flicker of sadness passed across her face. "I told him many times to stop smoking. But he said he needed it for thinking. What could I do?"

"I'm very sorry."

"Why are you telling me this? I'm not a doctor or a nurse. What can I do?"

"He's been ordered to move out of the house. He'll be homeless in a few days. Would you consider taking him in? He needs—"

Huang Yun held up a restraining hand. "We're divorced. He can't come here. We can't afford to get involved with—"

"You're his wife."

"Ex-wife."

"He's your son's father."

"We're not legally related to him anymore. He's a Counter-revolutionary. He's the Enemy of the People."

Jasmine felt anger rise through her chest. Suppressing her intense emotions, she softened the edge in her voice. "You know Li Ming. He's not—"

"Why don't you take him with you?" hissed Huang Yun, her tone full of contempt. "You two have communicated for years. He sent all kinds of food to your family. Isn't it time for you to do something for him?"

"You..."

"He loves you more than he loves me. He never admitted it, of course. But he was so happy every time he received your letters." Her bitterness was undisguised. "Don't tell me you didn't know."

Jasmine stood there, openmouthed.

"If you truly want to help him..." Huang Yun paused dramatically and put her hands on the sides of her hips, "marry him." With that, she slammed the door.

Jasmine staggered away, stunned, and wounded.

Of course, she knew that Li Ming was infatuated with her. He'd proposed to her. But that was sixteen years ago. She'd seen affection in his eyes, yet she'd told herself that their feelings were innocent— feelings of a brother to a sister or vice versa, feelings between two people who had shared life-and-death experiences.

Jasmine was shaken that her closeness to him had affected his marriage. Li Ming had never complained or talked much about his wife. His son was his concern and his pride. But the few times he mentioned her, his comments were all positive. From the way Huang Yun looked, life's hardship had never touched her. *How could she say she wasn't loved?*

Jasmine trudged home in deep thought. It was snowing again, specks of white landing on her head and shoulders. The cold penetrated to her bones, and she shivered. Halfway home she stopped abruptly. Without hesitance, she hurried back to the police station.

"What do we need to get married?" she demanded of the uncouth officers.

Chapter 54

—— —— —— —— —— —— —— ——

"I found a way," exclaimed Jasmine as she returned home. She was carrying a bag of noodles, cabbage, and a quarter pound of pork strips. After putting the food in the kitchen, she approached Li Ming.

Half sitting, half lying on a sofa, he lifted his head.

"If we get married,"—she took a deep breath, quelling her excitement—"we can leave here. You can go to Yunnan with me!"

A glimmer of hope leaped to life in his dark eyes. But within seconds, the sparks were gone. He shook his head.

She sat down by the side of the sofa. "We can't stay here for long. They're going to kick us out in a few days."

"I'll move to one of the classrooms. The students won't come back anytime soon."

"You can't live without someone, and they won't let me stay—"

"Don't worry about me, Jasmine. You've done enough. I'll manage..." He swallowed several times. "Worse comes to worst, I'll follow Tan Yin. I owe him an apology anyway."

"Please, don't think that way. A long time ago you told me that life is worth living, even if just for a few more months, or days. Don't think about...death. Let me take care of you. Let—"

"I'm a burden. Don't you see?" He pointed to his broken body. Sadness strained his once handsome features.

"No, you're family. That's what family members do for each other.

Please! Let me...let me have you just a little longer. Don't leave me."

"I love you, Jasmine." Li Ming lifted his arm and smoothed a strand of hair back away from her eyes. "It's been a dream to be with you. But not now. Not when I can't offer you anything. No money. No protection."

"I don't need—"

"You may run into trouble because of me." He grabbed her hand. "I can't put you through... God knows, I'll regret it, even after I'm dead. You saved me once—that's more than enough."

"I saved you; you saved me. Our lives were fused long ago." Jasmine placed her other hand on top of their interlocked hands.

"Think about Little Tiger. Huang Yun left me because of our son. Even if you don't worry about yourself, what about him?"

"He has one Counter-revolutionary father already. How bad can it be to have one more?" Jasmine tried to joke yet failed miserably.

Li Ming looked into her eyes. "Remember I proposed to you?" A soft chuckle broke through his lips, but it was a dull and bitter sound. "I thought you'd need protection. Look at us now. I can no longer protect you..."

"Years ago, our neighbors called me Mrs. Li. Remember? Finally, I'll be Mrs. Li for real." This time she managed an uneven smile.

———

Jasmine and Li Ming were married. There was no ceremony. No celebration. No friends or family to attend. With the required *Hukou—household registration permits*, they went to the police station. After a few stamps on a certificate, they were husband and wife. Later, the newlyweds went to a small restaurant and ordered two dishes for dinner. That was luxurious enough. Li Ming had enough money saved, but his bank account was frozen. No one could access the funds except for the government.

When they returned home, Li Ming retreated to his room. His health wouldn't allow him to stay up late. Jasmine packed their suitcases for their trip and sorted the things needed to be sold. After everything was done, she stepped into his room.

She'd been so determined during the day. She'd had one goal and one goal only—to help Li Ming no matter what it took. She wouldn't let him die alone. It was the love for a family member. It was due to *Yi—morality, duty, loyalty, decency, and brotherhood* to a dear friend, to a big brother, to the man who had saved her, to the man who had tried his best for his country, even though his best wasn't enough and clearly not appreciated.

Yet she hesitated when it was bedtime. Where should she sleep? With him? Or in the separate bedroom where she'd stayed?

Li Ming was already in bed, but he was wide awake. She walked over and stood, hands self-consciously clasped in front of her.

"Come here," he said, patting the edge of the bed.

Jasmine sat down and angled her body to face him. He captured her hand, pressing it to his mouth. She lowered her head and felt the heat creeping onto her face. Gently, he lifted her chin. Their gaze came together and locked. She could see his eyes overflowing with naked emotions—tenderness, longing, love.

She stiffened, feeling a warmth that originated in the pit of her stomach.

"Relax," he said. He skimmed a knuckle down her jaw. "I dreamed of making love to you. Many times. I…can't anymore." A sad smile turned his lips downward. "See, you're safe."

Jasmine felt terrible. It was their wedding night. Although she married him to help him, marriage was sacred to her. She was his wife. "I'm so sorry. I didn't mean—"

"You have nothing to apologize for, Jasmine. What you've done is above and beyond. I'll forever be in your debt. When everyone abandoned me, when the country betrayed me, you showed up. You took me in when I had nothing except a damaged reputation and a failing body." His fingers lightly caressed her hair. "I have no right to ask anything of you. I saw the sparks in your eyes whenever you talked about Danny. That kind of love… I have to be honest—I used to envy him. But not anymore. You're a woman with a heart as large as the sky."

She took his hand, lifted it to her mouth, and kissed his palm.

Li Ming sucked in a sharp breath. His eyes drifted shut, and he let out a low, content sound.

Her heart reached out to him.

When he opened his eyes, moisture gathered in them. "Jasmine, I can never repay—"

She laid a finger over his mouth. "Shhh… Don't talk about repayment. You're my husband now." She slipped under the cover and lay down at his side. Threading her right arm under his neck, she put her left hand on his upper body, her fingers caressing his chest in slow circles.

Jasmine could hear every beat of his heart, every swallow, every breath he took. *Soon, his heart will stop beating. Before long, he won't take another breath.* And she wouldn't be able to hold him anymore. At that thought, her heart responded, tightening in her chest, aching with sharp pain.

Li Ming turned to face her. In the dim light, his eyes glistened with tears. Tenderly, he placed a kiss on her forehead. She nestled against him. Her cheek touched his cheek, and her tears blended with his tears. A sense of urgency threatened to overpower her. *Love him,* she shouted in her mind. *Love him as he deserves to be loved before it's too late.*

So, she reached out and placed her hand on the back of his head. Gently, she turned him toward her and fused her mouth with his. His lips gave the slightest tremble beneath hers, and encircling her upper body with his right arm, he drew her closer. His fervency made Jasmine wish she'd kissed him much earlier.

For as long as he lived, she promised silently, she would kiss him every day and try to make his life, however short, worth living.

Chapter 55

— — — — — — —

During the next few days, Jasmine managed to sell everything in the house to a secondhand store so that they would have enough money to travel. The night before their departure, they slept on the floor in the empty room. It was raining. Raindrops pounded the window and roof, and the house was very cold. Without blankets or coverlets, they wore heavy jackets and wool hats. Li Ming slipped an arm around Jasmine and pulled her close to keep her warm.

"How did we get to this point?" Tucked under his arm, she asked the same question he'd asked many years earlier. "The idea of communism seemed quite enticing. I first learned about it from Leng Xue. Remember her?"

He nodded.

"She was so excited when she shared her knowledge. A new world. A new beginning. A place where everyone is equal and sharing all the commonwealth…"

He sighed. "Many people, including Leng Xue, died for this ideology." Taking a ragged breath, he asked, "Do you know that the eight-year-old boy was Shen Shen?"

"I guessed it." A lump formed in the back of Jasmine's throat. "He was such a fine kid. Polite. Kind. Smart. Every time I saw him, I thought about Bai Ge. I drew…"

"Oh, I forgot to tell you. I saw those drawings."

"You did?"

"He showed them to everyone." A ghost of a smile flickered across Li Ming's face. "One day, I woke up with pain all over. There he was standing outside my cell with his big curious eyes."

She laid her head against his shoulder, feeling the lump in her throat expand.

"He asked where I was hurting. He had such a sympathetic look that was too mature for his age. He…" His voice cracked. "He asked if I could get closer so he could show me something. I crawled closer to the door. He showed me a picture of him and his mother. Right away, I knew you had drawn it. But I still asked. When he said your name, tears came to my eyes. He…"

Jasmine patted him. "Shhh…"

"He squatted and stuck his short arm in between the metal bars. He patted me just like you're doing." His chin quivered. "I cursed and screamed when they beat the hell out of me, but I never shed a tear. This skinny little boy… His small hand made me cry."

She wept, for Shen Shen who would forever be eight, for his graceful mother who had high hopes for a new country, for Li Ming who had been so tough but had been moved to tears by a child's soft touch.

"Actually, Shen Shen was the one who told me that you'd been released."

Jasmine couldn't speak for a few beats, and then she asked, "All those people died for the idea. I was excited, too. The Nationalist government had its problems. I thought it could be a great new beginning for China. How could everything go so wrong?"

"It's the system. One man runs our entire country."

Even in the isolation of their home, she laid a finger over his lips. "Chairman Mao is the greatest leader—"

"That's the problem. Now tell me: what's the difference between this system and the feudal systems we had for thousands of years?" He waited a few seconds before he continued, "Nothing! He's like an emperor. No, he *is* an emperor! With one speech, he can change the rules. With one wave of his arm, he can accuse and convict a person who has worked all his life for the Party."

In the faint light, Jasmine stared at him, openmouthed.

Li Ming wasn't done yet. "Most senior members of our party have been accused as Counter-revolutionaries and removed from power."

"I wondered about it, too. How could so many people turn out to be traitors?"

"The system is faulty and fatal. The entire country is in the hands of a cruel dictator."

The heavy rain pounded the roof, and the winter cold came in through cracks in the windows.

"Don't talk to anyone about this, Jasmine. I'm going to die soon, so I don't give a damn anymore." Li Ming took her cold hand, pressed it on his mouth, and placed a series of kisses to warm it. "I'm worried about you. You're not even fifty. You still have a long time to live. The village is safe for now. But will it be safe forever? I'm afraid—"

"Don't worry. I've been through worse..." She rose onto one elbow and faced him. "I used to think about death a lot. I didn't value life much. Now that I'm older, life has a different meaning to me. I'd like to see Little Tiger get married. I'd like to hold Bai Long's baby. I still have the dream to find...Danny. And I'll wait for your wrongful conviction to be overturned."

"That's a tall order."

"We've seen so many changes in our lifetime. Anything is possible."

"Fair enough..." The knot in his Adam's apple rose and fell a few times. "I won't see the change, but you may. When it comes..." He stuck his hand into the pocket of his heavy jacket and took out a *cun zhe*—deposit book. "This is my life savings. The account is frozen. It's useless right now. But if that day comes..." He placed it in her hand.

"I promise to give it to Li Dong."

"No!" Li Ming shook his head, his face stern. "I want you to have it. I understand what Huang Yun and my son have done. That doesn't mean I approve." He coughed and paused to draw in several breaths, his chest rising and falling rapidly.

Jasmine sat up and patted his upper body. "Slow down."

"I know you don't want me to speak of repayment, and by no

means can this repay what you've done for me. But at least I'll feel better knowing that I might be able to take care of you in some small way."

She felt the weight of the *cun zhe* in her palm.

"It's not worth anything right now, but if it ever becomes usable, treat yourself! Life has been so hard on you. Promise me!"

She gave a small nod.

A grin teased the corners of Li Ming's lips and an impish sparkle came into his eyes. "Use the funds to find Danny," he said.

Jasmine just stared at him.

"I'm your husband, but Danny is the love of your life." He held up his hand to stave off her protest. "I'm proud to stand with him."

Jasmine cradled his face with both of her hands. She looked into his eyes: light danced on his dark pupils. His gaze touched her soul. She lowered herself toward him. On the floor in the empty house, she kissed him—long, hard, deep. Li Ming reciprocated with equal ardor. His kiss transported her into a sphere where all sorrow and ugliness receded, and only she and this remarkable man existed in the world.

Outside, the wind wailed.

Chapter 56

▬ ▬ ▬ ▬ ▬ ▬ ▬

After a week of exhausting travel, they returned to Tao Hua Chu. Living with Jasmine in the peaceful village put a smile on Li Ming's worn-out face. "I've only been here twice. Who knew that it would become my resting place? Isn't life unpredictable?"

When Little Tiger and Bai Long learned that Li Ming wanted his ashes to be scattered at Angel's Pass, they insisted on carrying him to the gorge in the bamboo-pole sedan chair. Facing the breathtaking scenery, Li Ming said with a genuine smile, "I think of Birch as a brother. So, Danny is also my brother. I'm lucky to rest here with him." He eyed the statues of an angel and the Flying Tiger.

"You're also a Tiger," said Bai Long.

"That's right. You're all Tigers," exclaimed Xiao Hu.

With a lopsided smile, Li Ming corrected, "I'm the only wingless Tiger. Think about it. Danny, Birch, Jack, Meng Hu—they all had wings."

"Oh, I'm writing a story." Eagerly, the boy told him about the book that the family was working on.

"I'm so glad. It's a fascinating history, and it should be told," said Li Ming. "Have you heard about the bombing of Formosa?"

Jasmine and the young men shook their heads.

"Well, I should say the bombing of Taiwan. Formosa is an old name." They were near the statue of the Flying Tiger. Sitting in the sedan chair, Li Ming stretched his arm and touched the ivory-white marble. "It was November 25, 1943—American's Thanksgiving Day. The mission was a secret. Even the pilots didn't know a thing until they were about to take off."

Jasmine listened with bated breath.

"Are they the Flying Tigers?" asked Bai Long.

"Okay, let me clarify. The nickname was initially given to the pilots in the American Volunteer Group. Later on, it extended to all American pilots who fought the Japs in China."

The trio nodded in unison.

"This particular mission was carried out by the Fourteenth Air Force. Thirty aircraft containing sixteen fighters and fourteen B-25s—"

"B-25s? What's that?" asked Little Tiger.

"Bombers. They flew two-and-a-half hours from Suichwan Airfield. In Jiangxi Province, that is. The last one hundred miles or so, they had to fly at extremely low altitudes to avoid radar detection. They were crossing Taiwan Strait. The weather was perfect."

"It's like God was on our side," chirped Little Tiger, eyes blazing.

"Once they reached the Jap's airdrome, one unit of fighters took the lead. They knocked out the enemy in the air. Other fighters protected the bombers. Together they bombed and strafed the Japs. Soon, the area was lit up by fireworks."

The young men cheered while Jasmine unleashed a smile.

"Only one pass was made by each unit. But the brief encounter left fifty-eight Japanese airplanes—bombers and fighters—in smoking ruins," Li Ming said. Unsteady, he stood up from the sedan chair. Stepping two paces away, he clicked his heels together and saluted the Flying Tiger.

Both young men followed suit.

"Guess what kind of damage we had?"

The trio looked at him, their eyes wide open, anxious to hear the answer.

"A bullet hole in one of the fighters. A single bullet hole!"

"Hurrah!" Bai Long punched his right fist into the air.

Little Tiger jumped up and down a few times. "Long live the Flying Tigers!" he yelled at the top of his lungs. His voice echoed throughout the canyon.

Jasmine gave Li Ming a smile of gratitude and asked, "How can you remember so clearly?"

"Are you kidding me? It was the most successful raid the Allies carried out in the China-Burma-India Theater. I read the report again and again and imagined I was with them." A smug grin turned his mouth up. "Danny Hardy was one of the unit leaders."

Surprise widened Jasmine's eyes. Her heart swelled with pride. "How come you never told me?"

Li Ming offered a sheepish smile. "Danny was already a larger-than-life hero to you. How could I tell you more about his jaw-dropping victories when I was trying to impress you?" He picked up her hand. "Forgive me that I wasn't a bigger person."

All the way back to the village, he shared more stories he'd heard and held everyone spellbound. When they arrived home, Bai Long showed him the pictures he and Jasmine had drawn. Li Ming beamed and then warned, "You've got to hide them."

"We keep an extra set in the cave," Little Tiger assured him.

———————

Unlike most Chinese men, Li Ming displayed his affection for Jasmine in front of the family. He genuinely loved her and was grateful to her. He also had a sense of urgency that most people didn't have. His love made her feel like a blushful teenager, and she wished that it could last forever. His public display of affection made the young men chuckle. Every night, the couple went to bed, holding each other. Not a day passed that they didn't kiss as if it were the last day of their lives.

But his health deteriorated quickly. He'd been able to walk when they left Chungking. A couple of months later, he started to stumble and soon had trouble moving. Jasmine fed and bathed him when he could no longer take care of himself. Linzi gave him herbal medicines to ease his pain and discomfort. Li Ming put on a brave face, which made her job more manageable, but at the same time, broke her heart. They talked as much as he was able and shared stories and dreams.

Whenever she kissed him, he summoned every ounce of energy within him to reciprocate. In the end, it was no more than a tremble of his lips. The last time she kissed him, she noticed a fleeting spark came to his eyes before he closed them and took his final breath. A single tear leaked from the corner of his right eye.

Four months after their marriage, Li Ming passed away. His thin body was covered with all kinds of scars—gun-shot wounds from the Japanese, tortures by the Nationalist Secret Police, beatings from the Communists. The last thing he'd said before he lost his ability to speak was, "No enemy. Never an Enemy of the People!"

Even though she'd known the outcome and had several months to prepare herself, when the time came, Jasmine broke down. *Don't leave me*, she cried in her mind as wrenching sobs racked her body. *You did make me happy. I do love you.* Now, she had one less family member in her life.

A Communist Party official at the provincial level would have had a funeral of hundreds of mourners, with dozens of elaborate floral wreaths and tribute banners at the service. Mourning music—a Funeral March—would have been played, and his casket would have been covered by a Communist Party flag. Other important party officials would have praised him by listing his impressive titles and achievements.

But there was no funeral, no memorial, no eulogy, no music, no crowd. Li Ming was a Counter-revolutionary, an Enemy of the State, who deserved to die unremembered.

Only Jasmine, Little Tiger, and Bai Long went to Angel's Pass to scatter his ashes. They were all in dark-colored clothes with black armbands around their upper left sleeves. The sixteen-year-old Little Tiger walked at the front of the small procession, holding a plain wooden urn. With a somber expression, Bai Long followed. Jasmine dragged her feet while clutching a bundle of forget-me-nots. None of them said anything as they hiked up the mountains.

It was a gorgeous summer day, and the gorge was as breathtaking as ever, but neither the sunlight nor the beautiful scenery lifted anyone's spirit.

Who was Li Ming? With tears in her eyes, Jasmine wondered as his ashes sprinkled down the deep chasm. He'd been a young Nationalist Army officer fighting the Japanese when she first met him. Disappointed with the Nationalist government, he joined the Communist guerillas after the Nanking Massacre. He was a Communist spy when they met again in Chungking, and he became an important Communist official for nearly two decades. Now, he was accused as an Enemy of the People by his own party.

Li Ming had been married three times. His first wife disappeared during the war against Japan after she'd accidentally killed their two-year-old son. His second wife left him when he was in political trouble; she took their son with her. Jasmine had become his third wife, but only as his health declined and he approached death. He died in this remote village with only his new family at his side.

What if I hadn't saved him in Nanking? The image of an attractive, athletic young man came to her mind. Dressed in ill-fitting clothes, he'd stood before a group of armed Japanese soldiers. What if she'd never claimed him as her cousin? *He would've been killed with hundreds of thousands of innocent souls. But then he wouldn't have been accused as a criminal at the end of his life.* Knowing the undesirable outcome, what would he have wanted her to do?

The injustice and the irony stung her eyes, but Jasmine didn't shed more tears. Only silently and deep inside did she weep for this Big Brother. That was the man she knew—someone she'd saved and someone who had saved her—a Big Brother and now her husband.

When her cousin was so far away and out of reach, when Danny, the love of her life, was long gone, Li Ming had remained in her life for thirty years. *If I'd never saved him in the first place, what would have happened to me when I had no one?*

That night, Li Ming came to her in a dream. He held her close to him, and his warm body touched her frozen heart.

Chapter 57

━ ━ ━ ━ ━ ━ ━

In the fall of 1967, a dozen Red Guards and several armed police-men showed up in the village. Along with them came Yaya, Linzi's younger daughter, who was a sophomore at a local college. They didn't go into people's houses to destroy things as most of the Red Guards had done throughout the country. Instead, they herded Jasmine and Little Tiger to the herbalist's front yard.

Many villagers had already gathered around. Everyone seemed on edge. The place and the situation gave Jasmine high anxiety. The sky was a dull gray, just like the day of the massacre. A flow of pet-rifying memories slammed into her mind. A premonition flashed through and rattled her.

A policeman in his late twenties was obviously in charge. He exuded an air of authority and self-assurance typical to men in official positions. He was tall, wide-shouldered, and had a broad nose and heavy brows. "Tell them what you told us," he said to Yaya with a booming voice.

The petite girl scooted closer to a young man with acne. Like other Red Guards, she was dressed in an olive-green military uniform with a red armband. Her pigtails were gone, replaced by a bob cut. Barely above a whisper, she said, "My father saved…an American soldier—"

"Speak up!"

She wet her lips and took a nervous breath before reciting part of the story Linzi had told Jasmine fourteen years earlier.

Now Jasmine understood why the policemen were involved. Saving an American soldier in the Korean War would be a capital crime. It could send Linzi to his death. Her heart rate exploded as she remembered that Yaya had sat at the front step when they had the conversation.

Does the girl know the gravity of her accusation? Does she say it because she's trying to show her loyalty to the Party or to save her own skin? Since 1949, the Communist ideology permeated every human relationship, and in recent years, family members were encouraged to inform on one another for the good of the Party.

"Does anyone else know about this?"

Yaya wound the hem of her uniform around her thin fingers, unwound it, and then pointed at Jasmine.

A flicker of fear flashed in Linzi's eyes.

"No!" Without missing a beat, Jasmine denied it. "I've never heard such a ridiculous story."

"You..." The girl's lips remained parted, but she was speechless.

"You were only five when your father came back." Jasmine softened her voice. "Your father told me lots of stories." Taking a deep breath to calm her nerves, she said, "They were stories about how he saved our countrymen and how...brave the People's Volunteer Army was."

"She's lying. That's not all."

"I swear..." Jasmine was going to use the old term "a liar will be struck by lightning" but changed her mind. She quoted the saying that was popular at the time, "I swear to Chairman Mao."

The policeman didn't seem to be convinced.

"Comrade Wang Linzi became a member of the Communist Party over there. He was awarded for his bravery. Go inside his house." Jasmine urged them, "You can find his medals."

"We're aware of all that."

"I'm not saying that the girl is lying, but she was five. You can't accuse someone based on the memory of a five-year-old."

"It's better than counting on you. You saved an American Devil.

That's a fact. You can't deny that. Everyone knows—"

"Danny Hardy was a brave man! How dare you call him a Devil!" All the grief, rage, and despair she'd experienced for twenty-five years erupted like hot lava. "He fought the Japs for China. He died for us. You should be grateful to him and other Americans. They saved us, saved you."

"Hardline Counter-revolutionary!" With an open palm, he slapped Jasmine across the face so hard she lost her footing and almost fell if it weren't for Bai Long grabbing her arm. Blood trickled from her nose and the side of her mouth.

Kicking and shouting, Little Tiger fought to extricate himself from the grasp of two stout policemen. "Rot in hell!" Anger infused his sun-tanned face with hot color, and every inch of his body radiated fury.

Bai Long yelled, "Don't hit or swear at people—that's in *the Three Main Rules of Discipline and the Eight Points for Attention.* How dare you not follow what Chairman Mao said!"

"No hitting my villager!" Linzi frantically waved his hands. "I'm still the Party Secretary in the Village."

All the villagers shouted in protest.

Storm clouds turned the sky black and cast an ominous shadow over the area.

Ignoring the crowd, the policeman faced Jasmine. "You're *lou wang zhi yu—the fish that escaped the net.* You should've been punished a long time ago. Your uncle and cousin are Nationalist military officers. Your husband is a Traitor, an Enemy of the People."

"Damn you!" she snapped. Wiping the blood from her face, she glared at him.

"You're a cunning woman. You hid in this remote village to avoid being caught. But people's eyes are sharp. You can't escape."

"You'll all go to hell." Little Tiger released a string of expletives.

"His father"—the young man with acne pointed to Little Tiger—"was also a hardline Nationalist."

"We've done our homework," a girl with short hair informed. "His father was executed in jail during the Campaign to Suppress Counter-revolutionaries. He's the son of the Enemy of the People."

"My father was a fighter pilot. He fought the Japs for eight years." Shoulders back, head held high, Little Tiger stood his ground. "Without my father, Uncle Birch, and Uncle Danny, you and your families would not have survived."

"Look at him." The acned-man sneered. He took a step away from Yaya, who crossed her arms and hugged her elbows. "Even now, he's a diehard Counter-revolutionary."

"Down with the hardheaded Counter-revolutionaries!" one of the Red Guards shouted, and all of them joined him, "Long live our greatest leader Chairman Mao! Long live our Communist Party!"

Little Tiger held his head high. His undaunted posture reminded Jasmine of Meng Hu. For a moment, she regretted telling him his father's stories, yet she was sure that Meng Hu would have wanted his son to learn the truth. His son was a Tiger, just like him.

"What about her other son?" The policeman regarded Bai Long.

"He's not my son," Jasmine blurted. She glanced at Bai Long and saw hurt in his eyes. But she had no choice. "I picked him up by the side of a road. He was hungry and alone, so I brought him here. Check my *Hukou*." She was referring to the essential household registration permit. Indeed, she'd never put his name on it. During the Great Famine, tons of people had died. Registration became less important compared to more urgent issues such as hunger and death. Officially, she had only adopted Little Tiger. "He calls me Teacher Bai. Everyone here knows that."

There was nodding all around.

"What about his family? Tell us the truth."

Jasmine felt the weight of the policeman's stare. "I don't know anything about his family." She couldn't believe that she had to lie so much to protect her loved one but was relieved to hear no tremor in her voice. She had to conceal Bai Long's family background. If anyone found out that he was the son of the richest man in Anning, his life would be ruined.

A sudden gust of wind blew through the nearby trees, sending dead leaves falling to the ground.

Chapter 58

━ ━ ━ ━ ━ ━ ━

Jasmine, Little Tiger, and Linzi were taken from the village and locked in a penitentiary near Anning. It was late at night when they arrived. With the creak of a key and the squeal of hinges, Jasmine was brought to a long, narrow room. In the dim light, she could see two rows of sleeping platforms along the walls. Each "bed" had more than a dozen people. She was given a blanket and pointed to an empty slot.

With so many people in one space and lying on the hard surface, Jasmine had trouble sleeping. She heard faint sighs and cries. No one else seemed to be bothered.

In the morning, she said hello to her cellmates. One of them was pretty. A beauty mark on her right cheek created a permanent dimple. But she seemed dispirited. Her eyes were red and puffy. Jasmine believed that the cries she'd heard had come from her. "My name is Bai Moli. What is your name?"

The woman didn't lift her head.

"She won't speak," said another cellmate. She was thin and had a narrow face.

"Is she...mute?"

"She got into trouble by talking..."

Jasmine wanted to ask but swallowed her curiosity. *I'll learn from her.* She wanted to scream but stifled the urge. Venting would only get her into deeper trouble. And it would be meaningless. The ones with power wouldn't listen to her, and the sympathetic ones were powerless. *I'll keep my mouth shut.*

"She was a movie star. I'm Mouse," the thin woman said with a wink. Seeing Jasmine's bewilderment, she explained, "*Dan xiao ru shu—As timid as a mouse.* That's me. I don't mind being called Mouse."

———

Soon, Jasmine's plan to keep quiet was put to the test.

Two days later, she and her cellmates were brought to an auditorium. Except for a few male guards, there were only female prisoners, probably several hundred. Political slogans were posted all around them. On stage sat two men. She knew one of them—the policeman who had arrested her.

"I'm the prison chief," said the other man. In his forties, he had a large, round face with graying hair at his temples. Oddly, his voice was smooth and silky. "Come up when you hear your name."

Jasmine and her two cellmates were among the dozen being called.

"Admit to whatever they say. Don't argue," whispered Mouse.

Once on stage, each prisoner was forced to wear a tall cone-shaped hat. A piece of cardboard was also strapped to one's neck, dangling in front of the chest. Both items were used to humiliate their victims. Jasmine couldn't see the writing on her hat, but her cardboard had Counter-revolutionary in black ink, and the words were crossed by bloody red lines.

Others had similar signs, except the actress received 'Traitor' and Mouse obtained 'Capitalist Roader.' Jasmine believed that the signs were issued randomly. Nowadays, anyone could be called Counter-revolutionary, Traitor, or Capitalist Roader.

"Repeat after me." The policeman stood, assuming a militant posture with feet apart and shoulders braced. He punched his fist high in the air as he shouted, "*Tan bai cong kuan, kang ju cong yan.*"

The inmates followed him with low, downhearted voices, "*Lenient treatment to those who confess; severe punishment to those who remain stubborn.*"

The man in charge was dissatisfied. "Say it louder," he demanded, "if you don't want to be punished. Why do I have to reiterate?"

The women repeated, a little louder this time.

One by one, the selected prisoners confessed their crimes. One lady spoke with a blank look on her face while another stuttered and shook like a leaf.

With defeated eyes, Mouse said in her timid voice, "I'm sorry I was born in a bad family. My father was a capitalist. He hired dozens of men to work for him. He got up before sunrise every day and didn't come home until dark, of course, keeping the poor workers with him." She spoke in a monotone as if a schoolgirl reciting from her textbook, "He exploited his employees so he could send his sons, my brothers, to America. They also became capitalists. One opened a restaurant, and the other managed a laundromat. They lived in Chinatown in New York. After attending many struggle sessions, I realized the bad influence of my relatives. I'll…I'll stay away from them…"

She went on condemning her husband, who was a Communist but became a Traitor and Capitalist Roader. "He was too weak to be a true Communist," she concluded.

But the actress just stood there, twisting her hands. Her eyes were empty, devoid of all feelings. Her head lowered to the cardboard on her chest.

"*Huo cong kou chu—Misfortune comes from the mouth.* Good. I think she's learned her lesson," taunted the prison chief. His moon-face opened into a grin.

"Too bad. No need to make a silent movie anymore," said the policeman. "Otherwise, she could be a star once again." He laughed at his own joke, exposing crooked front teeth.

Jasmine fought the impulse to object to their cruel statements. She understood, though, that shaming was their tactic.

Then, it was her turn.

"We have a newcomer today," said the moon-faced man in his silky voice. "We welcome her, and hopefully she'll be reeducated and transformed into a law-abiding citizen in a short time."

With great fortitude, Jasmine clamped her teeth, curbing the urge to argue.

The prison chief turned to the policeman and said, "Tell them what Bai Moli has done."

The policeman listed her crimes. Her uncle was a general in the Nationalist Air Force; her cousin was a Nationalist fighter pilot; her husband was a Counter-revolutionary; her adopted son was the child of a Nationalist who was executed in jail.

The man went on to Americans, especially Danny Hardy. "She was hell-bent on saving him. Look at her scars." He eyed her with contempt. "She was willing to die for the American Devil."

Jasmine had to bite down on her lip to prevent herself from shouting back.

The policeman curled his lips. "It was for love, said an article in an old Nationalist newspaper. I think he just wanted to…you know… bang her. She probably wanted to go with him to live in Capitalist America. Hey, they could have a little Devil if he didn't…"

Jasmine shot him a venomous look. She couldn't let him stain Danny's name. Against Mouse's advice and her own decision to stay silent, tossing caution to the wind, she said through gritted teeth, "You know nothing about these Americans. You were just a little kid when they gave their lives to keep you safe."

She turned to the crowd. Despite the degrading hat and the cardboard, she squared her shoulders and raised her head. Her half-gorgeous, half-disfigured face was infused with color. "During the Nanking Massacre, it was a group of Americans who saved thousands of people."

Jasmine heard collective gasps. But she wasn't done. Resolve hardened her tone, and she continued, "In 1941, a group of American pilots came to China. They were volunteers. They risked their lives to fight the Japs. For us! They sacrificed so much; some gave their lives. We, the Chinese people, called them the Flying Tigers. Danny Hardy was one of those courageous American pilots—"

"Shut up!" the prison chief bawled, waving his arms madly in the air.

The guards tackled her. They twisted her arms behind her back. The pain stole her breath. It felt as if her arms were being wrenched from her shoulder sockets. They pushed her to her knees and shoved her head toward the floor. The strap attached to the cardboard cut deeper into her neck. A cloth was jammed into her mouth. Determined not to show her fear, Jasmine forced steel to her backbone.

"Down with the hardheaded Counter-revolutionary!" Thunderous shouts came from the loudspeaker. "Down with the cowardly, cruel American Devils!"

"Confess your crime! Come clean!" The policeman growled. Lifting his foot, he kicked Jasmine in the chest. She uttered a muffled cry.

"Bai Moli is stubborn," said the man in charge, "but I promise she won't remain stubborn for too long. Take her away!"

The guards dragged her off the stage and threw her into a tiny windowless room. Except for a waste bucket, there was nothing inside the room. It was icy cold. That night, lying on the concrete floor, Jasmine folded herself into a ball. *They're trying to break me. I won't let them. I've been through worse. I can handle this.* Shivering, she kept encouraging herself.

Twice a day, a small bowl of food and a cup of water were shoved in between the iron bars. Nobody talked to her. Not a living soul was around, except for rats. Jasmine had nothing other than her memories. Among them, a couple of sentences carved on the wall of the prison cell in Chungking came to her mind. "The will of the Communists is made of steel," and "Heads can be chopped. Limbs can be cut. The spirit of revolution is indestructible."

I'm not a Communist, but I have my spirit.

A month later, the guards took Jasmine out of confinement and returned her to the sleeping quarter. She was haggard. Dark circles shadowed her large eyes. Yet, a wisp of a smile graced her lips as she patted the hard-surfaced bed. "This is luxury. I'll sleep like a baby tonight." Resolve and strength emanated from her.

Her mood shocked everyone there. Very few people had come

out of isolation without being emotionally broken. Soon, her cell-mates called her *Bai Jie—Sister Bai*, regarding her as the heroine in a famous historical novel *Red Crag*. Ironically, the book was about life and death in a Nationalist prison in Chunking. The protagonist Sister Jiang was a valiant Communist who endured multiple rounds of brutal torture without giving up any information. She was portrayed as a Communist Martyr.

The novel was based partly on the author's experience. It had reminded Jasmine of Li Ming and the other Communists she'd known when she was incarcerated by the Secret Police in Chungking. Li Ming had told her later that the writer was one of the three survivors. He'd endured the Nationalist's harsh treatment, but he couldn't handle the mental pain of being wrongfully accused as a traitor by his own party. He took his life in the peaceful Communist society that he'd tirelessly worked to create.

Jasmine sympathized with those people. However, she'd never considered herself a heroine, let alone a Communist heroine. She'd done what she had to do to save the ones she loved. Her actions were never politically motivated.

She often wondered about those Communist Martyrs. If they'd survived, what kind of life would they have had? Did the author of *Red Crag*, in his final moment, regret his decision to join the Party which had betrayed so many of its own members?

Chapter 59

Chinese New Year was fast approaching, but there were no cheerful decorations in prison. The only thing unusual was the break they were allowed on New Year's Day. Since she'd adopted Little Tiger, Jasmine hadn't spent holidays without her family. This New Year would be hard.

"I plan to sleep in," said Mouse. She yawned. "This is the only free day. We've worked every day of the year."

Jasmine agreed. She'd been there for only three months, and she was bone-tired. On New Year's Eve, wrapped in the blanket, she listened to others talk about their favorite foods. She wished she could make dumplings for Little Tiger and Bai Long. The memory brought a feeble smile to her lips.

She hoped too that her uncle and cousin would have a great New Year, and Xiao Mei would join them. She was sure that the housemaid had gotten married by then and wondered who the lucky man was. *Xiao Mei is such a loving girl. Too bad for Birch. I wish they could have been together.*

She went on praying for her deceased family members. When she talked to Daisy, she asked her younger cousin to make dumplings for Danny. He was crazy about the pork and leek filling. She thought of Bai Ge and knew that Li Ming would take care of her son.

That night Jasmine dreamed of food. She woke to a street vendor's high-pitched cry. Opening her eyes, she realized that the scream wasn't part of her dream. More people started to shriek and cry, and the sound was bloodcurdling. She bolted upright. Everyone stared at the door, so she turned. Immediately, she paled. In the frigid cold room, she began to shiver. Above the door was a small window with iron bars. Below it hung a limp body. Even in the first light of dawn, she knew that it was the actress.

After the initial shock, Jasmine leaped out of bed and raced to the door. The icy cold concrete stung the soles of her bare feet. She clutched the woman's legs and raised the body so that she wasn't hanging by the neck. "Help me take her down!"

Her appeal jerked the other inmates out of their daze. Frantically, they took the actress down. But the woman had already departed this life. Her eyes were open and fixed. Her tongue protruded, and her skin was cold to the touch. On the only day they were given a break, she chose to rest permanently.

Jasmine felt numb.

"Don't feel too bad," mumbled Mouse. She thrust her hands into the pockets of her gray cotton coat. "Her spirit was long gone."

"What did she do?"

Mouse looked around and lowered her voice to a confidential pitch. "She said that Chairman Mao was just a human being. She said that the slogan 'Long live Chairman Mao' wasn't logical, and that he'd die one day like everybody else."

"She was jailed because of that?"

Mouse gave a small nod.

The poor woman had simply stated an inescapable fact, but that observation had cost her life. At the time, 'Long Live Chairman Mao!' was the first phrase a child learned. Mao Zedong was God. Obviously, no one was permitted to say that God would die one day.

"Truth is, she only talked to her best friend, in private—"

"Let me guess; the friend sold her out?"

Mouse nodded again.

"But that's not a reason to kill oneself…"

"She was put in isolation for two days, and after that, she stopped speaking." Mouse shook her head. "She lost hope. She knew she would never be a movie star again."

"Maybe no one is waiting for her."

"That's also possible." Mouse paused. "I'll never kill myself. I can't. My husband couldn't take it. He drank rat poison." Determination raised the chin of her narrow face. "No matter how hard it is, I have to stay alive…for my daughter. I won't let her be an orphan. Whatever it takes: I'll lie; I'll say anything they want to hear. I just have to get out of this godforsaken place. Alive!"

Although Jasmine didn't agree with Mouse's method, her determination to survive touched her. Suicide hadn't crossed her mind for many years; as she had told Li Ming, life had become a lot more precious as she grew older. So many lives had been cut short. She had to live for her departed family and friends, the two boys, and her remaining dreams.

The prison held a couple of thousand people from all over Yunnan Province. The males and the females were separated. Jasmine had not seen either Little Tiger or Linzi for a long time. She was worried about them, especially the boy. Indomitable and unyielding, he would break before he would bend.

Once, she saw him in the distance. He was carrying two wooden buckets suspended at the ends of a shoulder pole. She could only see his back. Yet she recognized him and could hardly breathe. His tall frame was silhouetted against the sunlight, and his hair tousled in the wind. He was much thinner. The buckets swayed with each step.

"Xiao Hu!" she cried out.

But he didn't hear her above the sound of the wind.

A thousand cherished memories dragged her into the past. How she wished she could talk to him and to hold him! She'd raised the boy since he was a toddler. He was her son. Jasmine had already lost one child, not being able to see either Little Tiger or Bai Long broke her heart. They were a few steps away, yet they were a world apart.

Once, Jasmine saw the boy face to face during one of the struggle sessions that everyone had to attend. Apparently, he was looking for her. They stared at each other across rows of people between them. Their eyes locked. For an ecstatic moment, everyone else faded away, and only her son existed in the world. Tears sprang to her eyes and blurred her vision. She blinked to clear her vision so she wouldn't miss this precious opportunity. Little Tiger cracked his usual carefree smile before he had to turn away and continue moving to his assigned area.

On a chilly evening, Mouse stuck something in Jasmine's palm and then squeezed her hand with both of hers. "Be careful." Her voice was barely above a whisper. Turning around, she picked up her flashlight and handed it to Jasmine. Despite her curiosity, Jasmine didn't check the note until she went to bed. Pulling the blanket over her head, she unfolded the paper.

Her heart swelled as she stared at the familiar handwriting in the dim light. It was Little Tiger's script. Without wasting a second, she started to read. It was part of the novel he'd been writing. There were only two pages, but his story touched her soul. That night, after reading it over and over again, she fell asleep, holding the precious gift to her chest.

From that day on, instead of surviving, Jasmine had something to look forward to. Papers of different sizes and types secretly circulated within the prison. She read everything she obtained.

And she wasn't alone. The handwritten sheets were passed hand to hand, leaving joy and excitement in the detention center. At the time, stories like his were strictly forbidden.

The Wind Beneath His Wings was a heroic tale where ordinary Chinese risked their own lives to rescue and safeguard a downed American pilot during the war against Japan. Since the Communists had taken over the Mainland, no one talked about the vital contributions that Americans had made during the war.

Older generations had heard about it, yet they didn't dare to say it out loud. The topic was prohibited. One could be put in jail or even killed if one spoke positively about Americans. The younger generations had no idea that the Westerners had participated in the war. The youths were brainwashed, and they believed that Americans were Devils. The novel was provocative and eye-opening.

It was also a love story about the brave Flying Tiger and a beautiful Chinese woman who tried to save him. Love was now seen as a sign of weakness, a feeling felt only by Counter-revolutionaries. It did not conform to the unbending toughness that the Communists demanded. Revolutionaries would get married because of their shared political goals, but no one talked about love, let alone the love between an American warrior and a Chinese girl.

No matter how authentic his novel was, in Communist China it would remain as a *shou chao ben—underground handwritten manuscript*. If the authorities found it, not only would the book be destroyed, but the author would be severely punished. So everyone was careful.

Jasmine was thrilled that Little Tiger's story moved his readers, but at the same time, she was out of her mind with worry. Whenever there was an unannounced inspection, her heart beat out a frantic rhythm, and it wouldn't calm until the search was over. Inevitably, some of the pieces were destroyed by the prisoners in order to protect the audacious work.

Two years after her imprisonment, she was summoned to a questioning room. The prison chief sat at a desk. Behind him, a massive portrait of Chairman Mao hung on the wall. "We've learned something," he said. He rested his hands on the edge of the desk, laced his fingers, and slowly rubbed his thumbs together. "Something bad. Counter-revolutionary." He paused for emphasis. "A secret manuscript is being circulated throughout the compound."

Her heart drummed rapidly in her chest. Her first thought was that Little Tiger had been exposed. She sat very still, trying to control the terror underneath her calm surface.

"It's about an American pilot. Who else knows that topic better than you?"

Jasmine heaved a silent sigh of relief. Her son wasn't their target. "I haven't read anything like that." Fending off her anxiety, she asked matter-of-factly, "Could you please let me see the writing?"

The man crossed his arms and cocked a skeptical eyebrow. "You're walking a tightrope, Bai Moli. We'll keep a close eye on you. If you are the author," —his voice lowered to an intimidating pitch—"we'll catch you, and you'll be sorry."

This incident rattled Jasmine but it also gave her an idea. Afterward, whenever she received a piece of the text, she copied it, imitating her son's handwriting. If the manuscript was discovered, she was ready to take the blame.

As an artist, she had the advantage of taking on this incredible job. Under her blanket and in the weak light of a flashlight, she labored through the night; and with each copy she made, she felt rejuvenated with a sense of purpose as the duplicated copies also filled the gaps in the damaged work.

Chapter 60

"Bai Moli, you have a visitor. It's your son."

Jasmine was pleasantly surprised. It had been three years since they were imprisoned. Could it be possible that Little Tiger was released? He would be twenty by now.

No visitors had been allowed until a couple of weeks earlier. Even when it was permitted, not many people came to visit. It wasn't wise to associate with the accused; most families chose to distance themselves. But Xiao Hu was different. He'd been the "guilty one." When she walked into the meeting room, her nerves tingled in anticipation of seeing her son after several years.

It wasn't Little Tiger. With a baby in his arms, Bai Long stood in the temporary visitation area.

"Bai Long!" Jasmine stretched her hands and grabbed the young man. She checked him up and down. "How are you? Why are you here?" She scanned the room and lowered her voice. "I'm so happy to see you. But leave! Don't come back again. It's not safe for you or your family." She touched the baby's head. Her eyes turned softly.

"It's okay. Don't worry about me. Don't always think about others."

"Have you seen Little Tiger?"

"I'm going to after..."

That meant that Xiao Hu was still locked up. She felt a stab of disappointment and hurried to say, "Tell him I love him! Tell him

275

to be strong. Please visit him. He needs a brother."

Bai Long nodded.

"How's Linzi? I've been out of my mind with worry. I haven't seen—"

"No need to worry. He was released several months after his arrest. He was rehabilitated"—Bai Long made quotation marks with his hands—"because of his awards and your adamant denial of Yaya's story. He's the Party Secretary in the Village again."

Jasmine released her breath in a sigh of relief.

"But..."

She noticed a nervous tic in his upper lip, and her stomach tied itself into a knot. "What is it?"

"My mother-in-law passed away."

"Lili's mother? No!" she grunted with agony and surprise. "When? How? She wasn't even fifty."

"After Uncle Linzi's arrest, she became very ill. She couldn't keep anything down. We sent her to the hospital in Anning, but..."

"Poor Linzi. Poor Lili and Yaya."

"Yaya..." Bai Long stuttered, "She doesn't know better. She lost her mind."

"Good heavens!"

"After her father's arrest, she was ridiculed by her fellow Red Guards, especially the boy—"

"The boy with acne? She had a crush on him, didn't she?"

"Yes. Yaya told him about her fuzzy memory of the conversation. Everyone was supposed to search deep inside his or her soul to look for anything suspicious. He pressured her to sell out her father. Yaya was heartbroken and ashamed about the whole thing. She's back home now, but...but she's like a...toddler. Don't worry. Lili and I have been helping Uncle Linzi to take care of her."

Jasmine felt a pang of sympathy for Linzi, for his wife, for his daughter. Insane times created insane people, and many lives had been irreversibly changed. She placed a hand on his arm. "It must be so hard on you."

Bai Long gave a clipped nod. "Another bad news." He lowered his head. "Red Guards damaged the statues."

"How?"

"They tried to push them down but couldn't. So, they smeared the sculptures with black ink. I'm sorry, I couldn't stop them."

"We'll clean them one day. We'll repaint."

He dipped his head. "I miss you…" He paused. His Adam's apple bounced as he worked his throat to swallow. "May I call you mother? You've saved me. Twice. You've been a mother to me for many years."

Tears gathered in Jasmine's eyes. She took both the young man and the baby in her arms. In this chaotic and dangerous time, when other families had broken apart, she had gained a family member.

"Uncle Li, before he passed away, told Little Tiger and me about Bai Ge. I'm a parent now. I can't imagine…"

Her lower lip began to tremble, and tears pricked her eyes.

"He asked us to be nice to you. We told him he didn't have to worry about it. That goes without saying. We love you."

She nodded, not trusting herself to express anything without a torrent of emotion.

"I was born the same year as Bai Ge. I know I can never replace him, but I'll be a good son."

She squeezed his arms.

"Remember what my father said?" A grin teased the corners of Bai Long's mouth. "He said you could be my mother."

The memory brought a faint smile to her face. Bai Fu's slip of the tongue had gotten her in trouble with An Kong, who was apprehensive that her husband would take Jasmine as his concubine. Two decades later, it seemed almost comical. Relaxed, she tickled the baby's tiny palm who giggled in response. "How old is she? What's her name?"

"Eight months. Her name is Bai Zhizi."

"White Gardenia? It's also called—"

"Cape Jasmine. I hope she'll grow up like her grandma."

A new kind of satisfaction thrummed through her, and her spirit soared.

The visit turned out to be a pivotal moment. More than ever,

Jasmine was determined to survive. As a result, the nightmares that had tormented her for years unexpectedly disappeared. Instead, Danny and Li Ming took turns showing up in her dreams.

The Flying Tiger would take her soaring to the snow-capped mountains and the meadow carpeted with forget-me-nots. His cheerful voice pulled her out of the darkness. His infectious smile and high energy reminded her of the joy of life.

Li Ming would hold her and whisper in her ear, "Remember your dreams. You will fulfill them." His lips softly grazed her cheek, her hair, and the trembling that had held her captive dissolved. His words gave her hope for the future.

In this gloomy place, Jasmine found inner peace.

Part Three

Light at the End of the Tunnel

Chapter 61

Ten years in the penitentiary dragged on like a foul dream. Every day was the same as the one before: scolding, beatings, studying, humiliation, hard labor. Yet life went on despite the injustices and terrors that were daily occurrences. And as Jasmine had said, no one could predict the future. The world wouldn't stand still, and finally, things started to change.

On September 9, 1976, Mao Zedong died, just as the actress had stated. No matter how many times people had shouted "Long Live Chairman Mao," he was, after all, just a man who had lived eighty-two years. Eighty-two years too long for Li Ming, Meng Hu, Wang Hong, Tan Yin, Bai Fu, An Kong, and millions of others, Jasmine thought.

On October 6, 1976, the Gang of Four—a political faction composed of four Communist Party officials, including Mao's wife Jiang Qing—was labeled as the Counter-revolutionary force and charged with a series of treasonous crimes. They were officially blamed for the Cultural Revolution, which had created societal chaos for a decade. Their downfall marked the end of a turbulent political era.

Afterward, Deng Xiaoping gained power in the Communist Party and started several reforms. Ironically, he'd been purged twice by Chairman Mao during the Cultural Revolution.

Jasmine read the news with enthusiasm and hope.

One summer day in 1977, she was summoned to the office. Behind a desk piled high with documents sat the prison chief in his usual olive-green uniform. The air in the room was stifling, and a sheen of perspiration covered his broad face. "Sit down, Comrade Bai." Mustering a hint of a smile, he pointed to a chair.

Excitement coursed through her body. For the first time in almost ten years, Jasmine heard someone calling her Comrade. It was a sign that she was no longer viewed as an Enemy of the People. She held her breath, trying hard not to fidget in anticipation of his next statement.

"According to our party's new policy, we reexamined your case as we've done with others." He patted the pile of files. "Many people were wrongfully accused. We're in the middle of correcting misjudged cases." He cleared his throat and cooled himself with a bamboo hand fan. Fidgeting in his seat, he said in an unusually small voice, "You…you're free to go, Comrade Bai."

Suppressing her joy, Jasmine asked, "Where is my son? I won't leave—"

The man looked at the door and waved his arm. Jasmine turned in time to see a young man walk inside. Her breath caught in her throat. She hadn't seen Little Tiger for almost ten years, except for occasional glimpses of him in the distance. He was no longer the teenager she remembered. At twenty-six, with broad shoulders, he was tall, sinewy, and head-turning handsome—a straight nose, a firm mouth, dark eyes, shiny black hair. He was the very image of Meng Hu, who had come to her rescue forty years earlier.

Tears flooded her eyes faster than she could prevent them. She couldn't move, couldn't speak, and her heart squeezed tightly in her chest.

"Mom!" called out the young man. His face lit up with joy. In several huge strides, he leaned down and scooped her in his arms.

Jasmine had been so determined to survive that she hadn't allowed herself to cry since she'd arrived there. Ten years. She'd been strong and resolute. She wouldn't show her weakness and vulnerability in front of the bullies. Now, in her son's warm embrace, she lost her battle against tears. Joyous tears for a change.

Little Tiger patted her back. "It's over. We can go home now."

Jasmine had dreamed countless times of the peaceful village. It had seemed so far out of reach. Now, once again, she would return to the place that held her heart and soul and her loved ones.

The man in charge stood as he wiped the beads on his forehead with a handkerchief. "Our party is great and wise. We admit we've made wrong decisions. We'll right all wrongs."

Little Tiger kicked open the door. "Let me lock you up for ten years. Then you can tell me how great and wise I am when I release you."

As the mother and the son left the place where they were imprisoned for a decade, fresh air mixed with the sweet scent of honeysuckle greeted them.

―――――――

After losing freedom for almost ten years, Jasmine found that life in the village was better than ever. At fifty-eight, she enjoyed every minute of being with her sons and grandchildren. Soon after her return, she started painting again. When she was locked up, it had been her dream to pick up the paintbrushes. She also wanted to earn money. Her dream of searching for Danny had never died. If anything, it grew stronger and more urgent as she got older. Years of hard living and lack of proper nutrition had taken a toll on her. She often felt dizzy and every now and then threw up for no reason. Linzi gave her herbal medicines, but it would take time to heal her.

One day in the autumn of 1977, as usual, Jasmine checked the newspapers after preparing for dinner. Her lips parted in wordless surprise as she stared at a front-page story. Quickly, she scanned the article, stood up, and walked outside. With the newspaper in hand, she paced back and forth in front of the house.

The sun was setting, beaming warm light over the village, casting the surrounding forest in gold. The soft wind rustled the nearby hardwood trees, where birds flitted and twittered. Under the sunlight, the lush hillside and the remote village were as picturesque as ever.

Jasmine waited. As soon as her sons showed up, she greeted them in an excited tone and waved the piece of newspaper. "The government has decided to resume the college entrance exams. You can take part this winter. You may get into a university!"

"Seriously?" asked Little Tiger, mopping sweat from his sun-tanned face.

Jasmine nodded. She could hardly contain herself.

Little Tiger snatched the newspaper and read it with Bai Long.

Titled "After a Decade, the College Entrance Exams Resume," the article stated that since 1966, the Cultural Revolution had swept the nation and college examinations had been suspended. Students were mobilized to participate in the revolution. For ten years, normal learning at schools was interrupted, and all the universities were closed as professors and school officials were publicly humiliated and beaten, some driven to suicide. Since 1968, following Chairman Mao's instruction, millions of young people were sent to the countryside to be reeducated by peasants. Now, as part of his reform, Deng Xiaoping, the paramount leader of the People's Republic of China, had decided to tackle problems in the education system.

"Unbelievable!" said Bai Long. "Too late for me," he sighed. Disappointment showed in his voice. At thirty-four, and with two young kids, a college was beyond his reach. "But you've got a chance." He turned to Little Tiger and slapped his back.

"Me?" He was still gawking at the paper.

"It's a once-in-a-lifetime opportunity," said Jasmine, "for both of you." She lifted a hand to forestall Bai Long's protest. "Look here, they're going to waive the age restriction. You've got a chance too!"

"I can't. I don't have enough education. But Xiao Hu can!" Bai Long had had education for only two years before his father was killed. He was fifteen when Jasmine took him to the village, and since then, he'd mainly studied art. Although Little Tiger had never had a day in school, she'd taught him before they were arrested.

"Yes, he has a better chance. But you've got a chance, too." She paused, one corner of her mouth twitching with the need to smile. "You can apply for Art Colleges!"

Hope leaped to life in Bai Long's eyes.

The sun had already sunk behind the mountains. Its last rays crowned the distant peaks with a hazy orange halo, and the sky blazed amber, rose, and peach. Jasmine looked at her two sons; their zestful faces bathed in the sunset's glow. Her heart swelled.

From that moment onward, even though they still worked in the fields during the day, the young men spent countless hours in the evening preparing for the exam. It was exhausting, but they were in high spirits and never complained. The bothers had been denied so much in life, and they appreciated the opportunity as much as life itself. Jasmine also stayed up late, helping them with problems, testing their knowledge, or making delicious snacks for them.

There was an air of excitement and hope.

Chapter 62

━ ━ ━ ━ ━ ━ ━ ━

February 1978 was cold and gloomy in the mountainous area of Yunnan Province.

One after another, all the universities to which Little Tiger applied rejected him. His score of literature was the second-highest in the province, and his scores for other subjects were good enough. By academic merit alone, he could have entered any universities in the country. However, he was denied. He failed at *zheng shen—political background check*. Even though he'd been released from the penitentiary, his father was still labeled as Counter-revolutionary. Children of Counter-revolutionaries were deprived of opportunity simply because they were born into the wrong families.

Disappointment and frustration enveloped the family. Their spark of hope was snuffed out. No matter how hard he worked or how great the scores he achieved, Little Tiger would never enter a university. That saddened Jasmine. Among them, she felt the worst since she'd had the highest expectation.

"Don't worry, Mom," Little Tiger comforted her. "Out of 5.7 million people that applied, only about 300,000 got in. I'm not alone." A determined expression tightened his mouth. "I can still write. Many writers in history never had formal education. I won't give up." He'd written a lot while he was in jail, but most of the writings were on pieces of papers scattered all over the compound. He had to rewrite the book from scratch.

"It's so unfair!" hissed Jasmine. Her sadness and disappointment gave way to anger. "I was hoping things would be different now."

"It *is* different. I'm not locked up. I have a notebook to use." His seriousness vanished, replaced by his typical levity. "Hey, lucky I'm not obsessed with science. It would be impossible to do lab work here."

She was awestruck by his unsinkable spirit.

Bai Long was luckier. Although his art had received an extremely high score, his scores in other subjects were too low to be accepted into college. However, one professor in Kunming was so impressed by his work that he offered him a job as his assistant. "If you accept," the professor wrote in his letter, "you could start in the coming semester."

"You'll be working at a college." Little Tiger punched his brother on the shoulder, his face glowing. "That's better than being a student."

"I just hoped, you know, that we could go together."

"One is better than zero." Little Tiger's smile broadened.

His devil-may-care and happy-go-lucky personality reminded Jasmine so much of Meng Hu, and she was delighted and proud. Being educated at a university would be ideal, but having such a positive outlook on life, after everything that had happened to him, was invaluable. At moments like this, she wondered who the lucky girl would be to marry this delightful young man.

Yet, she wished that there was something she could do for him. Little Tiger wasn't just her son. He was Meng Hu's son and Birch's godson. He was the offspring of that group of fighter pilots, many of whom had perished, including Danny and Tan Hu.

A year after her return, Jasmine would once again separate from one of her family members—Bai Long. But this time, she was elated. Her son was going to work at a college.

"Your grandpa was a professor and the head of the Art Department at Nanking University. I was an art student before the war forced me to quit school." She held his arms and said with a barely contained excitement, "I'm thrilled that you're continuing the family tradition of studying art."

"I'll do my best."

"You've got the family name." Little Tiger poked a playful finger at his brother's arm.

"I wish you could—" mumbled Bai Long.

"I'll visit you one day."

"Hey, why don't you send your brother to Kunming?" Jasmine said, feeling a sudden lift of her spirits. "You'll get a chance to see the city."

"Now? It's almost summer. We're busy here—"

"Yes, but it won't take more than a few days. You want to be a good writer. You need to see the world. 'It's better to travel ten thousand miles than to read ten thousand books,'" she quoted a famous proverb.

"I'm like the frog at the bottom of a well. I've never been anywhere except Anning."

"Come with me!" Enthusiasm flooded the older brother's face.

"But—"

"You're writing a book about the Flying Tigers. Their headquarters was in Kunming," said Jasmine.

That convinced Little Tiger. His dark eyes brightened with an eagerness that he couldn't hide. "Perhaps I should look for Professor Lin when I'm there."

"Great idea. Hopefully, she's back to work."

———————

A week before their trip, as the family had dinner together, a teenager brought their mail. There was still no postal service to the community, but the villagers shared a mailbox at the post office in Anning. The boy was responsible for picking up mail twice a week.

Besides the newspapers that Jasmine had subscribed to, there was a thick envelope from Yunnan University in Kunming. She didn't think twice before handing it to Bai Long.

After reading the letter, he let out a cheerful hoot. The generally reserved and quiet man stood up and pulled Little Tiger to a stand-ing position. Before anyone could blink, he picked up the taller and heavier brother, and in the tiny room, he twirled a few times.

"What's going on?" Jasmine asked with an amused smile.

"He's going crazy," laughed Xiao Hu, struggling to stand still. "Did they give you a raise before you start?"

Bai Long beamed, unable to suppress his delight and pride, but he didn't say anything.

She picked up the letter and drew in a quick breath before her mouth made a perfect O. When she looked up, tears trickled down her cheeks.

"What the heck?" Little Tiger took the letter from her. Once he started reading, he, too, was dumbstruck.

"Congratulations, Xiao Hu!" Jasmine said in a voice thick with emotion.

"You're going to be a college student, after all." Bai Long punched his brother's arm a few times. Exhilaration infused his face with color.

Little Tiger lifted his head. For the first time since he was a tod-dler, he had tears in his eyes. Reaching down, he wrapped his arms around her. "Thank you, Mom! Thank you so much."

She patted his back. "You deserve it," she said, not trusting herself to elaborate without great emotion.

It turned out that Jasmine had written a letter to Deng Xiaop-ing, the leader of the country. She thanked him for all the positive changes in recent years. She told him Little Tiger's situation and his family background. "Meng Hu was wrongfully accused. As a fighter pilot, he fought the Japanese for eight years, and he was a flight instructor during the Civil War. He couldn't possibly be an Enemy of the People." She'd included the suicide note the policeman had written to Wang Hong before he jumped in front of a bus. His bloody fingerprint was still clearly visible.

"Even if Meng Hu were a Counter-revolutionary, this shouldn't affect the future of his son who has never met him." She asked the leader of the Party to intervene in the unfair and discriminatory treatment of Xiao Hu and others like him.

The staff in Deng Xiaoping's office had taken this case seriously, and after their investigation, they'd made an exception. Based on Little Tiger's academic merit and a professor's recommendation, he was accepted by Yunnan University. This professor was Lin Ling. She was once again the head of the Literature Department. Little Tiger's exceedingly high score had caught her attention, and she'd recommended him. The thick envelope included all the information.

Xiao Hu said, "It's so…surreal."

"I can't believe it, either." Jasmine beamed. "I had no idea if anyone would take it seriously when I wrote the letter. Thank God!"

"Thank Deng Xiaoping," corrected Little Tiger.

"Yes! Thanks to his reforms and his open mind." She wished that Meng Hu, Li Ming, Birch, and Danny could witness this moment. This was beyond her dream. *Wang Hong, I told you I'd take care of your son.* Now, she'd fulfilled her promise.

"Well, I've already packed."

"Yeah, adding a few more clothes, you're ready to go," grinned the elder brother.

"After all, you can't get rid of me." Little Tiger threw a fake punch at Bai Long's arm. "You're stuck with me, Big Brother."

Chapter 63

Neither Bai Long nor Little Tiger came home during the winter break.

Bai Long was working on an assignment in Dashan. Although it was only a one-day hike to the village, the thick blanket of snow made the path impassable.

Little Tiger wanted to research for his book about the Flying Tigers. During the school year, he had barely had time for anything except his homework. When he asked for her permission, Jasmine quoted a famous saying, "Great ambitious men travel far and aim high." She missed them dearly, but their futures were more important to her.

She waited. The summer of 1979 was fast approaching, but it wasn't fast enough for her. She hadn't seen her sons for over a year and couldn't wait for them to return home.

The reunion was as sweet as she'd imagined. Both men were in great shape and high spirits. Little Tiger picked her up and twirled her around while Bai Long scolded him. Although they'd never stopped communicating by mail, they had so much to talk about. The entire village threw a party in the herbalist's front yard. There were many dishes, rice wine, music, and storytelling. The delicious aroma of food and the sweet scent of honeysuckle and other wildflowers lingered in the air.

Little Tiger stayed with Jasmine while Bai Long lived with his wife and children at Linzi's house. Once a week, the three of them would have dinner together as they used to. A few days later, she cooked pork and leek dumplings, their favorite dish. As they enjoyed their meal, the teenage boy stopped by to deliver the mail. There was an official-looking letter from Chungking.

Her heart thudded in her chest when she started to read.

It was "Resolution on the Rehabilitation of Comrade Li Ming" issued by the Provincial Committee of the Communist Party in Chungking. It declared his ouster to be unwarranted and removed all labels of "Traitor, Capitalist Roader, and Counter-revolutionary" that had been attached to him at the time of his death.

The case regarding Li Ming and the other two survivors in the 1949 prison break had been reexamined. The conclusion was that they'd been unjustly accused. It was a case of misconduct. All of them, along with Tan Yin, were posthumously "rehabilitated," and their names were cleared.

The document also stated that "Comrade Li Ming was a great Marxist and Proletarian Revolutionary" and recognized him as one of the important provincial leaders of the Party in Chungking. The followers of the Gang of Four were blamed for concocting false evidence against him and subjecting him to a political frame-up and physical persecution.

Even though Jasmine had been waiting for this news, she was so emotional that her hands started to shake. For the past two years, many cases had been reexamined, and countless people had been "rehabilitated" throughout the country, including Liu Shaoqi, the former Chairman of the People's Republic of China and Peng Dehuai, the former Defense Minister.

"Are you okay, Mom?" mumbled Little Tiger with a mouthful of dumplings.

Tears spurted from her eyes. "I'm okay." She handed the first page of the letter to him. "I'm more than okay!" She wished Li Ming could see this. He was no longer branded as an Enemy of the People. She knew how thrilled he would be. One more dream on her list was achieved.

"Finally!" exclaimed Little Tiger.

"Finally," sighed Bai Long. "Twelve years too late for Uncle Li."

On the second page, Jasmine was informed that Li Ming's bank account had been unfrozen. "He gave me his deposit book." She told them about their discussion. "He didn't want Li Dong to have it. But I know how much he loved his son. The day we left Chunking, we took a detour and stayed outside his ex-wife's house for half an hour, just to see his son in the distance for one last time. I'd like to give part of this to Li Dong. What do you think?"

"Uncle Li gave it to you. Whatever you do, we'll support you." Little Tiger turned to his brother, who nodded.

She hitched in a deep breath. "Believe it or not, he told me...I could use the funds to find...Danny." Her heart was filled with warmth as she relayed their conversation. Once again, her admiration for Li Ming deepened. *He said that I had a heart as large as the sky. He had a heart greater than the sky.*

"Uncle Li was an incredible man," said Bai Long in a respectful tone.

"That's awesome! Now we have the funds." Little Tiger patted his brother's shoulder excitedly. "We can go tomorrow to find—"

"Go where? To find what?" asked Jasmine.

His expression turned contrite. He probably realized his slip of the tongue.

"Go where?"

"It's my fault. I should've told you," admitted Bai Long. "You know I had the assignment in Dashan during winter break. I remember you said that Uncle Birch had found out about a Jap prison northeast of the town. So, while I was there, I went to the nearby villages and asked around. I found an old gentleman who told me he knew about a mass grave. He and two other farmers had saved a man from it. I—"

Jasmine's eyes rounded. She clutched his arm. "Did you find it? The grave?"

He tipped his head.

"Dear God!" was the only thing she uttered. After the initial shock, she asked with a shaky voice, "Did you see—"

"No!" Bai Long interrupted her. "The old man took me there.

He told me there were probably fifty or sixty people buried there. It can't be the one… That's why I didn't say anything."

Jasmine turned to Little Tiger. "You knew it too, but you—"

"I'm sorry, Mom," murmured the young man. "Bai Long told me as soon as he returned from Dashan. He wanted to search for… Uncle Danny. But we didn't have enough money to do anything, and the school was starting again. He asked me if we should tell you, but we decided… you know." His Adam's apple bobbed up and down. "We didn't want to give you false hope. We didn't find him. We were going to wait—"

Jasmine sighed. She knew they meant well. "Now that I know, and we have the funds, let's go as soon as we can."

"Yes, but you really shouldn't go," said the elder brother.

"You stay here. Let us do it for you, Mom."

She shook her head. Years of hard living had taken a toll on her, and she'd been in bad shape after her release from the prison. She was doing better after taking Linzi's herbal medicines, but at age sixty, she wasn't in good enough condition to hike a long distance.

"I must go!" she said, sitting ramrod straight. Determination raised her face. "No negotiation. I'll be there, even if I have to crawl."

The two men exchanged a helpless look.

"Let's compromise." Bai Long paused and exchanged another understanding look with Little Tiger. "Let's carry you." He held up a hand to prevent her from arguing. "Anyway, we'll need a way to transfer Danny's body once we find him."

Little Tiger agreed. "You don't want us to carry an empty sedan chair with us, don't you? We need the exercise. Otherwise, you'll have two fat-bottomed sons pretty soon." With a goofy smile, he tilted his head back and popped a dumpling into his mouth.

Chapter 64

Bai Long took Jasmine, Little Tiger, and Lili to an abandoned Japanese prison near Dashan. "The villagers think there are too many ghosts around the area. It hasn't been occupied since the war against Japan ended."

The small camp was surrounded by a rusty barbed-wire fence. They walked through a wooden gate. Nearby, a teetering watchtower loomed above them.

The midday sun beat down on the empty courtyard. In the back stood a mud-brick building with six rooms, clearly prison cells. Each had bolted windows and a heavy lock on the door. Inside, straw was scattered everywhere, some rotted. The walls were covered with dust, and spider webs dangled from the low ceiling. Two wooden buckets were tucked in a corner. A foul stench flooded the air. Only slivers of sunshine filtered through the windows. Jasmine's heart tightened at the thought that this was the place Danny and Birch had been locked up for weeks.

In a separate building, the rooms were much nicer with bigger windows and wooden beds. Obviously, this was the sleeping quarters of the Japanese guards.

"I can't stay here," she said, new hatred for the Japanese soldiers boiling up from deep inside her gut. These were the people who had tortured and shot Danny, Birch, and other prisoners.

Little Tiger nodded. His face creased with revulsion. "No way in hell I'll sleep on those beds..."

There was no objection. The group walked back to the prison cell and cleaned two of the rooms. The tarps they'd brought with them became their temporary beds.

After they settled, Bai Long led the group to a place not far from the compound. "The old gentleman told me..." He pointed to a sign sticking out of the ground in an area covered with grass. A few characters were carved upon the aged wooden plaque: *These Nameless Heroes Will Never Be Forgotten.* "He told me he and two villagers found a wounded man right here and took him to a military base. We know now that the man was Uncle Birch."

There was nodding all around.

"He said there were fifty or sixty people. The villagers had no idea who they were except that they were killed by the Japs. So, the villagers buried the bodies and put up this sign."

How many people still remember those who fought the Japs for our freedom? How many people care about them? The words on the commemorative plaque seemed poignant to Jasmine. Shaking her head, she asked, "They don't know anything about the other grave?" She'd already heard the answer, but she couldn't resist double-checking.

"I'm sorry."

Little Tiger spun around, scanning the area. "So, where do we start?"

They looked at each other. No one had any good ideas.

Grass and shrubs covered a considerable stretch all along the fence. The area was dotted with white, yellow, and magenta flowers in full bloom, and the long grass swayed and danced in the breeze. Beyond it lay the dense forest. The grave shouldn't be in the woods. But if it was in this relatively open field, where would be its exact location? After three decades, the growth of vegetation made it impossible to identify. They tried their best to look for any sign but to no avail.

Jasmine fell ill. Sadness, exhaustion, and frustration took a toll on her already frail body. She couldn't get out of bed for days.

"Let's go home, Mom," proposed Little Tiger. "You need medicines and rest."

"Yes. We'll come back." Bai Long and Lili spoke in unison. "We may find a better lead by then," he added.

Jasmine shook her head; the movement made her feel dizzy. Her face had an unhealthy pallor, but she wouldn't leave. *We're so close. Danny is right here!* She could feel his spirit all around her. It had been her dream for thirty-six years. How could she give up now? She wouldn't fail him in death as she had in life.

A few days later, a short, wiry villager showed up. He was in his late sixties and balding. "I heard that you're looking for a grave. I used to pass this area at night. I've seen *gui huo* around here many times."

"Will-o'-the-wisp?" asked Jasmine.

He nodded. "According to our ancestors, where you see *gui huo* is where you'll find bodies. They are the light from the ghosts." His weathered face tightened a little. "It scared the living daylights out of me."

Hope brightened Jasmine's bleak mood. She knew that mysterious pale lights could be seen on some nights. In the dark, they danced over the ground, eerie and ghostly. It was due to the spontaneous combustion of chemical compounds produced from decomposing organic matter—human bodies included. If the grave were shallow, then some of the bones might be exposed over time. The ancient belief wasn't too far from the mark, except that the lights didn't come from ghosts. "Can you show us where you saw it?"

The villager scratched his bald head. "It happened many years ago, but I can try."

The next day, the young men started digging according to the villager's fuzzy memory. They found ten corpses; none wore a Flying Tiger's flight jacket.

Through her disappointment, Jasmine wondered, how many people died in this prison? *How many bodies do we have to exhume in order to find Danny?* She shaded her eyes to block the bright sunlight as she scanned the open field. The balmy July morning had given way to a rising temperature. Frowning, she was worried that

297

she would never see a resolution.

"Don't be discouraged," said Little Tiger. His hair was damp from perspiration, and his shirt was soaked through.

"There's one more place we can check," added Bai Long, wiping the sweat from his face. "It seems the old man is pretty accurate."

———————

Jasmine awoke with aches all over her body. It had been a couple of weeks, and she was still not completely recovered from her illness. The room lacked proper circulation, even after the wooden planks had been removed from the windows. Sleeping on the hard floor further aggravated her problem.

A shaft of light from the open window indicated that it was well past dawn. No one was around. She figured that her sons were busy searching for the grave while Lili had probably gone shopping for food. Flattening her palm on the wall to stabilize herself, she stood, and dragging her feet, she walked outside.

Brilliant sunlight splashed across the empty compound. Not a breath of wind disturbed the stillness of the day.

She squinted. After a moment of waiting for her faintness to pass, she started to move. Her gait was awkward and uneven. When she reached the gate of the compound, she watched her sons squat not far away in front of piles of dirt. "Xiao Hu. Bai Long," she called out.

Little Tiger leaped to his feet. He exploded into a full sprint toward her, raising a trail of dust from the gravel lane behind him. A rag tied over his face covered his nose and mouth but couldn't disguise his grim expression. "We found—"

Without hearing the rest, Jasmine limped forward.

"Don't go." He grabbed her arm, blocking her way. "Mom, please don't!"

Bai Long joined them. He took hold of her other arm. A similar rag shielded his darkened face. "You shouldn't see—"

"I must..." She straightened and stretched her spine, and resolve raised the chin on her heart-shaped face.

Chapter 65

Three decades had passed, but grief had no time limit, and the pain of Danny's death remained deep in her heart. Jasmine missed him—his high spirits, his infectious smile, his handsome features, his tall frame, his gold-speckled brown eyes. Throughout the years, she'd drawn countless pictures of him, so his face was crystal clear in her mind. Not many days had passed that she hadn't thought of him. For over three decades, she'd dreamed of this moment, the moment of seeing him again.

But the reality was too cruel. Although Jasmine was eager and determined, it took everything she had to look at the grave.

Her Danny was gone. Only his skeleton awaited her. Amongst the partially uncovered remains of other prisoners lay his body. Worms and bugs were crawling in the dirt around them. With visible damage from shooting and stabbing, his familiar flight jacket was tattered and shredded in places. A hole rotted through the image of a winged tiger leaping out of a Victory "V" on his left chest. Next to it rested his right fist.

Jasmine couldn't breathe. Logically, she'd known what to expect, but the gruesome image sliced into her like a knife and ripped out her heart. Danny was not only the love of her life but also a courageous American who had made the ultimate sacrifice for her country. No one, except her family, talked about him and his friends. No one appreciated the freedom obtained by the help of the Flying Tigers. No one remembered the brave exploits of this group of American pilots. Instead, the American soldiers had been labeled as Devils for three decades. Looking at the grave with sad eyes, she crumpled as if a crushing weight had been pressed upon her shoulders.

Little Tiger caught her arm, stabilizing her.

Cicadas shrilled their high-pitched, incessant buzz in the nearby grassy field. The putrid stench of decay and death permeated the air. Bile climbed into her throat, and Jasmine had trouble holding it. Stepping aside, she bent over and vomited. Even after she emptied her stomach, she continued to dry heave.

Bai Long handed her a water carrier.

"Go back inside," begged Little Tiger, squeezing her arm.

"Xiao Hu is right." The elder brother patted her back. "There is nothing you can do here. We'll—"

"Let me say goodbye..." Jasmine murmured. She dropped to her knees in front of the grave and bowed down. Her sons knelt beside her. Their heads knocked against the ground three times, using the traditional way to show their highest reverence.

She didn't get up for a long time. Her forehead touched the ground; her hands gripped the dirt from the grave that had covered Danny for years. *Goodbye, my dearest. I love you!* The blade in her chest twisted. *Until the end of my life.*

"Look," said Little Tiger. "There's something in his hand." He reached out. Gingerly, he removed the item and opened it. It was the remnant of a red scarf. The color had faded. The silk fabric had deteriorated, giving it a ghostly texture.

Jasmine's face went pale as she recognized it. "It was mine, a gift from Birch. He gave a pink one to Daisy." It had flown away when the Japanese tortured her in Linzi's front yard. The last time she'd seen it was in the newspaper. She guessed that Birch had found it in the village and had given it to Danny.

The ghostly scarf transported her into a long-ago world where love, sacrifice, kindness, and bravery had all played a part during one of the darkest hours of their history. The past rushed forward and seized her, a relentless assault of sights and sounds stirred her soul.

"I think…we should put it back," mumbled Little Tiger.

Bai Long agreed. "It must have been very important to him."

Jasmine nodded. *In the last moment of his life, he was holding my scarf. He was thinking of me!* If she hadn't been so scared and ashamed, if she'd returned to the village earlier, she could have given Danny her love. Now, even on a sunny day, she felt chilled. The familiar guilt and regret gripped her with full force.

Through blurred vision, she stretched out her hand, trying to touch the scarf before it disappeared from her life once again. However, a sudden wave of giddiness came over her, and stars appeared in front of her eyes. Her arm fell to her side as the world dropped out from under her.

———————

Nightmares haunted Jasmine. She was kneeling by the side of the grave. The full moon dusted the area in a gunmetal-blue hue, casting insidious shadows on the ground. Tears trickled down her face as she gazed at Danny's remains. Ghostly pale-green lights danced around her.

"Jasmine…" Someone was calling her from behind. She knew the voice. It was the Flying Tiger. But how could it be? He was lying in front of her in the shallow grave.

"Why are you so sad?" he asked.

"I saw you in a…" She was about to turn her head when he cradled her face in his hands. "Don't look." He tightened his grip. "It's okay. Birch is safe."

"I haven't seen him in years. I'm worried about him."

"Don't be. He's a tough man. He can handle it."

"What about you?" She was about to recheck the grave when Danny slipped an arm around her and pulled her close. "Fly with me." He lifted them into the sky. Instantly, they were above Angel's Pass. His eyes twinkled with mischief.

Hand in hand, they flew over and under the suspension bridge. The endless abyss took Jasmine's breath. He set her down near the statue of the Flying Tiger and kissed her, long and deep.

The next moment he was gone, only his voice echoed in the canyon. "Remember me. I'm forever in this place!"

Jasmine awoke with tears in her eyes and a smile upon her face. Even in death, the Flying Tiger had found a way to cheer her. And that was how she would remember him.

Jasmine remained in bed for days. The event had been so traumatic that she'd drifted in and out of consciousness. Lili took care of her while the young men dealt with the remains. She learned later that they'd found a body wearing a pair of broken eyeglasses and guessed that he was Mr. Ding. They got in touch with Old Ding in Dashan and helped him to cremate his son's remains. The old man was grateful beyond words. Since they didn't know anyone else, the brothers covered the bodies, marked the sight, and informed the local government about the two graves they'd discovered.

"Thank you so much for everything!" Jasmine said with a knot in her throat.

"No need," said Little Tiger. "Nothing I do will ever repay what you've done for me. I was just a kid, but I remember. I…" His Adam's apple slid up and down a few times. "I've never thanked you."

"Me either," choked Bai Long. "Thank you, Mother! Without you, I'd have starved to death or been thrown into jail."

Hearing their words made her lifelong struggle worthwhile, and her chest expanded with warmth. Perhaps she'd survived and suffered so that these two children could be saved? Reaching up, she drew both of them into her embrace.

Several days later, when Jasmine felt better, they started for home.

It was overcast. The sun was obscured by clouds that shrouded the mountain tops. The gray sky reflected her mood. Sitting in the bamboo-pole sedan chair carried by the brothers, she held a ceramic urn tightly in front of her chest. A few characters were engraved on the pearl white cremation container: "Beloved Bai Hu, 1914 – 1945, Forever Missed, Forever Loved."

She'd been taken aback when she first saw the words. Although the country had started to open, the relationship between China and the United States was still complicated. To avoid any potential trouble, and they'd had more than their fair share of trouble, the brothers had come up with this idea. They told the crematorium that the man was their uncle. No one would check the identity of the deceased's remains. The name was fitting in many ways: Bai was Jasmine and Birch's family name, Danny was born in the year of *Hu*—*Tiger*, and he was a *Fei Hu*—*Flying Tiger*.

It was ironic and poignant that Danny had tried to locate her remains. Now it was Jasmine who had found his body. The thought brought a stab of pain, and she groaned.

"Are you okay?" asked Little Tiger. He carried the sedan chair in the front whenever they were going downhill. The creaky bamboo poles rested on his shoulders.

"I'm all right." She pulled in a long breath. "My next goal is to locate Danny's family. But I only know that he lived in San Francisco."

"You don't know the address?" questioned Lili, walking along with the sedan chair.

"No, it never occurred to me to ask. I have no idea how to look for them." Jasmine lowered her head. "I'll keep his ashes for as long as I live. If I can't find them by the time I die, I want you to scatter my ashes with his at Angel's Pass."

Little Tiger protested.

Jasmine held up her hand. "'None can escape from death since ancient times,'" she quoted a famous saying. "Promise me?"

The brothers replied in unison, "We promise."

Just then, a slat of sunlight fought its way through the leaden clouds.

Chapter 66

Finding Danny Hardy's remains fulfilled the promise Jasmine had made, but her job was far from over. Now, she had to locate his family and send his remains home.

She'd befriended several Americans many years earlier. Peter Peterson was her art teacher in Chungking, who had fallen in love with her and proposed to her. They had not communicated since he left China. During the Nanking Massacre, Father John and Professor Valentine had helped to protect hundreds of thousands of people, including Jasmine, Li Ming, and Xiao Mei's family. But she lost contact with Father John once she moved to this remote village, and the professor had taken her own life. Jasmine didn't know anyone else in the United States.

"Where can I start?" she asked after they were back in the village.

"How about the American Embassy?" ventured Little Tiger.

"They might be able to help if they know that we found the remains of an American citizen," said Bai Long.

"I don't even know where the American Embassy is located." Jasmine had been living in this remote village for over three decades. The outside world was largely unfamiliar. From newspapers, she learned that Mainland China and the United States had established diplomatic relations in January 1979. In March, the two countries had established embassies in each other's capitals.

"Let me go to the college in Anning," volunteered Little Tiger. "I need to check a few things for my book anyway."

Since she was still feeling weak, Jasmine nodded her appreciation. She knew how much her son was eager to help. It was the beginning of August, and his school wouldn't start until September.

That evening, Little Tiger came back with a dispirited look. "The librarian stared at me as if I'd come from another planet," he grunted. "I looked for books. None—"

"Let me guess," said Bai Long. "None of them say anything positive about the U.S."

"The library only has propaganda books."

Jasmine handed him a cup of water.

Little Tiger finished it in a few gulps. Wiping the water from his face, he continued, "I also called an operator asking for information. There was a long silence. Then, she said, 'Hold please.' I waited and waited and almost gave up. Finally, a man's voice came on the line. He asked several questions. 'Who are you? What do you do? Why do you need the American Embassy's number?' I hung up without saying anything."

"You did the right thing. The world is changing. But it's better safe than sorry. Don't raise any red flags." Alarmed and disappointed, she heaved a long-winded sigh. "We'll have to wait."

"We'll check with our library once we're back in Kunming," promised Bai Long.

"They might be more open-minded in a bigger city," observed Little Tiger.

———

Little Tiger had written *The Wind beneath His Wings* as a novel during his imprisonment. Professor Lin suggested that he write it as a true story. "You told me it's ninety percent real. Why don't you write it as nonfiction? This already incredible story would be even more remarkable and touching," she said. "It may not be easy to get it published, though. Not because your writing isn't good enough, but because the subject is too sensitive."

He understood. The country had just started to open. Americans were no longer labeled as Devils, but there weren't any books or articles describing their involvement in the war against Japan. And a story about the rescue of an American pilot by the people, including a Nationalist officer, would be controversial, to say the least. The contribution of the Nationalists in the war was another forbidden subject. According to the authorities in Mainland China, the Communists alone had fought the Japanese. This was far from the truth, but history was often written and slanted by the winners.

Despite the obstacles, Little Tiger worked tirelessly.

Jasmine provided more detailed information, and both she and Bai Long were his first readers. Professor Lin spent countless hours working with the young man.

In the summer of 1980, the manuscript was finally done. Writing word by word by hand, Jasmine and Bai Long helped Little Tiger to make copies. By winter break, he'd sent the book to half a dozen publishers. The family waited. For weeks nothing happened. Not even a rejection letter. It was like he'd thrown a rock into the middle of the ocean.

In the late spring of 1981, he received a letter from an editor. "I love your story. It's beautifully written and very moving. I didn't know that part of history and thank you for educating me. Unfortunately, I can't accept it. The subject is too debatable and risky. Do you have anything else? Would you consider writing a book with a less sensitive subject? I'd love to work with you."

Little Tiger thanked the editor but stated that he had to tell the truth. He'd just started writing another book. *Roar of a Feisty Tiger* was about his father Meng Hu—his life as a fighter pilot, his friendship with Tan Hu, Birch, and Danny, his love for his wife Wang Hong, his wrongful imprisonment and death.

"Bai Long took me out to dinner," Little Tiger wrote in his letter to Jasmine. "He said he'd take me out every time I receive a rejection letter. I'm not discouraged, and I won't stop writing. But his kind gesture meant so much to me."

As the country opened its door even further, Professor Lin made connections in Hong Kong. In 1982, she helped Little Tiger to get in touch with a publisher there. Soon, Jasmine received a letter from him.

> *Dear Mom,*
>
> *You won't believe this. My book has been accepted for publication! I jumped up and down a few times as I shouted, waving my arms like a crazy man. Then, I ran to Bai Long's classroom and barged in. He apologized to his students while I grabbed him and pulled him outside. I couldn't help it. I was so excited that I had to share it with someone. God! I wish you were here!*
>
> *It was 1966 when I first had the idea. Do you remember? I've worked on this book for over fifteen years. It's been my dream to get it published. It's still so surreal. Can you believe it? I'm going to be a published author.*
>
> *Thank you, Mom, for everything! Despite the danger, you adopted me, raised me, and always put my well-being above yours. You told me the truth about the Flying Tigers and my family history when those were forbidden topics. If Danny Hardy was a larger-than-life hero, you're a real-life hero. Your unbendable courage and undying love for the Flying Tiger are the inspiration and the foundation for this book. Words can never describe my gratitude and respect.*
>
> *Love,*
> *Xiao Hu*

Jasmine was brimming with joy. Once again, she wished his biological parents were there to witness his success. Dying of cancer, Wang Hong had traveled a thousand miles to bring her son to this remote village in the hope that he would be safe here. Meng Hu had taught his child to live with integrity, even in the face of injustice and death. They would be so proud of their son.

More great news arrived.

Readers loved *The Wind Beneath His Wings*; many were deeply touched by the story. It was so well received that a publishing house in the United States translated it into English. People, including some Americans, started to contact Little Tiger.

"I'm so glad you taught me English," he said. "Remember I didn't do well at first? Thank God you didn't give up on me. How could anyone imagine the country would actually open its door to the outside world?" Before the summer of 1984, Little Tiger told Jasmine that he would bring several new friends to visit the village.

Chapter 67

Jasmine hadn't had visitors for two decades. The last one was Professor Lin, who had stayed for three months in 1964. Using the leftover funds from Li Ming, she hired young villagers to remodel the house, which had been built in the 1930s by her uncle. The day the guests arrived, Linzi and Lili helped her to prepare the meal. They made dumplings. She hoped that Little Tiger's friends would like them.

Around noon, her sons stepped into the courtyard, and she flung herself into their arms.

"Mom," chirped Little Tiger when he broke from the embrace, "look who is here." He stepped aside, and a petite woman in her early sixties moved forward.

Jasmine was startled. She'd expected to see a group of young people. Politely, she extended her hand.

The woman grabbed her hand with both of hers. "Miss Jasmine!" she cried out, her voice quivering with emotion. "It's me. I'm Xiao Mei."

"Xiao Mei?" she stumbled over the name. *Is this real?* It had been over forty years since she'd parted with the housemaid in Chungking in 1941. She studied the woman's face, seeking the once familiar features and remembering her eyes full of kindness and sincerity. "My God! You are Xiao Mei! You were twenty when I last saw you."

The two hugged, tears swimming in their eyes.

"She's also Mrs. Bai," Little Tiger proudly announced. "She's Uncle Birch's wife."

Jasmine squeaked in surprise. "Birch's wife?" A smile lit up her face. "Thank God!" She clutched Xiao Mei's arms. "I knew how much you loved him. I've always wished that the two of you would be together."

"Me, too," beamed Linzi.

"Where is Birch?" Jasmine looked behind the other woman, searching for her cousin's tall figure.

Xiao Mei's face darkened.

"Where is he?"

"He's…gone, Miss Jasmine. He passed away."

"No!" she wailed. "Not Birch!" She'd waited four decades to reunite with her family. She knew that the chance of seeing her uncle alive became slimmer as time passed—she'd expected that as he would be in his nineties—but Birch was only five years older than she. He would be seventy this year. The last memory she had of him was of a tall, strong, and athletic young man. She'd clung to a sliver of hope that she would meet him again. "How…?" She could hear her own voice sliding out of control.

"Emphysema."

Tears streamed down her face.

"He never stopped thinking of you," choked Xiao Mei. "He'd be over the moon if he could see you now. So sad he didn't know. He searched for your body many times. How could he have known that you were still alive?"

Jasmine shivered as profound sadness and guilt engulfed her. Birch had had a strong influence on her. They'd grown up together, practically like brother and sister. He'd taught her to swim, to bike, and to play tennis. He'd encouraged her when she had doubts. She'd always called him *Birch Ge—Big Brother Birch*.

It just dawned on Jasmine that almost all the men close to her, even though they were different in age, race, career, and political belief, had similar traits to her cousin—decent, kind, courageous, principled, determined, passionate…

LEGACY OF THE TIGERS

A wave of dizziness swept over her. Little Tiger and Bai Long each grabbed an elbow to steady her.

"Don't be too sad, Miss Jasmine. Look…" Xiao Mei summoned a young woman standing behind her.

Jasmine staggered a step back and then stood transfixed with astonishment. In a carmine red T-shirt, blue jeans, and hiking boots, the young woman was in her late twenties. She was gorgeous—suntanned skin, delicate features, almond eyes. She looked just like Daisy!

"I'm Phoenix. Birch is my father."

Jasmine seized the young woman's arms, checking her up and down. *She also sounds like Daisy.*

"Birch named her Phoenix because of you and Miss Daisy. He wanted her to rise from the ashes of the war. He wanted her to become an incredible woman like…her aunts."

Tears clogged Jasmine's throat, so she nodded.

Pride was written all over Xiao Mei's face. "She became a pilot. Can you believe it?"

"A rescue pilot in the U.S. Coast Guard," added Little Tiger with admiration.

"So impressive. Your father…would be very proud."

"I'm not the only one Dad encouraged to learn to fly," Phoenix said with a gleam in her eyes. "My husband is also a pilot." She moved aside as a Westerner stepped forward.

The man was in his early thirties, tall and athletic. He was attractive—a straight nose, a firm mouth, and gold-speckled brown eyes. A white scarf was wrapped around his neck. He bore a striking resemblance to Danny Hardy.

"I'm Danny Greene, Danny Hardy's nephew."

Jasmine couldn't divert her attention from his face. Her eyes, shiny with recent tears, rounded.

"It's such an honor to meet you, Auntie Jasmine. I've heard so much about you…since I was a little kid." He spoke fluent Chinese. His smile was warm and infectious.

"Danny?" She lifted her arm, her hand lightly touching his hair.

"Oh, please don't tell me this is a dream."

"No. I'm real. My mom is Susan Hardy, Danny Hardy's sister. She'd be so happy to meet you!"

Jasmine trembled with joy. "How can it be? You live in the States, but…but Birch lived in Taiwan…"

"He found us in San Francisco almost twenty years ago."

"Soon, we moved to the States," explained Xiao Mei. "He knew he wouldn't live much longer and wanted to spend as much time as possible with Susan and young Danny."

"Ever since then, we're together." Phoenix clutched her husband's hand.

Jasmine was beyond excited. She was lit up from inside, and she couldn't hide it.

The young American took the white scarf off his neck and laid it over his hands. "Do you remember this?"

She blinked a few times. It was the gift she'd given to the Flying Tiger on his twenty-eighth birthday.

"Uncle Danny left it to Uncle Birch before…"

Tears returned to her eyes. *That's why it wasn't with him.* She'd wondered when she found his remains.

"Dad had it when he was shot." Phoenix pointed to a hole in the middle of the scarf. "That bullet hit his right shoulder."

With a shaky hand, Jasmine touched the scarf, feeling the silky smoothness of the material between her fingers.

"Mother told me to wear it on the day we find either Uncle Danny or you." The young American presented the scarf to Jasmine. "This belongs to you."

Jasmine took it with both hands and pressed it to her chest as if she were holding the man she loved. From Yunnan to Taiwan, then from Taiwan to San Francisco, this scarf had traveled over forty years, and now it had returned to its original owner. She closed her eyes and savored the extraordinary gift that attested to their undying love and friendship. When she opened her eyes, she handed it back to Danny Greene. "I gave it to your uncle. Now it belongs to your family."

"I'll wear it again on the day we scatter my uncle's ashes. Mother told me to keep half and scatter the other half at Angel's Pass with Uncle Birch."

"You know we found…"

"Little Tiger told us."

Jasmine turned to her son. "Everyone knows everything, except me. Why didn't you say something in your letter?"

"Don't be mad at me, Mom. They got in touch with me only a couple of months ago. I didn't…"

"We didn't want you"—Bai Long butted in—"to face the emotional rollercoaster alone."

A whispery sigh escaped her. *They were right.* She'd been whirling in a vortex of emotions. It would have been harder to deal with them by herself.

"You're amazing," said Danny Greene with a look of open admiration at Jasmine. "You never give up. No matter how long and how hard, you never go back on your promise. You're a…tigress."

A smile spread across Jasmine's slender face. She knew the young American meant to praise her. But *Mu Lao Hu—Tigress* was used to describe a woman with a hot temper in China.

Everyone there grinned.

"Don't just stand here," said Linzi. "Let's go inside and sit down." He turned to Little Tiger and Bai Long. "Your mom made lots of dumplings. Go get them from the kitchen."

Chapter 68

"Almost everyone here knows my uncle better than I do," said Danny Greene, standing at Angel's Pass with the people related to Danny Hardy and Birch Bai. The white scarf was wrapped around his neck, flapping slightly in the breeze.

He turned to Jasmine and handed the urn to her. "You're the one who rescued him once and found him again. I'm related to him by blood, but you," he paused, the knot of his Adam's apple rose and fell, "you're connected to him on a much deeper level. I think you should be the one..."

She held the urn close to her chest, quivering from a vast array of emotions too complicated to name.

"Wait!" Xiao Mei moved a step closer to Jasmine. She was holding the urn with Birch's ashes. "For years, Birch wished he could find his brother. Now, both of them are here." She looked up, her eyes shining with unshed tears. "Let's pour their ashes together. In this way—"

"They'll always be together," Jasmine finished.

Everyone nodded.

They were standing near the statue of the angel where Daisy had perished. Looking across the gorge, Jasmine stared at the Flying Tiger. In his flight jacket, he stood facing them, holding a model airplane in his right hand high above his head.

She learned what Danny Hardy had said before his death.

Inhaling deeply, she cited the same ancient Chinese poem as she scattered their ashes, *"Feng xiao xiao xi yi shui han—Wind rustled across the desolate land. Water in the river turned icy and cold."*

Everybody joined her, *"Zhuang shi yi qu xi bu fu fai—A warrior, knowing he wouldn't return alive, walked straight forward without so much as a backward glance."*

The cadence of the words drummed with her heartbeat. As the ashes floated down the gorge, disappearing forever from her life, Jasmine said her silent goodbye to the two men she loved most.

In 1942, Danny Hardy and Birch Bai had become sworn brothers after the heroic rescue of the Flying Tiger. For the next three years, they'd taken many courageous missions together, lived through countless life-and-death situations, and tried to save each other's lives. Finally, four decades later, the two brothers were reunited at the gorge that meant so much to them, and now they would never be separated again.

How thrilled they would be if they could see each other alive! A shudder tore through her as years of longing, grief, and guilt rushed back with brutal force.

"Take it easy, Mom." Little Tiger patted her back.

"Dad always wanted to return here," said Phoenix. "He'd be elated, knowing you're here, knowing you found Uncle Danny."

Jasmine nodded, not trusting herself to say anything without breaking down. This place already had a special meaning to her. Her loved ones and friends were here—Daisy, Li Ming, Meng Hu, and Wang Hong. Now, Danny and Birch joined them.

"I've got great news to share. We waited for this moment to tell you all," continued the young woman. Her heart-shaped face spread into a huge smile. "Danny and I..." She interlocked her hand with his. "We're going to have..." She paused for effect.

It worked. The group held its breath, waiting, expecting.

After a moment of intense silence, she blurted it out, eyes glowing, "We're going to have a baby."

The group cheered.

Fat tears rolled down Jasmine's cheeks.

Xiao Mei let out a whoop of glee. "I'm so happy. Your dad would be crazy. How far along are you?"

"Just over three months."

"Have you thought about the baby's name?" asked Bai Long.

Phoenix and Danny exchanged a look. "If it's a boy," she answered, "he'd be Barkley. It means—"

"Birch tree meadow," Jasmine blurted out with enthusiasm.

Xiao Mei cried out. "Yes! He'd be Barkley Hardy Greene."

There was nodding all around.

"And a girl?"

Phoenix grinned, sinking two dimples on her cheeks. "Dad told us that Uncle Danny had never considered having a girl. He only imagined he'd have a boy."

Xiao Mei's eyes were bright with tears, but she chuckled. "Major Hardy was so confident in everything. He had no idea he'd have no control of that."

Everybody broke into gales of laughter.

They were basking in the glorious sunlight on this beautiful summer day. The sky was blue, only wispy clouds hovering above the distant peaks. Over the rocky rims, lush forests stretched as far as the eye could see. White, yellow, and raspberry-colored flowers dotted the edge of the woods. The fragrance of wildflowers and pine trees permeated the atmosphere.

"So, if it's a girl, she'd be Aster," said Phoenix.

Jasmine nodded. "Your grandma would be so pleased that you kept her tradition of using flora names."

"Yes. But Aster is more than a flower's name. In Ancient Greek, Aster means star."

"I'll be that bright star's uncle," chimed in Little Tiger. The thought brought a gamine smile to his lips.

"Me, too!" remarked Bai Long. He turned to his children. "You'll have a baby cousin soon."

"What about me?" Linzi scratched his head, amused. "Grand Uncle?"

"Yes. And there's more," Phoenix said. "Have you seen Aster

flowers? They look very much like daisies!" She lowered her head and caressed her stomach. "Dad had never gotten over the guilt of killing Daisy. Even at the end of his life, he kept calling her name. He…" She swallowed a few times, opened her mouth, but nothing came out.

"He mistook me as my uncle and Phoenix as you." Danny Greene faced Jasmine, his protective arm circling his wife's shoulders, pulling her close to him. "He took our hands and pressed them together. 'Finally,' he said, 'you're together.'"

"He smiled." The young woman squeezed Jasmine's arms. "Dad was so happy. He thought we were all in heaven and asked for Daisy. He wanted to make sure she was with us—Danny and Jasmine. I think he was worried that his little sister would be left out."

Jasmine blinked a few times to remove the moisture from her eyes. She understood that Daisy would forever be Birch's soft spot. Gently, she touched Phoenix's stomach. The baby was too small to make any movement, but she felt it in her heart.

In the summer of 1942, Danny Hardy had been shot down in this remote part of China. To protect him, many people had been killed. *What if I'd never rescued the Flying Tiger?* Then Birch might not have survived, and Phoenix might not have existed, let alone marrying Danny's nephew and having their child. In a cosmic way, the bond formed between the American pilot and the Chinese woman forty years earlier was so strong and indestructible that it extended to the next generation. A new life was created.

Jasmine's chest expanded with tenderness.

Between sheer rocky cliffs, the two sides were connected by a suspension bridge built by Birch and the villagers. Nearby, a hawk drifted, swooped, and dove for the pure joy of it.

The bird reminded her of the marvelous dream—flying with Danny over and under the bridge. She inhaled the perfumed air and listened to the soft whisper of the wind, detecting the gentle heartbeat of the forest, feeling the spirits of the ones she loved.

Jasmine wiped the salty streaks from her face and lifted her head. "No more tears." She stood taller and straighter, and with her steady gaze, regarded the people around her. "We've cried enough." Pride and dignity outshined the scars on her cheek. "Danny, Birch, and Daisy would be happy for us. And for Barkley or Aster!"

About the Author

Iris Yang, Ph.D. (Qing Yang) was born and raised in China. After graduating from Wuhan University, she was accepted by the prestigious CUSBEA (China-United States Biochemistry Examination and Application) program. At age 23, with poor English, little knowledge of the country, and 500 borrowed dollars, she came to the United States.

Later, she received a Ph.D. in molecular biology at the University of Rochester and worked at the University of North Carolina. Although she has published a number of scientific papers, she has a passion for creative writing. *Wings of a Flying Tiger and Will of a Tiger* are the first two books of the Tiger Saga series. She has been interviewed on National Public Radio and invited to speak at the Flying Tigers WWII Veterans 78th Anniversary Reunion.

Besides writing, Iris loves hiking, dancing, photography, and travel. She holds a private pilot license. Her website is www.irisyang-author.com.

An Interview with the Author

What inspired you to write the third of the Tiger Saga series?

At the end of *Wings of a Flying Tiger*, I left a small window of opportunity to bring back Jasmine Bai. I loved this character so much that I wanted to write more of her story. However, I couldn't do it. I knew her life wouldn't be easy. I've already given her so much trouble that I didn't have the heart to hurt her any further.

On June 29, 2019, Greg Alexander attended my presentation at Sedona Public Library, bringing in his father's flight jacket. His father, Ed Alexander, had fought the Japanese in WWII in China as a pilot, just like my hero, Danny Hardy.

Greg thanked me for writing books about American heroes. Two days later, he finished reading *Wings of a Flying Tiger*. "My eyes blurred with tears... You reached me, touched me in a way I haven't felt for ages..." Before sleep, he asked his father, who passed away many years ago, to give him permission to share the jacket with me, and he woke up the next day by the tapping of a pure yellow bird on his window.

Someone offered to buy the jacket for $5000; he didn't sell. A WWII museum asked him to donate; he didn't donate. His son wanted to have it; Greg didn't give it to his son.

Yet, he gave it to me.

Greg told me the reason:

The similarity between Danny Hardy and his father is striking: Both were shot down in southern China and lost their best friends during the mission. Both had leg injuries and malaria. Both were rescued by Chinese villagers, who treated them with herbal medicines and sheltered them for several months while the Japanese soldiers searched for them.

The flight jacket played a vital role in *Wings of a Flying Tiger*—a Blood Chit was sewed to the back of the jacket. In Chinese, it reads: "This foreigner has come to China to help in the war effort. Soldiers and civilians, one and all, should protect him." Jasmine Bai realized that Danny Hardy was an American pilot because of the Blood Chit.

Since he promised his mother that he would keep the jacket in the family, Greg asked me to be his sister. So, on July 4, 2019, I became the little sister of a Flying Tiger's son. I'm part of a Flying Tiger's family.

I wrote the books because the Flying Tigers' stories touched me. I wanted to thank them for their bravery and sacrifice. I have never imagined that one day a Flying Tiger and his son would walk into my life and touch me in such a profound way.

This heartwarming event inspired me so much that I started writing the third of the Tiger Saga series. Even though Danny Hardy is gone, his fighting spirit lives on through Jasmine Bai and the next generation.

Is any character in your novel based on a historical figure?

In December 1936, Chiang Kai-shek, the leader of the Nationalist government, was detained by his subordinates in Xi'an. Generals Zhang Xueliang and General Yang Hucheng held him captive until he agreed to an alliance between the Nationalists and the Communists. After the Xi'an Incident, the two parties formed a united front to counter the Japanese invasion. But later, General Zhang was detained and spent over fifty years under house arrest, first in Mainland China and then in Taiwan.

General Yang was arrested, along with his wife, children, and some of his staff members. He remained in prison for twelve years until Chiang Kai-shek ordered him executed in September 1949, shortly before the Communists took over the Mainland.

Song Qigun was General Yang's secretary. As a member of the Communist Party, he was secretly sent to the Nationalist Army. After Xi'an Incident, he was one of the staff members arrested by the Nationalist Secret Police. His wife, Xu Linxia, and his son, Song Zhenshong, were imprisoned with him. Leng Xue and Shen Shen in my book were based on them.

Song Zhengshong, nicknamed Sen Sen, was only eight months old when he went to jail with his parents. On September 6, 1949, he was butchered by the Nationalist Secret Police in Chungking at age eight, and he became the youngest Revolutionary Martyr bestowed by the Communist Party. He was a minor character in a historical novel *Red Crag*, but he left such a long-lasting impression that I brought him back in my book.

On November 28, 1949, the Nationalist Secret Police carried out a massacre in jail in Chungking, shooting prisoners with machine guns, and over two hundred people were slaughtered. Yang Qindian was a jailer who participated in the killing of the eight-year-old boy, Song Zhengshong. Feeling remorseful and awakened by humanity, he opened the doors and set nineteen detainees free, including Luo Guangbin, one of the two authors of *Red Crag*. During the Cultural Revolution, Yang Qindian was labeled as a Nationalist spy and sentenced to twenty years in prison. Tan Yin, in my novel, was partly created because of him.

Red Crag is a Chinese novel published in 1961. It was set in Chungking during the Chinese Civil War in 1949 and based partly on the experiences of its authors Luo Guangbin and Yang Yiyan—both were imprisoned by the Nationalist Secret Police. This novel has played a critical role in the heroism culture of that era. As a kid growing up during that time, I was inevitably influenced by the story.

During the Cultural Revolution, *Red Crag* was labeled as a Counter-revolutionary book, and both authors were wrongfully accused as Traitors. After enduring public humiliation and physical persecution, on February 10, 1967, Luo Guangbin committed suicide by jumping off a tall building. In 1978, like my character Li Ming and countless other cases, Mr. Luo was posthumously "rehabilitated," and his name was cleared. The Cultural Revolution was a crazy time, and many tragedies like this have happened.

The political movements you described in the book are devastating and incredible. Are they true? Did your family suffer from them?

Yes, they are true. From 1949 to 1976, there have been two dozen campaigns launched by the Communist Party in Mainland China, some of which had enormous negative impacts, resulting in extreme terror and millions of deaths. While I wrote the book, I felt sorry for my parents and grandparents, who went through all those tough times.

My grandmother, Yuan Changying, was the first Chinese woman to receive a master's degree in the UK, and she became a famous writer and a professor at Wuhan University. During the Anti-Rightist Movement in 1957, she was wrongfully accused as a Counter-revolutionary Rightist and fired from her job. Allegedly, she'd criticized the Party in the Hundred Flowers Campaign the previous year, during which the Communist Party encouraged citizens to express their opinions of the government and its ideology. Like a minor character in my novel, my grandma only expressed her views privately to her friend, who gave her up under pressure to save his own skin. During the Cultural Revolution, she was kicked out of her university housing and sent back to her hometown, a remote rural village hundreds of miles away. She died there alone.

My aunt, Yang Jingyuan, received her master's degree from the University of Michigan in 1948 and became a famous translator. She translated *Peter Pan*, *Jane Eyre*, *Wuthering Heights*, and other classics into Chinese. Eager to help build the new China, she returned to the Mainland at the end of the Chinese Civil War. During the Anti-Rightist Movement, she was also wrongfully accused as a Counter-revolutionary Rightist and sent to a labor camp for many years.

As professors, my parents also had tough times during the Cultural Revolution. My father, Yang Hongyuan, spent several years in a labor camp while my mother, Zhou Chang, took care of my sister and me, who were little kids. My father was allowed to come back home only once a year. I remember him bringing home eggs and peanuts, which were precious since food was limited by ration coupons. To this day, I still can't imagine how he stood on a bumpy bus or the back of a truck for seven hours, holding a basket full of eggs and trying to make sure the eggs would be intact.

Like a character in my novel, my friend's father said that Chairman Mao was just a human being. He said the slogan 'Long live Chairman Mao' wasn't logical, and Chairman Mao would die one day like everybody else. Because of this comment, he was sent to prison. Unable to handle the mental and physical torment, he killed himself there.

Even I, a little girl during the Cultural Revolution, felt the oppressive atmosphere. Shao Xian Dui, the Young Pioneers of China, is a mass youth organization for children aged six to fourteen, and each member wears a red scarf. Having the red scarf was, and still is, a symbol of being a good kid. Most of my classmates joined Shao Xian Dui in the first grade, but I wasn't accepted until the third grade, simply because my grandma was a Counter-revolutionary Rightist.

One day when I was in the first grade, several school officials showed up in our classroom. They made us write several sentences and sign our names and then took the papers away. A couple of days later, a boy was kicked out of school. Rumor had it that he wrote "Counter-revolutionary" slogans. Why would a seven-year-old boy write such a thing was beyond me and was never explained. Things like these affected me tremendously, and I learned to be extremely careful. I was shy and fearful, partly because of the environment I grew up in.

Is it true that after stopping it for ten years, Mainland China resumed the College Entrance Exam in 1977?

Yes, it is true.

In 1966, the Cultural Revolution swept the nation, and the

college examination was suspended. For ten years, normal learning at schools was interrupted, and all the universities were closed as students were mobilized to participate in the revolution, and professors were publicly humiliated. Since 1968, following Chairman Mao's instruction, millions of young people were sent to the countryside to be "reeducated" by peasants.

After the Cultural Revolution, Deng Xiaoping, the paramount leader of the People's Republic of China, decided to tackle the problems in the education system, and the College Entrance Exam resumed in 1977.

One of my friends passed the exam in 1977. But like Little Tiger in my novel, he wasn't accepted by any university—he failed at *zheng shen—political background check*, simply because his father was wrongfully accused as a Counter-revolutionary Rightist. He wrote a letter to Mr. Deng Xiaoping. The staff in Deng's office took his case seriously, and the following year, a prestigious university accepted him.

In 1979, I passed the College Entrance Exam and became a student at Wuhan University. It is hard to imagine what my life would have become without this life-changing opportunity.

Check my website https://www.irisyang-author.com/ for more information about my books, interviews, and presentations.

Acknowledgments

‒ ‒ ‒ ‒ ‒ ‒ ‒ ‒ ‒ ‒ ‒ ‒

My deepest appreciation to Greg Alexander and his wife Mullika Alexander. They gave me his father's flight jacket and inspired me to write this book (see Interview with the Author).

Huge thanks to Marywave Van Deren and Gary Jacobson. They came to my aid when I needed it the most. Words cannot express my gratitude.

I'm eternally grateful to Tiffany Frankovich, Lauraine Stewart, and Anne Crosman for their help and support.

Thank you, Gloria Haddad, for being curious about Jasmine's fate. I told you her life would be hard, and now you know.

I owe thanks to three writing groups led by Naxie Reiff, Sy Brandon, and Robin Harris. Their feedback made my book better. I appreciate Tanya Marcy and Janie Macintosh for reading the story to the groups. I'm grateful to Cottonwood Public Library and Sedona Public Library for their invaluable resources.

My sincere thanks to all the readers of my first two novels, *Wings of a Flying Tiger* and *Will of a Tiger*. Special thanks to those who went out of their way to support the books: Carolyn Francis, Phil Sullivan, Melinda Collis, Heidi Moore, Bertie Boston, Brian Daniel, Jeanie Valentin, Michael Chek, Charlene Gier, Becky Coltrane, Virginia Storey, Allyson Tilton, Wendy Bratzel, Jade Vincent, Christine Weir, Martin Vann, Doug McDaniel, Lindy Parr, Richard Parr, Dee

Holliday, Walt Holliday, Jeff Skelley, Martha Skelley, Paul Steffy, Paul Falk, Roy Murry, Les Gee, Susan Sage, Emit Blackwell, Mary Anne Yarde, Gale Zasada, Karen Bernard, Sharon Clayton, Priscilla King, Píaras Cíonnaoíth, Anna Casamento Arrigo, Rebecka Jager, Denis Mcgrath, Cynthia Hamilton, Carol Marrs Phipps, Jess Combs, Meg Stivison, Padgett Gerler, Denice Josten, Larry Stoffers, Terrie Frankel, Yuli Wang, Lingna Li, Jiaxin Liu, Hong Zhang, Jiaqing Liu, Wu Xia, Yongqing Yang, Peter Wang, Xiaoying Yin, Dave Kerr, and Jim Wilfong.

Thank you, Sammy Xu, for designing a beautiful website: www.irisyang-author.com. I love it.

Dozens of organizations have offered me the opportunities to present, and I'm grateful to all of them. Special thanks to Lydia Rossi (Executive Secretary of the Flying Tigers Association), Michelle Clouthier (President of the Flying Tigers Association), T.J. Hicks (Program Coordinator at Rancho Mirage Library and Observatory), Jenny Levine (Humanities & Adult Programming Coordinator at Durham County Public Library), Sarah Willadsen (Adult Services Librarian at Prescott Public Library), Judy Poe (Assistant Director at Sedona Public Library), Jolene Pierson (Library of Congress Veterans History Project in Sedona), Fred Borns (President of the Classic Airplane Association of Arizona), Tracy Wu (Director of Alliance of Chinese Americans San Diego), and Alice Osborn (Organizer of Wonderland Book Club).

Once again, thank you, David Ross and Kelly Huddleston, for publishing my books. Words can never describe my gratitude.

I thank Kurt Stevens for his friendship. The quotation, "Courage is doing something when you're scared half to death," came from our conversation.

Danny Hardy, the larger-than-life hero in this series, was inspired by Danny Walker in the movie *Pearl Harbor*. I'm grateful to Josh Hartnett, the actor, for creating such a memorable character.

Finally, I give thanks to my family. I'm indebted to my mother Zhou Chang and father Yang Hongyuan. My heartfelt thanks to my sister Jin Yang, daughter Jessie Xiong, niece Alison Zhang, nephew Justin Zhang, and best friend Libby Vetter for their encouragement and support.